DAMAGE
CONTROL

DAMAGE CONTROL

J. A. JANCE

WM

WILLIAM MORROW

An Imprint of HarperCollinsPublishers

HarperCollins books may be purchased for educational, business, or sales promotional use. For information please write: Special Markets Department, HarperCollins Publishers, 10 East 53rd Street, New York, NY 10022.

FIRST EDITION

Designed by Susan Walsh

Library of Congress Cataloging-in-Publication Data
Jance, Judith A.
    Damage control / J. A. Jance. — 1st ed.
        p.   cm.
    ISBN 978-0-06-074676-6
    1. Brady, Joanna (Fictitious character)—Fiction.   2. Cochise County (Ariz.)—Fiction.   3. Policewomen—Fiction.   4. Sheriffs—Fiction.   5. Arizona—Fiction. I. Title.
PS3560.A44D36 2008
813'.54—dc22   2007037121

08   09   10   11   12   WTC/RRD   10   9   8   7   6   5   4   3   2   1

For Jim

DAMAGE
CONTROL

PROLOGUE

LAUREN DAYSON WAS SLEEPING SOUNDLY WHEN SOME SMALL noise in the front room of the apartment disturbed her. What actually awakened her was the sound of Mojo barking. Mojo, an unlikely cross between a Chihuahua and a chow, was a pint-sized, laughable dog, but this time she was barking in her ferocious big-dog voice, and Lauren knew what it meant. Rick Mosier was here. Somewhere in her apartment. Somewhere in her home. He had broken in and he was coming for her.

Rick had warned Lauren that he would be. He had sworn that if he couldn't have her, nobody would. He swore he would kill her before he would let her go, and Lauren had reason to believe him. He told her that it didn't matter to him if she moved or changed the locks on the doors or put bars on her windows or papered Pima County with restraining orders against him. He said she could never hide from him—that he would find her anyway; that if Rick Mosier wanted her, he would have her. End of story.

When Lauren had first fallen for the guy, that kind of exclusivity hadn't bothered her. It hadn't been a problem. She had loved him with all her heart. She had been intrigued by the fact that Rick walked on the wild side; that he lived an edgy existence that was beyond the scope of her limited, girl-next-door experience. She had been fascinated by the idea that when he sped around campus on his skateboard like a modern-day whirling dervish, he had carried at least one handgun and often several knives along with the schoolbooks in his backpack.

Lauren came from a family where the very idea of owning guns was unacceptable. According to her father, only "right-wing yahoos owned guns." Rick was, in fact, the antithesis of "right wing," but knowing he was armed to the teeth every moment of every day was part of what made him appealing in a forbidden-fruit sort of way. For Lauren, the "good-girl daughter," as opposed to her older sister, the "rebellious one," Rick was an idea whose time had come at a point when Lauren was a naive freshman and Rick a "mature" twenty-one.

She had found him utterly fascinating and charming in those early days, especially when Rick told Lauren she was "the fair princess" to his "dark prince." Over her parents' strident objections and because she knew it would drive them nuts, Lauren had moved in with him at the end of her junior year. Their romance had stopped being charming on the day three years later when Rick had blackened one of Lauren's eyes because he claimed she'd been flirting with a guy playing pool at the Red Garter when they'd gone there for a burger. The truth was, she hadn't even noticed the man, but that didn't matter to an insanely jealous Rick. Two months after that, he'd broken her arm for the same reason—because he thought she was flirting with someone else. That wasn't the end of the relationship, but it was pretty much the end of the fascination.

Eventually Lauren had taken her worldly goods and moved out. The best she could afford on her own was a much cheaper apartment in a not-so-good part of town. So she had done all those other clichéd things as well. She had convinced her new landlord, Mr. Ford, to put bars on her windows, jamb-bars in the slider, and dead bolts on the front door. Lauren had also managed to sweet-talk her way around Mr. Ford's "No Pet" rule. He had finally reluctantly gone along with letting Mojo move in by saying she was such a worthless little sample of muttdom that she didn't really qualify as a pet, let alone a canine.

In addition to all that, Lauren really had gone to Legal Aid and gotten herself a restraining order, but she'd done one thing more—the one thing her parents would never tolerate or forgive. She'd gone to Best Deal Pawn, just up First Avenue, and bought herself a used Glock 26 semiautomatic. Then she'd made it her business to learn how to use it. She'd taken the classes and passed the necessary tests so she could have her very own concealed-weapon permit as well. And that was where her Glock was at the moment—concealed and loaded—directly under her pillow.

The first chambered round was full of bird shot. That was supposed to function as a deterrent—as a nonlethal warning shot. After that, though, all bets were off. The others were hollow points. Her instructor had told her, "If you draw a weapon, you'd better plan on shooting to kill." And that's what she was going to do. If the first bullet didn't stop Rick, one of the others sure as hell would.

Mojo was closer now, still barking frantically, still raising the alarm. The phone was right there on the bedside table. Lauren could have reached for that, but she knew the statistics. Rick had come to kill her. She'd be dead long before Tucson PD could respond to an abortive 911 call. Instead, Lauren reached for her weapon and pulled it free of the bedding and free of the holster. Then she turned over and propped herself up on the pillows.

She could have switched on the lamp, but she didn't. The full moon outside glowed in through the window, suffusing the room in an eerie silvery light. She hoped it would make it easier for her to see him and harder for him to see her. With her heart pounding a quickening drumbeat in her chest, she sat, with the gun trained on the open doorway, waiting.

Suddenly Mojo's barks were punctuated by a sickening thump. The dog gave a startled half-yip and fell momentarily silent.

My baby, Lauren thought fiercely. *My poor baby. That son of a bitch kicked her!*

Mojo whimpered then. The sound of the injured dog only served to strengthen Lauren's resolve.

I'll get you for that! she swore to herself.

Lauren had already decided that this was where Rick Mosier would meet his "fair princess" match. This was Lauren's home, her castle, and she was going to make her last stand here no matter what. Not that there was time for her to move or run away even if she'd wanted to. Besides, where would she have gone— out through her carefully barred window and then down a twenty-foot drop to hard-packed bare dirt? Not a good idea.

Then suddenly he was there—a dark silhouette looming in

her bedroom doorway. Lauren saw the moonlight dance off something in his hand. She knew at once what it was—what it had to be—a knife blade shimmering in the moonlit room.

The cops on TV always warn the people they're about to shoot, but in Lauren's book, Rick Mosier didn't deserve any warning—none at all. Armed or not, he was an uninvited intruder in her home. She simply held the weapon with both hands and squeezed down on the trigger. Rick squawked once in surprise when the bird shot hit him. He staggered and turned aside as if to protect himself, and then he grunted when the first hollow point hit him as well. But just because he was falling didn't mean Lauren stopped pulling the trigger. She fired away, one shot after another, following him as he fell. None of the shots went wide of their mark. Every single one of them hit him, even though he was dead before the last one struck.

Only when he lay still and the clip was empty did panic finally hit. Lauren suddenly found that her trembling hand and arm could no longer support the weight of the weapon. She dropped it and reached for the phone, but her hand didn't seem to be attached to her arm or her brain. Instead of picking up the phone, her fumbling, clumsy fingers knocked it off its stand and sent it spinning across the room, where it came to rest under her chest of drawers.

Lauren crawled out of bed to retrieve the phone. Just then Mojo came limping into the room, still whimpering. Forgetting the phone, Lauren scooped up the trembling dog and held her close.

"Oh, my baby," she murmured over and over. "My poor, poor baby. Are you hurt? Are you okay?"

Mojo, for her part, wagged her tiny tail and kissed Lauren's nose.

When Lauren finally managed to retrieve the fallen phone, it took three separate tries before her shaking fingers finally managed to key in the proper number.

"Nine-one-one. What are you reporting?"

"A man was in my room. My ex-boyfriend. He broke into my house."

"Is he there now?"

"Yes. He's here. I shot him."

"You say he's injured?"

"I don't know," Lauren answered. "He isn't moving. He could be dead."

"Units are on the way. What's your name?"

"Lauren. Lauren Dayson."

"Are you hurt?"

"No. I'm okay. But Mojo isn't."

"Mojo?"

"My dog. My little dog. She was barking at him. I'm pretty sure he kicked her. She may have a broken rib."

"You say you know the intruder's identity?" the operator asked.

"Yes. His name's Rick Mosier. He used to be my boyfriend."

"Does he have a pulse?"

"I don't know. Do you want me to check? Do I have to?"

"Please."

Still holding the dog in one hand and the phone in the other, Lauren managed to get to her feet. Using the back of the phone hand, Lauren reached over and switched on the light. That was when she finally got her first clear look at the man lying dead in her bedroom doorway.

After he had spun away from that first hit, one of the hollow points had entered the back of his head and exploded out the front, taking part of his face with it. Lauren stared in astonishment at the bloodied, sandy-blond-haired mess that was left behind. It wasn't just that the man was dead—that she had killed him in cold blood—it was that she couldn't make sense of what she was seeing.

Rick Mosier had been her "dark prince" because he was dark. His hair was chemically augmented black. He was olive-complexioned. Swarthy. From what was left, Lauren could tell that this man was light-haired, light-skinned.

No matter how much Lauren wanted it to be true, the dead man wasn't Rick Mosier! This was someone she had never seen before. Lauren had gunned down a total stranger. As for the threatening knife she had seen in his hand, the blade glinting in the moonlight? That had tumbled from the dead man's hands as he fell, and lay at the tips of his lifeless fingers. It was a harmless kitchen table knife, probably from her own silverware drawer, with flecks of peanut butter and jelly still attached to the blade.

As the awful, appalling realizations hit home, Lauren gripped Mojo so tightly that the little dog finally yelped in pain. Now she was sure one of her puppy's ribs was broken. Lauren eased her hold, but still she couldn't believe she had done this. How was it possible? She had shot some poor man who had broken into her apartment to help himself to a peanut butter sandwich? Lauren had killed him for that? Because no matter how she looked at the dead man lying there on her floor, he wasn't Rick Mosier.

"No," she whispered hoarsely into the phone. "No, this can't be."

"Miss?" the emergency operator asked. "Are you all right?"

But by then Lauren had dropped the phone and her whispered no had become an anguished wail. "Noooooooo!"

"Miss Dayson, are you still there? Are you all right?"

Even though Lauren didn't hear the question, her answer was correct. "No! No! No!"

Because she wasn't all right and would never again be all right. In trying to protect herself, Lauren Dayson had killed the wrong man.

CHAPTER 1

"THANK YOU SO MUCH, MR. CAMPBELL," CLAIRE NEWMARK SAID AS the disgruntled speaker returned to his seat. As head of the Cochise County Board of Supervisors, Claire was chairing that Friday morning's meeting. "Do you have anything to say in response, Sheriff Brady?"

Joanna snapped awake. One of the things about being a sleep-deprived working mother meant that she could fall asleep anywhere—in front of her computer, at her desk, in church, and definitely in front of the TV set on those rare occasions when she actually tried to watch a show. In this case, she had dozed off during a Board of Supervisors Friday morning meeting.

Randy Campbell was one of Joanna's constituents. A prominent local rancher, Campbell was also one of Joanna's most vociferous critics. He had come to the Board of Supervisors meeting that morning armed with his usual litany of complaints.

Joanna had considerable sympathy for the man. His ranch, located on Border Road just east of Bisbee Junction, was also border-crossing central for illegal immigrants. Campbell's house had been broken into on numerous occasions. His wife and children had been held at gunpoint and threatened by armed robbers who had taken the time to load several television sets and power tools into Randy's pickup truck before driving off in it. His fences had been cut, letting his livestock loose. Once outside the fence, his daughter's prizewinning bull had been hit and killed by a passing Border Patrol vehicle.

So even though Joanna may have allowed herself to doze during the course of Randy Campbell's tirade, she knew what he had said—almost by heart—because she had heard it all before.

"Thank you, Madame Chairman," Joanna said, rising to her feet. "And thank you, too, Mr. Campbell. I appreciate the fact that you're willing to bring your concerns to the attention of this board and also into the public arena. I live in a rural setting myself. Although we haven't had the same number of incidents Mr. Campbell has had, our property, too, has been damaged by illegal crossers.

"The problem is this. We're dealing with something that is well beyond the scope of my department to handle. We've done our best to increase patrols in Mr. Campbell's area. Because of that, we've also managed to decrease our response time. But the truth is, the border-enforcement problem is a national issue. It requires a national solution as opposed to a local one. Our mission is to handle criminal complaints, and we do that to the best of our ability, but that ability is limited by both budgetary and personnel considerations.

"There are eighty miles of international border inside Cochise County. That's a lot of territory to cover. It's also a lot of crime to cover. My department does the best it can, and I'm sure Border Patrol and Homeland Security are doing the best they can to interdict illegal entrants. No one agency caused this, and no one agency can fix it. Thank you."

Randy Campbell was still glowering at her as Joanna resumed her seat. The public-comment part of the meeting had come at the very end of the day's agenda. A few minutes later, as Joanna walked toward her car in the parking lot, Claire Newmark fell into step beside her.

"Sorry to have to let him dump on you like that," Claire said. "But you just stood for reelection. Mine is coming up. If I hadn't given him a forum, he'd come looking for me next. I figured you could handle him, and you did. Very nicely, as a matter of fact. It sounded a little like a stump speech, but not too much. Way to go."

The exchange caught Joanna by surprise. She had gradually come to understand that although the office of sheriff was theoretically nonpartisan, it was definitely not nonpolitical. Everything Joanna did or didn't do was grist for someone's mill, and this was no exception. What she hadn't realized, however, was that somehow the political climate in Cochise County had changed. There was now an established old-girls network capable of wielding its own particular brand of power. To Joanna Brady's astonishment, she was in a position to reap some of the benefits of that unexpected sea change.

"Thanks," she said.

With that, Joanna headed back to her office at the Cochise County Justice Center. She'd had her weekly ordeal by bureaucracy.

Now it was time to go do battle with her other daily headache—paperwork. Crime fighting was supposed to be her main focus. Too bad it took so many dead trees to do it.

———+———

Alfred Beasley had pretty much of a death grip on the steering wheel of the decrepit old Buick as he nursed it up the steep winding mountain road toward Montezuma Pass. He and Martha had bought the Buick new, fifteen years earlier. At the time they made the purchase, they had also discussed the very real possibility that this would be their last new vehicle—that this final Regal would be their "toes-up" Buick. Back then they hadn't expected it would last nearly as long as it had. Of course, they hadn't really thought they'd make it this far, either. Martha had just turned ninety-one and Alfred himself was eighty-eight. She'd outlived her parents by forty years; Alfred had surpassed his by almost as many.

Throughout their long marriage, they had always loved road trips, and this one was no exception. Martha had insisted that they do Montezuma Pass at the bottom of the Huachuca Mountains "one last time," as she said, and they were doing it, come hell or high water—and not necessarily in that order. The rains had come two days late—on the sixth of July rather than the fourth. Once they were off the paved road and onto gravel, there were places where there were already washouts. In one spot a small boulder had fallen onto the road. Afraid the Buick would high-center if Alfred tried going over it, he carefully steered around it, praying that no one would come barreling downhill toward them when their left rear tire—far more worn than it

should have been—was within mere inches of going over the
edge. Alfred breathed a heartfelt sigh of relief once they were
back on the right-hand side of the narrow road. No matter what
else was going on with him, at least he could still drive.

By the time they were around the boulder and the tight hair-
pin curve that followed, Alfred looked in the rearview mirror
and counted at least four cars lined up behind him. A hot little
sports car of some kind was right on his bumper. Behind that
was a Jeep Cherokee, followed by a pair of behemoth pickups.
No doubt the last two were four-wheel-drive numbers—Tundras
or Dakotas or some other tough-sounding name.

Too bad, Alfred thought. *You're not going up this damned mountain any faster than we are, so take an old cold tater and wait.*

Martha sat beside him, quiet and unperturbed. That was the
way she'd ridden with him for all these sixty-nine years—seventy
next month. She seemed to be keeping watch on the passing
scenery out the window—the scrubby pines, the red-hued dirt,
the ragged burned-dry grass—but he didn't know how much she
was actually seeing. Macular degeneration had robbed her of
much of her sight, but certainly not all of it. There was enough
vision left to her that she still read Alfred the riot act whenever
he tried clearing the table without first cleaning his plate.

"That's what I like about this spot," Martha said at last. "The
sky's always so blue up here."

And that was true. Far off to the east, somewhere over New
Mexico, stood a tiny fringe of white cumulus clouds. No doubt
those would build up during the day, rising higher and higher. By
late afternoon they'd tower overhead and would probably grow
into another fierce monsoon storm, but for now the sky above
the Huachuca Mountains was a vast expanse of brilliant blue.

"Yes," Alfred agreed.

They both knew that Alfred was totally color-blind. He wouldn't have known blue from green if it had come up and slapped him in the face. But Alfred Beasley was no dummy, either. After all these years he was smart enough to know that if Martha said something was blue, he agreed completely, no questions asked.

The sign back at the highway had said it was three miles from the turnoff to the viewpoint. To Alfred's way of thinking, today this seemed like a very long three miles. By the time they turned into the parking lot and stopped in the first handicapped space, the needle on the Buick's temperature gauge was hovering right at the H. Alfred let go of the steering wheel and turned off the key. "Well, Buttercup," he said. "Here we are."

It took several minutes for him to wrestle her wheelchair out of the backseat. At home Martha could get around on a walker for short distances, but outside the house they used the chair. There were times Alfred could have used a walker himself. Pushing Martha's chair gave him the benefit of a walker without having to admit to his wife that he maybe needed one.

Alfred was relieved to see that the nearest picnic table—only a matter of a few feet from the parking lot—was still unoccupied. Once he had Martha in her chair and the picnic hamper on her lap, he made straight for that. The path was steeper than he would have thought, but he made it, wondering as he went if, when it came time to leave, he would be strong enough to push her back up the hill to the car.

He parked Martha's chair at the end of the table, set the brake, and then settled down on the end of the bench to watch while she took charge of setting out forenoon coffee. First came the red-

and-white-checked oilcloth tablecloth. It was old and almost frayed through in spots, but it still worked. Then came the stainless-steel thermos they'd bought for three bucks at a Kiwanis rummage sale. After that came the paper napkins and the school cast-off cups and plates.

Martha had spent twenty years cooking and dishing out food in the high school cafeteria. When the school had unloaded its old, indestructible plastic dishes, Martha had dragged a set home. By then, years of hot water and detergent had scrubbed away the shiny surface. Now they boasted a matte finish. Martha claimed they were pink. As far as Alfred was concerned, they were no particular color at all.

Once the dishes were set out, it was time for their midmorning treat. Once a week, at Safeway, they bought a package of eight sweet rolls which Martha would put into individual Tupperware containers so she could dole them out one at a time, one day at a time, with an extra half apiece on Sunday. She did so now, bringing out the roll she'd brought along in the hamper. Placing it on one of the two plates, she felt with her fingers and then carefully divided the roll in half with the paring knife she kept in the hamper for just that purpose. Then, after placing one half of the roll on the other plate, she set that one in front of Alfred and turned her attention to pouring coffee.

Watching Martha as she concentrated somewhat shakily on her self-appointed tasks, Alfred couldn't help being struck by how much he still loved her and by how lucky they were to be still together. Most of their couple friends were gone now. Only a few widows remained. Alfred was pretty much the last of the Mohicans when it came to the men. When he had met Martha working in that diner in Omaha back in 1934, he was a cocky seventeen-year-old and she a dark-eyed beauty of twenty. At the time those three years had seemed like an insurmountable obstacle. Now those critical three years were just a drop in the bucket. They didn't mean anything.

"Are you just going to sit there daydreaming and let your coffee get cold?" Martha demanded.

The coffee was cooling rapidly because, compared with the hot valley floor, the mountain was downright chilly. At sixty-five hundred feet, the midmorning sun wasn't nearly as warm on this July day as one would have thought, and Alfred was glad they both had sweaters. Once they finished their roll and coffee, Martha reached into the hamper again and pulled out a tattered brown book and handed it over to him. *The Treasury of the Familiar,* its frayed cover now held together with duct tape, had been the one book, other than the Bible, that Martha had owned when they married. And they still read from both volumes on a daily basis, in the mornings though. Not in the afternoons. These days Alfred wasn't good for much in the afternoons.

"What would you like me to read today, Buttercup?" Alfred asked.

"*The Song of Hiawatha,*" she said. That was the one he turned to, although the book opened to that page pretty much on its own. The poem was Martha's particular favorite. She had learned it when she was in sixth grade in Kearney, Nebraska, and could still recite most of it by heart. Alfred had read it to her so often that he almost had it memorized as well. Eventually, though, Albert noticed that Martha's mind had wandered. She was no longer repeating the familiar words along with him.

Alfred closed the book. "What is it?" he asked.

"We've been really lucky," Martha said, pouring second cups

of coffee. He marveled that she could still see well enough to do that without spilling any.

"Yes," he agreed. "I was thinking that very thing a few minutes ago."

"What about the girls?" she asked. "Will they ever be friends?"

Their two daughters had had a falling-out in high school when they'd both been interested in the same boy—a Bisbee High School bad boy who hadn't married either one of them. But the bad blood between the two sisters, Sandra Louise and Samantha Ann, had stuck. They still didn't speak—couldn't come to the same holiday celebrations. Their estrangement was going on forty years now. Alfred knew that no matter how hard Martha tried to fix it, their daughters' continuing feud was the one stark failure in his wife's life—the one intractable problem that no amount of prayer or effort or hard work had been able to solve.

Alfred could have said, "Of course. They'll grow out of it." But it was too late for that kind of empty-headed crap. "I doubt it," he said. "They're both too set in their ways."

"Is it time?" Martha asked a little later.

Alfred straightened and nodded. "Pretty much," he said.

Just then a young woman in hiking attire approached the table. "Excuse me," she said in heavily accented English. "I am watching you. You remind me of my grandparents in Germany—Bernkastel. Would you mind so much if I took your picture?"

"Why on earth would you want to do that?" Martha asked.

"To help me remember them," the young woman said.

"Come on, Buttercup," Alfred urged, smiling and putting his large hand over Martha's small one. "Let's do it."

Martha sighed and arranged her face in the tight grimace that passed for a smile. She had always been ashamed of her crooked, misshapen teeth. Even though the false teeth she had worn for the past twenty-five years were as straight as could be, she had never managed to change her lifelong habit of not smiling when faced with a camera.

Once the picture was taken, the young woman stayed on, chatting gaily with Alfred while Martha repacked the hamper and folded the tablecloth. Alfred had always been the gregarious one in the family—someone who made friends easily wherever he went. And when it came time to push Martha's chair back to the Buick, the young woman—whose name was Trudy—helped out by carrying the hamper. In her younger days, Martha might have been a little jealous.

"Trudy and her friends are here to spend two weeks hiking the Pacific Crest Trail," Alfred explained as he helped Martha into the car.

"What a bunch of foolishness," Martha said. "Why walk when you could ride?"

Alfred didn't have an answer for that one, so he said nothing.

Once in the car, Martha automatically reached for her seat belt, then thought better of it. "I don't suppose we need those this time," she said.

"No," Alfred agreed. "I suppose not."

With a fond glance in his wife's direction, Alfred put the car in reverse and backed out of the parking space. There were more cars in the lot now, but there was still a single empty spot in the line of cars parked so they looked out over the San Pedro Valley far below. There was a low rock wall positioned as a guardrail in front of the cars, but Alfred knew if he picked up enough speed before he got there, the Buick would either smash through the wall or jump over it.

Keeping the emergency brake on, Alfred pressed his foot on the gas pedal. The Buick's old V-6 came to life. Only when the engine was a full throttle did Alfred shove it into gear and release the hand brake. Once he was sure they'd make it through the space between the other two cars, he let go of the steering wheel and sought Martha's hand, squeezing it hard enough that the thin bones ground together.

And that's what Alfred and Martha Beasley were doing when their Buick went screaming over the wall and plunged down the steep mountainside—they were holding hands. They were still holding hands when the Buick came to earth the first time in an explosion of metal and glass and dust. The car hit once and then turned end over end. The force of that first blow drove them apart. Alfred tried to hold on, but he couldn't.

The last thing Alfred Beasley knew, Martha's hand was lost to him, but strangely enough, he felt like he was flying.

And he was.

—+—

The 911 calls reporting the horrific accident started coming in just after eleven that morning. Several witnesses dialed in almost simultaneously, all of them calling to report seeing the same thing—a vehicle at the Montezuma Pass Overlook in the Coronado National Forest had gone racing through the parking lot with an elderly man at the wheel and with an equally elderly woman in the passenger seat. The speeding Buick had plowed through a retaining wall and then plunged off the side of the mountain, ejecting both passengers in the process.

One of the frantic witnesses, a German national, took it upon herself to clamber down the steep mountainside to check on the two victims. When she finally managed to reach them—at some considerable risk to her own life and limb—she called back up to her hiking companions and reported that neither of the two victims had survived.

When the calls first came in, Joanna was at her desk and was just starting to wade through the morning's mail. Knowing that the appropriate departmental assets had been dispatched to the scene, Joanna's initial reaction was to stay where she was and keep her nose to the grindstone. An hour or so later, however, Ernie Carpenter, her chief homicide detective, called in for reinforcements.

"Sorry to bother you, boss," he said, "but we need some help out here."

"What kind of help?"

"We've got two bodies lying on rocks halfway down the mountain in terribly difficult terrain," he said. "Deb was able to drag her butt down there to take a look at the situation. I didn't even try."

Deb was Debra Howell, Joanna's recently promoted newbie homicide detective.

"She says it's dangerous as hell down there," Ernie continued. "One false step and the rescuers will be done for, too. Not only that, it looks like there's a serious storm blowing in. If you want those bodies picked up before they get washed down the mountain and end up floating away to who knows where, it's going to take a miracle to get them hauled out of here. That or a helicopter."

Of course, the perpetually strapped Cochise County Sheriff's Department didn't have a helicopter of its own. Fort Huachuca, a U.S. Army military installation located entirely inside Joanna's jurisdiction, did have helicopters available—more than one, in fact. They also boasted a well-trained search-and-rescue team, but getting folks from the fort to cooperate with their nonmilitary neighbors was never an easy sell. They weren't what you could call big on providing mutual aid.

First Joanna took herself out to the scene so she could assess the situation with her own eyes. Herding her Crown Victoria up the narrow winding road was challenging. Then, once she got to the viewpoint, one look was enough to put her in total agreement with Detective Carpenter's opinion. Having deputies use stretchers to hand-carry broken bodies up the steep mountainside was utterly out of the question. The idea of risking fully half a dozen workers' comp claims at the same time would have sent her budget-conscious chief deputy Frank Montoya into a fiscal spasm.

"I guess I'll put on my best poker face and go to Fort Huachuca to talk to whoever's in charge," she said.

"Want me to call Doc Winfield?"

Dr. George Winfield was the Cochise County medical examiner. Now married to Joanna's mother, Eleanor, he also happened to be Sheriff Brady's stepfather.

"Not yet," Joanna said. "He can't climb down there either, and there's no sense having George standing around with nothing to do until we're somewhere near ready to hand over the bodies."

Once on post, it took two hours of going through channels and across desks before Joanna finally made her way to Colonel

Donald Drake, someone with enough brass on his uniform to make a decision to bypass any number of prohibitive rules and regs.

"That's very rugged terrain out there, Sheriff Brady," he observed somewhat patronizingly. "Even setting aside the problems of using military equipment and personnel for an essentially civilian purpose, I'm not sure you understand some of the extensive technical difficulties involved in that kind of operation."

Donald Drake wasn't a large man, but he was stern-faced, hawk-nosed, and imposing. Joanna half expected that, at some point in the conversation, he'd look at her over his reading glasses and call her a "little lady."

Running the Cochise County Sheriff's Department had given Joanna Brady considerable experience in dealing with the cool macho dudes of this world. Many of them could be brought into compliance with a smile along with a short-enough skirt and a well-displayed bit of leg. She recognized at once, however, that none of that would work with Colonel Drake. Here her uniform and badge helped level the playing field. So did not backing down.

"I just came from the scene," she told him. "I'm well aware of the difficulties posed not only by the terrain itself but also by the severe crosswinds that will most likely accompany the storm that's currently blowing in from the southeast. According to the weather service, we should start seeing the first serious gusts from that at around sixteen hundred hours. I was hoping we could have the situation wrapped up before then."

Drake gave her a piercing look. "We'd have to use our own personnel," he said. "I wouldn't want some untrained yahoo on the ground who wouldn't have the foggiest idea of how to use our slings. If they're not fastened properly, we could end up dropping one of those bodies instead of hauling it out."

This sounded like a major concession. "Absolutely," Joanna agreed quickly. "That would be dreadful."

"From what you're saying, I assume this is strictly a recovery operation. My guys go in, pick up the bodies, drop them off at a prespecified point, and then we're out of there. Correct?"

"Understood," Joanna said.

Drake thought about that for a moment. "What's the situation again?" he asked. "And where?"

"Several hundred yards straight down from the viewpoint at Montezuma Pass. The victim drove through the parking lot, over the wall, and down the side of the mountain."

"How many victims total?"

Obviously Drake hadn't bothered to listen to her to begin with, because he hadn't expected to be involved. Joanna found it heartening that he was asking her to repeat the details.

"Two," she said. "An elderly man and woman."

"What happened?" Drake asked. "An accelerator problem?"

"I don't know," Joanna answered. "It could be. Or it might even be a homicide/suicide."

Maybe the incident was the result of a mechanical failure in the Beasleys' car, but Joanna suspected that Drake and his commanding officer would be far more interested in being involved in a possible homicide investigation than in the aftermath of a mere accident.

"That's why we need to get the bodies of the victims out of there before the rain hits," she added. "To help preserve the evidence."

Drake stood up. "All right, then," he said. "I'll take this to my CO. Maybe I can pass it off as a training exercise."

Joanna knew this was a hint for her to leave his office and keep a low profile until he came back with his answer. "I'll wait," she said with a smile, and refused to budge. Since Joanna wasn't leaving, Colonel Drake did. He returned less than five minutes later.

"All right," he said. "It's a go. Let's understand going in that we're not going to make a habit of this, Sheriff Brady. Where do you want the victims taken?"

"There's a gravel turnaround right at the junction with Highway 92. It's on the flat, but it's only about three miles from where the bodies are now."

Drake smiled. "Probably less than that as the crow flies—which we do."

Joanna smiled back. "I'll have the medical examiner waiting there with vans," she said. "How long?"

Drake glanced at his watch. "Let's say an hour to an hour and a half to scramble my people, check out their gear, and arrive on the scene. One other thing, though. What about media involvement?"

"What about it?" Joanna asked.

"My CO was wondering if there was a possibility of getting some press," Drake said. "Good press, of course."

The homicide gambit had worked. *I called that shot,* Joanna thought.

"I'll see what I can do," she said. In actual fact, she already knew the press was already either en route or on scene. She had encountered two camera vans from Tucson stations lumbering up the mountain road earlier, as she was coming down. No doubt there'd be plenty of opportunity for positive PR for the Fort Huachuca Search and Rescue Team from whoever was doing the local stand-up news commentary.

Feeling just a bit smug, Joanna hurried out to her Crown Victoria and dialed George Winfield.

"Not you," he said when he picked up. "Not on Friday."

"What do you mean, not me and not on Friday?" Joanna asked.

"I mean your mother and I have plans," George replied. "We're supposed to drive up to Tucson to have dinner with friends."

"You also have two dead bodies that'll be flown out of the Coronado National Forest right around four P.M."

"Two!" he exclaimed. "Hell of a time to have two at once. Bobby's on vacation at the moment. Won't be back until the end of next week."

Bobby Short was George's only full-time assistant.

"And if I miss dinner again, Ellie will kill me. But you say they're being flown out? From where? What's going on?"

And that was the real problem for Joanna's mother, Eleanor Lathrop Winfield. With her new husband, she was perpetually at war with her daughter. When it came to George's choosing between dinner with his wife's friends or tackling a homicide investigation for his stepdaughter's department, Joanna always held the trump card.

"Car drove off the Montezuma Pass Overlook late this morning," Joanna explained. "Two people are dead. The bodies were thrown from the vehicle in incredibly rough terrain. Fort Huachuca's search and rescue unit is bringing in a helicopter and crew to fly them off the mountain. I told Colonel Drake that you'd have vans waiting at the junction where the road from Montezuma Pass meets Highway 92."

"And exactly how do I go about producing a second van?"

George demanded. "They don't grow on trees, you know. I suppose I'll have to rent an ambulance. The Board of Supervisors won't like that. I'll probably have to go there, hat in hand, and beg for money to pay the bill."

Joanna thought about Claire Newmark and wondered how George would fare with her when it came time to plead his budgetary case.

Better you than me, Joanna thought with a slight smile. *Just make sure it doesn't sound like a stump speech.*

CHAPTER 2

WHILE STOPPING OFF TO GRAB A QUICK LUNCH IN SIERRA VISTA, Joanna called Ernie to let him know the helicopter and crew would be there eventually. "That's good news," he said. "Better them than us." Which was the same thing Joanna had just told herself about George Winfield.

"How are things?"

"It's a damned zoo. The local LEO is here and helping out," Ernie said, referring to the national forest's federally funded law enforcement officer. "But there are far too many people in too small a space. I've called for a tow truck to retrieve the vehicle once we get the bodies out of there, but I just ordered two television news camera crews to clear out. I'm tired of them being under hand and foot. Most of our witnesses aren't just from out of state, they're from out of the country. They're here with an international climbing club from somewhere in Germany, I believe. If we don't interview them and get their statements now, we're going to miss out."

"Call the news teams back," Joanna said.

"Call them back?" Ernie sounded stunned. "Are you kidding? Did you hear me? I said 'television news camera crews.'"

"I heard what you said," Joanna told him. "The question is, did you hear me? I want you to call them back. We need those cameras. We're getting Fort Huachuca Search and Rescue for free as long as they can come away with some good PR. Do not send any more news crews packing!"

"Hey," Ernie shouted, blasting a hole in Joanna's ear. "Hey, you with the camera. Forget it. I take it back. You don't have to leave after all." Then he came back on the line. "You owe me," he said.

"No, I don't," Joanna said. "Because otherwise you'd be one of the guys scrambling down the mountain on your hands and knees to retrieve those bodies."

"Point taken," Ernie agreed grudgingly.

"Any ID on the victims yet?"

"Tentative. The vehicle is registered to Alfred Lawrence Beasley. Deb found a wallet with his name in it. Do you know them?" Ernie asked.

"I've probably met them, but I don't know them," Joanna said. "I'm pretty sure he worked in the post office, and I believe she was a cook in the high school cafeteria."

"Know anything about next of kin?"

"I don't," Joanna said. "My mother might. She's a fountain of information about everyone in Bisbee, but right now probably isn't a good time to ask. And what did the witnesses say about our victims?" Joanna continued. "Were they quarreling? Was there some kind of disagreement?"

"None whatsoever," Ernie replied.

"And the woman got in the car willingly?"

"Absolutely. No sign of force whatsoever. One of the witnesses was standing in front of his vehicle which was parked right next to the spot where they went over. He swears they were holding hands when they went by him."

"A suicide pact, then?" Joanna asked.

"Maybe," Ernie said.

By 3:00 P.M. Joanna was standing next to her Crown Victoria at the bottom of the road leading to Montezuma Pass. The sun was unbearably hot, and the high humidity made the air almost too thick to breathe. Off to the east, thick dark clouds were building. A storm was definitely brewing. Watching it, Joanna uttered a small prayer that high winds, which were an automatic prelude to an approaching monsoon, would hold off long enough for the helicopter crew to work its search-and-rescue magic.

Knowing how long it would take to sort things out, Joanna called home to check on Butch and on Dennis, who had passed the four-month mark two days earlier. Now that Joanna's maternity leave was over, Butch had been doing a good job of being Mr. Mom, but she knew there were times when he was overwhelmed. She also knew he was up against a deadline for finishing the review of the copyedited manuscript for his second book, *Collateral Damage*. Unfortunately, taking care of the baby was getting in the way of Butch's being able to work.

"I finally got the little twerp down for a nap," Butch Dixon grumbled. "Obviously he's a chip off his mother's block. He can get by on minimal amounts of sleep, but that means I'm not getting anything done."

Jenny was fourteen now, and this summer she had been a godsend, helping care for her little brother. But Joanna also remembered how it had felt to be at home looking after Jenny as a baby while Andy, her first husband, had been away at work. There were times when she had felt she was losing her mind. There had been countless days when nothing got done—when clothes didn't get folded, dishes didn't go in the dishwasher, and when the idea of taking even a quick shower was an impossible dream.

"Anything I can do to help?" she asked.

"Yes," Butch said. "Bring home a pizza. I haven't had a chance to get to the store. That way I won't have to worry about dinner."

"It may be late," she said. "I'm on the scene of what could turn into a double homicide."

"What's late?" Butch returned. "I didn't manage to eat lunch until just a few minutes ago."

"I'll see you then," she said. "I love you."

"I love you, too," he said. "But I'll love you more if you bring me a double pepperoni."

A few minutes after three, George Winfield arrived in his county-owned, specially outfitted Dodge Caravan, followed by a green-and-white aid car with Sierra Vista's logo on the doors.

"How'd you do that?" Joanna asked, nodding toward the second vehicle.

"Pulled in a marker," George said. "The city manager owed me a favor."

"How's Mother taking this?" Joanna asked.

George shook his head. "Don't even ask," he said mournfully. "I'll be in the doghouse for weeks on this one. Do we have names on our victims?"

"Tentative," Joanna told him. "Alfred and Martha Beasley. Longtime Bisbee residents."

"Did you know them?" George asked.

"Knew of them more than knew them. Mother might be a better source of information."

George grunted. "Never mind," he said. "I doubt she'd be inclined to help. So tell me. How did this happen? These people just drove their vehicle right off the cliff?"

"According to witnesses, they had a little picnic. Then they got back in the car, with the husband behind the wheel. Once they backed out of the parking place, he put the pedal to the metal and then went screaming through the parking lot, through the wall, and over the edge."

A few minutes later Joanna heard the noisy *thump-thump-thump* of an approaching helicopter. Pulling a pair of binoculars out of her glove compartment, she saw the aircraft coming south following the Highway 92 right-of-way. Just as it passed over Joanna's head, the helicopter turned sharply to the right and seemed determined to fly directly into the face of the mountain. At last it came to a hovering stop. Seconds later, Joanna could see a figure being lowered to the ground in some kind of harness. The first person was followed by a second. Finally a basket contraption was lowered to the ground as well.

The two crew members wasted no time. Only a few minutes passed before the basket, loaded with a body bag, was winched back into the waiting helicopter. As soon as it disappeared inside, the aircraft changed positions. It shifted to another spot slightly below the first one and then hovered in place while the empty basket was lowered once more. Finally, once the second body bag and the two crew members had been retrieved, the helicopter wheeled away from the mountain and headed back down toward the junction where Joanna and the medical examiner waited.

When the aircraft came to a noisy stop next to the two vans, Joanna was surprised to see that a grinning Colonel Drake was the first person to exit. "I saw the cameras," he said. "Two of them at least. I hope they got some good footage."

So do I, Joanna thought, but she was grateful the cameras were on the top of the mountain and not there where the bodies were being transferred into the waiting vans.

Within minutes the vans headed for the morgue in Bisbee, and the helicopter took off on its return flight to Fort Huachuca. As it turned into a dot on the horizon, Joanna felt the first puff of breeze that signaled the approaching storm. Grateful that it had held off as long as it had and having done what was needed, Joanna left her investigative team in charge and headed back to the office. On the way she stopped and picked up the pizza. She knew that, as far as Butch was concerned, his pepperoni didn't have to be hot to be good.

It was after five by the time she returned to the Cochise County Justice Center. The temperature had dropped. When she got out of the car, no precipitation was in evidence, but the wind whipping around her was heavy with the smell of approaching rain. Joanna was a child of the desert. There was something about that distinctive and heady fragrance that made her heart lighter no matter what else was going on around her.

Joanna's plan was to stop by her office just long enough to

check on things and then head home. By then, Kristin Gregovich, Joanna's secretary, had already left for the day. Kristin, another relatively new mother, had to be out the door by five on
the dot in order to pick up her daughter, Shaundra, from day
care. Shaundra's daddy, Terry, happened to be Joanna's K-9 officer. Seeing the juggling act Kristin and Terry did every single
day never failed to leave Joanna counting her blessings that she
had Butch Dixon to manage the home front.

Marveling at the peace and quiet, Joanna sat down at her desk
and closed her eyes. Parents of infants often get by on far too little sleep. The working mother nursing-pump routine hadn't
worked well for her. (Having Ernie barge uninvited into her office one day when she'd been in the middle of things hadn't
helped.) So Dennis was now a bottle-fed baby, thriving on formula and rice cereal. That meant that Joanna and Butch could
take turns with overnight feedings, but it also meant that neither
of them was getting a full night's sleep.

Within minutes Joanna found herself mired in the day's stack
of unfinished paperwork. Caught up in that, she didn't notice the
deteriorating weather outside until a fierce clap of thunder shattered her concentration. She looked up to find that the promised
storm had started in dead earnest. Rain pelted down so hard that
it almost obscured the limestone cliffs on the steep hills beyond
her office window while almost continuous bursts of lightning lit
the sky to the south and east.

Hurriedly she stuffed the most important of the day's reports
and her laptop into her briefcase. Then she grabbed her purse,
shut off the lights, and left by the back door. The rain had come
so hard and fast that the downspouts were already working at
full capacity. Water poured off the roof. Just crossing the two

steps from the covered area to the door of the Crown Victoria was enough to leave her drenched.

When the first of the seasonal summer rainstorms had arrived two days earlier, the water had all disappeared as the parched earth lapped it up. Now, though, the downpour was so severe that the water lay in thin puddles on the desert floor. Joanna knew what that meant. Rather than soaking in, the rain would turn to runoff, filling the shallow gullies and deeper washes with swift-running brown water. Unfortunately, between the Justice Center and High Lonesome Ranch there were several of those that would have to be crossed. Joanna had no intention of being one of those hapless motorists who failed to heed posted warnings that said DO NOT ENTER WHEN FLOODED. Every year some drivers who did that merely had to be rescued, while others drowned. Joanna knew that if she didn't make it home before water in the washes got too deep, she'd be stuck waiting on the far side until the levels subsided.

I hope I'm not too late, Joanna thought, and she was right to be worried.

The first two washes on High Lonesome Road were dry. The third and fourth had a tiny trickle of water, but the last one—the one after she turned onto their own private road—was actually starting to run. Taking a deep breath, she rammed her foot onto the gas pedal, counting on momentum to finish carrying her across the streambed. She drove the rest of the way to the house with her hands alive with needles and pins.

As she approached the house, another flash of lightning lit the sky, followed by a fierce boom of thunder. The lights in the house flickered slightly and then went out. By the time she made it to the garage door, however, their emergency generator had rumbled into action. The interior lights flashed back on and the garage door opened when she pressed the clicker.

Still drenched from getting into the car back at her office, Joanna was grateful that she could pull inside the garage. The family's three dogs were all waiting just inside the door that led from the garage into the laundry room. Jenny's two, the incredibly ugly Tigger, a half golden retriever/half pit bull, and Lucky, a boisterous but stone-deaf black Lab, gave Joanna a joyous greeting. Lady, Joanna's far more dignified Australian shepherd, held back. Once Joanna set the pizza box on the kitchen table, however, it was clear that the dogs were far more interested in the possibility of pizza than they were in greeting their newly arrived human.

Butch's laptop and stacks of manuscript pages sat unattended on the kitchen table. From several rooms away, Joanna heard Dennis wailing at the top of his lungs.

Butch appeared a moment later with the squalling baby propped on one shoulder and with a bottle gripped in his other hand. "He's mad as hell and isn't going to take it anymore," Butch said. "The poor little kid was in bed and asleep, but that last crack of thunder woke him up. Do you want him?"

After slipping out of her wet clothing and putting on a robe, Joanna took both the baby and the bottle. When she tried offering him the bottle, Dennis wasn't the least bit interested. He screwed his angry little face up and kept right on screeching.

With a sigh Butch went over to the table and helped himself to a piece of pizza. "Had to turn off the computer. Didn't want it to get fried. The power went off, too," he said. "I'm sure glad we bit the bullet and sprang for a generator. The lights came back on without a hitch a few seconds later, just the way the brochure says they should."

At the time Joanna and Butch had been building the house, they debated whether or not to take on the expense of adding a liquid-propane-powered generator. Because their house was so isolated, however, they knew that when electrical outages did occur, High Lonesome Ranch could end up a long way down the priority list when it came to having power restored.

"So am I," Joanna said. "Where's Jenny?"

"Sleepover at Cassie's house, remember?"

Cassie Parks, Jenny's best friend, lived a few miles away near Double Adobe at a decommissioned KOA campground her parents had turned into a mobile home park.

"Didn't," Joanna said.

Butch went over to the fridge and pulled out a beer. "Want one?" he asked.

"No, thanks," Joanna said.

"How were the roads?"

"They're fine," she said. That was a little white lie, but Butch didn't need to know she had crossed a possibly dangerous wash on her way home. "So far," she added. "But it's raining enough right now that they could be bad by morning. My Crown Victoria doesn't have a whole lot of clearance."

Butch looked at her and grinned. "But tomorrow's Saturday. You won't need to go in, will you?"

Her department was currently dealing with a homicide/ suicide. It seemed unlikely that Joanna would be able to take all of Saturday off. "Maybe not," she hedged.

Most of the time Butch was really understanding about the demands of her job, but at the moment his job as a mystery writer was demanding its own kind of attention.

"That's a relief," he said. "The reviewed copyedited manuscript needs to be in New York by Tuesday at the latest, and I could sure use some help with little troublemaker here in the meantime." Butch helped himself to another piece of pizza, then he came over and kissed the top of Joanna's head. "This is food for the gods, by the way," he added.

Joanna tried the bottle again. This time Dennis took it. The sudden silence in the kitchen was almost deafening. The pizza was calling to her, too, but with the baby in one hand and the bottle in the other, Butch's double pepperoni would have to wait.

"I do have some bad news," Butch said. "The check bounced."

"What check?"

"The renter's check—from the ranch. It was due on the first and didn't get here until the fifth. I deposited it yesterday. The bank called this afternoon right after I talked to you to say Bob Baker's checking account was closed."

Between them, Butch and Joanna had two rental properties, a house he had rehabbed in Bisbee and the original house on High Lonesome Ranch, one Joanna and her first husband, Andy, had purchased from his parents. Over the course of the past few months they had learned that being landlords wasn't a trouble-free proposition. Bob Baker had rented the property six months earlier, claiming he was putting together an important import/export company that would be based in Agua Prieta, south of Douglas.

"Closed," Joanna echoed.

"So I loaded Dennis into his car seat and drove over there to raise hell with him. He's long gone, Joey, and the place is a pigsty. I don't know how long he's been gone. It looks like illegals have been using it as a stopping-off place for quite some time. In fact, I'm starting to wonder if Bob Baker's supposed import/ export business wasn't just a cover for whatever else he was really doing."

"You think he was a coyote?"

In the parlance of southern Arizona's law enforcement community, coyotes were more often the two-legged kind involved in smuggling illegal immigrants rather than four-legged ones, who were generally law-abiding.

Butch nodded.

"And he's been using our property as a base for that kind of illegal activity?"

"Right again," Butch said. "I'd bet money on it. I locked the place up as best I could. We'll have to bring in a whole crew to muck it out. Baker gave us a cleaning deposit along with his first and last month's rent, but that's not going to come close to covering the costs. And by the time we get it cleaned up enough to rent it again, I'm guessing we'll be out another month's rent, maybe even more."

"Great," Joanna said.

"And whatever that bill turns out to be," Butch continued, "I want to go after him for it."

"Go after him?"

"You bet," Butch said. "I already called Dick Voland and asked him to do a skip-trace."

Richard Voland had once served as one of Joanna's chief deputies. Since leaving the department, he had hung out his shingle and now worked as Bisbee's only private investigator. Even though Voland's going rate was far under what was being charged in Tucson and Phoenix, Joanna knew it wasn't an inexpensive proposition. On the other hand, she couldn't very well turn anyone from her own department loose on investigating something that was essentially a private matter, coyote or not.

"Dick Voland's a private eye. He'll end up charging us way more than the cleaning is worth," Joanna pointed out, "and more than you'll ever get back from Baker, either."

"I don't care," Butch insisted. "It's the principle of the thing."

Since Butch handled the rental properties, Joanna didn't argue the point. And if Baker had been using their property as a cover for illegal activities, Butch was more than justified in being pissed at the man.

"Fair enough," Joanna said finally. By then Dennis had drifted off to sleep. "I'm going to put him back in the crib. Don't eat all the pizza while I'm gone."

—+—

By the time Joanna and Butch were finishing their pizza, the wash between their house and High Lonesome Road was running at full flood stage. Ten miles to the south and west was another gully, Greenbush Draw. That one, near the tiny border community of Naco, had also turned from a sandy creek bed into a rushing torrent.

The transformation happened gradually. At first there was only a tiny trickle of water in the middle of the sandy bed, but as more and more water drained off the desert floor, the flow increased. Within minutes it expanded from being inches wide to more than a foot. Eventually a wall of water five feet deep came roaring downstream, carrying in front of it the flotsam and jetsam—discarded backpacks, food wrappers, water containers—deposited by the unending army of illegal border crossers who also had to scramble through the usually dry creek bed and across that portion of the Sonoran Desert in their quest to gain entry into the United States.

At first the water rushed over the sand, but as the flow deepened and strengthened, the sand in the gully's bed liquefied and began to move—and so did something else, something that had long lain undiscovered in that desolate, sandy wash.

Two black plastic bags, held together with a swathe of duct tape, had been buried deep enough in the sand that it took time for the anchoring weight of the sand to rise up and drift away. As the sand rose, so did the bags.

Time, the elements, and ravening insects had done their work well. The contents of the bags weren't nearly as heavy as they had been when they'd first been placed there. Holes chewed in the material—also the work of industrious insects—did their part to keep the grisly package from actually floating, but the bags did move. They tumbled along in the murky red flood like some evil-looking bottom-dwelling fish.

Then, where the streambed curved sharply to the right, the roaring water overflowed the steep banks and surged out across hundreds of yards of flat desert floor. The trash bags were carried along there as well. They came to rest finally, caught up in the low-hanging branches of a scrawny mesquite tree. In the course of the night, as the storm moved northward, the water gradually receded. By morning the desert was a desert again, but the tattered bags were still there— sodden and stinking—waiting patiently for some poor unsuspecting passerby to see them and uncover the horror lurking inside.

—+—

After being up with Dennis twice overnight, Joanna was sound asleep the next morning when Butch shook her awake at two minutes past six. "Up and at 'em, sleepyhead. There's a deputy waiting for you outside. Didn't you hear the dogs bark?"

"A deputy?" Joanna mumbled groggily. "This early? Which one, and how come? What's he doing here?"

Butch shook his head. "I'm not sure which one," he said. "I believe he said his name is Raymond."

That would be Deputy Matt Raymond, Joanna thought.

"According to him, our landline phone is currently out of order," Butch continued. "And lightning took out two cell-phone towers up on Juniper Flats."

Joanna sat up and tried to put her feet on the floor. They landed first on Lady, who refused to sleep anywhere but next to Joanna's side of the bed. "That means my cell phone isn't working either?"

"What it really means is that nobody in Bisbee has a working cell phone."

"Great," Joanna muttered. "So why's Deputy Raymond here? What's going on? Has something happened?"

"There's evidently been some kind of incident down near Double Adobe," Butch answered. "A fatality mobile-home fire. Dispatch thought you'd want to know about it."

Joanna's heart constricted. Jenny had spent the night with Cassie Parks in her family's mobile home a few miles from Double Adobe. "Not Cassie's—" she began.

Butch shook his head. "No," he reassured her quickly. "I already checked. It's not Cassie's folks' place. The fire's within half a mile or so of there, but Jenny's fine."

"Thank God," Joanna breathed. She got up and staggered toward the bathroom. "So much for having Saturday off. Tell Matt to go on ahead. I'll be there as soon as I can."

"No can do," Butch said. "That storm parked itself right over the Mule Mountains and stayed there most of the night. Our wash is still running. So are the ones down on High Lonesome Road. Raymond managed to get through them in his four-wheel-drive Explorer. Your Crown Vic doesn't have four-wheel drive and won't do the job. It's stranded here for the time being. He's waiting to take you."

"Even better," Joanna muttered. Still shaking her head, she hurried into the bathroom. By the time she had showered and dressed, Deputy Raymond was in the kitchen drinking coffee and having an earnest conversation about the ins and outs of APUs—alternate power units—and the overall reliability of electrical generators. Dennis, already dressed and breakfasted, snoozed peacefully in his infant swing.

Red-haired and pink-cheeked, the baby looked for all the world like a sweet little cherub—nothing at all like the red-faced demon who had kept both his parents awake for much of the preceding night. That was the distressing reality about babies, Joanna realized. They got to nap at will off and on during the day while their poor zombielike parents did not.

Grateful that Butch wasn't giving her any grief for abandoning him on a Saturday, she took the travel cup of coffee he offered her and headed for Deputy Raymond's Explorer. "Butch said there's a fatality," she said as she buckled up. "Any idea who's dead?"

Matt Raymond shook his head. "Dispatch may know the names. I don't. From what I've heard, a woman, two kids, and a dog all survived. The man, confined to a wheelchair, didn't."

"Anything else going on that I should know about?" Joanna asked.

Deputy Raymond didn't answer until after he'd picked his way across the rocky expanse of creek bed that was still running several inches deep with reddish-brown water.

"Most of the county got two-plus inches of rain. The Mule Mountains above Bisbee got the worst of it," he replied finally. "Three and a half inches up there. We've spent the whole night dragging stranded doofuses out of flooded washes and dips all over the county. Phone and power lines are down between here and Douglas and between Bisbee and Tombstone. People are without power from Douglas east to the state line and there are spotty outages around Sierra Vista and Benson and over by Elfrida and Willcox as well. It's a mess."

"No wonder the phones are out," Joanna said.

"Exactly," Matt Raymond agreed. "Just what we needed."

As they turned off High Lonesome onto Double Adobe Road, Joanna looked several miles to the east, where the remains of what must have once been a dark smudge of smoke were still visible against a cloudless blue sky. The fact that the smoke appeared to be white and dissipating meant that the fire was most likely fairly well under control.

Reaching for the car's radio, Joanna called in to Dispatch, where Tica Romero was holding down her usual weekend shift. "Deputy Raymond got to you, then?" Tica asked. She sounded relieved to hear Joanna's voice. "When I couldn't reach you by either of your phones, I started to worry."

"The washes by our house are still running, but we're fine," Joanna said with a laugh. "And thanks for sending Deputy Raymond to come get me. I won't be able to drive the Civvie out until after the water goes down."

"Don't feel like the Lone Ranger," Tica returned. "You're not the only one with no phone and lots of running water. This storm was a doozy. There are crews out working on downed phone and electrical lines all over the county. They're getting things back on line, but it's slow going. Where are you?"

"Headed down Double Adobe Road toward the scene of that fire. What can you tell me about it?"

"Not much. The phones were out. A passerby saw the flames. He stopped long enough to pound on the doors and help the survivors out. Then he drove down to Double Adobe and reported the fire at four-twenty this morning. By the time their volunteer fire department responded, the structure was fully engulfed. Afraid the fire might spread to other nearby structures, they called for backup from Bisbee and Douglas both."

"What about the survivors?" Joanna asked. "Any injuries?"

"The woman who lived there, her two grandsons, and a dog are all fine," Tica replied. "The woman's husband was disabled. He was trapped in a back bedroom and couldn't get out. We're assuming he's deceased. The mobile home is a complete loss."

"Cause?" Joanna asked.

"It's all speculation so far," Tica returned. "We called out Detective Carbajal. If he's not on the scene, he's on his way. I believe Doc Winfield is headed there as well."

Wonderful, Joanna thought. *Another hitch in whatever plans Mother made for the weekend. George and I will both be in the doghouse.*

"Anything else I should know about?"

"We're still operating on backup generators here at the Justice Center," Tica continued. "Chief Deputy Montoya is coming in to keep an eye on the situation here."

It sounded as though Joanna's department had been managing to keep things together in the face of a damaging storm, even with Joanna out of the picture. *But is that a good thing or a bad thing?* she wondered. Did it mean she had succeeded in creating a department where things could be delegated to the right people in the right jobs? That was one side of the coin. Or did it mean that she was really extraneous and they could get along fine without her?

Joanna pushed aside that nagging bit of insecurity. "Tell Frank I'll come in as soon as we're finished here. Ask him to pull together a briefing. I'll let you know when we're headed in that direction."

They drove past Mountain View Mobile Estates, the former KOA campground Dick and Susan Parks had re-created as a mobile home park. In the wintertime the place filled up. Countless snowbirds in their fifth-wheel campers or RVs crammed their vehicles in cheek by jowl, parking next to tiny concrete pads where they could throw out a patio chair or two. In the dead of summer, though, the place was virtually deserted, except for the modest double-wide where the Parks lived with their daughter, Jenny's best friend.

Joanna knew the smoke and flames would have been visible from the Parkses' front door, and someone had perished in the inferno. It was likely the two boys, grandsons of the man who had died, would turn out to be friends of Jenny's and Cassie's or, at the very least, acquaintances from riding the school bus.

Having a family tragedy come this close to her own daughter's existence made Joanna uncomfortable. It was one thing for Joanna herself to deal with death, murder, and mayhem. After all, that was her job, but she would have liked to protect her daughter from that kind of ugliness.

I'll keep my fingers crossed, Joanna thought hopefully. *With any kind of luck, maybe Jenny and Cassie slept through the whole thing.*

CHAPTER 3

HALF A MILE BEYOND THE MOBILE HOME, PARK DEPUTY RAY-mond's Explorer came even with a collection of emergency vehicles, augmented by a number of private vehicles. The shoulder of the road was peppered with neighbors, curiosity seekers, and passersby, all of them hoping to catch a glimpse of what was going on.

Matt drove across a cattle guard and then headed down a bumpy dirt road toward a grouping of three different fire trucks. Suited-up firemen were in the process of unpacking hoses from two of them. Crew members from the third were using lengths of hoses that had been strung from a stock tank to pump water onto the smoldering ruin. What little remained offered scant testimony that a few hours earlier a fully habitable mobile home had stood in that spot.

Catching sight of Detective Jaime Carbajal standing next to

his Econoline van, Joanna directed Matt Raymond that way. Once the wheels stopped moving, she hopped out and hurried over to Jaime. "Any word?" she asked.

"Morning, boss," Jaime replied. "Yes. The word for the day would be stupidity. I haven't talked to the survivors yet, but the fire chief told me the dead guy was a smoker. He was also on oxygen. The miracle is that he's the only one who died."

"Do we have any names?"

"Sunderson," Jaime answered. "Leonard and Carol Sunderson. I don't know the grandkids' names. The grandparents were evidently raising the two boys."

Joanna surveyed the scene and saw no one. "Where are they?" she asked.

"In their van," he said, nodding toward an older-model VW bus with an empty wheelchair holder attached to the back. "They're all pretty broken up. Reverend Maculyea just went over to talk to them. I thought I'd give them a little private time with her before barging in with a bunch of questions."

It was only then that Joanna caught sight of Marianne Maculyea's sea-foam-green antique VW Bug tucked in among the hulking fire trucks. Marianne was the pastor at Tombstone Canyon United Methodist Church, which Joanna and Butch attended. More than that, though, she and Joanna had been best friends since junior high.

In the past several months, in the wake of disasters that had overtaken other small towns around the country, Bisbee's various clergy members had joined together to create an emergency response team of their own. They had established an on-call duty roster so that, in a crisis, one of them could roll out at the same time the first responders did.

As if on cue, Marianne emerged from the van. Two boys, bare-foot and wrapped in blankets, followed. One of them clutched a black-and-white mongrel dog to his chest. Marianne turned back and helped a gray-haired woman out of the dilapidated vehicle as well. Wearing a pair of what looked like oversized men's pajamas, she too was barefoot. That was all these three unfortunate people had left in the world, Joanna realized. The clothes on their backs, the dog the one boy carried, and noth-ing else.

The two boys appeared to be several years younger than Jenny—one about seven and the other one maybe nine. Both were still wide-eyed with shock. The traumatized dog, a sheltie mix, shivered uncontrollably. The woman was fairly heavyset and somewhere in her late fifties to early sixties. Her frizzy gray hair stuck out in all directions, and her sunken, careworn face was twisted with grief.

Breaking away from Ernie, Joanna hurried up to them. "I'm Sheriff Brady," she said, holding out a hand to the bereaved woman. "I'm so sorry for your loss, Mrs. Sunderson."

Biting her lip, Carol Sunderson nodded somberly. "Thank you," she murmured.

The younger boy stared as if mesmerized at the remains of what had been their home.

"Where will we go, Grandma?" he asked plaintively. "What's going to happen to us? Where will we live?"

"Hush, Danny," the distraught woman said determinedly. "Don't worry. We'll manage somehow. We always have."

Jaime walked up behind Joanna. "This is one of my investi-gators," Joanna said, stepping aside to introduce him. "Detec-tive Jaime Carbajal. He'll need to talk to you," she explained.

"Get some background, find out what happened, that sort of thing."

Jaime handed Carol his card. She studied it for a long moment. As she did so, the look on her face changed abruptly. Joanna knew that was when the word "homicide" finally registered. Carol gave Jaime a beseeching look. "Do the boys have to be there while you do it?" she asked.

Unasked, Marianne immediately stepped into the breach. "I'll bet you two are hungry," she said, addressing the boys. "How about if I take you down to the Mini-Mart at Double Adobe and get you something to eat—doughnuts, cupcakes, juice, and maybe some chocolate milk?"

The younger boy's face broke into a sudden smile at the proffered treat. "Real chocolate milk?" he asked. "Like in a carton?"

The older boy—the one holding the dog—shook his head and tightened his grip on his still traumatized pooch. "Only if Scamp gets to come along," he declared.

"Great," Marianne said. "By all means bring Scamp with you. He's probably hungry, too. We'll get him some food as well. That's my car—the little green one over there by that last fire truck. Why don't you go get in. I'll be there in a minute." As the boys walked away, taking the dog with them, Marianne turned back to Carol Sunderson. "Would you like something?" she asked. "We can bring it back here."

"Coffee, please," Carol said. "Black coffee would be nice, but don't get me anything to eat. I'm not hungry."

And won't be for a long time, Joanna thought. In the days and weeks that had followed the shooting death of her first husband, Sheriff Deputy Andrew Roy Brady, food had been the last thing she had wanted.

Leaving Carol with Jaime Carbajal, Joanna followed Marianne back toward her car. "Anything we should know?" she asked.

"The older boy is Rick; the younger one is Danny," Marianne said. "Their father isn't in the picture. Hasn't been since Danny was born. Their mother, the Sundersons' daughter, got caught up in the drug trade and is doing time for manslaughter back east somewhere. The grandparents have custody and have had since the boys were three and five."

"And the grandfather?"

"A retired coal miner. Dusted. Came out here for his lungs."

Bad lungs were a health hazard for miners everywhere. Copper miners used the code word "dusted." In other places it was called "black lung disease." Joanna wasn't a smoker. Never had been, but the idea that a man whose lungs were already compromised would exacerbate the problem by smoking cigarettes was something that left her shaking her head. And lighting up a smoke in a room where oxygen was in use was, as Jaime Carbajal had already pointed out, downright stupid.

Marianne herded the boys into the car and directed them to buckle up. "I think she's afraid he did it on purpose," Marianne added quietly once the door closed behind them.

"On purpose?" Joanna asked.

Marianne nodded grimly. "Lenny Sunderson was in a wheelchair, and his health was deteriorating more and more. They've been scraping by on his Social Security and some pittance of a pension. Mrs. Sunderson says she thinks he decided he didn't want to be more of a burden to her."

"Offing himself and leaving his family homeless isn't what I'd call helping," Joanna observed.

Just then a battered pickup roared up behind them. As soon as it came to a stop, an outraged man sprang out of the driver's seat. "What the hell is going on here?" he demanded. "How did this happen?"

Joanna recognized the newcomer as Tom McCracken, an eccentric old codger who was Cochise County's resident slumlord. Over the years he had bought up distressed properties everywhere from Pirtleville to Kansas Settlement. Without ever doing much to improve them, he rented them out to people of limited means. He had come to Joanna's department on more than one occasion seeking help in carrying out eviction notices.

Jaime, holding one of Carol's arms, was leading her toward his van, where they'd be able to talk with a semblance of privacy. Tom McCracken, wearing a frayed cowboy hat and down-at-the-heel boots, strode after them.

"What the hell did you people do?" he raged at Carol. "Set fire to the place? Is this the thanks I get for renting to poor white trash?"

Joanna hurried to cut him off. "Excuse me, Mr. McCracken," she said. "Enough. Leave her alone."

"Leave her alone? Why should I?" he went on, his face twisted in fury. "They've burned down my trailer! Those ratty little kids of hers probably torched it. Playing with matches, I'll bet. Worthless little buggers!"

With a shake of her head, Marianne started her VW and drove away, taking the two boys safely out of earshot. Carol, pulling free of Jaime's arm, turned back to face McCracken.

"I'm sorry," she said. "I really am."

"You're sorry?" he repeated. "My mobile is gone, and all you can say is that you're sorry?"

"Come on, Mrs. Sunderson," Jaime urged. "Ignore him."

Joanna knew Tom McCracken to be a canny businessman. She had no doubt whatsoever that his rental mobile home was fully insured. Whatever settlement he received would be more than enough to purchase another run-down mobile home to replace the one that was gone. The Sundersons' losses, on the other hand, were just exactly that—overwhelming, uninsured losses that wouldn't be easily recouped.

"Please, Mr. McCracken," Joanna said. "The fire was reported a little after four this morning, at a time when the two boys would have been in bed asleep. I doubt they had anything to do with it."

"Who the hell—" the man began, turning his anger in Joanna's direction. Then, recognizing her, he stopped. "Oh," he said, a bit more reasonably. "Sheriff Brady. What are you doing here?"

"We believe your renter, Leonard Sunderson, died in the fire," she told him. "That's why we're here. People from my department are investigating."

It took a moment for Joanna's words to penetrate McCracken's fog of outrage.

"Sunderson died?" he repeated at last, sounding far more subdued. "My phone isn't working. A friend of mine, Mason Timbers, was driving into town and saw the fire trucks. He came by the house to let me know what was going on. He never mentioned someone was dead. I had no idea."

Joanna was relieved to see that hearing the news seemed to bring McCracken back to his senses. He might be an obnoxious old coot without enough good breeding to come right out and say he was sorry, but at least he backed off some. So did Joanna.

"That's because your friend didn't know," she said. "No one did, and we haven't actually confirmed the fatality at this point. The wreckage is still too hot to search."

McCracken walked back to his pickup truck and leaned against it. He took off his hat and wiped beads of sweat from his forehead with his shirtsleeve. The sun was fully up now, and with the humidity still off the charts after the previous night's rain, Joanna could tell the day was going to be a scorcher.

"If the kids didn't do it, what caused it, then?" McCracken asked.

Now was not the time to tell him Carol Sunderson was afraid her husband had deliberately caused the fire. "No way to know that until we're able to do more investigating."

McCracken nodded. "All right, then," he said. "No sense in my hanging around here." He opened the passenger door, reached into the glove box, and produced a business card that read "Mc-Cracken Enterprises." He handed it over to Joanna. "If your people need to contact me, those are my numbers—once they get the phone service working again." With that, he entered the pickup, slammed the door, started the engine, and drove away.

George Winfield had arrived unobserved during Joanna's confrontation with Tom McCracken. "Good riddance to that little turd," the medical examiner said now from just behind Joanna's shoulder. "I liked the way you got rid of him. I'm here way too early to look for a body. What have we got?"

Joanna gave him a brief overview of what Marianne had said. "Two possible suicides in as many days, and one collateral damage," George said. "This is starting to get old."

She wondered if George even remembered that was the title of the book Butch was working on. Joanna was about to mention it when Deputy Armando Ruiz, one of Joanna's relatively new hires, came up and tapped her on the shoulder.

"Excuse me, Sheriff Brady," he said. "There's someone over there who says she needs to speak to you right away. She said she tried to call you, but her cell phone isn't working."

Joanna glanced in the direction Deputy Ruiz was pointing and spotted Jenny standing on the far side of the cattle guard leading into the Sunderson place. She stood next to Kiddo, her sorrel gelding quarter horse, with the reins clutched in one hand. With the other, she gave her mother a halfhearted self-conscious wave.

Without another word to anyone, Joanna hurried toward her daughter. "Jenny," she demanded. "What are you doing here?"

"I wanted to know what was going on," Jenny began. "I tried calling, but—"

"I know, I know," Joanna interrupted. "The phones aren't working. But this is a crime scene, Jenny. You have no business—"

"Are Danny and Ricky all right?" Jenny asked.

That brought Joanna up short. "Danny and Ricky are fine."

Jenny's face flooded with relief. "Great," she said.

"You know them, then?" Joanna asked.

Jenny nodded. "They're good kids. Cassie takes care of them sometimes at her place when Mrs. Sunderson has to take her husband to the doctor or when she needs groceries or something." By then Jenny's boot was already in the stirrup. "I'll go," she added. "I know you don't like having me around stuff like this. And I told Butch I'd come home early to help with Denny."

Jenny was the only member of the family who routinely called the baby by that pet name. Jenny and Denny.

"Butch has a bunch of work to do on the book this weekend," Jenny continued. "And since you're not there, I'd better go. I'll stop by Cassie's and tell her that the boys are okay. She was worried."

With that, Jenny wheeled Kiddo around and threaded her way through the parked vehicles. Once she was clear of them, she gave the horse a light jab in the ribs that brought him to a swift canter.

Watching her daughter head home, Joanna was flooded with yet another rush of insecurity. It wasn't just her department that was more than capable of functioning without her. The same thing seemed to be true of her family as well.

Boy, Joanna told herself. *Isn't it great to be needed.*

—+—

Luis Andrade opened his eyes. The sun was up, boring in through the open bedroom window. That was what woke him—the sun and the heat. For a few minutes he lay there, listening. In Tucson, with the air-conditioning running, he had never paid attention to the birds. But the AC in this place didn't work. Luis had learned that the birds woke up early, just as the sun came up. The quail were especially noisy, but they were comical and fun to watch.

Luis had fallen asleep last night during the height of the storm, reveling in the cool wind that had blown in through his window. A little rain might have come in through the window, too, but Luis hadn't minded that. He was grateful not to be too hot for a change. His mother kept telling him that their landlord was going to get their AC fixed one of these days. That had been the story for over a month now, but it still hadn't happened.

His mother, Marcella, had come home at her usual time—

around three in the morning or so. He had heard her laughing when someone dropped her off. That probably meant she'd had too much to drink and was too drunk to drive herself home. That was all right. Luis knew they'd find the car eventually, even if they had to walk to do it. They'd done that often enough before, and they always knew where to look—outside one of the bars down in Naco. Marcella might have gone trolling for customers up in Bisbee. A lot of tourists came through town now, but Old Bisbee was where his mother's brother lived, and Luis knew she didn't want to run into him. So she stayed away from Bisbee proper, limiting her trolling to the broken-down bikers and toughs who preferred hanging out in Naco or even at that place outside Huachuca City. Luis hoped she hadn't gone there. It was a long way away and it would make getting the car back a lot tougher.

Luis was a smart kid. At fourteen, he knew the score. He understood what his mother did for a living. Everyone else in town could pretend that Marcella Andrade kept her head above water by selling cosmetics for Avon, but Luis knew that was a lie. His mother was a whore. Men paid money to have sex with her—unprotected sex. The more men Marcella saw, the more money she and her son had for rent and groceries and gas.

Luis had learned enough in his eighth-grade sex ed classes to be scared to death about that. When his mother was drinking too much—as she usually was—she never bothered to wear her seat belt. He doubted she made her customers wear condoms, either. Marcella liked to say she was a "free spirit" and she wasn't going to be forced into doing anything she didn't want to do—like being a grown-up, for example. Apparently she also didn't much like being a parent.

Sometimes Luis envied his cousin Pepe. He had two parents instead of one. They both went to Pepe's baseball and basketball games and to his parent/teacher conferences at school. As far as Luis knew, his mother had never attended a single one. And that was probably just as well. Luis was smart and got good grades, whether she was there or not, and if Marcella showed up drunk or high, it would have been far worse for Luis than not having her there at all.

But it was his mother's line of work, along with the hot pressing rays of the sun, that drove Luis out of bed early that Saturday morning. Careful not to make any noise so he wouldn't disturb her, he pulled on his clothes and shoes. Then he crept out through the door, closing it softly behind him. He knew Marcella would sleep until noon at least. That gave him several hours to do what he wanted without anyone being the wiser.

Once out of the house, Luis cut out across the desert at an angle, making straight for the wash. The sooner he was in it and out of sight, the less likely he was to attract anyone's attention. They had one neighbor in particular, Mrs. Dumas, who was always watching him and threatening to call Child Protective Services when his mother left him home alone. Not that Luis wasn't used to that. He'd been taking care of himself for a very long time. Now, though, he was hoping to find a way to take care of his mother.

One of the things Luis did when he was home alone was watch TV. At least his mother had sprung for Basic Cable, and what Luis liked to watch more than anything was news—all kinds of news. CNN. Fox. He didn't care. Luis liked them all.

He knew everything there was to know—at least everything

that was reported on television—about the War on Terror and the War on Drugs. He knew about the army of illegal immigrants that came through his neighborhood every day of the year, and he knew all about what some of those border crossers had to leave behind as they lightened their loads, abandoning backpacks and debris along the way.

And that was what Luis Andrade was doing that steamy July morning—scavenging for whatever leavings there were to find. He knew it was likely that plenty of illegal travelers would have been tempted to take advantage of the previous night's storm. They would have set out in the face of the lightning and pouring rain in hopes of evading the hordes of Border Patrol agents whose job it was to keep them from moving north. Everyone knew that Border Patrol agents were the same as everybody else. They naturally preferred sitting in the comfort of their dry vehicles to stomping around in mud and rain in search of prey.

Luis understood that when the floodwaters receded, the newly settled sand would form itself into a hard, damp surface that made for far easier walking than when it was dry. He marched along inside the wash until he was well beyond the reach of Mrs. Dumas's prying eyes. Then, using an overhanging branch of mesquite, he clambered up the steep bank and set off across the desert with his eyes scanning back and forth for any sign of something useful or valuable that might have been left behind.

This was something Luis did often, and he was good at it. Through the months, he had made several reasonably valuable finds. One discarded backpack had yielded a zippered case with ten hundred-dollar bills in it. He had given his mother three of those. Worried about a possible emergency, he had kept back the remaining seven. They were still hidden away in the bottom of his sock drawer. Since Luis washed his own clothes, there was never any danger that his mother would go looking there.

Once Luis had come across an abandoned backpack stuffed full of marijuana. He could have taken it home. No doubt his mother would have known how to unload it on one of her many unsavory friends, but he hadn't wanted to run that risk. What his mother did for a living was bad enough. If she got caught dealing drugs, no telling what would happen to her—or what would happen to Luis, either.

He wondered occasionally what he would do if, on one of these expeditions, he came across an even larger cache of cash. Both the drug trade and the transportation of illegals evidently involved impossibly large amounts of money. Luis sometimes fantasized about coming home with a real fortune—enough to buy his mother a decent place to live; enough for her to stop selling her body; enough for Luis to be able to think about going to college.

And that was what he was thinking about when he saw the chunk of something black caught in the branches of a mesquite tree.

At first he was afraid someone was sitting there—that someone had sat down under the tree and had simply fallen asleep. But then, as he came closer, he could see that he was actually looking at a shapeless mass of something made out of black plastic, some of which had torn and was now flapping in the occasional blasts of hot wind that blew across the desert floor. Only when he came much closer could he tell that he was looking at two separate garbage bags that had been welded into one with yards of duct tape.

When Luis saw the duct tape, he actually began to hope. Maybe Border Patrol had stumbled across some smugglers, startling them and forcing them to abandon their payload. Luis worried a little that the bags might turn out to contain a stash of drugs. If that happened, he didn't know what he'd do next. But if the contents of the bag turned out to be just plain money . . . ? No problem.

As Luis approached the bag he picked up a stick. When he prodded the plastic, a once small tear suddenly gave way and expanded. What rolled out onto the ground wasn't at all what Luis had hoped or expected. It wasn't a sheaf of cash or a plastic-wrapped packet of drugs. It was, instead, an empty-eyed human skull, its tooth-filled mouth gaping open.

Too shocked to breathe, Luis shrank away from the bone, stained red and still plastered with mud. For a moment, all he could do was stand there, staring and trembling. His legs seemed to have forgotten how to obey his mind. He willed them to move, but they didn't. Couldn't. Finally, one halting step after another, Luis managed to back away until he blundered, unseeing, into a mesquite. The shock of the branches unexpectedly brushing up against him filled him with such terror that it knocked him out of his stupor. He turned and ran then, racing back across the desert the way he had come, tearing toward home without caring if Mrs. Dumas saw him; not caring if he awakened his mother.

As he ran for the house, Luis knew there was no way he could keep this awful discovery a secret. He had to report it—he had to call his uncle. His mother's big brother was a homicide detective for the Cochise County Sheriff's Department. Uncle Jaime would know what to do.

When Luis got back to the house, he was relieved to find that his mother was still asleep. She wouldn't want him to get involved in whatever was going on. He picked up the phone. When it was dead, he didn't assume it was out of order. He thought, instead, that his mother had simply forgotten to pay the bill. That had happened often enough in the past.

Quietly, Luis left the house once again. This time he made his way on foot to the golf course. In the wintertime, the trailer park across the street was crammed with campers. Now, in the dead of summer, the place was almost deserted, so Luis kept on walking. When he reached Naco Highway, he stopped and waited. He realized as he stood there that his clothes had taken a beating during his run through the desert. He worried that someone from Border Patrol might see how he looked, assume he was an illegal, and pick him up, but that didn't happen. Two marked Border Patrol vehicles drove past without giving him even a second glance.

Finally a private vehicle came toward him. Luis stuck out his thumb and a beat-up Chevy Lumina with Sonora plates pulled over and stopped.

"Where to?" the driver asked in Spanish.

"To town," Luis replied.

"You have a funny accent," the man told him.

That's because I'm not a real Mexican, Luis thought.

The man was on his way to Wal-Mart in Douglas. He gave Luis a ride as far as the end of the Warren cutoff. There, Luis got out, thanked the driver, and headed for the Cochise County Justice Center. Luis had never been inside the place; he had only driven by, but he knew this was where Uncle Jaime worked—Pepe had told him. Someone there would be able to help him.

The buildings were painted pink on the outside. They looked bright and clean and cheerful—not at all like a jail, even though Luis knew the jail was there. As he walked up the gravel drive toward the parking lot, he began to have second thoughts. What if this was a bad idea? What if bringing this to Uncle Jaime's attention also brought attention to Marcella? What if doing this somehow ended up causing trouble?

Even though he was beset with doubt, Luis kept walking—through the parking lot and up the long wheelchair ramp to the front door, which turned out to be locked. Unsure what to do next, he was about to turn away when a disembodied voice asked him, "May I help you?"

That's when Luis realized there was a speakerphone of some kind attached to the door. The woman was speaking to him through that.

"I'm looking for my uncle," he said. "I need to talk to him."

The door clicked. "It's unlocked now," the voice said. "You can come in."

Luis entered the polished lobby area. At the far end was a glass-fronted display case full of pictures of people wearing guns and badges and cowboy hats. Over to his right, from behind another thick wall of glass, a woman beckoned to him. She didn't look very friendly. In fact, Luis thought she was going to tell him to go away.

"You say you're looking for your uncle?" she asked. "Is he a prisoner here?"

It didn't surprise Luis that she would make that assumption. He shook his head. "He works here," he said.

"What's his name?"

"Jaime," Luis answered. "Jaime Carbajal. He's a homicide

detective, and that's why I need to talk to him. I just found a body."

The expression on the woman's face changed remarkably. "Oh, my," she said. "You poor thing. I believe Detective Carbajal's out on a call right now, but please have a seat. Someone will be right with you."

CHAPTER 4

BY THE TIME JOANNA LED CAROL SUNDERSON BACK OVER TO HER boys, her cell phone buzzed with a voice mail notification. She was relieved to know that at least the telecommunication situation had improved.

Marianne was talking on her own phone when they got there. "All right, Mrs. Sunderson," she said, once the call was completed. "We've talked to the Red Cross and made arrangements for you and the boys to have vouchers so you can stay at Crocker's Motel out in the Terraces for the next five days. We're using that one because they allow pets and also because the rooms have kitchenettes. We've also arranged for gift cards for you to both Target and Safeway. That way you should be able to get the basics as far as food and clothing are concerned. And Mr. Morales, who runs the Chevron station on the traffic circle, says you have fifty gallons of free gas coming. Just go by there and fill up whenever you need to."

Carol Sunderson's eyes filled with tears. "I can't thank you enough," she said.

"Don't thank me," Marianne replied. "That's what small towns are good for. When there's a problem we all pull together. The trick is getting those solutions in place before something bad happens instead of doing it after the fact."

Joanna knew there was indeed no trick to it at all. What it took was hard work, organization, and lots of pre-planning. Fortunately for Carol Sunderson, Marianne Maculyea was good at all three.

By then the last fire truck was finishing its mopping-up operation. As Joanna directed deputies Raymond and Ruiz to put up a crime scene barrier, her phone rang, reminding her that she had not yet checked her voice mail messages, either.

"Frank here," Chief Deputy Montoya said.

"What's up?"

"To begin with, Jaime's nephew showed up claiming to have found a body. The kid was too spooked to speak to anyone but Jaime. I've asked Dispatch to send Ernie out to the Double Adobe fire so Jaime can take his nephew down to Naco to check out his story," Frank said. "Jaime said he'd stay on the scene until Ernie gets there to take over.

"But that's only part of the problem," Frank continued. "Now I've got a crazy woman here at the office who's demanding to speak to you and nobody else."

As sheriff, Joanna had dealt with more than her share of crazies. Some of them were such regulars that they were practically on a first-name basis. "Which one?" Joanna asked. "And is she armed or not?"

"Not," Frank said. "She says her name is Edwards, Samantha Edwards. She wants to know why her sister received the next-of-kin notification about their parents' deaths and she didn't."

Joanna waved at Matt Raymond, miming that it was time to drive.

"Where to?"

"Back to the Justice Center," Joanna told him. "She's one of the Beasleys' daughters, then?" Joanna asked Frank.

"Yup."

"And who was in charge of doing notifications?"

"Detective Howell."

Deb Howell was Joanna's newest detective. It was possible that inexperience had led to some kind of error in judgment.

"Where's Deb right now?" Joanna asked.

"Up at Doc Winfield's place," Frank said. "She's scheduled to be there most of the morning—for the official ID, and then she's supposed to hang around and sit in on the autopsy as well."

"Okay," Joanna said. "Speaking of Doc Winfield. He can't deal with any remains here until what's left of the fire cools down. I'm going to leave Deputy Ruiz on-site to maintain the scene. When I left the house earlier, our wash was still up, so my Crown Victoria is stuck at home. I'll have Deputy Raymond give me a ride to the office. Before I get there, though, I'll try to talk to Deb and get her version of what happened."

"She'd better have a hell of a good story," Frank said. "This woman is not a happy camper."

"So what's all this about Jaime's nephew and a body?"

Frank gave her a quick overview. "Like I said, Jaime's on his way there and will call once he has had a chance to scope things out and let us know if he needs more people."

"We don't *have* more people," Joanna pointed out. "According to my count, we're already two homicides over capacity, and the weekend's barely started."

Rather than calling the medical examiner's office and risking interrupting George, Joanna scrolled through her phone until she located Deb Howell's number. Detective Howell answered after the third ring. She didn't sound good.

"What's wrong?" Joanna asked.

"Autopsies," Deb replied weakly. "I'm still not very good at them."

"Nobody is at first," Joanna assured her. "And I'm still not. But which autopsy, Arthur Beasley's?"

"That's the one," Debra replied. "Doc Winfield started on him just a few minutes ago. I was glad when my phone rang. It gave me an excuse to step outside. Madge said I'm a bit green around the gills. I'll probably never hear the end of it."

Madge Livingston was George's tough-as-nails clerk/receptionist. She made fun of anybody who couldn't handle the nitty-gritty of what went on in the medical examiner's office—Joanna Brady included.

"It turns out the Beasleys are why I'm calling," Joanna told Detective Howell. "Chief Deputy Montoya just told me that one of their daughters, Samantha Edwards, is waiting for me at the office. According to him, she's pissed as hell that her sister was notified about her parents' deaths and she wasn't. Do you know anything about that?"

"Samantha Edwards is at your office?"

"That's what I just said."

"But Sandra Wolfe told me she was dead."

"Who's Sandra Wolfe?" Joanna asked.

"Sandy Wolfe. The Beasleys' other daughter. When I talked to her, she told me her sister was dead."

"Either Sandy is mistaken, or her sister is risen from the dead," Joanna said. "I'll try running both those options past Samantha when I see her. I have a feeling they won't go over very well."

At the Justice Center Joanna directed Deputy Raymond to drop her off on the far side of the building near her private back entrance. Using the keypad, she let herself in. Even though it was not yet ten in the morning, the heat outside, combined with sky-high humidity, was downright brutal. Everyone always talked about Arizona's "dry heat," but as soon as the summer monsoons arrived, the whole idea of dry heat went right out the window.

Joanna set her purse and briefcase down on the credenza behind her desk. Then, with the door shut, she unbuttoned her blouse and slipped off her Kevlar vest. She required that all her officers wear bullet-resistant vests when they were out in the field. In an effort to lead by example, Joanna wore hers as well, but the damned things didn't breathe, especially not in weather like this. Rebuttoning her blouse over her damp skin, Joanna dropped into her chair and allowed herself a moment to revel in the luxury of air-conditioning and to be grateful that somehow full electrical power had been restored to the Justice Center.

Finally she called Frank. "Okay, I'm here," she said. *And dressed,* she thought. "Now where's the dragon lady?"

"Out by Kristin's desk," he told her. That meant Samantha Edwards had left the public lobby behind and was seated directly outside the door that led to Joanna's office.

"So I guess I can't act like it's business as usual and pretend I don't know she's here."

"Nice try," Frank said. "I guess not."

"Bring her in, then," Joanna said. "Let's get this over with."

The woman Frank ushered into Joanna's office a few minutes later was a small, well-put-together lady who appeared to be somewhere in her early sixties. Her iron-gray hair was cut in a short pixie style that accented the sharp angles of her face. She was thin to the point of being bony, well dressed in a stylish pant-suit, and utterly furious.

"I want to know who's responsible for my not learning about my parents' deaths in a timely fashion," she said. "And once I know who the responsible party is, I want him or her fired. Immediately!"

Since Alfred and Martha Beasley had been dead for less than twenty-four hours, Samantha Edwards had obviously, one way or another, learned about the incident in what most of the world would regard as "a timely fashion."

But she's just lost both her parents, Joanna reminded herself. *No point in being churlish about all this.*

"Your sister would be the responsible party," Joanna said aloud. "And since she's not an employee of my department, I can't exactly fire her, now can I."

"My sister?" Samantha repeated.

"Yes," Joanna replied. "Sandra Wolfe is your sister, correct?"

"What about her?"

"She told my investigator, Detective Howell, that you were dead," Joanna said. "That made notifying you pretty much impossible."

"She said what?" Samantha demanded. "As you can see very well, I'm anything but dead. I'm standing right here in front of you, aren't I?"

"Indeed you are," Joanna agreed. "Unfortunately my investigator relied on the information she was given. She had no way of knowing—"

"That my sister is a lying sack of crap?" Samantha returned. "Sandy stopped telling the truth sometime within the first minutes of birth, and nothing has ever changed. Of course she lied. When hasn't she lied? So what actually happened to my parents? According to the news reports, Dad hit the accelerator when he meant to hit the brake and went off a cliff."

"We won't know for sure what happened until after the autopsy," Joanna said quietly.

Samantha's narrow jaw dropped. "Autopsy!" she repeated. "Someone is doing an autopsy? Who said anything about an autopsy? Who authorized that?"

"Ms. Edwards," Joanna said patiently. "Please have a seat. Your parents' deaths qualify as sudden and unexplained. As such they are currently under investigation. I'm the one who authorized the autopsies. In situations like this, they're a routine matter."

"Cutting my parents to pieces is not routine!" Samantha objected. "And their deaths are anything but unexplained! In fact, they're perfectly understandable. They died in an automobile accident."

"We don't know that for sure," Joanna explained. "The autopsy will tell us whether or not your father was suffering some kind of physical impairment that might have interfered with his being able to operate a vehicle in a safe manner. Toxicology screens will let us know if he was under the influence of drugs or alcohol at the time of the incident."

"That's a laugh," Samantha returned. "My father never had a drop of liquor in his life!"

"But he may have been overmedicated," Joanna said. "That's

something that happens fairly often with the elderly. They take so many medications from so many doctors that they end up operating under the influence of drugs without even knowing it."

"If you want to check for toxic substances," Samantha advised, "check out my sister. That woman is poison—absolute poison. She's the one who turned my parents against me, by the way."

"Are you saying you were at odds with your parents?" Joanna asked. It was an innocuous question, asked more because it seemed a polite way to keep the conversation going rather than with any expectation of an answer. To her surprise, Samantha Edwards's features seemed to collapse in response to that solitary question.

"Yes," she said, her voice breaking into a wrenching sob. "As a matter of fact, my parents and I were estranged," she managed. "I never meant for it to happen. I was trying my best to fix it, really I was."

Caught momentarily off guard by Samantha's unexpected outburst of grief, Joanna searched in her top drawer until she found a box of tissues which she pushed across the desktop toward her weeping guest. At that same moment, Joanna's cell phone, lying directly in front of her, began to ring insistently. Joanna could see from the readout that the caller was Jaime Carbajal. As much as Joanna wanted to pick up the phone, she couldn't very well do that in the face of Samantha Edwards's very real need. Instead she let the call go to voice mail.

"I'm very sorry for your loss, Ms. Edwards," Joanna said quietly once Samantha seemed to have regained control of her emotions. "And I'm doubly sorry that you and your parents were having difficulties at the time of their deaths. That makes something like this that much more traumatic and harder to bear."

Nodding, Samantha collected another handful of tissues and mopped her eyes. "It does make it worse," she agreed.

"But I can't understand why your sister would tell my detective you were dead," Joanna said. "Why would she make such an outrageous claim?"

"It's a long story," Samantha said sadly. "I suppose it's because I am dead to her. I have been for a long time, ever since we were in high school—since she was a senior and I was a sophomore."

So this was a family fracture of long standing, Joanna realized. The brouhaha over the missing next-of-kin notification was merely the tip of the iceberg. The challenge for Sheriff Joanna Brady would be handling this unfortunate incident while, at the same time, keeping her department out of the cross fire between two perpetually feuding siblings.

"Were your parents in good health?" Joanna asked.

"As far as I know they were," Samantha said. "For someone their ages, that is. But, as I said earlier, we'd had some disagreements in recent years. Once Sandy and her husband moved back here from Texas, they stayed in closer touch with the folks than I did, so I may not have been completely in the loop with everything that was going on with them. Why do you ask?"

Joanna had just come from Lenny Sunderson's burned-out mobile home. It was possible that the man's failing health had caused him to choose suicide as a way of avoiding being more of a problem to his already overburdened family. It seemed likely that Alfred Beasley's plunge from the Montezuma Pass parking lot fell in that same category.

"Would someone have told you if they weren't?" Joanna asked.

Samantha thought about that for a moment. "Probably not,"

she said finally. "I would have had to find it out on my own, just like I did with this. One of the neighbors might have let on to me eventually. That's what happened this morning. After I saw the item on the news, I called Maggie Morris. She's lived next door to my folks for the past thirty years. She was the one who told me Sandy was already here in Bisbee last night."

Joanna decided to steer away from that particular topic. "What was the rift with your sister all about?" she asked. "What went wrong between you?"

"The usual, I suppose," Samantha said. "We both fell in love with the same guy, Norbert Jessup. Sandy was hoping he'd invite her to the senior prom. He asked me instead."

In terms of jaw-dropping, now it was Joanna's turn. She knew Norbert Jessup. He had run a family-owned construction company in town for as long as she could remember. Maybe in his high school days he'd been a hot item, but now he was a butt-sprung old guy with a dual reputation, as a hard worker and as a hard drinker. He was also known for being a bit of a brawler when he'd had one too many. And for as long as Joanna had known Norbert, she'd also known his wife. Sally Jessup was a legitimate character in her own right, a cigar-smoking, tough-talking dame who handled the office-work part of Norbert's various business enterprises and kept a notoriously close rein on her husband as well. It was astonishing to think that a dissolute old rogue like him could possibly be the cause of a decades-long feud between Alfred and Martha Beasley's two daughters.

"So what kind of difficulty did you have with your parents?"

Samantha shrugged. "Once Sandy came back here with her new husband, our parents wanted the two of us to kiss and make up. I told them no way."

"But didn't you say earlier that you were trying your best to solve the problem? How exactly did you expect to accomplish that?"

Samantha looked away and didn't answer.

"What were you doing to fix it?" Joanna pressed. "Did you come down to visit them? Write them letters? Did you ever tell your sister you were sorry and get rebuffed?"

Samantha Edwards squirmed uncomfortably in her seat. "I prayed about it," she said at last. "I prayed that our quarrel would be healed, but it wasn't."

"It's not too late," Joanna pointed out.

"What do you mean?"

"It may be too late for your parents to know about it, but it's not too late for you and Sandy to bury the hatchet," Joanna said. "Praying about it is a good thing, but my mother-in-law is always telling me, 'God helps those who help themselves.' Maybe instead of praying and waiting around for a miracle to happen, you should be actively doing something about it."

In actual fact, those words of wisdom came from Eva Lou Brady, Joanna's first mother-in-law, not her somewhat troublesome current one. After Andy's death, Joanna's close relationship with his parents had never faltered. Jim Bob and Eva Lou Brady had remained an important part of her life and her in-laws of choice regardless of Joanna's marital status. Their commonsense approach to life had helped see Joanna through more than one serious crisis, but in this instance, Eva Lou's words didn't seem to resonate very well with Samantha Edwards.

The woman's narrow features hardened. "Sheriff Brady, how dare you imply this is all my fault. You don't even know me, yet you think you can decide I'm the one who's supposed to fix it?

Why? Sandy sure as hell didn't pick up the phone and call me when she found out what had happened. She knew about the folks yesterday afternoon—soon enough for her to drive down and be here last night. Did she let me know? Not on your life."

Joanna sighed. *Isn't this where I came in?* she wondered. Her phone rang again. Once again Jaime Carbajal was calling.

"Look," Joanna said. "I'm very sorry to interrupt, but I'm going to have to take this call." She picked up the phone. "Hang on," she said into the receiver, then she looked back at Samantha. "Are you going to be staying in town?"

Samantha nodded.

"When you go out, then, please stop by the desk in the outer office and leave your local-contact information. That way, if one of my investigators needs to speak to you, we'll know how to reach you."

"All right," Samantha said, rising to go. "Thank you," she added. "You really have been very kind."

Just doing my job, Joanna thought.

She went back to the phone. "Jaime? What's up?"

"We need assistance," he said.

"Where are you?"

"Out in the middle of nowhere," Detective Carbajal grumbled. "I didn't want to bring anyone else along in case this turned out to be some kind of wild-goose chase. Luis assured me he remembered exactly where the body was and could lead me right to it. That didn't quite happen, but we're here now, and it wasn't a wild-goose chase."

Up to that very moment, Joanna had hoped that somehow Jaime's nephew would have been mistaken—that whatever he had found and assumed to be human remains would turn out to be something else—anything else.

"You did find a body, then?" she confirmed.

"What's left of a body," Jaime replied. "The skull's all I've been able to see so far. There are probably additional remains, but they're stuck inside what's left of two torn garbage bags along with about fifty pounds of wet sand. If Doc Winfield is coming out, have him bring along some kind of body board. That's the only way we're going to be able to lift this mess without losing some of it. And it's going to take a four-wheel-drive vehicle to get in and out of here. No roads."

"If there aren't any roads to the site, how did the bags get there?"

"I'd say the bags were left somewhere else and got washed here during last night's rainstorm."

"Doc Winfield's van doesn't have four-wheel drive," Joanna pointed out.

"We can't carry it by hand," Jaime said. "What about Dave Hollicker? We're most likely talking skeletal remains, rather than a corpse. I doubt the M.E.'s presence is required. CSI can probably handle it."

The Crime Scene Investigation unit at the Cochise County Sheriff's Department was limited, to say the least. It consisted of two officers—Dave Hollicker, the officially designated crime scene investigator, and Casey Ledford, the latent fingerprint tech. In practice, the two shared lab space and worked together as a team more often than not. In this particular case, if retrieving this set of remains was going to be as strenuous as Jaime was hinting, it was probably a good idea if Joanna sent Dave. He was several decades younger than George Winfield and in much better physical shape.

"I'll give Dave a call," Joanna said. "Can you give me your exact location?"

"We're about two miles north of Naco, off Wilson Road and on the west side of Greenbush Draw. Tell him if he comes due west from there, we'll hear him coming and wave him in."

Once off the phone with Jaime, Joanna tried calling Dave's extension. When there wasn't any answer she got up, let herself out the back door, and walked across the steamy parking lot to the department's barbed-wire-enclosed impound lot. There, as expected, she found Dave bent under the crumpled hood of the almost unrecognizable hunk of shredded metal that had once been Alfred Beasley's Buick.

"Find anything?" Joanna asked.

Dave straightened up and cleaned his hands with a paper towel. Then he wiped the sweat off his brow as well. "Not much, mechanically speaking," he said. "Other than a set of very bald tires, there's nothing amiss. I did find something interesting, though. It was in the glove box, which somehow managed to stay closed the whole time the vehicle was tumbling down the mountain."

Walking over to a rolling tool cart, Dave picked up a see-through evidence bag, which he handed to Joanna. Inside was a single piece of paper covered with handwritten script done in shaky pen and ink:

To Whom It May Concern: Martha and I are done. My mother had Alzheimer's. She was helpless at the end. I know it's coming for me, too. Martha doesn't want to be alone, and I don't blame her. We've decided to go together. Tell the girls we love them. Tell them good-bye. That's my only real regret in life, and Martha's, too—that our daughters couldn't be friends.

The note was signed "Alfred Beasley" and "Martha Beasley."

When Joanna finished reading the note, she found herself blinking back tears. Alfred and Martha had, indeed, succeeded in going together. She wished she had known the contents of the note prior to her emotional meeting with Samantha Edwards.

"I'm no homicide detective, but it all looks like a pretty straightforward case of suicide pact to me," Dave said. "I called Ernie's cell and left a message about what I'd found."

Joanna returned the bag to Dave. "You've already put this in the evidence log?"

"You bet."

"So now I've got something else for you. Jaime Carbajal is out in the desert down near Naco with the remains of what will probably turn out to be a homicide victim. The skull fell out of some plastic garbage bags, and we're assuming the rest of the bones are still inside. He says you'll need to take along a body board of some kind. He also says you'll need four-wheel drive to get there."

"Busy Saturday," Dave observed as he started putting away his tools.

That's the truth, Joanna thought. Overtime pay for this weekend alone was going to be off the charts.

"There's one thing more," she added, after giving Dave Jaime's detailed directions. "Do you happen to know any arson investigators?"

"Not up close and personal. Why?"

"Because that's the other thing that's going on this morning—a fatality mobile home fire down by Double Adobe. Nobody has been able to get close enough to tell for sure, but the man we're assuming died in the blaze was in poor health and confined to a wheelchair."

"Another possible suicide?" Dave asked.

"That's what I'd like to know. So would the guy's landlord, Tom McCracken."

"That jerk?" Dave returned.

"You know him?"

"I helped out on a couple of his evictions. He's a real piece of work."

"A politically well-connected piece of work," Joanna countered. "And that's why I want to make sure we have certifiable experts handling the fire investigation. I don't want anything missed."

"I'm pretty sure the Department of Public Safety has some arson investigators on staff—one in Tucson and maybe a couple in Phoenix. I think we can send through a request for one of those."

"Thanks," Joanna said. "I'll look into it."

Joanna made her way back into the building through the public entrance, letting the people who ran the front end of the building know she was on the premises. When she reached the office area at the back of the building, however, she could hear Frank Montoya's raised voice.

"This is absolutely outrageous. You can't possibly expect us to pay this. It's highway robbery!"

Joanna's chief deputy was anything but excitable. Curious

about the cause of this unaccustomed uproar, Joanna made her way into his office and waited in the doorway while he finished up with a phone call.

"What?" she asked when he slammed down the receiver.

"That!" he exclaimed. He sailed a piece of paper—a receipt or a bill of some kind—across his desk.

Joanna plucked it out of the air as it flew past. Ordinarily Frank would have congratulated her on making a good catch. Today he was in no mood for pleasantries.

"They know they have us over a barrel," he said. "So they're sticking it to us."

It was a bill—from Ajax Towing in Sierra Vista. When Joanna saw the figure written in pen at the bottom of the page, she couldn't believe it, either. "Four thousand five hundred fifty-three dollars and sixty cents? For towing?"

Frank Montoya was Joanna's budgetary watchdog. He was the one who tried to make sure her department stayed within its fiscal means. He was the one who watched the payroll expenditures, letting Joanna know when overtime hours were outstripping the money designated for that purpose. No wonder Frank was taking this very personally.

"They claim it took two drivers and two trucks fifteen hours to drag the Beasleys' car back up the mountain so they could bring it here," Frank said. "They say because the accident happened inside a portion of the national park system, they had to comply with federal rules and regulations, blah, blah, blah. And when they delivered it to the impound lot this morning, the new girl out in the public office signed off on it. They say her signature on their form means we accepted the billing at the time the vehicle was delivered, and now we're stuck with it."

"But it's over forty-five hundred dollars!" Joanna objected. "That's ridiculous. We can't afford that. Think about it. That's enough money to pay a good portion of the jail's monthly food bill. Or to buy ten or so brand-new Kevlar vests."

Frank nodded bleakly. "Or to keep gas in a pair of patrol cars for a couple of weeks."

"And all because poor Alfred Beasley decided to end it all," Joanna said.

Her chief deputy's face brightened slightly at those words. "He did?" Frank asked. "We know this for sure?"

"We're reasonably sure," Joanna told him. "Dave Hollicker found what sounds like a handwritten suicide note in the glove box of the Beasleys' Buick. It'll have to be verified, of course, probably by a certified handwriting expert, but in the note Alfred said that he was worried about the possible onset of Alzheimer's and that he and Martha wanted to go together so she wouldn't be left behind. That sounds like a suicide pact to me."

"It may give us an out," Frank observed.

"What do you mean?"

"If we can prove this wasn't an accident at all—that it was a deliberate illegal act on Alfred Beasley's part—maybe we can bill his estate for the cost of the towing. That would make Alfred responsible. Recovering his vehicle from the mountain would be Alfred's problem, not ours."

Frank had met Samantha Edwards and escorted her into Joanna's office, but she was the one who had actually dealt with the woman. So far neither Frank nor Joanna had met up with Samantha's sister, Sandra Wolfe. From what had been said, Joanna surmised that the older sister would be every bit as much of a handful as Samantha was. Joanna also suspected that any attempt on their part to pass the towing bill along as a charge against the Beasleys' estate would be greeted by the two feuding sisters with a possibly united front and with predictably explosive results—a lot like tossing a live hand grenade into a pond covered with a layer of gasoline.

"Are you sure you want to do that?" Joanna asked.

"Why not?" Frank returned. "If this is a result of a deliberate action on Alfred Beasley's part, what have we got to lose? Did Ms. Edwards tell you who handled her parents' last will and testament?"

"She didn't," Joanna said. "From what she said, I doubt she knows."

"I'll try to find out," Frank said. "I'll contact whoever it was and try to get the ball rolling. The worst that will happen is we'll be turned down and end up having to pay the bill. I'm betting if we turn the county attorney loose on this, though, that he'll be able to make it happen."

Joanna had known Arlee Jones, the Cochise County attorney, for years. Other than having an uncanny ability for getting himself reelected, Arlee didn't come with a long list of career accomplishments. Joanna thought Frank's assessment of the man's capabilities in this particular instance seemed wildly optimistic.

"Maybe so," Joanna said doubtfully. "But for the record, I'm declaring you point man on this scheme, Frank. From here on, I'm out of it."

"Don't you worry about a thing, boss," Frank said with his most reassuring smile. "I'm on it."

CHAPTER 5

BY NOON JOANNA HAD THINGS AT WORK AS MUCH UNDER CONTROL as they were going to be. With a Department of Public Safety arson investigator being dispatched from Tucson and with her own people handling what needed to be done, Joanna wanted to be home to give Butch a much-needed break.

When she was ready to head out, Frank offered her a lift. On the road up to the house, Joanna was relieved to see that the water had finally quit running. The tire tracks from Deputy Raymond's four-wheel-drive Explorer were still clearly visible on either side of the sandy wash, but so were the imprints of another set of tires. A passenger vehicle of some kind had plowed its way through the wash when it still had water in it.

Once at the house, Joanna was surprised to see that her mother's robin's-egg-blue Buick was parked next to the backyard fence.

Joanna wasn't overjoyed to see it. If Butch was trying to work, the last thing her husband needed was having Eleanor Lathrop Winfield wandering in and out and gumming up the works.

Frank saw the car and recognized it at the same time Joanna did. Having worked together with Joanna for years, her chief deputy had a fair understanding of his boss's complicated relationship with her mother.

"Did you know you were having company?" he asked.

"Not until just now," Joanna said.

"Good luck, then," Frank said cheerfully as she got out.

Joanna laughed. "Thanks. I'm probably going to need it."

She let herself in through the garage. The counter in the laundry room was stacked full of folded laundry, enough to indicate that someone had run several loads through both the washer and dryer. With the time clock ticking on the due date for Butch's reviewed manuscript, it seemed unlikely that he would have devoted his morning to getting the laundry done. That didn't make sense. And the fact that Tigger, Lucky, and Lady didn't come racing to meet her struck Joanna as odd as well.

"Hello," Joanna called out in her best *I Love Lucy* fashion. "Honey, I'm home."

Butch didn't answer, but Eleanor did. "In here," she called from the living room.

Joanna followed the sound and found her mother sitting in the rocking chair with Dennis in one hand and a nearly empty bottle of formula in the other. Naturally, the baby was asleep.

"Where's Butch?" Joanna asked.

"In the office," Eleanor said. "Working. He needed some peace and quiet in order to get anything done. This little guy isn't big on peace and quiet."

"Oh," Joanna said. "And Jenny?"

"She took the dogs and went for a ride up in the hills," Eleanor told her. "So if you're home this early, does that mean George is done working as well?"

Joanna sat down on the couch. "Most likely not," she said. "He had at least one autopsy to do this morning. There was also a fatality fire down by Double Adobe, but the debris from that was still too hot to handle earlier. I believe that's where he's headed next—to the site of the fire to retrieve whatever human remains can be found in the ashes."

Eleanor grimaced. "He spends so much time at work I don't know why he doesn't just move into his office and forget about me."

Joanna bit back the temptation to apologize. Why should she? After all, it wasn't her fault that Cochise County had turned into murder/mayhem central for the weekend. Besides, George Winfield had taken on the job of medical examiner all on his own and long before he knew either Eleanor Lathrop or her daughter.

"Busy weekend" was all Joanna said.

"I noticed," Eleanor groused. "But with George out of the house and totally preoccupied, why should I spend the whole day hanging around on my own? When I talked to Jenny and heard she was going to be stuck babysitting all day long, I decided to come over and pinch-hit."

Joanna started to say, *Jenny likes taking care of her baby brother, and we actually pay her for it.* But Eleanor was on a roll, and she kept going.

"She's only a child, too, you know," Eleanor added disapprovingly. "She shouldn't have to pay for your mistakes."

"Excuse me?"

"Come on, Joanna," her mother said. "You know that for someone with a small baby, you're working way too many hours. As for expecting Jenny to look after the baby so Butch has time to do his work? It's just not right. And what's going to happen when September rolls around, when Jenny's back in school and Butch has to go off on tour? How do you plan on handling your childcare dilemma then?"

The fact that Joanna worked outside the home had been a bone of contention between Joanna and Eleanor for all of Joanna's adult life. Although she had loads of experience in dealing with her mother's constant interference, this was entirely new territory. Joanna couldn't quite get her mind around the idea that Eleanor had come riding to Jenny's and Butch's rescue and Joanna was now cast as the bad guy. This was so unusual that Joanna was momentarily stunned to silence.

"It's what your father always did," Eleanor continued, undeterred. "I haven't forgotten him, you know, and I haven't forgiven him, either. Hank was a great one for hiding out at work. He put in plenty of hours that were entirely unnecessary. All he was doing was keeping himself out of the house."

And out of harm's way, Joanna thought.

By then she was gearing up to deliver a heated response of her own—one that would defend both her father and herself—but something held her back. For one thing, Hank Lathrop had been dead for years. It seemed likely to Joanna that Eleanor's current tirade had far less to do with her daughter's working or with her first husband's long-ago marital transgressions than it did with some of George Winfield's current ones.

"What's going on, Mom?" Joanna asked.

Just then, Dennis gave an involuntary little jump. It wasn't enough to awaken him, but it was enough of an interruption to allow Eleanor to fall silent in an attempt to disregard her daughter's question.

"Mom?" Joanna insisted.

To Joanna's astonishment, Eleanor's eyes suddenly filled with tears. She set the baby bottle down on the side table next to the rocker and plucked a tissue from a nearby box.

"I just wanted to spend the weekend with my husband, that's all," she said, dabbing at her eyes. "It feels like I'm living through exactly the same thing—same song, second verse."

Seeing her mother dissolve into tears of self-pity was almost as unexpected as hearing Frank Montoya lose his temper on the telephone. In Joanna's experience, both were wholly unprecedented.

"Mom, I'm sorry things are so busy right now," Joanna said placatingly. "And I'm sure George is, too. Four unexplained deaths occurred inside our jurisdiction this weekend. Four. All of them are George's and my responsibility. I have a whole department of people working for me. George has to make do with one full-time clerk, weekdays only, and one assistant who's currently off on a two-week vacation."

"Madge doesn't do all that much," Eleanor said. "She's next to useless. George should definitely have more people working for him—more qualified people."

Tell that to the Board of Supervisors, Joanna thought. "Yes, he should," she agreed.

"At his age, he shouldn't be working so hard," Eleanor added.

He likes working this hard, Joanna thought. *He actually enjoys it.* "He likes being useful," she said aloud.

"Well, so do I," Eleanor said. "That's why it's a good thing I was able to come here and help out today—so I can feel useful, too. You're almost out of laundry detergent, by the way."

As Eleanor made the sudden shift back to business as usual, the effect on her daughter was jarring. Joanna didn't think there was any purpose to be served in mentioning that Butch was the one who handled most of the grocery shopping and that their need for laundry detergent should be added to his list rather than hers.

"Thanks," Joanna said. "I'll make a note of it."

"And I gave the rest of that dead pizza to the dogs. It looked ghastly."

That one hurt. With a growing teenager in the house, left-over pizza was an unusual and welcome treat. Joanna had been hoping there might still be a single piece of double-pepperoni lingering in the fridge that she could grab for her lunch.

Eleanor turned her attention back to the sleeping baby. "Have you noticed that Dennis looks just like you?" she asked. "Those long reddish-blond eyelashes. That funny half-smile when he's sleeping. George thinks he looks like Butch, but then George didn't know you when you were a baby."

First the tears and now this? Joanna wondered. Sentimentality on her mother's part was totally out of character.

"Mom," Joanna said. "What's wrong?"

"Nothing," Eleanor said abruptly. "Nothing at all."

Her sharp-toned denial was enough to startle Dennis out of his doze. His bright blue eyes popped open, and he looked around. Focusing on his grandmother's face, which was familiar but not familiar enough, he started tuning up for a good bawl. Before he managed that, however, Eleanor rose to her feet and handed him over to his mother.

"There you go," she said. "Here's your boy. I'll head out, and give you some privacy."

Eleanor let herself out the back door while Joanna turned her attention to Dennis. Did he look like her? The hair, yes. Eyes? No. How he looked when he slept? If that was anything like the way Joanna looked when she slept, it was news to her. But what really puzzled her as she sat there playing with her son was what was going on with his grandmother. Something wasn't right with Eleanor. Yes, she had always wanted her daughter to be able to be a stay-at-home mom, but this seemed to be more than that. What it was exactly, Joanna couldn't fathom.

Half an hour later, when Joanna was in the nursery and finishing cleaning up what Dennis's father liked to refer to as "a complete wardrobe malfunction," Butch appeared in the doorway. He was holding a FedEx box, sealing it shut, and looking enormously pleased with himself.

"Done!" he announced. "If I leave right now, maybe I can catch up with the FedEx truck as it comes back from Douglas."

"You can't e-mail it?" Joanna asked. "Isn't that what you did last time?"

"That was for the editorial letter. For that one they want an electronic file. For the review of the copyediting it has to be hard copy."

"Well, do it, then," Joanna said. "Let's get it out of here. Maybe we can both take the rest of the weekend off."

Butch came over and gave her a peck on the cheek. "Thanks," he said. "I'll be right back."

"Mom says we're out of laundry detergent," Joanna said.

Butch nodded distractedly. "Maybe not *right* back, then," he amended. "I'll stop by the store on the way and pick up some detergent and a few other things we need. It'll go a lot faster if I do that on my own. When I'm trying to run errands, buckling the kid in and out of his car seat is a major pain in the butt. It takes forever. Come to think of it, I may stop by the hardware store while I'm out, too. I need some new locks for the other house. Having new keys made isn't something that'll be simple if I have Dennis along."

Joanna remembered very well how doing anything at all with a relatively new baby in tow was always much more complicated than doing the same thing on her own. She picked Dennis up and followed Butch into the kitchen.

"I'm sorry if Mom was in your way while you were trying to work," she apologized as he pocketed his car keys.

"In my way?" Butch returned. "Are you kidding? Your mother was a regular lifesaver today. I never would have finished working on the manuscript if she hadn't been here looking after the baby. And she's done all the laundry, too. Amazing."

Joanna found Butch's unstinting gratitude about Eleanor almost as baffling as her mother's bizarre behavior. "So you don't mind that she showed up uninvited?"

"Not at all. And she wasn't uninvited, by the way. I'm pretty sure Jenny told her she was more than welcome to come pitch in. She did and she was—welcome, that is."

With that Butch took his manuscript and headed for his Subaru. Joanna stowed Dennis in his swing—one of the new battery-operated ones that was not only self-swinging, it also came equipped with lights and music—all of which Dennis seemed to enjoy.

Having him occupied for a time gave Joanna a chance to put away all that folded laundry. In the process she noticed, with some consternation, that the usually brimming ironing basket was also empty. In the course of several frenetic hours, Joanna's mother had not only managed to look after the baby, she had also done all the laundry, ironing included. If Eleanor was burning off that kind of excess energy, Joanna suspected George Winfield was in far more trouble than he knew.

Working in fits and starts, she eventually managed to open her briefcase and spread two days' worth of accumulated paperwork out on the dining room table. She was still attempting to sort that—not easy with a baby on one knee—when Jenny and the dogs came into the house. Panting, Tigger and Lucky flopped down on the cool tile floor next to the wall. Lady came over and lay down at Joanna's feet. Without a word, Jenny took Dennis from his mother and then sat down with him on the floor, where she initiated a game of peekaboo that sent the baby into spasms of delight.

"Grandma thinks we're picking on you," Joanna told her. "She's afraid we're forcing you to look after the baby when you don't want to."

"But I like taking care of him," Jenny said. "Besides, you pay me. Where else could I find a job?"

"She thinks we're taking advantage of you."

"Mother," Jenny said. "That's just Grandma. You know what she's like."

Yes, Joanna thought. *Yes, I do.*

"What's for lunch?" Jenny asked.

Not leftover pizza, Joanna thought. "Butch isn't here. He went to mail his manuscript. How about peanut butter and jelly sandwiches?"

"Sounds good."

They ate their sandwiches in the dining room. "What about

Danny and Ricky Sunderson?" Jenny asked as she bit into one corner of her sandwich. "Where are they right now?"

"At Crocker's Motel out in the Terraces," Joanna said. "Marianne got them vouchers to stay there for five days."

Jenny made a face. "That old place? It looks like a dump."

"It's better than nothing," Joanna said. "At least they'll have a roof over their heads. It's the only motel in town that takes dogs."

"Oh," Jenny said. "But where will they go when the five days are up?"

Joanna liked the fact that Jenny was worried about the displaced family, but it concerned her, too. People who cared too much sometimes got hurt.

"I have no idea," Joanna told her daughter. "Marianne's working on the problem, but the fire just happened this morning. Sorting out those kinds of arrangements takes time."

Jenny wasn't ready to drop the subject. "What about our house?" she asked. "Our other house. Butch told me this morning that the renter moved out and left the place a mess. Maybe Mrs. Sunderson and the kids could live there."

Joanna had an idea that the reason the Sundersons had settled on Tom McCracken's hovel of a mobile home was that the price had been right—the rent, that is. And if the family had struggled financially when Mr. Sunderson was alive, Carol and the two boys would most likely be having to make do on less than they'd had before, now that he was gone.

"I doubt they'd be able to afford it," Joanna said.

"Oh," Jenny said again.

The rest of the afternoon was fairly quiet—as quiet as afternoons get when there's a baby in the house. Butch returned finally with a carload of groceries, including steaks for dinner. "Doesn't look like it'll rain tonight," he said. "But they're expecting another storm tomorrow."

Let's hope it's not as bad as yesterday's, Joanna thought.

George Winfield called a little after four. "Where are you?" she asked.

"Back at the fire scene on Double Adobe Road," he said. "Ted is about to finish up. Then I'll have a go at it."

"Ted?" Joanna asked. "Who's he?"

"Ted Carrell's the arson investigator from Tucson," George said. "I thought you called him in."

I did, Joanna thought. *But that doesn't mean I know the man's name.*

"Anyway, he and Blackie have been here for some time. Ernie and I are waiting them out."

"Blackie?"

"The accelerant-sniffing dog. They've been combing through the ashes."

"Finding much?" Joanna asked.

"Evidently not," George said. "The heat at the far end of the trailer was incredibly intense."

"The end with the victim's bedroom?"

"That's right. He said what we'll find will be more like cremains than anything else. Ashes to ashes, as it were."

One of the things Joanna appreciated about George Winfield was his ability to use a light touch in what were often really tough circumstances. As far as Joanna was concerned, picking through a burned-out trailer in search of scorched body parts was tough.

"While I'm hanging around waiting, though," George continued, "I thought you'd want to know about this morning's autopsy. Since Alfred was driving, I did him first. With everything else that's going on, Martha's going to have to wait until Monday."

"Find anything?" Joanna asked.

"About what you'd expect in this kind of incident," George returned. "The man had multiple injuries. Lots of broken bones. What actually killed him, however, was a severe blow to the side of the head. The air bags deployed as soon as the car hit the first time, but the car went end over end several times. It was one of those later flips that slammed Alfred's head into the door frame."

"Any sign of Alzheimer's?" Joanna asked.

"Not in what I saw," George said. "I suppose there might be microscopic evidence of plaque that will turn up in later tissue analysis. It wasn't visible to the naked eye."

"Have you talked to Ernie?" Joanna asked.

"Yes. He was already at the scene when I got here."

"Did he tell you about the Beasleys' joint suicide note?"

"Yes, he did," George answered. "But if Alfred Beasley was developing Alzheimer's, it was very early on."

"You're saying he overreacted?"

"I'm saying he did what he thought he had to do. Maybe Alfred forgot where he left his car keys that morning or what he had for breakfast. But after he saw what happened to his mother, the idea that he might be developing Alzheimer's scared the daylights out of him. Worried that his ailing wife would be left behind with no one to take care of her, he took what looked to him like the easy way out. And I can't say that I blame him. If I'd been in his place, maybe I would have done the same thing. When Annie and Abby were sick and dying, if I'd thought I was coming down with Alzheimer's or Lou Gehrig's, I probably would have done something along that same line."

George didn't talk about his previous family much, but Joanna knew that both his wife and his daughter had died of cervical cancer. She also knew that he had shouldered most of their end-of-life care. Leaving them alone would have been unthinkable. From that perspective Joanna wasn't sure she could fault Alfred Beasley's actions, either.

"Speaking of overreacting and mothers," George went on. "Have you heard from yours this afternoon?"

"Not in the last couple of hours," Joanna answered. "She was here helping Butch with the baby earlier this morning, but she left around one or so, shortly after I got home. Why?"

George sighed. "I've tried calling her cell several times. She isn't answering. The calls go straight to voice mail. I know Ellie's bent out of shape that I messed up her dinner plans last night, but it's not like her to miss an opportunity to give me a piece of her mind."

Joanna had to agree that keeping quiet was *very* unlike her mother. In that regard, George's misgivings about what was going on at home seemed to jibe with her own.

"Did you quarrel?" Joanna asked.

"It takes two to quarrel," George observed. "Ellie evidently isn't speaking to me. She was closeted in the guest room when I came home last night, and she was up and out this morning before I woke up. Did she say anything to you about what's got her all riled up?"

"Not really," Joanna admitted honestly. "I noticed she wasn't herself, but I got the feeling she was upset about something—mostly that you're working too hard."

"If people would stop dropping like flies around here, maybe I wouldn't have to. Anyway, I suppose she'll get around to letting me have it eventually. In the meantime, here comes Ted. That probably means it's time for Ernie and me to go to work. If you happen to hear from her, ask her to give me a call."

"Sure, George," Joanna said. "Will do." *Not that it'll do any good.*

"What's up?" Butch asked when Joanna put down the phone.

"George and Mom are evidently on the outs. He was wondering if I knew anything about it, and I told him I don't. Do you?"

"Me?" Butch asked with a smile. "I'm Eleanor's son-in-law, remember? I got the feeling she showed up to help me today because she's of the opinion that I'm reasonably incompetent. But just because she's willing to lend a hand doesn't mean she'd be willing to confide in me."

"If it's any consolation," Joanna said, "Mom thinks I'm reasonably incompetent, too, and she doesn't confide in me, either."

"Good," Butch said. "If there's something going on between them, we'd best not get in the middle of it. No Kevlar vest in the universe will protect you from that kind of cross fire."

An hour later, when the phone rang again, Joanna expected the caller to be either George or her mother. Instead Dave Hollicker was on the line.

"Hi, boss," he said. Joanna appreciated the fact that most of her people referred to her that way. "Thought you'd want to know that we finally got Jaime's bags of bones hauled back to the lab. No easy thing, by the way. I tried to do it in the van. Without four-wheel drive, that didn't work out too well, but we're here now."

Joanna seemed to remember mentioning four-wheel drive, but there was no point in reminding Dave of that right now.

"So what have you got?"

"As Jaime said, mostly skeletal. We've got a good fifty pounds of sand in the bags with the bones. I've been going through all that with a fine screen and a brush to see what else might be in there. So far, I've found a few remnants of clothing—what looks like part of a T-shirt, what's left of a pair of jeans, size twenty, and a pair of woman's Keds. Size nine. From the condition of those I'd say we're dealing with something that's months old rather than years."

"But a female victim, then," Joanna said. "A wide-load female victim. Any signs of homicidal violence?"

"Plenty," Dave replied. "In my opinion, at least, although we'll leave it to Doc Winfield to have the final word on that. Evidence of some stab wounds to the ribs, but I doubt those were fatal. From what I see, our victim has a thoroughly crushed skull—from several different blows. I found some pieces of duct tape inside the bags. One single strip and two that were formed into bands. Since the bones were no longer connected to each other, it's hard to determine where the tape was or what it was used for. If I were a betting man, I'd say the two bands were probably used for restraints on her hands and legs."

"And the flat strip was probably used as a gag?" Joanna asked.

"Seems like," Dave agreed.

"What about blood? Did you find any evidence of that?"

"Luminol says yes," Dave replied. "Lots. I'd say the victim exsanguinated while inside the bags."

Joanna didn't have a lot of patience when Dave or anyone else started tossing around crime lab jargon. "You're saying she bled to death inside the bags; that the victim was alive when her killer taped her inside?"

Dave paused for a moment before he answered. "Yes," he said finally. "Affirmative on that."

His reluctant confirmation left Joanna feeling half sick. Unsuccessful at stabbing Jane Doe, her killer or killers had trussed her, stuffed her inside the bags, and then finished her off with blows to the head. No matter how many times Joanna encountered man's inhumanity to man, it was always shocking; always troubling; always disturbing.

"Anyway," Dave continued, "I'd like to call Casey and ask her to come in to help out. I'm guessing that once the sand got inside the bags, any fingerprints on the inside of the plastic probably got scrubbed off, but with all the duct tape, maybe we'll be able to find evidence on some of that. The tape may have protected some trace evidence—DNA evidence and/or fingerprints—from being washed away."

Casey Ledford was the department's resident latent fingerprint expert. Joanna knew that duct tape used in the commission of crimes often proved to be a good collection source for both DNA and fingerprints. Between the two of them, though, Joanna was hoping for the latter. Yes, DNA results could nail crooks with astonishing reliability, even on cases that were decades old. The problem with DNA evidence was not so much a matter of reliability as it was the time it took to get results. DNA testing often required months, if not years. With the advent of the Automated Fingerprint Identification System, a hit on an unidentified fingerprint could be accomplished in a far more timely manner— in minutes, as opposed to months.

"Thanks for checking with me on this, Dave," Joanna said. "I'll let Frank know I've personally authorized the overtime."

The rest of the evening was reasonably quiet. Butch grilled the steaks and boiled some fresh corn on the cob. Once the baby was in bed and Jenny was in her room with her dogs and her TV set, Joanna and Butch settled down on the swing on the outside patio and shared a bottle of wine. It was quiet. The day's heat had burned off and the humidity had dissipated. A slight breeze was blowing from the south, and the black velvet sky overhead was littered with stars.

Lady sat with her head in Joanna's lap, soaking up some individual attention that didn't have to be shared with a baby or the other two dogs.

"I heard from Carole Anne today," Butch said.

Carole Anne Wilson was Butch's editor at Hawthorn Press.

"And?" Joanna asked.

"She asked again if I'd be willing to go on tour for *Serve and Protect.*"

That book, Butch's first, was due out at the end of September. It had been finished for a long time as opposed to the one in manuscript form that had been shipped to New York earlier that day.

"What did you tell her?" Joanna asked.

"That I'd need to talk it over with you. For one thing, these days it's unusual for publishers to send beginning authors out on tour. I'm gratified that they're still thinking about it, especially since I already told them no. Twice."

"Carole Anne's never been very good at taking no for an answer," Joanna said.

"True," Butch agreed, "and I'd like to do it, but how would we manage? More importantly, how would you manage? I'd only be gone for two weeks, but still, that's a long time for you to get along on your own with both kids. This summer Jenny's been a huge help, but once she goes back to school . . ." He paused. "What about your mother?"

"My mother?" Joanna repeated.

"You should have seen her with Dennis this morning. She was great with him."

Joanna was already shaking her head. "No way," she said. "I couldn't deal with my mother for two full weeks. Either I'd end up killing her or it would be the other way around."

"I thought as much," Butch said. "I'll call Carole Anne back first thing Monday morning and tell her to forget about it. I'll tell her there's no way I can go."

One of the things Joanna and Butch had discussed often was the reality that she was an elected official. Being sheriff wasn't a lifetime job. She served at the whims of her constituents. She and Butch were both hoping that his career as a writer would take off while Joanna's job situation was still stable. And going on book tours was one of the prices of success.

What about all those months when Butch was here keeping the home fires burning when I was out running for office? Joanna thought. *Doesn't he deserve a little of his own back?*

"Don't do that," Joanna objected. "Don't call her and turn it down. A book tour on a first book sounds like an opportunity you shouldn't pass up. No matter how much we have to scramble, we'll figure out a way to make it work."

Butch studied her for a long time. "Are you sure?" he asked.

"Absolutely," Joanna said firmly and with far more confidence than she felt. "I'll talk to Jim Bob and Eva Lou. They're always willing to pitch in and help out. This can be done, Butch," she added. "One way or the other, we'll make it happen."

"Thanks, Joey," Butch said softly. "This means more than I can say."

CHAPTER 6

JOANNA AND BUTCH WERE IN BED BY NINE AND ASLEEP BY nine-thirty. When the phone rang an hour later, Butch groaned, pulled a pillow over his ear, and flopped onto his other side. Hoping to catch the phone before it awakened Dennis, Joanna groped on her nightstand until she managed to lay hands on the offending instrument.

"Not another one," she grumbled into the phone. "We can't handle another one."

Late-night call-outs usually meant someone had died unexpectedly somewhere in Joanna's jurisdiction.

"Don't worry," Larry Kendrick said hurriedly. "Nobody's been murdered—so far."

Larry was the department's lead dispatcher, and it was unusual for him to be pulling a weekend nighttime shift. "Why are you working?" she asked. "Aren't you usually off on week-ends?"

"With vacations coming up, we're doing some shift trading."

"Sounds good," she said, "but if nobody's dead, why are you calling me?"

"We got called to a bar fight at the Branding Iron tonight. Two deputies responded. Both were assaulted."

The Branding Iron was a relatively new establishment in the area and an unexpected success. Fueled by incurable optimism, a newly retired couple had bought a dead motel near Paul's Spur, transformed the room area into a dining room and the office area into living quarters. Then they had opened the place as a steak house complete with an immense wood-fired grill. They served three sizes of steaks, one kind of grilled chicken, ranch beans, salad, and tortillas—flour and corn. They also served booze, but the Branding Iron had a reputation for selling more food than booze. Bar fights were unusual among its clientele, which included regulars who came from as far away as Tucson.

Joanna moved Lady out from under her feet and then made her way into the living room, so her being on the phone wouldn't disturb Butch any more than it already had.

"Which deputies?" Joanna wanted to know.

"Brophy and Butler," Larry answered.

"Are they all right?"

"According to the patrol supervisor, they're fine. A few scratches and a pair of bruised egos. There's nothing like being beaten up by a couple of women to make you feel like you're a piss-poor excuse for a cop, if you'll pardon the expression."

Joanna was taken aback. "Deputies Brophy and Butler were beaten up by some women?"

"That's right," Larry said. "A pair of them. The two suspects are being transported back to the Justice Center right now. Tom Hadlock wanted me to ask you what you want him to do with them."

Tom Hadlock was Joanna's jail commander.

"If they assaulted my officers, that's a felony. Lock them up and throw away the key until we can get around to having a preliminary hearing sometime on Monday. They can cool their heels until then. What I can't understand is why anyone's bothering to ask me about this."

"Tom wanted you to be aware of the situation, is all. With their parents dead, Tom's afraid locking them up might come back to bite the department in the butt."

"Their parents," Joanna repeated. "You mean these women are sisters?"

"Yes," Larry said. "Their folks are the people who took that header off the mountain out in the Huachucas yesterday."

The light dawned. "You're talking about the Beasley girls—Sandra and Samantha?"

"That's right. Sandra was evidently there having dinner with some friends. Samantha showed up. First the two started arguing, then it got physical. Glasses and dishes were thrown. Hair was pulled. When the waitstaff couldn't break it up, they called for the owner, who doubles as the bartender, to come help. As soon as he showed up, the women stopped fighting each other and turned on him. By the time Deputies Brophy and Butler responded to a 911 call, the fight had moved into the bar. It took both officers and several customers to finally bring the situation under control. The dining room is a shambles. So is the bar."

"And now they're being brought to my jail," Joanna said.

"Yes. In separate patrol vehicles. But Tom wants to know what we should do with them when they get here."

"Are they hurt?"

"Some scratches, cuts, and bruises. One of 'em is going to have a real shiner."

"Do either one of them need to see a doctor?"

"Probably not."

"Drunk?"

"Don't know that for sure, but it sounds like one or both of them has had quite a bit to drink."

"Fine, then," Joanna said. "Tell Tom I want him to clear the other inmates out of one of the cells. Once the two sisters are booked, lock them up by themselves in the same cell and leave them there."

"Together?" Larry asked. "Are you sure?"

"That's what I said—together. They've been carrying on this blood feud for forty years or more. Their parents couldn't bring them together, but I'm willing to try a dose of enforced friendship. Maybe when Sandra and Samantha sober up, they'll figure out it's time to talk about whatever's bothering them."

"What if they hurt each other?"

"That's a risk I'm willing to take," Joanna said. "Tell Tom if he has any questions, he should call me back."

When she hung up, Joanna leaned back against the couch, intending to wait a few minutes to see if Tom would call her back. She was still sitting there with the phone in her lap and sound asleep when Butch, with Dennis and a bottle in hand, nudged her awake at 2:00 A.M.

"I got up to feed the baby and you weren't in bed," Butch said. "What are you doing out here?"

"There was a problem at the jail last night," Joanna said. "I'm waiting for Tom Hadlock to call me back."

"If the man has any sense, he's probably in bed asleep by now," Butch said. "And you should be, too."

"Thanks," Joanna said. "You're right." With that, she staggered back into the bedroom. When she woke up next, the sun was shining in through the window and bacon was frying in the kitchen. When Joanna showed up there, Butch seemed to have the baby and breakfast well in hand. Pausing long enough to pour herself a cup of coffee, she kissed Butch on her way to the table.

"Thanks for letting me sleep in."

"You're welcome, but what was the problem at the jail that had you up half the night?"

"A barroom brawl down at the Branding Iron," she said. "Two sisters got into it. They beat the crap out of the bartender, two of my deputies, and each other. I decided they should sleep it off in the same cell. Since no one's called to say otherwise, they must not have killed each other overnight."

They were about to load into the car to head for church when Joanna's phone rang. "We've identified our trash-bag Jane Doe," Dave Hollicker announced.

"Who is she?" Joanna asked. "And how did you do that?"

"Her teeth," Dave replied. "There's that new program that keeps computerized dental records on missing persons. Doc Winfield came in early this morning to take charge of the remains so he could examine them and issue a death certificate. He was the one who thought to enter the dental records into that Missing Persons database, and that's how we ID'd her. The victim's name is Wanda Louise Mappin. She was age thirty-one and developmentally disabled. Her mother, Lucinda Mappin, lives in Eloy. Wanda was reported missing from her residence, a group home in Tucson, on March twenty-first of this year."

Joanna knew that having George at work so early on a Sunday morning probably meant that he and Eleanor were still on the outs.

"Does Detective Carbajal know about this?" Joanna asked.

"Yes, ma'am. He does. All of it. He's actually spoken with the mother. She's driving down here. She should be at the Justice Center a little after one. She may be able to identify some of the items we found in the bag along with all that sand—the Keds, some bits and pieces of clothing, an earring, and a little gold locket."

Joanna sighed. Of all her duties as sheriff, meeting with homicide victims' bereaved family members was one of her least favorite responsibilities. She did it because she felt she had to—because it went with the territory. If Lucinda Mappin was coming to meet with the officers investigating her daughter's death, Joanna would be there as well.

"Let Jaime know I'll be there at one to meet with the mother, too."

"No Sunday afternoon off, then?" Butch asked when she ended the call.

"Doesn't look like it," Joanna told him.

"But we're supposed to go to Jim Bob and Eva Lou's after church."

Joanna had known that; she had also forgotten. "We should probably take two cars, then," she said.

On the way into town in her Crown Victoria, Joanna called in to the on-duty jail supervisor.

"How's our sister act doing this morning?"

"Samantha and Sandra? They seem to be fine. I've been check-ing on them regularly with the monitor. Looks like they're not speaking, which, under the circumstances, is probably just as well."

"Probably," Joanna agreed.

Next she tried calling George. "I hear you were at work bright and early this morning," she said. "Good work on the ID."

If George heard Joanna's compliment, he didn't acknowledge it. He was too focused on his own difficulties.

"I never went home," he said miserably. "Well, I did stop by for a while after I finished up with Leonard Sunderson, but since Ellie still wasn't speaking to me, there wasn't much sense in hanging around. I have a fold-out couch here in the office, so I came back up the canyon and slept here. I don't know what's go-ing on with her," he added. "I missed a dinner party on Friday. So what? It's not as though that's the first time it's ever happened. I can't imagine why she's making such a big deal of it. Do you have any ideas about this?"

"Sorry, George," Joanna said. "I can't help you there. My mother's been a mystery to me my whole life. What about Sun-derson?"

"We found him in what was left of his bed. I doubt he even woke up before his oxygen tank exploded. Once that happened, it was too late for him to get out."

"Smoking in bed, then?" Joanna asked. "Suicide?"

"Neither one. We'll most likely have to chalk this one up to aluminum wiring. According to Ted Carrell, the DPS arson investigator, aluminum wiring in those old mobile homes is a disaster waiting to happen. He thinks the wiring overheated, smoldered in the wall for a long time, and then finally broke out and set the place on fire—starting with Mr. Sunderson's oxygen tank."

"And Jaime's Jane Doe?" Joanna asked. "What's her name again?"

"Wanda," George replied. "Wanda Mappin. I've just done a preliminary on her remains, but it looks like Dave called it about right. Several superficial stab wounds to the ribs, but what killed her was blunt-force trauma from repeated blows to the head."

By then Joanna was pulling into the church parking lot. "I've got to go now, George," she said.

"But if you hear from your mother and she tells you anything about what's going on—"

"I'll let you know, George," Joanna said. "I promise."

Once Joanna was seated next to Butch in the pew, she checked out the bulletin and saw that the topic for that day's sermon was "My Brother's Keeper." Joanna stayed focused on the proceedings long enough to make it through the opening hymn, the Scripture reading, and the announcements—including the one that mentioned that the Ladies' Auxiliary would be accepting donations of food, clothing, and cash to benefit a family whose home had been burned down the day before. Joanna was glad that Marianne was continuing to look out for Carol Sunderson and her family, but once the actual sermon started, Joanna was far too busy *being* her brother's keeper to pay much attention to the message.

Would Carol Sunderson be relieved to know that her husband hadn't deliberately taken his own life? Or would she be devastated because the home she'd managed to create for her family, the one with the bargain-basement rent, had turned into a death trap? And what about Alfred and Martha Beasley's daughters? Joanna knew she'd have to speak to them that afternoon. What would she say? And then she'd end up having to speak to Lucinda Mappin as well. What comfort could she offer to the mother of a brutally murdered child? Would Joanna be able to find any words of consolation adequate to that painful task?

After the service they went downstairs to the church social hall for coffee hour. Marianne's two-year-old son, Jeffy, had escaped from the nursery and was playing a shrieking game of toddler tag, terrorizing the place by dodging in and out between people juggling cookies and coffee cups. No doubt within months, Dennis would be walking and he, too, would join that noisy parade. Meanwhile, eight-year-old Ruth, the daughter Marianne and her husband, Jeff, had brought home from an orphanage in China, clung shyly to the sleeve of her mother's robe.

Joanna found it reassuring to know she wasn't the only woman there dealing with work and family issues. Marianne's mother was no longer on speaking terms with her daughter. That rift came with an unexpected side benefit. It meant Marianne didn't have to deal with the kind of constant meddling Joanna was forever having to endure from her own mother on the subject of family and career.

"Are you okay?" Marianne asked, seeking Joanna out. "You looked preoccupied." It was a nice way for Marianne to say she had noticed Joanna wasn't paying attention to the sermon.

"Sorry," Joanna said. "There's a lot on my plate right now."

"I know how that goes," Marianne said with a laugh. "Some of the ladies were talking about doing a fund-raiser to benefit Carol Sunderson and the kids. What would you think about that?"

"It's fine with me," Joanna said. "As long as I'm not the one doing it. I'm overbooked as it is right now. Adding one more thing to the mix just isn't possible."

"That was my take on the situation, too," Marianne said. "Go ahead and knock yourselves out. Just don't expect me to run it."

Someone came up to talk to Marianne just then. As Joanna turned away, Marliss Shackleford-Voland caught her eye and came hurrying toward her. That was one of the problems with living in a small town—you found yourself thrown in with people you'd much rather avoid, Marliss being a prime case in point.

Long a columnist for the local paper, the *Bisbee Bee,* and now married to Joanna's former chief deputy, Dick Voland, Marliss was always on the prowl looking for fodder for her column, "Bisbee Buzzings." This Sunday-morning coffee hour was no exception.

"Joanna," she said with a delighted smile. "I heard that the Beasley girls ended up in the slammer last night. Any truth to that?"

"Since no one's been charged with a crime at this point, it wouldn't be fair for me to comment one way or the other," Joanna told her.

"But there were plenty of witnesses," Marianne said. "One of my friends was having dinner in the dining room at the Branding Iron when the fight first broke out. She saw the whole thing."

"And you're welcome to write it up that way if you want, Marliss," Joanna said. "I certainly can't tell you what you should or shouldn't publish. All I can control is what I will or won't comment on. Without formal charges, this is a definite won't. Once charges are filed, you're welcome to ask again."

"You don't have to be snippy about it," Marliss said.

"I'm not being snippy," Joanna returned. "I'm being firm."

Joanna was relieved when, moments later, Butch gave her the high sign. He had collected Dennis from the nursery and was headed for the door. Joanna hurried after him.

"Thanks for rescuing me from Marliss," she said.

Butch smiled. "I could see you needed it."

While he stowed the diaper bag, Joanna buckled Dennis into his car seat.

"You're sure you don't have time to stop by and grab some lunch with the Gs before you head off to work? I know Jim Bob and Eva Lou won't mind if you eat and run."

It pleased Joanna that Butch had taken to calling her former in-laws by Jenny's pet name for her grandparents—the Gs. She glanced at her watch and shook her head. "Better not," she said. "Have fun."

Even though Joanna drove straight to the Justice Center from church, Lucinda Mappin was already there. Jaime Carbajal and Dave Hollicker were ushering her into the conference room as Joanna arrived.

"Sorry to be late," she said, extending her hand. "I'm Sheriff Joanna Brady. And I'm so sorry for your loss."

Lucinda Mappin was a heavyset woman in her late fifties or early sixties. Her shoulders drooped; the features of her broad jowly face were distorted by sorrow; her red-rimmed eyes looked bleary and haunted.

She nodded numbly. "Thank you," she murmured. "Wanda's been gone for months now. It shouldn't be that much of a shock, but it is. It's hitting me pretty hard."

Joanna nodded.

"I guess I always hoped she was alive and well somewhere," Lucinda continued. "She was developmentally disabled, you see—functioned at a three- or four-year-old level. I hoped and prayed that she was with someone who was being good to her and that she just wasn't able to communicate well enough to tell them where she belonged. Unrealistic, I know. But that's what I told myself. Otherwise I would have gone crazy. This is all my fault, you see," Lucinda added. "If I hadn't had to put her in that place to begin with—in that group home—none of this would have happened, but my husband, my Bill, was so terribly sick at the end. He was bedridden and required round-the-clock nursing care. What with working and looking after him, I just couldn't take care of Wanda, too. It was too much, and now I've lost them both. What happened to her? Did my baby suffer?"

"The medical examiner says she most likely died from a blow to the head," Jaime said quietly.

"So maybe it was quick, then?" Lucinda asked hopefully.

Jaime nodded. Joanna appreciated his understated answer. That was what murder victims' survivors always wanted to know and always hoped—that their loved ones had died quickly and painlessly. That they hadn't been forced to endure incredible suffering. Joanna was grateful that Dave Hollicker had the good sense to keep quiet about the bloodstains he had found inside the bag.

Lucinda swallowed a sob. In order to give her some space, Jaime offered the grieving woman a bottle of water. She picked up the bottle, looked at it blankly, and then set it back down without drinking any of it.

"Will I be able to see her?"

"As I told you on the phone," Jaime continued, "there's not

much point, although you can if you wish. The remains we found are primarily skeletal, and they've been moved to the morgue. The Cochise County medical examiner, Dr. George Winfield, is the one who entered your daughter's dental information into a Missing Persons database. That's how we tentatively identified her. But there are a few items that we found among her personal effects that you might recognize."

Jaime nodded to Dave, who opened an evidence box that had been sitting beside his chair. He reached inside, removed a pair of Keds, and set them on the conference table. They were stained a muddy reddish brown and were still shedding sand, but some of the original color, a vivid shade of pink, still showed through. Lucinda picked one of them up and examined the bottom.

"They look like hers," Lucinda said with a nod. "They're the right size, and Wanda loved pink. It was her favorite color. She also loved Keds."

Next Dave handed the woman a see-through glassine envelope. Lucinda held it up to the light, nodded, and handed it back. "That's one of her earrings," she said. "Rose zircon. Her birthstone. Also pink. Do you know anything about people who are developmentally disabled?"

Her question was directed at Joanna, who nodded, thinking of Junior Dowdle at Daisy's Café.

"The only one I know personally," she said, "is the adopted son of people who own a restaurant in town. He helps out there, busing tables, handing out menus, and washing dishes."

Lucinda nodded. "He must function at a higher level than Wanda. She was never quite potty-trained, which made things complicated."

Joanna vividly remembered the night she had picked Junior

up after his supposed caregivers had abandoned him at an arts and crafts fair in Saint David. He had said, "Go. Go. Go," over and over. Joanna had thought he was telling her to drive when in actual fact he'd been talking about another kind of going altogether—one that came with disastrous consequences for the interior of Joanna's vehicle.

"Believe me, Junior has his difficult moments, too," she said.

Lucinda nodded. "Anyway, Wanda loved sparkly things. When she wanted something badly enough, she had a way of making her feelings known. When she was about twenty or so, she met someone who had pierced ears, and she decided she wanted hers pierced, too. At first her father was absolutely dead set against it, but finally Bill relented. Not only did Wanda have her ears pierced, we bought her a pair of birthstone earrings—rose zircon— because they're not that expensive, and they're pink, too. Eventually, Wanda lost one of the first pair we gave her, and she was devastated. So we bought several sets that were all just alike. That way if she lost one, we'd be able to replace it without any fuss. I still have two and a half pairs of these left," Lucinda added as she handed the glassine bag back to Dave. "All of them are just alike and just like this one. This is hers. I'm sure of it."

"And this?" Dave asked, passing over yet another bag.

Lucinda held it up to the light. "What is it?"

"A heart-shaped locket," Dave said. "There's a place for two tiny photos, but there weren't any photos inside it."

Lucinda shook her head. "I have no idea where Wanda would have gotten something like this. I certainly never gave it to her. Maybe one of her friends at the group home gave it to her. Are those rhinestones?"

"No," Dave said. "They may be small, but I believe they're

actual diamonds that have been designed and set so they spell out two separate sets of initials. HRC and KML."

"These are all real diamonds?" Lucinda asked. "That many? Something like that would be expensive, wouldn't it?"

Dave nodded, and Lucinda shook her head. "I can't imagine where it would have come from—not from her dad and me. We didn't give it to her."

"And the initials aren't ones you recognize?" Jaime asked.

"Not at all."

"Tell us about the group home," Joanna said.

"It was the best I could do at the time," Lucinda answered. "It's on East Copper in Tucson. It's run by a company called the Flannigan Foundation."

"Does the home have a specific name?" Joanna asked.

Lucinda nodded. "It's called Holbrook House, I don't know why. Flannigan Foundation operates group homes for the mentally impaired, and for other kinds of people as well, all over Arizona. Maybe not all over. Mostly in Phoenix and Tucson. If there had been one in Eloy when I needed it, I would have put Wanda there—somewhere closer to home. The foundation buys up four- and five-bedroom places, mostly ones that are in less than wonderful neighborhoods. They fix them up and assign clients to them, complete with resident supervisors and caregivers. Living in a place like that with three or four other clients is supposed to be more like living at home, but of course it's nothing like home."

"How long was Wanda there?" Joanna asked.

Some detectives might have objected to having Joanna join in the questioning process. Jaime Carbajal seemed to welcome it. It was clear to all of them that Lucinda's own mental state was so fragile at that point that a womanly touch was a help rather than a hindrance.

"She lived there a little over two years," Lucinda answered.

"And she was happy there?"

"Not at first, but she adjusted all right. Eventually. By the time Bill died, she was settled enough that bringing her back home would have required another huge adjustment. Besides, I needed to work all the hours I could."

"And when she disappeared?" Joanna asked.

"That would be on Monday, the twenty-first of March. They called me at home at nine that morning. I was asleep because I had just come home from working a double shift at the Trucker's Café in Eloy. Whoever called me said Wanda had been missing at her midnight bed check. They had reported her missing to Tucson PD right away—at twelve forty-five that morning. They said they didn't call me until several hours later because they were hoping that maybe she'd just wandered off somewhere and that she'd turn back up."

"But she didn't."

"No."

"When was the last time you saw her?"

"Saturday of that week. That's when I always drove down to see her—on Saturdays. If it wasn't too cold or too hot, I'd take her to visit the Reid Park Zoo. That's really close by, and she loved going there. Or, if the weather didn't cooperate, I'd take her to Park Mall or to a movie. She didn't like movies all that much, though. She had a hard time sitting still long enough to watch them."

"And was everything all right when you saw her that last time?" Joanna asked.

"She was upset. She said her friend had gone away. His name was Wayne, and she was sad that he was gone. Wanda didn't have many friends, you see."

"What happened to him?" Jaime asked. "Where did he go?"

Lucinda shrugged. "I asked, but I never found out. At first I thought that he might have had something to do with it—that wherever Wanda was, Wayne was there, too. But the people I talked to at the group home said they didn't know anyone named Wayne—that Wanda must have made him up. That wasn't true, though."

"What do you mean, it wasn't true?"

"Wanda had Down's syndrome. People like that deal with the world in a very simple way—things are either black or white; real or not; yes or no. They don't think in abstracts. They don't imagine things. They don't make things up."

"So you think Wayne was a real person, then."

"Yes, I do."

"But the Flannigan Foundation wouldn't provide you with any information about him?"

"They said they have a responsibility to protect patient privacy, but that no one named Wayne had been involved with Wanda's particular group home. Ever."

"And you just let it go at that?" Joanna asked.

For the first time Lucinda Mappin bristled. "What else could I do?" she demanded. "If I had gone to the police, what would I have told them? Without Wayne's last name, they wouldn't give me the time of day. And I couldn't hire a private detective because I couldn't afford one. I'm a waitress, Sheriff Brady. I work for minimum wages plus tips. If I ever get around to retiring, I'll be living on whatever comes in from Social Security and that's it.

There was some life insurance that came to me when Bill died, but I ran through most of that just paying his final expenses. And I used the rest of it to pay Wanda's way at the group home because by then she liked it there. Flannigan Foundation may be a charity, but the care they provide in their facilities isn't free. Not even close."

Having the woman's whole financial situation laid bare in those few sentences left Joanna feeling as though she'd somehow overstepped. With a glance in Jaime's direction, Joanna handed the process off to him.

"So, other than the fact that Wayne had disappeared, there was nothing else out of the ordinary in your daughter's life in the days before she went missing?" Jaime asked.

"Nothing that I know of," Lucinda said.

"And she didn't mention having any kind of difficulties with her caregivers or with any of the other residents."

"No, but then she wouldn't have. Wanda was a sweet child," Lucinda responded. "A sweet, loving person. She wasn't the kind who would get mad at someone or carry a grudge. That didn't make it easy to care for her, though. She would get into things she wasn't supposed to occasionally. That meant she had to be looked after all the time—like a toddler almost. After she disappeared, one of my friends—someone who used to be a friend—said to me, 'Well, Lucinda, maybe it's all for the best.' But it isn't for the best. Wanda was my baby, and I loved her, and now she's dead."

With that Lucinda Mappin lowered her head onto her arms and then sobbed into them as though her heart was broken, and Joanna Brady had no doubt in the world that was true.

"I'm so sorry," Joanna said to her again. "And I promise you that my people and I will do our best to see that whoever did this is brought to justice."

Joanna looked around the room and saw both Jaime Carbajal and Dave Hollicker nodding in solemn assent. Joanna meant it, and so did they.

"Thank you," Lucinda said, straightening up and wiping the tears from her face. "That's the best I can hope for and the best Wanda can hope for—that you'll find whoever did this and put him away."

CHAPTER 7

TO JOANNA'S SURPRISE, WHEN THE INTERVIEW ENDED LUCINDA
Mappin insisted that she wanted to view her daughter's remains
before heading back to Eloy. Joanna couldn't help thinking that if
skeletal remains were all that was left of Wanda, there wouldn't
be much for her mother to see.

"You may not be able to do that," she warned instead. "Today
is Sunday. There's a good chance Dr. Winfield, our medical examiner, won't be available."

But Lucinda wasn't easily dissuaded. "Would you mind checking?" she asked. "Please."

Hoping George wouldn't be there, Joanna picked up her
phone and dialed his number. George answered on the second
ring. "Have you heard from Ellie?" he asked.

"This isn't about that," Joanna said. "I have Wanda Mappin's mother, Lucinda, with me. She drove down from Eloy this morning and would like to view her daughter's remains before she goes home."

"I'm not at all sure that's wise," George said. "There won't be anything she'll recognize, and the last thing I need is to have some hysterical woman—"

Although Joanna was inclined to agree with the medical examiner on this subject, it seemed only fair that Lucinda's wishes should take precedence over theirs. "Ms. Mappin's daughter has been missing for months," Joanna interrupted. "She's been apprised of the condition of Wanda's remains, but she still wants to view them. It's her choice."

"All right, then," George agreed reluctantly. "Tell her she's welcome to stop by. That way I'll be able to discuss whatever final arrangements she'll want to make once I'm ready to release the remains. Will the mother be alone or with someone?"

"She'll be accompanied by Detective Carbajal."

"And about your mother—" George began.

"We'll have to deal with that later," Joanna interrupted. "For right now, let's focus on Ms. Mappin."

Once Jaime and Lucinda left the room, Joanna reached across the table and picked up Dave Hollicker's evidence bag, the one with the heart-shaped locket in it.

"Fingerprints?" Joanna asked.

Dave shook his head. "Casey says not."

Peering at the locket through the clear material, Joanna studied the diamond-studded monograms on either side. Using the tip of her finger, she began to count them.

"There are fifty altogether," Dave said. "Originally there were fifty-two. Two of them must have come loose from their settings and gotten lost along the way."

"But even with these tiny baguettes, that's a lot of diamonds," Joanna observed. "How much do you think the locket is worth?"

"The last time I priced diamonds was when Shannon and I were engaged and we were out shopping for her ring," Dave said. "From what I saw back then, I can say with reasonable certainty that this little piece of jewelry is worth a lot of money—several thousand dollars at least."

"Someone's treasure, then," Joanna said. "It looks old-fashioned and a little clunky—more like an heirloom rather than a piece that would be worn on a regular basis. So the question remains: Where did this come from and why did Wanda have it? Was it something she was wearing at the time of her death, or is it something that was thrown into the bags with her?"

"No way to tell," Dave said.

"It's pretty distinctive," Joanna said, handing the bag over to Dave. "Maybe it was lost and Wanda found it somewhere—on the street or in a park. With her intellectual deficits, she might have picked it up because she thought it was pretty without having any idea about how valuable it was."

"On the other hand, it could be stolen," Dave said as he put the bag with the locket back in the evidence box. "It might even be on a stolen-property list somewhere, but I don't know how we'd go about finding it. Since Wanda lived in Tucson, I can start with the property guys at Tucson PD, but I'm not sure if they maintain a computerized list. Without something like that to work from, we're looking for a needle in a haystack."

Joanna grinned at him. "But isn't that why I pay you the big bucks—to look for needles in haystacks?"

Nodding, Dave took the box and went to return it to the evidence room. As Joanna started into her own office, the telephone was ringing. When Joanna answered, Lisa Howard, the weekend desk clerk from the public office in the outside lobby, was on the phone.

"Sheriff Brady," she said, "I know you're in right now, but since it's Sunday, I didn't know if you're really in, if you know what I mean. There's someone out here who's asking to see you."

"Who is it?"

"Says his name is Irwin Federer. He's an attorney hired to represent one of the 'sister' inmates in the jail. He's made a special trip down from Tucson, and he says that it's urgent that he speak to you in person."

"Which one of the Beasley girls are we talking about?" Joanna asked. "Sandra or Samantha?"

"Sandra," Lisa replied. "Sandra Wolfe."

"And he's already stopped by to visit his client?"

"Evidently."

"Is Tom Hadlock anywhere around?"

"Not as far as I know."

In other words, Joanna was on her own on this one. "All right," she said. "Can you bring him back to my office?"

"Sure thing."

The man Lisa escorted to Joanna's office a few minutes later was casually dressed in Dockers, a Boss golf shirt, and a pair of high-end loafers, no socks. He looked to be in his early forties. From the studied casualness of his hairstyle to his artificially whitened teeth, Irwin Federer appeared to be immensely impressed with himself. Joanna didn't like him on sight. Nonetheless, she stood to greet him. Federer, however, didn't seem inclined to be civil.

"Sheriff Brady," he announced brusquely. "I'm here to protest your casual disregard of my client's safety and well-being. Considering the fact that Samantha Edwards viciously attacked Sandra last night—a completely unprovoked attack, I might add—it's entirely irresponsible for you and your department to have those two women locked in the same cell. It's irresponsible, and totally uncalled for."

"That's a matter of opinion," Joanna returned calmly. "Once Sandra Wolfe and Samantha Edwards were placed under arrest, I'm the one who determined where they'd be held. For as long as they've been here, the guards in charge of my jail facility have been monitoring the situation in that cell very carefully—the same way they monitor all the other cells, by the way. I can assure you there's been no problem between the two women, none whatsoever, but if there had been, my people would have moved in to put a stop to it. Keeping the peace among prisoners is a major part of their job description."

"There may have been no problem so far," Irwin said ominously, "but that doesn't mean there won't be. And if something bad were to happen to Mrs. Wolfe as a result of your actions here—if Samantha Edwards were to harm Sandra in any fashion—I must warn you that there would be very serious consequences . . . very costly consequences."

Joanna Brady, a woman with a flash-point temper that matched her bright red hair, had never reacted well to being patronized or threatened.

"You're saying you'd sue me?" Joanna asked. "Let me be sure I have this straight. You would prefer that we keep your client locked up with inmates in the regular jail population—with my two accused female murderers, for example, or with several assorted drug dealers and DUI offenders—rather than being confined to a cell with her very own sister? I'd say we were being incredibly lenient with your client instead of the other way around."

Federer remained unconvinced. "As I said, that 'very own sister,' as you call her, viciously attacked my client last night. When she did so, she was intent on inflicting serious bodily harm."

"It turns out there was plenty of bodily harm to go around," Joanna interjected. "Neither of the two sisters is what you could call blameless. I happen to have copies of their individual booking sheets right here, and I was reviewing them while I waited for you to come down the hall. Yes, two separate booking statements and the results of two separate Breathalyzer tests. As it turns out, at the time Samantha Wolfe and Sandra Edwards were busy breaking up housekeeping at the Branding Iron Restaurant dining room and bar, assaulting my officers, and resisting arrest, both of them were more than legally drunk. Now that they're sober, I think it's a lot less likely that they'll do each other any additional bodily harm."

"But you can't guarantee that it won't happen," Federer asserted. "Besides, my client was simply defending herself. People in this state are allowed by law to do that—to protect themselves in the event of a physical attack."

"So are my officers," Joanna pointed out. "According to statements from my two deputies, when they arrived on the scene they were assaulted by both Samantha and Sandra. That's what often happens in domestic-violence situations, Mr. Federer. Feuding family members stop fighting with one another and turn their ire on the officers who've been sent to intervene in their dispute. That's why Ms. Wolfe and Ms. Edwards landed in jail—for assaulting my officers and for disturbing the peace. As for their being locked up together? If your client was assigned to a cell with one of my two accused murderers—one of them a long-term drug user—I couldn't guarantee her safety in that instance, either."

"So you're not going to move her?"

"I'm not going to move either one of them," Joanna replied. "The preliminary hearing is tomorrow, probably ten A.M. or so. I'd suggest you come back then and do what you can to bail your client out."

"But, Sheriff Brady," the attorney sputtered. "I really must protest—"

"You can protest all you want, Mr. Federer, but I don't believe we have anything further to discuss," Joanna said evenly. "Sandra Wolfe and Samantha Edwards aren't media stars, and this isn't Hollywood. In addition, I'm quite busy at the moment, so if you don't mind, I'll let you see yourself out."

She gave the man enough time to get back down the hall to the lobby. Then she went over and slammed her door shut behind him. "Arrogant jerk," she muttered under her breath.

Joanna didn't like Federer and, by extension, she didn't like his client, either. Lucinda Mappin, faced with the tragedy of her daughter's murder, was responding to the crisis in her life with considerable dignity and grace. Dealing with a similarly tragic loss, Alfred and Martha Beasley's bickering daughters came up short. Behaving like aging spoiled brats and caught up in their own selfishness, all they were capable of was broadcasting their decades-old feud far and wide. Joanna sat at her desk for a few moments, contemplating the vast difference.

I think Alfred and Martha deserve better, she told herself finally.

Picking up her phone, she dialed Lisa Howard's extension. "I'll be out of the office for a while," she said. "I'm going over to the jail."

Managing the jail and its attendant difficulties was a troublesome job all its own. Joanna's first jail-related crisis had occurred less than a month into her tenure as sheriff, when the then cook, who had been skimming food and money to his own advantage, had decamped, taking the jail's supply of Thanksgiving turkeys with him. Since then, Joanna had been doing what she could to improve conditions inside the county's lockup facility. She had allowed the establishment of a jail ministry and had encouraged inmates to participate in GED classes. On one occasion, when the need had arisen, she had even used the jail as an emergency shelter for pit bull puppies rescued from a puppy mill. In the process Joanna had come to see the inmates as individual people rather than nameless prisoners—two of whom happened to be female and also accused murderers.

One of them had come home from work and found her philandering husband in bed with another woman. She had shot her husband dead on the spot and had chased his stark-naked lover out of the house. The other, a drug-dealing prostitute, had plugged her pimp in the course of an argument over money. Joanna had implied to Irwin Federer that Sandra Wolfe would be safer if kept apart from the two accused killers, but that had been more for effect than anything else. Joanna doubted either of those unfortunates posed an actual threat to anyone other than the two people they'd already done away with.

Joanna hadn't been concerned about protecting the two sisters from any particular risk when she had locked them in the same cell. She had done so for one reason and one reason only: that's where she thought they belonged—together.

After crossing the parking lot and securing her weapons in a locker, Joanna waited while the guards, using video monitors and remotely operated electronic locks, allowed her access to the women's unit.

As she approached the cell, Joanna saw someone she assumed was Samantha Edwards sitting at the table reading a paperback book. The other woman lay on the top bunk with one arm slung over her eyes to shut out the light. It was only when Joanna came closer that she realized she had no idea which sister was which. The two women looked so much alike that they might have been twins. The fact that they were both dressed in identical orange jail jumpsuits didn't help, either.

"I'm Sheriff Brady. Which one of you is Sandra Wolfe?" Joanna asked.

The woman at the table put down her book and turned to face her. Her left eye was seriously black and blue. "I am," she said.

"Your attorney just came to see me."

"Irwin? Yes," Sandra said. "My husband must have called him. Are you going to get me out of here so I don't have to put up with *her* any longer? Doesn't locking us in here together constitute cruel and unusual punishment or something?"

"Oh, cut the crap and shut the hell up, Sandy," the woman on the bunk groused down at her. "I'm not the one who's blabbing here."

"Come down, Samantha," Joanna ordered. "I want to talk to both of you."

Rolling her eyes, Samantha climbed down from the bunk. She came over to the front of the cell and stood with her back to her sister, staring out through the bars without really looking Joanna in the eye. Joanna noticed that she, too, was more than a little worse for wear. There was a long straight scratch on the side of one cheek, and she had a distinctly fat lip that had nothing to do with collagen.

"About what?" she asked disdainfully.

"About your parents," Joanna answered. "About what the two of you are doing to their memory."

"They're dead," Samantha said. "What does it matter?"

"It matters because people from around here knew them. The fact that you two were in a drunken public brawl last night with each other and with my officers is big news in town because your parents were well-respected and even beloved members of this community. Marliss Shackleford-Voland was asking me about your knock-down, drag-out fight at church this morning. She had already heard about it and wanted me to confirm some of the more salacious details."

"Who's Marliss?" Sandra asked. "If she was a friend of the folks, I've never heard of her."

"Marliss works for the *Bisbee Bee*," Joanna told them. "At this rate, the paper with your parents' obituaries will probably also contain news about your arrests. That should keep the gossip-mongers busy for weeks to come."

"Samantha started it," Sandy declared. "I was just sitting there having dinner with friends and minding my own damned business when Sammy showed up and lit into me for absolutely no reason—"

"No reason my ass!" Samantha shot back. "You come riding down here without even telling me that our parents are dead? How dare you! If that isn't the lowest of the low!"

Joanna was appalled. Here were two women in their sixties acting like a pair of out-of-control juvenile delinquents.

"It doesn't matter who started it," Joanna returned. "And whatever 'it' was, it certainly didn't start yesterday because the two of you have been at war for a lot longer than that. You're old enough to know better and you're both responsible for what happened. Here your poor parents have died, apparently for no good reason, and the best the two of you can do is beat each other up in a bar fight? That's pretty pathetic."

For the first time Samantha turned toward Joanna and met her gaze. "What do you mean, they died for no reason?" she demanded. "You told me they were in a car accident. They went off a cliff, didn't they?"

"Have you spoken to Detective Howell since yesterday?"

"I haven't," Sandra said.

"Neither have I," Samantha interjected, "but then why would I? It seems someone—some lying bitch—told the good detective that I was dead, so why would she bother trying to contact me about what was going on?"

"Oh, shut up, Sammy," Sandra said wearily. "Let Sheriff Brady finish."

"Your parents did go off a cliff," Joanna said carefully. "But it wasn't an accident."

"What do you mean, it wasn't an accident?" Samantha asked. "What was it, then? Did someone mess with their brakes? Are we talking murder here?"

"My crime scene investigator found a suicide note in the glove box of their vehicle," Joanna replied. "It was signed by both of your parents. It wasn't notarized, but I'm sure we'll be able to verify that the handwriting on each of the signatures is legitimate."

"Suicide?" Samantha repeated. "You're saying Daddy killed himself, and Mother, too? That's crazy. It's just not possible. Why would he do such a thing? And they both signed this supposed note? Are you telling me that's what Mother wanted, too?"

"According to the note, your father thought he was developing Alzheimer's," Joanna explained. "He was worried about what would happen to your mother if he became too ill to look after her. He didn't want to leave her unattended."

"That's ridiculous," Sammy said. "Utterly ridiculous."

"No, it's not," Sandra said. "Not after what happened to Grandma. The poor woman spent years living like a vegetable without knowing up from down. She was totally helpless. Dad and Mom both wore themselves out taking care of her while some people I can name never lifted a finger to help them."

"You wouldn't let me lift a finger, remember?" Samantha returned. "Every time I tried to help, whatever I was doing was wrong. It wasn't good enough."

"Had your parents discussed any of this with either one of you?" Joanna asked.

"Not with me," Sammy said, "but then they didn't discuss much of anything with me. *She* saw to that."

"Oh, spare me," Sandra said. "Can't I go stay in another cell somewhere? At least that way I wouldn't have to listen to her yammering."

"Getting back to your parents," Joanna said. "What about you, Sandra? Did you know anything about your father's health concerns?"

"I suppose he may have mentioned something about it," Sandy allowed, "but he didn't make a big deal of it. And I can't imagine him being so upset that he'd do something so drastic as to drive himself off a cliff."

"Yes," Joanna agreed. "Especially since it seems your father wasn't developing Alzheimer's after all—at least not according to the autopsy."

"He wasn't?" Sandra asked.

"Dr. Winfield didn't find any visible indications of it," Joanna replied.

The unmasked surprise that registered on Sandra's face was enough to make Joanna wonder if the woman hadn't known far more about her parents' health situation than she was willing to admit. Samantha Edwards seemed to arrive at the same conclusion.

She wheeled and turned on her sister. "I'll bet you knew all about this," Sammy said accusingly. "You always made sure that you were closer to them than I was. You always found ways to shut me out."

"Come on, Sammy," Sandra said. "Knock it off. Isn't it a little late for all this?"

"Both of you knock it off," Joanna interjected. "And you're right. It is a little late. For your information, the suicide note mentioned that, too—that the fact that you two were estranged was a continuing heartache for both your parents. Before last night, how long had it been since the two of you had been in the same room together?"

Samantha shrugged. "Forty years, give or take, but who's counting?"

"And who cares?" Sandra added.

"I do, for one," Joanna said. "What's your name?" she said to Sandra.

"You know my name. It's Sandra Wolfe."

"So presumably you have a husband?"

"Yes. His name is Larry. Lawrence, actually. Lawrence Wolfe."

"Of course," Samantha sniffed. "Lawrence sounds so much better."

"And what's your last name?" Joanna asked, turning to Samantha.

"Edwards," Samantha replied. "And no, I don't have a husband at the moment. I'm divorced."

"So since neither one of you actually married Norbert Jessup, isn't it about time the two of you grew up, put an end to this silly quarrel, and got over it? Isn't it more than a little ridiculous for you to still be feuding over some poor dolt who's been married to somebody else for as long as I can remember?"

"This was never about Norbert," Sandra exclaimed. "Whoever said it was?"

"Like hell," Samantha returned. "It was always about him. You never forgave me because he chose me over you when it came time to go to that stupid prom. You've been pissed about it ever since, and you've undermined me and bad-mouthed me to the folks whenever you had a chance."

"Nobody had to bad-mouth you to anybody," Sandy said. "Your actions always spoke louder than anything else. For the past ten years you've barely given Mom and Dad the time of day."

"So here's what we're going to do," Joanna interrupted. "It's just after two P.M. The preliminary hearing will probably be twenty hours or so from now. Judge Cameron isn't much of an early bird. He doesn't usually get started before midmorning. Between now and then, you're going to be here together in what I'm calling a dose of enforced friendship. I suggest you use the time together to come to some kind of understanding about how the two of you are going to get along in the future.

"Eventually your parents' bodies will be released for burial.

When that happens, it would be nice if the two of you could work together to make the proper arrangements. It would also be nice if you could manage to conduct yourselves with enough dignity that your actions wouldn't be a public embarrassment to the memory of your poor parents. They were both honest, hardworking, well-respected people, and they deserve better than what their daughters have given them so far."

"Just a minute here," Sandra declared. "You've got no right to lecture us like this, Sheriff Brady. This is a private matter."

"That's right," Samantha agreed. "It's none of your concern."

The sudden turnaround was astonishing. In an instant, the two feuding women stopped quarreling with each other long enough to join forces against Joanna. If Joanna hadn't seen it with her own eyes, she might not have believed it possible. She also understood that was exactly how Deputies Butler and Brophy had gotten into trouble.

Fortunately for Joanna, Samantha Edwards and Sandy Wolfe were sober now. There was also a sturdy set of iron bars between her and them.

"It stopped being private the moment the two of you started brawling in public," Joanna returned. "And it became my concern as soon as the two of you attacked my deputies."

"You shouldn't talk to us like that," Sandy said. "Aren't you supposed to say 'allegedly attacked'? After all, we haven't been convicted yet."

"Sorry," Joanna said. "It's my jail, my rules."

"But I'm old enough to be your mother," Samantha objected.

"More than old enough," Joanna countered. "Too bad neither one of you has brains enough to act your age."

With that she turned away from the cell door, walked back to the entrance of the cell block, and buzzed for the guards to let her out.

Returning to her office, Joanna was packing up to head home when Jaime Carbajal tapped on the door frame.

"Back already?" she said. "How'd it go?"

Jaime shook his head. "About how you'd expect," he said. "There wasn't much to see."

"Have you had any luck figuring out where the body was all this time?"

"No. I walked back along the bed of Greenbush Draw, but I couldn't see anything. If it hadn't been for that storm, we probably wouldn't have found the body for years, if ever."

"What's this about your nephew?" Joanna asked. "He lives in Naco?"

Jaime nodded somberly. "Luis," he said.

"I didn't know you had family living in Naco."

"I don't talk about them much," Jaime admitted. "Luis's mother is my sister, Marcella. She's five years younger than I am; divorced; pretty much the black sheep of the family. She has issues."

"Issues?"

"Chemical-dependency issues," Jaime returned. "Employment issues. Housing issues. Parenting issues. The whole ball of wax."

"So how did Luis find Wanda Mappin's body?" Joanna wanted to know.

"According to him, he likes to go out hiking and looking for stuff people might have dropped or left behind."

"So he's a scavenger who picks up the leavings of illegal crossers and coyotes, to say nothing of your basic ordinary drug smugglers.

Does he have any idea how dangerous that could be?" Joanna asked. "What if he got himself caught up in a deadly cross fire between Border Patrol and the bad guys?"

"Exactly," Jaime said.

"And I'm guessing he's done this before and found things of value?"

"I asked him about that. He turned very coy, which is probably a yes, but he wasn't talking. I tried to explain to Luis that if he happens to come between a drug dealer and his cash, his life won't be worth a plugged nickel, and neither will his mother's. I doubt he was listening. I'm betting he'll do it again the first chance he gets."

"What if his mother talked to him. Would he listen to her?"

"I doubt it. Besides," Jaime said despairingly, "I don't think she's that kind of mother."

"What do you mean?"

"Luis is a good kid. He's smart, he goes to school, and he gets good grades. But this is the first time I've been to Marcella's house since she moved back here—and I thought she was going to tear me limb from limb when I showed up. She went totally ballistic on me, screaming like a banshee, threatening to pull my hair out. She said I had no business coming there, no business interfering with her life; but her life is a mess, Joanna, and so's her house—that's a disaster.

"You should have seen the place. It's a wreck. It was filthy. Garbage everywhere. I don't think she's ever done the dishes. I don't know what they eat or where. There was no food visible anywhere in the house—at least no food that was fit to eat. There's so much dry rot in the bathroom, it's a wonder the toilet hasn't fallen through the floor. If Child Protective Services came and saw how they were living, they'd take Luis away from Marcella so fast, it would make her head spin. So what should I do about this? Do I call them? Do I turn her in?"

"Turn her in for what?" Joanna asked.

"You name it," Jaime replied. "Child neglect. Prostitution. Drug dealing. Take your pick."

As far as Joanna could remember, Jaime had never mentioned having a sister before—at least not in Joanna's presence. Now she knew why.

"If your sister went to prison or if she died," Joanna said, "what would happen to your nephew then? What about his father?"

"What about him?" Jaime answered. "Marco Andrade's idea of fatherhood stops at being a sperm donor. I've never met the man. I doubt Luis has, either."

"And what about your nephew?" Joanna asked gently. "What does he want?"

"He acts like he's the grown-up in the family," Jaime said. "Like he has to look after Marcella instead of the other way around."

"If it ever came to that, could you and Delcia take Luis in?" Joanna asked. "Would you?"

"I don't know for sure what we'd do," Jaime said. "We've never discussed it one way or the other."

"Maybe you should," Joanna said quietly. "Just in case."

CHAPTER 8

ANOTHER LATE-AFTERNOON THUNDERSTORM WAS PREDICTED. NOT wanting to have her Crown Victoria stranded on the wrong side of the wash at High Lonesome Ranch, Joanna stopped by the motor pool. Her department kept several older-model patrol vehicles in reserve for use when newer ones ended up in the shop. She left the Justice Center driving an overused Ford Explorer that was several years beyond its pull date but still ran. Unlike her sedan, it came complete with four-wheel drive and reasonably high ground clearance. During Arizona's monsoon season, high ground clearance was the order of the day.

The rain arrived in a pelting downpour before Joanna made it home. She was grateful that the attached garage enabled her to park and go inside without getting soaked. She went straight into the bedroom and peeled out of the clothing she'd worn to church. Back in the kitchen, she saw that Butch had things in hand. He was feeding the baby, and Jenny was helping herself to their traditional Sunday-night dinner fare of cocoa, toast, and cheese. Having missed lunch altogether, Joanna collected a cup of coffee and put two slices of bread in the toaster.

"How were Jim Bob and Eva Lou?" she asked, giving Butch a peck on the cheek as she passed his chair. "And how was lunch?"

"Great on both counts," Butch said. "They were sorry you couldn't come, but Eva Lou sent home some dessert for you—a piece of her pecan pie."

"I'll eat it if you don't want it," Jenny offered.

"No way," Joanna told her. "That pie is mine. I'm not sharing."

"But you always tell me sharing's a good thing," Jenny objected.

"Not when it comes to Grandma Brady's pecan pie."

Joanna's toast popped. She went to butter it.

"I asked them about the book-tour thing," Butch said, pausing to mop a stray dribble of rice cereal that had spilled down Dennis's chin. "The problem is, one of Eva Lou's cousins is celebrating her fiftieth wedding anniversary, which means Jim Bob and Eva Lou will be in Tulsa, Oklahoma, for a family reunion the second and third weeks of September. When I heard that, I was afraid it put us back to square one as far as the book tour is concerned, but when I told your mother about it, she said she'd be happy to come help out."

"You're sure you're talking about my mother?" Joanna asked.

"Who else?" Butch returned.

"When did she tell you that?"

"This afternoon," Butch said. "She stopped by a couple of

hours earlier this afternoon, just after we came home from Jim Bob and Eva Lou's. She wanted to know what I thought about Mazda Miatas. She's evidently thinking of buying one—a convertible, bright red."

The fact that Eleanor wanted to come and run roughshod over Joanna's household in Butch's absence was bad enough. The rest was beyond belief. "Wait a minute," Joanna said, holding up her hand. "You're saying my mother came to you—to Butch Dixon—for car-buying advice? And she wants a convertible?"

"That's right. I told her she should probably talk the Miata situation over with George. She said ordinarily she would but that she isn't speaking to him at the moment."

Joanna shook her head. "As you said earlier, whatever's going on between them, we can't afford to get in the middle of it."

"I'm afraid we already are," Butch said. "George called here looking for her. Twice. I told him she had been here earlier but that I didn't have a clue where she was headed after that. George asked me if she had given me any hint about what was going on with her. I told him no, because I didn't know what else to say."

"Does that mean you do know what's going on?" Joanna asked.

"I think your mother is jealous," Butch said.

"Jealous!" Joanna repeated. "Of whom?"

"The woman who works in George's office. She didn't mention any names, but she kept talking about 'that woman in his office.' Other than the car, that's *all* she talked about."

"You mean Madge?" Joanna blurted. "My mother is jealous of Madge Livingston? Are you kidding? That can't be."

"Why not?" Butch asked.

"Have you ever met Madge Livingston?"

"Never."

"She's a sixty-something peroxide blonde who's a bitch on wheels," Joanna said. "She drinks too much, smokes too much—unfiltered Camels—and rides her Harley to and from work."

"Hey," Butch observed mildly. "There's nothing wrong with people who ride Harleys."

With his beloved Honda Goldwing safely under cover and stowed in his section of the garage, Butch had an opinion about motorcycles and their riders that was widely at variance with Joanna's. There was nothing he liked better than to hit the road for a long solitary ride. Joanna, on the other hand, had adamantly refused Butch's every invitation to accompany him.

"Not on your life," Joanna had told him the last time he asked her to come along. "I'm not getting on that thing until hell freezes over."

"Madge has worked for the county for years, even though she's only been assigned to George for a matter of months," Joanna continued. "Every year she times her vacation so she can go to that big motorcycle week in Sturgis, North Dakota."

"South Dakota," Butch corrected.

"Whichever," Joanna returned. "But the point is, she and my mother are as different as night and day."

"Maybe that's why your mother is so interested in buying a Miata," Butch suggested. "Maybe she figures having a hot little convertible is one way of leveling the playing field with the competition's Harley."

"That makes no sense," Joanna said.

"Jealousy is an emotion," Butch observed. "It doesn't have to make sense. In fact, it usually doesn't."

He has a point, Joanna thought. *Think about Sandra Wolfe and*

Samantha Edwards still feuding over Norbert Jessup. None of that made sense, either.

Joanna reached in her pocket and pulled out her phone. "What are you going to do?" Butch asked.

"Call her," Joanna said. "Try to talk some sense into her head."

"Just don't tell her I told you," Butch said. "She swore me to secrecy."

"About Madge?"

"And about her wanting to buy the Miata. Once she knows I've let the cat out of the bag, I'll no longer be her favorite son-in-law."

"You're her only son-in-law," Joanna pointed out. Shaking her head in exasperation, she dialed her mother's cell phone number. It rang and rang and finally went to voice mail. Joanna hung up without leaving a message.

"She isn't answering," Joanna said.

"I know," Butch replied. "George already told me as much."

When she ended the call, instead of putting down the phone, Joanna dialed George's number. He answered immediately and without bothering to say hello. "Have you heard from her?" he asked. "Is she all right?"

"No," Joanna replied. "I haven't heard from her. What about you?"

"She hasn't called me, either," he said morosely. "I'm here at the house. Ellie's makeup is gone from the dresser. So are her toothbrush, hairbrush, and hair dryer from the bathroom. That means she's packed up and taken off for somewhere, but she didn't leave a note, Joanna, and she didn't say a word about where she was going or when she'd be back."

"Do you know anything about her wanting to buy a Miata?" Joanna asked.

"A what?"

"A Mazda Miata. You know, one of those sporty little convertibles."

"A sporty convertible? No way. Ellie would never let loose of that big Buick of hers. She loves that car."

That pretty much showed how much George knew about the situation—which was to say, *nada*.

Joanna decided to tackle the problem head-on—well, more or less head-on. "Butch seems to think Mom is jealous," she said.

"Jealous?" George repeated, as though the word were entirely foreign to him. "Jealous of what?"

"Of you and Madge."

"You mean Madge Livingston, my receptionist?" George managed. "You're saying your mother thinks something is going on between Madge and me? That's ridiculous. You know the woman, Joanna. She's a regular man-eater if I ever met one. Wherever would your mother come up with such a fruitcake idea? What's she been smoking?"

"You've been putting in some pretty long hours," Joanna suggested. "In fact, she was complaining to me about that just yesterday. She said your department needed to have more help."

"That's true. I could use more help, but believe me, when I'm working, I'm working. I don't have time to screw around with anyone, especially with one of my employees. That would be professional suicide. In addition to which, why would I? Your mother's more than enough woman for me. I knew that from the moment I met her. I also knew that she was the one. Compared with Ellie, Madge Livingston isn't even in the same ballpark."

"So what is going on between you and Mom?" Joanna wanted to know.

George's response was guarded. "What makes you think something's going on?"

"For one thing, you're calling here looking for her. For another, she's not speaking to you. For a third, she's suddenly treating Butch like he's the Second Coming or something. She even offered to come here to *babysit* this September so he can go off on a book tour when *Serve and Protect* comes out. Does any of this sound like the Eleanor Lathrop Winfield you know and love? It doesn't to me. I think someone's pulled a switcheroo on us. Otherwise, she's gone completely round the bend."

"She has been a little strange lately," George admitted.

"How lately?"

"The last few months. Certainly the last few weeks. Ellie hasn't been herself. She's been out of sorts—snappish and unhappy."

That didn't seem odd—or even out of character. As far as Joanna was concerned, snappish and unhappy was how Eleanor Lathrop Winfield was most of the time.

"What about being overly emotional?" Joanna asked, thinking of Eleanor's sudden bout of tears the day before.

"Well, yes," George agreed. "I suppose there's been some of that as well, but when the women in my life turn on me like that, I just assume it's something I've done wrong. Usually, if I wait around long enough, they'll let me know what it is. But the idea of Ellie taking off without saying a word about where she's going? This is something altogether new." He paused. "And as far as her talking about buying a new car? She's never said a word to me about that, either."

That was one of the tricky things about being married, Joanna realized. You had to be aware of and understand what your spouse was saying. But you also had to understand what he or she wasn't saying. And why. Text, subtext, invisible subtext. There was evidently a whole lot Eleanor hadn't been saying to George. And probably vice versa as well.

"I don't suppose I should report her missing," George mused at last.

"There's no sign of a struggle at your house?" Joanna confirmed. "Nothing to indicate that she didn't leave of her own volition, right?"

"No," George replied. "Everything's shipshape."

"Then I'd say there's no reason to report her missing just yet," Joanna told him. "Adults have every right to come and go on their own. You simply wait to hear from her. We all do."

"But it's not like her to be so unreasonable."

That, Joanna thought, *is a matter of opinion.*

"If she calls here, we'll let you know, George," Joanna assured him. "And if she calls you, you do the same."

"I still can't get over it," George said. "Ellie thinks I'm carrying on with Madge? That's unbelievable."

As Joanna hung up, she turned to look at Butch, who was busy plucking Dennis out of his high chair. "Now you've done it," her husband said. "We're right in the middle of it."

Joanna shook her head. "We already were," she replied.

Once the baby was down and Jenny closeted in her room, Joanna was kind enough to share her pecan pie with Butch. Lying in bed later, Joanna was still puzzling over her mother's odd behavior.

"Did Mother come straight out and say she thought George was carrying on with Madge?"

Butch had already rolled over on his side. "No," he said. "Not by name. She never mentioned anyone by name. Just 'that woman from George's office.'"

Joanna started to say something more, but by then Butch was already snoring. She lay awake for a long time thinking about it, and before she fell asleep she'd made up her mind. The next morning, as soon as she dropped her purse and briefcase in her own office, she made her way to Frank Montoya's.

A longtime deputy, Frank had been one of Joanna's original opponents when she ran for office the first time. Her decision to make him one of her chief deputies had been a wise political move. From an administrative standpoint it had been absolutely brilliant. Frank had a good eye for detail. He was her chief IT guy and a bulldog when it came to keeping track of budgetary concerns. For the two years since Dick Voland's departure, Frank had served ably as Joanna's sole chief deputy. He had a reputation for being the first one at his desk each morning, but not that particular Monday morning, when she was especially in need of his IT skills.

Joanna wrote a Post-it note and left it on his desk. "See me," the note said.

Out in the lobby, Kristin handed Joanna a stack of correspondence that was topped by that morning's edition of the *Arizona Daily Sun*. The paper was folded open to reveal a highlighted article headlined "Missing Group Home Patient Found Slain."

"Thanks," Joanna said. "Let me know when Frank shows up."

Back at her desk, Joanna disposed of most of the correspondence before finally turning her attention to the designated article.

Saturday morning, when Luis Andrade, a fourteen-year-old Naco resident, took himself out for an early-morning walk after the previous evening's torrential downpour, he had no idea that he would soon be embroiled in the homicide investigation of a developmentally disabled woman who disappeared from her Tucson home in March.

While walking in the desert northwest of Naco, Arizona, Luis stumbled upon the remains of a person who has now been identified as Wanda Louise Mappin, age thirty-one, a developmentally disabled woman who was reported missing from a Tucson area group home in late March. Ms. Mappin disappeared from Holbrook House, one of numerous facilities operated by the Tucson-based Flannigan Foundation.

"I was out walking and saw one of those black yard bags. I thought it might have something valuable in it, like clothes or something," Luis said. "I poked it with a stick to see what was inside. When a skull fell out, it scared me to death."

Luis immediately reported his disturbing find to his uncle, Cochise County homicide detective Jaime Carbajal. With the help of dental records, the Cochise County medical examiner, Dr. George Winfield, was able to identify the remains as belonging to Ms. Mappin, whose mother, Lucinda, lives in Eloy.

"I put her in that place because her father was dying and I couldn't take care of both of them," Ms. Mappin said. "They were supposed to take care of Wanda. They were supposed to look out for her. Instead they lost her, and now she's dead."

There was a tap on the doorjamb. Joanna looked up to find Frank Montoya standing in the doorway. "Sorry I'm late," he said. "Overslept. Did you need something?"

"Come in," Joanna said. "Have a seat. I wanted to talk to you about my mother."

"What about her?" Frank asked.

"She and George seem to be having a bit of a wrangle," Joanna said. "And she seems to have taken off without letting anyone know where she went. Since I haven't heard from George this morning, I'm assuming she didn't come back home overnight. He's not wild about doing a missing person report and neither am I, so since you always seem to have plenty of backdoor sources, I was wondering if you had any secret way—short of a court order, that is—of tracking her cell phone calls or maybe her credit card activity."

Instead of answering, Frank gave Joanna a long, searching look. Then, shaking his head, he flopped into one of the captain's chairs on the far side of her desk. He sat there studying his shoes, like an errant kid unceremoniously summoned to the principal's office.

"What?" Joanna said.

Frank raised his gaze and looked Joanna in the eye. "I know exactly where your mother is—or at least where she was up until about forty-five minutes ago. But I'm not sure I should tell you. There are some things you're better off leaving alone."

Joanna was dumbfounded. "You know where my mother is, but you're not going to tell me?"

"I don't want to tell you," Frank said. "I probably will, but I don't want to."

"What the hell is going on?" Joanna demanded.

Frank sighed. "Is it possible your mother is having an affair?"

"An affair? My mother?"

Frank nodded miserably.

"What would make you say such a thing?"

"You know the Westmoreland Hotel out on Highway 92?"

Joanna nodded. She knew a little about the Westmoreland. It was a nice enough place. She'd been to a couple of Kiwanis meetings there—in the restaurant part. For rubber-chicken fare, the food had been more than decent.

"I saw your mother's car parked there when we checked in last night," Frank said. "It was still there this morning when I left to come to work a little while ago."

There were two things in Frank's statement that didn't compute—the part about Joanna's mother's car being parked at a Sierra Vista motel and the part about Frank spending the night there.

"We?" Joanna asked.

For the first time, Frank glanced at her and grinned. "I finally got lucky," he said.

Over the years Frank Montoya had endured plenty of teasing for being a confirmed bachelor. Maybe that was about to change.

"Dr. Marcowitz," Frank continued, looking a little sappy. "Dr. LuAnn Marcowitz. She's the new ER doc at Sierra Vista Community Hospital. Well, relatively new. We met a few months ago when I did that presentation for the Sierra Vista Chamber of Commerce. She was the one appointed to introduce me, and the two of us really hit it off. We've been having fun ever since. She's divorced, with her mother and a couple of kids at home. LuAnn was on call last night, but it wasn't all that busy at the hospital.

We were able to get away for a few hours without raising any red flags with her mother and the kids. That's why we went to the Westmoreland. I didn't expect to see anyone there I knew. I'm sure your mother thought the same thing."

"I'm sure," Joanna told him. Without another word, she pulled her phone book off the credenza behind her and began thumbing through the pages.

"What are you doing?" Frank asked.

"I'm going to call the hotel."

"Don't do that," Frank urged. "Can't you just leave it be?"

"Would you?"

"Probably not."

Moments later, the hotel operator answered. "I was wondering if Eleanor Winfield is still registered there," Joanna said.

"Yes, she is. Would you like me to ring her room?"

"No, thanks," Joanna said. "No need." She put down the phone and picked up her purse, all in one smooth motion.

"But what about the morning briefing?" Frank began. "With everything that's gone on before—"

"You handle it, please," Joanna said. "This won't take long. I'll be back as soon as I can. In fact, I can probably read my mother the riot act and be back here long before you're done."

The Explorer she had taken home the day before had only the lamest of air-conditioning, so Joanna had stopped by the garage and retrieved her Crown Victoria on the way into the office. Heading for the highway, she was tempted to use her lights and siren, but she didn't. Instead, she turned the air-conditioning to full blast and hoped the cool air would help calm her down.

What is she thinking? Joanna asked herself as she drove, several miles over the limit, toward the coming confrontation. How was it possible for her mother to sink so low? Most likely that was why Eleanor had come up with that bogus charge about George and Madge. The best defense was always a good offense. As for George? He was a good man—a fine man. He certainly didn't deserve to be treated like that. And who was the low-down scum her mother was hanging out with? Was it someone Joanna knew? Someone from the Presbyterian Church, for instance? That would be rich. And incredibly hypocritical, but hadn't hypocrisy been Eleanor Lathrop's watchword all her life?

Instead of cooling down, Joanna found herself feeling more and more outraged. As the mother of a sometimes challenging teenager, Joanna now understood that in the years following Hank Lathrop's death, she had put her mother through hell. She had been out of control, determined to do things her own way. That was one of the reasons she had turned up pregnant without first being married to Andy. Her mother had pitched a fit at the idea of her daughter having a "shotgun" wedding.

For years after that—all during Joanna's marriage to Andy and even after his death—Eleanor had continued to anguish over what she considered to be her granddaughter's "unseemly premature" arrival. After Joanna had endured her mother's criticism all that time, it had come as a total shock to her when she had learned, a few years earlier, that she had an older brother—that her parents had had their own out-of-wedlock baby, a boy who had been given up for adoption long before Eleanor and D. H. Lathrop's much-later marriage.

That's you in a nutshell, isn't it, Mom, Joanna thought bitterly, turning the air-conditioning in her cruiser a few degrees lower. *You're always a good one for "Do as I say, not as I do."*

By the time she arrived at the Westmoreland Hotel, a steely

chill had settled over Joanna. Somehow the roles between mother and daughter had reversed. Joanna was now the grown-up and Eleanor the out-of-control teenager disregarding the rules and not caring who might be hurt in the process. Joanna had thought briefly about calling George but decided to put that off. She would tell him what she knew, but only when she knew all of it. He deserved that much—the whole story, with no holds barred.

Joanna found Eleanor's Buick parked in a prominent position at the end of the first row in the hotel's spacious parking lot. *In front of God and everybody,* Joanna thought, *just like Frank said it would be.*

She pulled into a ten-minute loading zone and then hurried into the lobby. "I'm here to see my mother," Joanna said to the young man standing behind the registration desk. "Eleanor Winfield." She wondered about that. Why had Eleanor registered in her own name? Why not under the name of the man—whoever he might be?

"Of course, Sheriff Brady," the man said with a smile, plucking Joanna's name off the badge pinned to her uniform. "Room 222. Take the elevator upstairs. Second room on the right."

"Thanks," Joanna said, hoping that the smile she gave him in return for the information didn't look as forced as it felt. She rode up in the elevator with her heart beating hard in her chest. Now that she was here, what would she say? Frank was probably right. She shouldn't have come. It was stupid. She should let her mother do whatever she wanted to do. She should let her mother go straight to hell.

There was a prominently displayed DO NOT DISTURB dangling from the doorknob of room 222. For an indecisive moment, Joanna stood in front of that closed door and listened for the sound of voices coming from inside. All she heard was the low drone of a television set—Diane Sawyer and her pals on *Good Morning America*.

How normal, Joanna thought. *They're cuddled up in bed watching the morning news.*

With that, she pounded on the door.

"Who is it?" Eleanor called from inside. "If it's housekeeping, can't you read the sign? Come back later."

"It's me, Mom," Joanna said. "Open the door and let me in."

It took a moment for Eleanor to unfasten the security locks and fling open the door. She was wearing her own terry-cloth robe and she looked astonished. "What on earth are you doing here?" she demanded.

Joanna swept past her mother into the room. "I could ask you the same thing."

She glanced around. While the place was clean enough and serviceable, it certainly wasn't the Ritz. And, other than her mother, as far as Joanna could see, the room was empty. A single cup of self-serve room-brewed coffee sat on the coffee table in front of a sagging couch. The bed had clearly been slept in, but on one side only. The other side was still much as the housekeeping maid had left it, with the bedding smooth and the bedspread still covering a hard slab of foam pillow.

"So where is he?" Joanna demanded. "Did he stand you up? Lose his nerve at the last minute and didn't show?"

"Where's who?" Eleanor asked with a puzzled frown. "Who are you talking about?"

"Your paramour," Joanna said with a snarl. "The person you're meeting here."

Eleanor's eyes widened in what seemed to be genuine

astonishment. "You think I'm here to meet a man? You think I'm having an affair?"

"Aren't you?"

For an answer and much to Joanna's dismay, Eleanor Lathrop Winfield began to laugh. What started as a small giggle evolved into full-throated, almost hysterical, laughter. Doubled over and with tears dribbling down her cheeks, Eleanor staggered backward and dropped onto the couch. After a few moments, though, the laughter stopped as suddenly as it had begun.

"No," Eleanor said finally. "No, I'm not. There's no one here but me."

"But why?" Joanna asked. "What are you doing here, then?"

"Running away," Eleanor answered. "I wanted to see what it would feel like to just kick over the traces and do something wild for a change. Go to a bar, pick up a man, take him home, and notch my bedpost with him. Why not? Everyone else does it."

"George hasn't," Joanna asserted. "He hasn't done anything wrong."

Eleanor studied her daughter's face. "What makes you say that?"

"I asked him," Joanna said. "I asked him straight-out if there was anything going on between him and Madge Livingston. He told me no, not with her and not with anyone else, either."

"And you believed him?"

"Yes," Joanna said. "Of course I did. Why wouldn't I? Whatever's wrong right now, I know that he loves you, Mom. He's worried about you and wants you back."

"You expect me to believe that, too?"

"Yes, I do."

Eleanor rose abruptly from the couch. She walked over to

the window, pulled the curtain aside, and stared out into the parking lot. A draft of stale air from the window-mounted air conditioner wafted across the room.

"It wasn't fair of George to give you your father's journals," Eleanor said without turning away from the window. "He shouldn't have done that without asking me."

For a moment Joanna felt as though she had fallen through a crack in the conversation. Months earlier, in a fit of garage cleaning, George Winfield had stumbled across D. H. Lathrop's collection of leather-bound diaries in boxes of books Ellie had consigned to the garbage dump. Rather than tossing them, George had handed the diaries over to Joanna. The connection between those and what was going on now left Joanna mystified.

"What do Dad's diaries have to do with any of this?" she asked.

"Everything," Eleanor said. "Have you read them?"

"I read some of them," Joanna allowed. "I was working one of Dad's cold cases then, and I scanned through the volumes that were related to that. But after that, once Dennis was born and I went back to work, there hasn't been time to even think about them. Why?"

"I tried to protect you from all of that, but now that it's all out in the open, or will be out in the open, what's the use? Once you get around to reading them, maybe you'll understand."

"Understand what?"

"Didn't you ever wonder why Mona Tipton didn't come to your father's funeral?" Eleanor asked.

Mona Tipton had been Hank Lathrop's secretary. An exotic creature with a ballerina-style hairdo and dark, luminous eyes, she had been stationed at a wooden desk just outside Hank's office up at the old courthouse. Joanna seemed to remember that Mona, born and raised in Bisbee, had left town shortly after high school to pursue a career of some kind back east. She had returned years later to help care for her aging parents. Somewhere along the line she had gone to work for the sheriff's department and had worked there for years.

Yes, Joanna knew that Mona Tipton had been a fixture of D. H. Lathrop's work life, but she wasn't someone whose presence had raised any alarms. Mona had simply been there, one of the colorful cast of characters—the various deputies and investigators and crooks—who had peopled Hank Lathrop's existence. As a consequence, Eleanor's question about Mona Tipton now, years after the fact, caught Joanna completely off guard.

"Mona?" she repeated. "I seem to remember you told me she had a conflict of some kind. Wasn't she out of town at the time of Dad's funeral?"

"There was a conflict, all right," Eleanor declared hotly. "I told her if I saw her anywhere near the funeral home or the cemetery, I'd use your father's pistol to plug her full of holes. And I'm telling you right now, if George's precious Madge Livingston doesn't mind her p's and q's—if she so much as looks at me sideways—I'll make her the same offer."

CHAPTER 9

THE STARTLING REVELATIONS ABOUT JOANNA'S FATHER AND THE clear threat Eleanor had directed at Madge Livingston left Joanna staring at her mother in slack-jawed amazement.

"Surely you don't mean any of that!" Joanna exclaimed.

"Don't I?" Eleanor returned. "Try me. You should know by now that I never say things I don't mean. Come to think about it, what are you doing here? How did you find me?"

Joanna wasn't about to blow Frank's cover by giving away his part in her Find Eleanor operation, so she ignored her mother's questions. "You need to talk to George about all this," she said doggedly. "You seem to have a serious communication problem at the moment. You two should probably talk to someone—to a counselor, maybe—and get things sorted out."

"Talking to counselors is a waste of money," Eleanor said.

"Compared to going to prison on a homicide charge, counselors are dirt-cheap," Joanna returned.

Eleanor looked at her daughter and actually smiled. "I suppose if I did that, it would put you and George in a real bind."

"Mother!"

"And now that I have his attention," Eleanor added, "I suppose I should give the old coot a call. It's nice to know he's been worried about me for a change." With that, Eleanor abandoned the window. She returned to the couch, picked up her purse, and rummaged through it until she found her cell phone, turned it on, and dialed. "Good morning, George," she said a moment later. "How are you?"

Having been astonished by her mother's behavior twice in as many minutes, Joanna did the only reasonable thing she could do—she left. Out in the car, she turned on the ignition and the air-conditioning but sat in the parking lot for several long moments before ever putting the vehicle in gear.

She had been fifteen when her father was struck and killed by a drunk driver while changing a tire for a stranded motorist. Joanna and her mother had never been on the best of terms. Joanna had been a daddy's girl. When Hank Lathrop died, it seemed to her that Eleanor had simply closed the book on him and on everything that had gone before. Joanna had been wild with grief. Her mother, on the other hand, had been dry-eyed and distant.

In the months that followed, Eleanor certainly hadn't tarnished her husband's memory. She hadn't spoken ill of him to Joanna. In fact, she hadn't spoken of him at all. Joanna had taken that to mean that her mother had cared for her husband too little or not at all, and it had resulted in ever-worsening relations between mother and daughter. In Joanna's mind, Eleanor turned into public enemy number one while her dead father morphed into something close to perfection itself.

In all the intervening years, Eleanor had never once hinted that her husband might have strayed from his wedding vows. Not until now.

Is any of this true? Joanna wondered. If her father had indeed been carrying on a passionate affair with his secretary at the time of his death, would he have been so naive as to write about it in his diary? Eleanor had certainly implied as much. And if all that was true, wasn't it possible that the uncaring mask Eleanor had shown to the world on the occasion of Hank's death might well have been calculated to conceal how much she had cared for him rather than how little?

Joanna's ringing cell phone jarred her out of her reverie. "You'll never believe it," Dave Hollicker announced. "I found the owner of that locket."

"Good work, Dave," Joanna said, switching gears. "How'd you manage that? Police stolen property reports?"

Dave laughed. "Nothing that organized. Since Wanda Mappin was living in Tucson at the time she disappeared, I logged on to the Internet. I went to the Tucson section for Craig's List and checked out the Lost and Found page. And there it was, right there, complete with a picture. It's the same one, all right, only in the photo none of the diamonds is missing. There's even a five-hundred-dollar reward."

"Police officers aren't allowed to receive rewards," Joanna told him. "Now whose is it? And where do they live?"

"The guy's name is Logan," Dave replied. "Richard Logan. I already tried calling, but there was no answer. I left word on the machine as to who I was, what I wanted, and why. I asked him to call me back ASAP. It's midmorning, so he's probably at work right now, but since he's offering a reward, I'm guessing he'll be in touch as soon as he gets the message."

"Any idea where he lives?"

"I looked him up, using his licensing info," Dave said. "He lives on Second Street, just east of Campbell. Once I had a name and address, I contacted Tucson PD to see if they had a stolen property report that matched. Came up empty there, so until Mr. Logan calls us back, we're pretty much stuck in neutral."

So am I, Joanna thought guiltily, putting her own vehicle in gear. She eased into traffic on Highway 92 and headed back toward Bisbee.

"Let me know if you hear anything," Joanna said. When that call ended, she phoned Kristin to let her secretary know she was on her way. "What's happening? Is the briefing over?"

"As far as I know it hasn't started," Kristin told her. "Frank postponed it until after the preliminary hearing on those two sisters, which only started a couple of minutes ago. He thought someone representing the department ought to be in the courtroom—just in case."

"I agree completely," Joanna said. She was about to hang up when she thought of something else. "Do you have a phone book handy?"

"Sure," Kristin said. "What do you need?"

"Look up Tipton for me, if you don't mind. Mona Tipton."

"No Mona per se," Kristin said. "There is an M. Tipton, on Quality Hill, up in Old Bisbee. Do you want the number?"

"Not right now," Joanna said. "I'm driving. I don't have any way of writing it down."

"I'll leave it on your desk," Kristin said.

"Thanks," Joanna told her. *I think.*

But what would she do with Mona Tipton's phone number once she had it? Call her? What business was it of hers? Joanna had grown to adulthood thinking that her father could do no wrong, but that was before she knew of her parents' out-of-wedlock teenaged pregnancy. Now, if Eleanor's accusations of her husband's infidelity proved to be true, then D. H. Lathrop's otherwise supposedly spotless reputation for perfection pretty well evaporated.

Part of Joanna's difficulty with her mother had always been based on her belief that her mother hadn't really loved Hank all that much. Now it seemed likely that Eleanor had been so crushed by her first husband's betrayal that it was still affecting her relationship with George Winfield.

Once again Joanna's ringing cell phone summoned her from her thoughts.

"Did you find her?" Frank Montoya asked.

"Yes."

"And?"

"She's all right. She was talking to George when I left, so maybe things are better. What's up?"

"The preliminary hearing just ended."

"And?"

"They both pled not guilty. No surprise there. Judge Cameron set bail at a hundred thou each. Larry Wolfe posted same for his wife, so she's out. At the moment Samantha Edwards is still in our lockup. She was represented by a public defender, so maybe she's having a problem finding someone to post her bond."

"At least we're rid of one of them," Joanna said.

"Don't count on it," Frank returned. "I overheard Larry Wolfe, Sandra's husband, and her attorney out in the hallway. They're hoping to file a suit charging police brutality."

"But we've got dozens of witnesses who saw the two women attack Deputies Brophy and Butler."

"You're right. We have plenty of witnesses for that," Frank agreed. "But the Wolfes are alleging that you personally engaged in brutality when you locked Sandra up with her assailant."

"That's ridiculous," Joanna declared. "I locked Sandra up with her sister. And we have the jail tapes that prove nothing went on between them while they were in our custody."

"It may seem ridiculous to you and me," Frank agreed, "but then you and I aren't personal injury lawyers. Where are you right now?"

"Crossing the San Pedro on my way back to the office."

"In that case, I'll ask everyone to hang around for a while. We'll do the briefing once you're here."

Twenty minutes later Joanna and Frank gathered in the conference room with all the members of her investigative team. It took only a matter of minutes to deal with the weekend's other routine patrol matters. The four fatalities were something else entirely. At Frank's suggestion they discussed them in chronological order.

"Doc Winfield has Martha Beasley's autopsy scheduled for one this afternoon," Detective Howell told the group. "Depending on what he finds, he's hoping to release the bodies to one of the daughters later on this afternoon or else tomorrow morning."

"Which one?" Joanna asked.

Deb shrugged. "For now I suppose it'll have to be the one who's out of jail."

"You've warned Dr. Winfield that there's a problem between the Beasleys' two daughters?"

Debra Howell gave her boss a rueful smile. "Yes," she said. "He knows there are two of them. He also knows they're at war. Final results from the toxicology screenings won't be back for weeks, and for right now he's found nothing. I've spoken to the Beasleys' neighbors and to as many of their friends as I could find. One of them, Maggie Morris, mentioned that Alfred didn't seem to be quite his old self in the last few weeks. Both he and his wife seemed to be slipping a little mentally, and recently there had been mention of their looking into a residential assisted living arrangement of some kind. As far as Ms. Morris knew, though, nothing definite had been decided. She said Alfred was shocked by how expensive that kind of care would be."

"Aren't we all," Ernie Carpenter muttered.

"But Alfred didn't talk to anyone about a possible Alzheimer's diagnosis?"

"Not that I've been able to find so far," Deb said.

"If it was something that worried him, Alfred probably wouldn't have talked about it," Ernie said. "Maybe not even with his wife. And with a pair of genuine fruitcakes for daughters, I can't imagine that he'd talk to either one of them about it, either."

Ernie was Joanna's elder-statesman detective who was still dealing with the aftermath of his own bout with prostate cancer. When it came to knowing what a man would or wouldn't do in that situation, Joanna was glad to defer to him.

"Was money a problem for the Beasleys?" Joanna asked.

Deb shook her head. "They never earned a lot of money," she said, "but from what I can tell, they managed what they had very well. Their house was paid for. They had no debts of any kind and lots of money in the bank."

"How much money?"

"Over half a million," Deb said. "Enough that they shouldn't have had to worry about how much assisted living cost."

"There's money cost and then there's the cost of losing your independence," Ernie said. "If I was in Alfred Beasley's shoes, I'd have been a hell of a lot more worried about the second one than I was about the first."

"So everything we see so far still points to suicide?"

Deb nodded.

"With both of them gone, who gets the money?" Joanna asked. "Split fifty-fifty between the two daughters?"

"That's what everyone's expecting, although no one has as yet laid hands on the will itself. It's supposed to be at their attorney's office, but Burton Kimball is on vacation this week and his office is closed."

Burton Kimball was Bisbee's premier criminal defense attorney, but he also did a fair amount of estate planning work.

"You can't reach him by cell phone?"

"He's doing one of those river raft trips down the Colorado," Deb replied. "That means he's not reachable by cell phone. Alfred was so careful about planning everything else, you'd think he wouldn't have done this when his lawyer would be unavailable, but Burton Kimball's paralegal, Monica Jones, is due back from a weekend trip to California later today. She should be able to help out."

"What do you mean about Alfred Beasley's careful planning?" Joanna asked. "What's that all about?"

"Their funeral service—a joint service, by the way—is all prepaid and all prearranged, down to the music, Scripture reading, and program, cremation arrangements and where to scatter the ashes," Deb said. "The only thing missing was the actual date."

"That's careful planning, all right," Joanna agreed. "Keep after it, Deb. If and when there are copies of the will available, bring me one if you can." Joanna turned to Ernie Carpenter. "You're up next, Ernie," she said. "You were the last one at the fire scene. What's up with the Lenny Sunderson case?"

Ernie slid a set of papers across the table. "That's Ted Carrell's preliminary report," he said. "Ted's the Department of Public Safety arson investigator," he explained for everyone else's benefit. "What he found is consistent with an electrical fire. There was a room air conditioner running, assorted medical equipment, and probably a few other devices as well. The load was too much for the aluminum wiring and it started to smolder. Flames finally broke through the wall, causing the oxygen tank to explode. But Sunderson didn't burn to death. According to Doc Winfield, he succumbed to smoke inhalation long before the tank blew."

"Aluminum wiring?" Dave asked. "Not copper?"

"That's right," Ernie said. "That particular model of mobile home was built back in the sixties, when they still used that junk because it was cheaper than copper. It's also not nearly as safe."

"Does Mrs. Sunderson know about this?" Joanna asked.

Ernie nodded. "I talked to her about it at length yesterday afternoon. She said she had noticed that the light switches in that room were warm to the touch, and she had sent a note to her landlord about it with her last rent check, asking if it was something she should be worried about."

"It turns out it was," Joanna said.

"Looks like."

"And this is most likely going to be ruled accidental."

"Yes."

"How was she when you saw her?" Joanna asked.

"Mrs. Sunderson? Broken up but coping. The kids were fine. They were actually outside playing in the motel pool and having a blast. She was inside trying to figure out where they're all going to live once they have to leave the motel. I've heard that some of the local churches are banding together to help them, but when you're having to start over from scratch like that—when you're left with nothing but the clothes on your back, it's not going to be easy."

When attending the briefings, Joanna always carried a leather-bound notebook with her. She jotted a note to herself. "See Tom McCracken."

"All right, then," she said. "That's three down. Two suicides and an accidental death. What's happening with Wanda Mappin?"

Dave Hollicker raised his hand. "I've spoken to the owner of the locket we found with her body," he said. "Richard Logan, the man who placed the Lost and Found ad on Craig's List, is actually the great-grandson of the people whose monograms are on the locket." Dave paused long enough to consult his notes. "HRC and KML stand for Helen Rose Campbell and Kenneth Michael Logan. The locket is a family heirloom that has been passed from one generation to the next. It would have been passed on to Richard's daughter, eventually, but it disappeared from his mother's home sometime in the last year or so. He doesn't know when or how.

"They live in Tucson with his mother in a casita on their

property. There was no break-in that anyone knows about, but Mama Logan evidently isn't the greatest at keeping her doors and windows locked. Months ago she told her son that she was sure someone had been in her house and had taken a carton of cigarettes out of her freezer. If someone was prowling through her house, that might have been when it happened, but nothing else was found to be missing at the time and no police report was filed. Mr. Logan wasn't at all sure that his mother wasn't mistaken. The woman's evidently a chain smoker. He thought she was claiming someone had stolen her cigarettes rather than admitting she had smoked them herself. Then, three weeks ago, when Logan's daughter was about to get married, his mother wanted the locket to be the 'something old' the bride wore on her wedding day. The problem is, the locket couldn't be found."

"Because it was buried in a plastic bag along with Wanda Mappin's body," Joanna observed. "But we have no idea when it was taken or by whom."

"I asked Mr. Logan about that," Dave said. "He couldn't remember exactly. He seemed to remember the missing cigarettes incident was early in the year—shortly after Christmas."

"And where do these people live again?" Joanna asked. "Anywhere near Wanda's group home?"

"It's several miles away," Dave said. "The Logans' place is in a neighborhood called Sam Hughes, which is a few blocks east of the university. The group home is on Copper, several grids to the north and east of there. That's a long way for someone like Wanda to travel on her own, to say nothing of finding her way back home again."

Jaime cut into the conversation. "And even if she did, I doubt she was the one pilfering from Logan's mother's house.

As soon as Dave told me about this, I called Lucinda Mappin and asked her. She was adamant. Wanda never smoked. She hated the fact that her mother did. Lucinda says Wanda never would have taken something that didn't belong to her and she most especially wouldn't have taken cigarettes. But she did mention something intriguing. Lucinda remembers Wanda telling her that her friend—that imaginary friend of hers named Wayne—smoked."

"The friend who disappeared smoked." Joanna mused. "The one who didn't exist."

"Right."

"So we need to find him."

"Yes," Jaime agreed. "We do."

"Have you talked to the people at the group home?"

"Flannigan Foundation? I've tried talking to them. It turns out they run all kinds of group homes, everything from Alzheimer's to halfway houses for sex offenders and druggies. They started out about twenty-five years ago as your basic do-gooders providing homes for people like Wanda whose families, for whatever reason, could no longer care for their loved ones. In recent years, though, Flannigan Foundation has expanded like crazy. They still take some private placements, as they did with Wanda, but mostly they're paid by the state. Apparently state contracts like that can be very lucrative."

"What do you mean, you've tried talking to them?" Joanna asked.

"Most of what I've told you so far I've been able to track down on the Internet," Jaime answered. "I have a call in to Donald Dietrich, Flannigan's executive director. So far he hasn't bothered to call back. The people I've spoken to on my way up the chain of command to his office have been less than cooperative. Based on that, I doubt Mr. Dietrich will be, either."

"Have you learned anything else about Wanda's disappearance?"

"I pulled a copy of the original missing persons report."

Jaime slid a set of papers across the conference table. While Frank passed copies to all the others, Joanna glanced through hers. The report pretty much squared with what Lucinda Mappin had told them earlier—that Wanda had missed her midnight bed check and had been reported missing to Tucson PD forty-five minutes later.

"No video surveillance?"

"Not at the group home," Jaime said. "And if there was video surveillance from any other businesses in the neighborhood, those are most likely taped over and gone now. I get the feeling that Tucson PD didn't waste a whole lot of manpower, time, or effort looking for Wanda Mappin."

"They didn't know she was dead," Joanna said. "We do."

Joanna turned to Casey Ledford, the latent fingerprint tech, who had been sitting quietly throughout the briefing. "What about you, Casey?" Joanna asked. "Anything on your end?"

"I'm going over the bags inch by inch," she said. "There's a chance that the place where the two bags were taped together didn't get as degraded as the parts that were exposed to the sand and water. But so far, nothing."

"Keep looking," Joanna said. Before she could say anything more, the conference room door opened and Kristin beckoned to her. Kristin seldom interrupted the morning proceedings.

Assuming this to be something important, Joanna gathered up her notebook and other paraphernalia and followed her secretary out into the lobby.

"What's going on?" she asked.

"Dick Voland is here to see you," Kristin told her. "He says it's urgent. He came in the back way and asked to wait in your office."

"In my office?" Joanna asked in dismay. "You left him there on his own?"

"Sorry. He told me it was important," Kristin said. "Important and confidential."

Joanna approached her closed office door and stopped outside long enough to compose herself before turning the handle. Joanna had never discussed with anyone the exact nature of the circumstances under which Richard Voland had left the sheriff's department. She had sent him packing when she'd come to realize that he had a romantic interest in her that made their working together impossible.

Since that abrupt departure, Dick had moved on. Not only had he opened his own private investigation business, he had also courted and married Marliss Shackleford. Because they all attended the same church, that meant there were occasional public encounters in what was mutually neutral territory. Over time those had become less difficult, but this was different. Having him show back up on Joanna's home turf and bluff his way into her office without an express invitation was an entirely different matter.

"Hello, Dick," she said, forcing her voice to remain even. "You needed to see me?"

He was seated in one of the two captain's chairs. "Do you mind closing that door?" he asked.

"I don't see why—"

"Sheriff Brady," he said formally. "I believe what I have to say is best said in private."

Reluctantly, Joanna pulled the door shut behind her and then made her way to her desk.

"If this is about the situation with our former tenant," Joanna began, "you should probably be talking to Butch. He's the one who hired you."

"It's not just about Bob Baker," Dick said. "It's also about you."

"Have you found him, then?" Joanna asked.

"I've located his vehicle," Dick said. "It's parked in the long-term lot at Tucson International. I've also managed to trace his movements beyond that. He left a week ago on a flight to Mazatlán on a one-way ticket, by the way. I'm assuming he has no intention of coming back."

Dick Voland's competency had never been in question.

"It sounds as though you've done what Butch wanted you to do, then," Joanna said. "If you'll stop by the house, I'm sure he'll be glad to give you a check."

"There's more," Dick said.

His tone of voice was dead flat. That was worrisome.

"What?" Joanna asked.

"Before he took off, Baker had come under the scrutiny of the FBI. They were getting ready to bust him for smuggling, but he gave them the slip before they got their ducks in a row."

"So?" Joanna asked.

"Now the FBI is trying to wipe the egg off their faces, and they're investigating you," Dick said quietly. "You and Butch."

"They're investigating us?" Joanna asked.

"That's right," Dick said. "I stumbled on it by accident, and I certainly can't say how, but with Baker gone, the feds are looking into whether or not you and Butch knew what he was doing out of the house he rented from you. They're trying to see if you were in on it."

"That's appalling!" Joanna exclaimed.

"Yes," Dick Voland agreed. "That's what I thought, too. It's also why I decided to come to you with it. It seemed only fair to let you know. And now that I have, I should be going." He got to his feet. "Don't bother," he added. "I know the way."

Dick let himself out through Joanna's private entrance. Stunned to silence by his words, she let him go. Bob Baker had been using their rental property for illegal purposes, so now Joanna and Butch were under investigation? The whole idea left Joanna with a pain in her gut.

Wanting to talk it over with Butch, she reached for her phone and punched the speed-dial number for the house, but she ended the call before it connected. If they were being investigated, what were the chances their phone calls were being monitored as well? After putting the phone down for a moment, she picked it up and redialed.

"How about lunch?" she asked when Butch answered.

"Lunch? Are you kidding?" he asked. "You're inviting me to lunch even though I'll show up with a squalling baby and dribble on my shirt?"

"Yes."

"Jenny can't come. She's over at Cassie's, but Dennis and I will be there. Where and when?"

"Daisy's," she said. "Eleven-thirty."

Joanna's Monday mornings were usually devoted to routine

administrative matters. She tried to do some of that now, but she had difficulty concentrating. The idea that she and Butch were under suspicion was profoundly disturbing. They had rented property to someone who had come with a whole raft of good references, but now that Bob Baker had taken off, she and Butch were somehow guilty by association. Regardless of the outcome, the fact that an investigation had been initiated could result in far-reaching complications. If Joanna came under a cloud of suspicion, so would her department. The actions of her investigators and deputies would all be called into question. Individual suspects were supposed to be considered innocent until proved guilty. Joanna knew that law enforcement agencies weren't always accorded that same consideration.

As sheriff, Joanna had occasionally worked on investigations that included various federal entities. Many of those relationships had been prickly at best. How likely was it that someone whose toes she had stepped on in the past was now looking for wrongdoing on her part?

Exasperated by her inability to concentrate on her work, Joanna left the office for lunch several minutes early. Junior Dowdle, smiling and holding a handful of menus, met her at the entrance. "Dennis?" he asked.

Junior loved babies of all kinds, but he was particularly enamored of Dennis.

"Dennis is coming," Joanna said, smiling at him and pointing at her watch. "He'll be here in a few minutes." Junior nodded and grinned. His cheerful attitude and unfailing enthusiasm were catching.

Joanna settled into a booth to wait while Junior went back to the door to meet the next set of customers. Watching him,

Joanna couldn't help thinking about Wanda Mappin. The murder victim's mental deficits might have been more severe than Junior's, but she must have been a lot like him—full of guileless wonder and straightforward opinions. Sitting in Daisy's, Joanna had no doubt that, had Wanda and Junior ever met, they would have become fast friends. Just like Wanda and her mysterious and supposedly nonexistent Wayne.

A few minutes later, beaming proudly, Junior lugged Dennis in his baby carrier back to the booth while Butch followed with the diaper bag.

"Look," Butch said, modeling for Joanna. "Do you believe it? A shirt that's been actually ironed instead of dragged out of the dryer and put on wrinkles and all? Your mother's a wonder."

"She's that, all right," Joanna observed. "And you don't know the half of it."

Barely waiting long enough for Butch to settle into the booth, Joanna launched into her story, but Butch held up a hand to stop her. "Dick came straight out to the house after he talked to you. I talked to him right after you called about lunch, so I already know what you're going to tell me."

Busying himself with settling the baby carrier into the booth and locating the pacifier, Butch seemed totally at ease.

"But doesn't any of this bother you?" Joanna asked.

"Not really," he said. "Let them look. What are they going to find? People involved in criminal enterprises need time to do bad stuff. We have a teenager and a baby. We both have full-time jobs. The money we have coming in and going out is documented down to the penny. We own a two-year-old Subaru and an aging Eagle. But if they're going to do any investigating, they'd best get a move on. I've hired a crew of kids from church to come in and start cleaning the place out to-morrow."

"If we clean it up, won't that look bad?"

Butch laughed. "It'll look a lot more suspicious if we don't."

While Butch perused his menu, Joanna studied him. She loved his sense of humor, his logical way of sorting through cri-ses, his unflappable calm in the face of whatever storm they hap-pened to encounter. And here he was, doing it again.

"In other words," she said finally, "if the FBI is after us, we cross that bridge when we come to it."

"Right." Butch grinned. "Works for me. So how about if we order and eat *before* Dennis starts crying."

CHAPTER 10

COMING BACK TO THE OFFICE AFTER LUNCH, JOANNA FOUND SHE was feeling better. The food had helped, but so had the fact that Butch hadn't been freaked out by the idea of their being the focus of a possible federal investigation. Doing her best to emulate his "What—me worry?" attitude, she turned to her desk and tackled the bane of her existence—the never-ending routine paperwork that had to be read, assimilated, and signed. She was making reasonably good progress when Kristin tapped on the door.

"Ms. Edwards would like to see you," she announced.

"Somebody bailed her out?" Joanna asked.

Kristin nodded.

Having already been threatened with a police brutality lawsuit by the husband of one of the Beasley sisters, Joanna wasn't eager to talk to the other one. For a moment she was tempted to call Frank to come into her office and run interference—or at least to serve as a witness.

"Did she say what she wants?" Joanna asked.

"To apologize," Kristin said.

"All right, then," Joanna said, relenting. "Send her in."

The Samantha Edwards who had walked into Joanna's office on Saturday had been totally put together. Then she had been dressed in a stylish pantsuit. This time she entered wearing a worn pair of jeans and a tank top, both of which were much the worse for wear. There were spatters of blood on the shirt and jeans, and there was a three-inch tear in the side seam of the tank top. These were evidently the same clothes she had worn during the Branding Iron bar fight. Whoever had come to post her bail hadn't bothered bringing along a change of clothing. And the visible damage wasn't limited to the way she was dressed. The cuts and scratches on her face and arms were starting to scab over, and the bruises were far more vivid than they had been the day before.

"Have a seat, Ms. Edwards," Joanna said. "What can I do for you?"

"Sammy," Samantha said, sliding into one of the captain's chairs. "Please call me Sammy. I came to apologize for my behavior yesterday. And for Sandy's as well."

Her contrition stood in stark contrast to her bloodied clothing and her distinctly fat lip. "You were both under a lot of stress," Joanna said graciously.

"I also wanted to say thank you," Samantha added.

Kristin had given Joanna some advance notice that an apology was in the offing. Samantha's heartfelt thank-you, however, came as a complete surprise.

"Thank me for what?" Joanna asked.

"For giving me back my sister," Sammy returned. "You were right. The two of us hadn't been together for any length of time in more than forty years. Being locked in the same cell like that finally gave us a chance to talk—to clear the air. I doubt we'll ever be close, but at least we're speaking. That's progress."

"You're welcome," Joanna said. "You said you had been praying about this, and it sounds like your prayers have been answered. I'm sure your parents would be pleased."

Sammy nodded. "I'm sure they would be. Surprised, too. You see, we never did get along, not even when we were kids. Sandy was always better-looking than I was, and smarter, too. When I came along, the teachers always expected me to be the same kind of brain she was, but I never measured up. I was never quite good enough."

Since the two sisters still looked so much alike as to be virtually indistinguishable, Joanna wondered where the bogus "better-looking" complaint came from. She doubted there was any merit to the smarter/dumber comparison, either, but it seemed likely that nothing anyone else said to the contrary would change Samantha Edwards's mind.

"So when I had a chance to steal Norbert away from her, I did it," Sammy continued. "That's the only reason I did it—because I could. I admit it was mean, and I never meant for it to turn into a war that would last a lifetime, but it did. Like a little snowball growing into an avalanche. By bringing up the subject of Norbert yesterday, you actually fixed it, Sheriff Brady. You got us started talking and helped us see how ridiculous it was. We ended up laughing about it, so thank you—thank you very much."

Due to Joanna's efforts, Sandra Wolfe and Samantha Edwards

were finally back on speaking terms. So were George and Eleanor. *That's me, all right,* Joanna thought. *Just call me Madame Peace Broker.*

"You're welcome," she said aloud. "I'm glad it worked out."

"As you said, I'm sorry our parents didn't live to see it," Samantha added. "But at least we can plan their funeral now without being at each other's throats. Well, not plan, really, since they already did all that. But we can schedule it."

"And your parents' will?" Joanna asked.

"That's been handled, too. A woman from Mr. Kimball's office is bringing a copy of it up to the Copper Queen, where Larry and Sandra are staying. I'm supposed to meet them there in an hour or so. That way we'll be able to go over it together. It'll be good to have that out of the way."

Samantha glanced at her watch and stood up. "I'd better go," she said. "Someone's taking me down to the Branding Iron to pick up my car." She held out her hand. "Again," she said, "I can't thank you enough."

In Joanna's experience as a police officer, there weren't many thank-you moments. This was something to be savored.

"You're most welcome," Joanna told her.

Samantha left. Joanna turned to her next paperwork challenge. More than a year earlier, the county's perennially under-staffed and overworked Animal Control Department had been unceremoniously dumped in Joanna's lap. At the time Joanna had been assured that the move, done as part of a "cost-cutting realignment," was strictly temporary. Unfortunately, "temporary" was now looking more and more permanent.

One of Joanna's key AC officers, Jeannine Phillips, had been severely injured in a shoot-out back in March. After weeks in the hospital and months of physical therapy, Jeannine had now been cleared by her doctor to return to work on a "light duty" basis, but her physical condition made it unlikely that she would ever again be able to handle the rigors of ordinary patrol. Not wanting to lose Jeannine entirely and hoping to divest herself of some of the Animal Control responsibilities, most specifically scheduling, Joanna had come up with a plan. She wanted to create a new administrative slot—half-time if need be—that would bring Jeannine back to work and put her in charge of handling Animal Control's day-to-day activities. With Jeannine out on disability, keeping the Animal Control duty roster up and running had been a major challenge. They had managed by juggling the schedules of existing officers. Putting Jeannine at a desk, however, meant that Joanna would need to hire a permanent patrol officer replacement. That created a major stumbling block.

Months earlier, the Board of Supervisors had imposed a countywide hiring embargo. With NNP—No New Personnel—as the watchword of the year, the idea of bringing Jeannine back in a different capacity while also hiring an additional officer was anything but a slam dunk. By moving money from one category to another, Frank Montoya had managed to carve out a complex system of budget wiggles that could conceivably provide an "expenditure neutral" way of getting the job done. Now, however, it was Joanna's task to boil down Frank's complex budgetary mumbo jumbo and arcane pie charts into something the Board of Supervisors would deem acceptable. Joanna had asked for and received a slot on this week's Board of Supervisors agenda. By Friday she'd need to have her presentation pulled together, polished, and ready for seamless delivery.

She was deep in the process of working on that when Jaime showed up in her doorway. "Got a minute, boss?" he asked.

Joanna pushed her laptop aside. "Sure," she said. "What's up?"

"Look what I found." He tossed a thin file folder across Joanna's desk.

"What is it?"

"I decided to check out the Tucson PD Missing Persons file for anyone named Wayne. I think I may have found Wanda Mappin's missing friend. His name's Wayne Leroy Hamm, age twenty-six. He disappeared on May 12, 2005, from East Twenty-fourth Street, off South Swan, Tucson, Arizona."

Joanna picked up the folder and glanced through it. "What makes you think this Wayne is related to Wanda's Wayne?"

"You have to read all the way through it before you come to the meat of it. Turns out that the address on East Twenty-fourth is for another group home, one that's operated by the same organization—the Flannigan Foundation—the same people who ran the one Wanda was living in when she disappeared."

"But if they weren't in the same one—" Joanna began.

"Maybe they had joint outings of some kind," Jaime suggested. "But what I'm thinking now is that Wanda's imaginary friend wasn't so imaginary after all."

Joanna nodded. "What kind of halfway house?" she asked.

"Flannigan Foundation is real coy about that," Jaime said. "Their Web site says they operate group homes to fill any number of 'critical needs' in the community—places for drug and sex offenders and for recently released inmates as well as homes for mentally and physically disabled adults. This particular one is called Warwick House. I got the number from the reverse directory. The person who answered the phone there, however, refused to give out any information, citing client confidentiality, of course. She referred me to the corporate offices, which ultimately led me back to Flannigan Foundation's CEO, Mr. Donald Dietrich. He hadn't returned my previous phone call, and he hasn't returned the latest one, either."

Joanna turned back to the papers in her hands and scanned through them. The details were sketchy. Wayne Hamm, a ward of the state of California, had been sent to Tucson for reasons that weren't specified in the missing persons report. There was no way for Joanna to tell from what was written there why the man had been remanded into a custodial setting.

"Has Mr. Hamm ever been found?" Joanna asked.

"Not according to Tucson PD," Jaime told her. "They still have the case listed in their active missing persons file—as active as those things ever are."

"Wanda missed Wayne enough that she complained about it to her mother, but the date Hamm disappeared is almost two months after Wanda Mappin herself went missing," Joanna pointed out.

"I noticed that, too," Jaime said with a nod. "Maybe he got moved from one facility to another, and Wanda was no longer able to see him the way she had before. Maybe it was just a matter of scheduling. But if Wayne Hamm is Wanda's Wayne, why did the people at Flannigan Foundation tell Lucinda Mappin that he didn't exist, that her daughter had made him up?"

"You're right," Joanna said. "That is very interesting. Where's Flannigan Foundation located?"

"They have properties all over in both Phoenix and Tucson," Jaime said. "But their corporate offices are located in a business park out near Tucson International Airport."

Joanna looked at her watch. It was verging on four, and Tucson International was a good two hours away. By the time they got there, the offices would most likely be closed, and Joanna didn't relish making a wasted trip.

"I'll tell you what," she said. "How about if the two of us take a ride up there tomorrow morning and drop by to see Mr. Dietrich in person? It's one thing to ignore requests for returned phone calls. It's a lot harder to ignore people who are milling around outside your office, especially if two of those people happen to be wearing badges."

Jaime grinned at her. "I was hoping you'd say that," he said. "You've been known to charm open a few closed doors on occasion. What time?"

"Eight-thirty or nine," she said. "As soon as we finish the briefing."

"I need to head out, then," he said. "Pepe's got a Little League game tonight. I try not to miss them."

"What about Luis?" Joanna asked. "Have you heard from your nephew?"

"I tried calling him a little earlier," Jaime said. "There was no answer. I thought tonight, after the game, Pepe and I would stop by and check on him. Marcella may let Pepe in to see his cousin even if I'm persona non grata."

Once Jaime left Joanna's office, she closed her computer and started packing up to go home. George called before she managed to get away.

"How did you do that?" he asked.

"Do what?"

"Find Ellie, for starters," George replied. "She told me this morning that you'd come to see her at a hotel out in Sierra Vista. What in the world was she doing in a hotel?"

"That I don't know," Joanna answered.

"Whatever you said to her must have worked. She's gone home. She called me from there just a little while ago. She wanted to know when I'd be home so she'll know when to start dinner. She acted like nothing out of the ordinary had happened and completely ignored the fact that she's been on the warpath for days. Weeks, even."

Should I tell him what she said about my father? Joanna wondered. In the end, she let things be.

"Don't look a gift horse in the mouth," Joanna advised. "Go home. Whatever you do, don't be late for dinner. You might even go for broke and stop by Safeway for a bouquet of flowers."

"Good thinking," George said. "I'm on my way."

This time Joanna made it out to the parking lot without the phone summoning her back inside. There was another storm building over the mountains to the east, and once again she took the Explorer home, just to be on the safe side of the water cascading down the walls of Mexican Canyon and into their wash. Butch's rain gauge reported that they'd had close to two and a half inches of rain in the past three days. With the ground saturated, that meant that it wouldn't take nearly as big a storm to create another torrential runoff.

At home, she and Butch both pitched in to make it through the evening chores—dinner, dishes, baths, bedtime. She had loved Andy, but their relationship had been far more tempestuous than her relationship with Butch. When Jenny was a baby, Joanna never remembered the two of them working together as a team to take care of her. Andy Brady had come to parenthood with a macho mind-set that child rearing was women's work. For a while Joanna had gone along with that program, but over time the world had changed. So had Joanna's expectations. Dennis Dixon's parents were older than Jennifer Ann Brady's had been—older and wiser both, Joanna hoped.

But the other part of the equation had to do with the way Butch Dixon viewed the world and his place in it. He had always longed to have kids. Now that he did, he was prepared to do whatever was necessary to make it work—including changing diapers and getting up for overnight feedings. Those two things alone made him exceptional.

When Joanna emerged from putting Dennis down in his crib, Butch was folding clean clothes at the kitchen table. "Are you going to read your dad's journals and check out what your mom said?" he asked.

Joanna had mentioned the Mona Tipton situation to Butch at lunch. "I haven't decided yet," Joanna said. "Maybe I should just leave well enough alone."

"Don't you think you should know for sure?"

If there was any truth to Eleanor's claim that Hank Lathrop had been fooling around, Joanna wasn't at all sure she wanted to know about it. "It happened a long time ago," she said with a shrug.

"That's true," Butch said. "But your mother's behaving like a nutcase now—in the present. Not that I mind her doing the ironing. She's welcome to stop by and do that anytime, but she's also keeping you and George upset in the process. I think we all need to know if what she claims happened really did happen or if she made it all up. If she's created this story out of whole cloth, George certainly needs to know what he's dealing with, and so do you."

"Why me?" Joanna asked.

"You've always implied that your dad was practically perfect in every way," Butch said. "But what if he wasn't? It's not easy being a paragon. What if Hank Lathrop turns out to have been an ordinary human being after all and ends up getting knocked off that pedestal you've kept him on all your adult life? If it turns out your father wasn't a halo-wearing angel, maybe your mother isn't the Wicked Witch of the West, either."

"I never said—" Joanna began.

"All I'm saying," Butch continued, "is that if Hank wasn't as good as you've always claimed he was, and if Eleanor isn't as bad, maybe the two of you—you and your mother—could find some common ground."

"What do you mean, I put my father on a pedestal?" Joanna asked.

Butch shook his head. "Look," he said, "twenty years or so ago, my father had an affair, too. It was with someone from work—someone who was much younger than my mother. When Mom found out about it because someone from his office called and spilled the beans, she was hell on wheels for the next six months. It's probably hard for you to think of my mother as being more difficult than she's been whenever you've been around her, but believe me, during those six months she was absolutely impossible. But then, for whatever reason, things died down. No one ever mentioned it again. My folks are still together, all these years later. What they think of as a solid marriage may not conform to your version of holy matrimony, or mine, either, but it suits them. They probably see each other as they were when they met, instead of as they are now.

"And maybe the same thing would have happened for your parents, too," Butch added. "If your father hadn't died being a

Good Samaritan and changing that flat tire, maybe your parents would have gotten through the tough times the same way my parents did. It's possible they might have split up over it, but it's also possible that their marriage would have weathered the storm. They might even have come out the better for it on the other side. Either way, your mother would have had a chance to get over it. As it is, she's stuck. Whatever happened between your father and Mona or whatever your mother *thinks* happened is still eating away at Eleanor Lathrop Winfield. It's hurting her relationship with George, and it isn't helping her relationship with you, either."

Those were more words than Joanna had heard Butch Dixon string together in a very long time, if ever. She stared at him in silence for several seconds. Her instinctive reaction was to dig in her heels and argue the point. But Butch's relationship with his parents was so treacherously similar to her own with Eleanor that she had to admit that he probably had a point.

"All right, then," she said. "I'll guess I'll go delve into my family's dirty laundry."

Later on she heard rain falling hard on the roof of the den as she stood studying the shelf where she kept her father's diaries. Since her mother had been so specific about forbidding Mona to attend Hank Lathrop's funeral, the last volume, the one he'd been writing in at the time of his death, seemed like a logical place to start. Joanna pulled out the last volume. Then, switching on the lamp, she sat down to read. She went straight to the final entry, the one written the night before her father's fatal accident:

The worst thing about making a decision is living with the consequences.

In an entry from a few days earlier, Joanna found a damning passage that seemed to show her mother's accusations had been well founded after all:

> *This is eating away at me. I'm not sleeping at night. Living like this isn't fair to Ellie. It isn't fair to Mona. And it isn't fair to me. But what will become of Joanna if we split up?*

Joanna's eyes blurred with tears as she read those words. In a matter of seconds everything Joanna had ever believed about her parents' relationship went out the window. Butch was right. Had her father lived, it was possible her parents really would have been divorced, making Joanna a child of divorce. Had that happened, how different would all their lives have been?

Knowing what seemed to be the worst, Joanna scanned through previous entries. In one from several weeks earlier, woven in among a series of general comments about what was going on in the office, Joanna found this:

> *Ellie's still pitching a hissy fit. Nothing I do is right. Nothing I say is right. The only time I have a moment's peace is when I'm out of the house. If I wasn't able to go to work, I don't know what I'd do. But work isn't exactly peaceful these days, either. M is pushing me to make a decision. I know what she wants. Part of me wants it, too, but not enough to hurt the other people I know will get hurt.*

That was what Joanna's mother had said—that Hank had used work as a way of avoiding her. And that was why now, all these years later, she was so susceptible to thinking George Winfield might be doing the same thing with work and with Madge.

But when had her father's illicit office romance started? Joanna wondered. Had it been going on the whole time Mona had worked for Hank, or had it happened only during the last few months before her father's death? The snippets Joanna found offered no specific clues about the timing. What they did make clear, however, was that although Hank Lathrop had cared deeply for Mona, he had also agonized over what his relationship with her would do to his wife and daughter.

M's dad is back in the hospital, and her mother is a basket case. The whole mess is squarely on her shoulders. I wish there were more I could do to help her. It hurts like hell to watch someone you love being run down by a train when there's not a thing you can do to stop it.

Joanna stared at the words: "someone you love." There it was in black and white, an admission written in Hank Lathrop's own distinctive handwriting. Joanna's father had fallen in love with someone who wasn't his wife and wasn't her mother. Somehow Eleanor had figured it out; found it out. For her that betrayal had been a life-altering experience, and the fact that Eleanor had decided to keep her husband's secret from Joanna had altered their daughter's life as well.

Sometime later, Butch appeared in the doorway to the office. "Well?" he asked. "Did you find anything?"

Unaware that she'd been sitting and staring off into space, Joanna was startled by the sound of his voice.

"Mom's right," she said. "It's real. It's all here in black and white."

"I'm sorry," Butch said.

Joanna was surprised to realize that she was still close to tears. Her father's betrayal had happened years in the past, but for her it was a raw, bleeding wound. "Me, too," she managed. "Do you want to read it?"

"Naw," Butch said. "No need. But it's late, Joey. Don't you think we should go to bed?"

Without another word Joanna switched off the lamp and followed him to the bedroom. By the time she had changed into her nightgown, Butch was already half asleep, but when she crawled into bed beside him, he turned over and enveloped her in a full body hug. Within a matter of seconds, he was snoring. Joanna was wide awake.

For a long time she lay there going over everything she remembered about her father's funeral. Joanna had been fifteen at the time and overwhelmed with grief. Her mother had been quietly stoic. If Eleanor had shed any tears at all, she had done so in private—away from her daughter's prying eyes and away from everyone else's as well. Joanna remembered hearing people saying how brave Eleanor was being in the face of her husband's senseless death. Joanna hadn't thought of her mother as brave— she thought her cruel and heartless. If she had really loved the man, how could she not show it?

Still, no matter how much Joanna had disapproved of her mother's behavior, she had also internalized it, modeled it, and made it her own.

Gradually, as the rain pelted down outside, Joanna stopped thinking about Hank Lathrop's funeral and started thinking about Andy's.

—◆—

At the time of his death, there had been so much going on in his life that Joanna hadn't known about that the two of them might as well have been living in separate universes. There was his closely guarded secret investigation into corruption inside Walter McFadden's Cochise County Sheriff's Department. Joanna had known Andy was running for the office of sheriff, but he hadn't told her what kind of malfeasance had prodded him into doing so. And there was money from a long-lost uncle that had suddenly come into Andy's possession. Joanna hadn't known about that, either—about the source of the money Andy had used to buy the diamond ring he had planned to give her as a surprise at the tenth anniversary dinner they never got to have.

Lying there next to Butch, Joanna remembered in freeze-frame, high-definition detail, that whole difficult time surrounding Andy's funeral. All of it remained imprinted on her heart. She saw herself sitting in the kitchen polishing Andy's boots and his badge. She remembered pinning the badge on his uniform, intending that it would be buried with him. Later she had changed her mind about that. She had called the funeral home and asked for them to remove the badge. She had saved Andy's badge for Jenny, just as Eleanor had saved Hank's for Joanna.

And then there were the people—hundreds of them, friends and complete strangers—who had come to the visitation and to Andy's funeral the next day. She remembered the funeral itself and the graveside ceremony—hearing the sound of the bagpipes, seeing the coffin being lowered into the grave, being handed the carefully folded flag, hearing the last call on the two-way radio. Through it all, Joanna had done her best to hold herself in check, behaving to the best of her ability as her mother had behaved under similar circumstances—emulating what Eleanor had done because Joanna didn't know what else to do.

All of those pictures were there in Joanna's head, but as she mentally scrolled through them, there was one more detail that had been there from the beginning but that she hadn't noticed before—or, more likely, had refused to let herself notice. Many of the frames from the funeral home and from the cemetery included the image of a young woman, a blonde a few years younger than Joanna, with the slightly thickened waist of a midterm pregnancy. Whoever the woman was, she was there suffering along with everyone else who had come, her face tear-stained and her features distorted by grief. And yet she had never once spoken to Joanna—not at the visitation or the cemetery nor at the reception afterward. She had never introduced herself to Andy's widow and had never offered her condolences.

Who was she? Joanna wondered now. *What was her connection to Andy?* Was she someone from work, perhaps? If so, the woman had disappeared from the sheriff's department long before Joanna had shown up there after her own election several months later.

The baby monitor squawked as Dennis stirred in the other room. Glad to escape the questions that were plaguing her, Joanna hurried out of bed and turned down the volume so the baby's fussing wouldn't disturb Butch. She went to the kitchen to get a bottle, then went into the bedroom where she pulled the wide-awake, screeching child from his crib. She changed him, soothed him, and fed him, but then, long after Dennis had fallen back to sleep in her arms, Joanna continued to sit in the rocker, holding him and rocking, with all those questions and more once again roiling in her head.

Who was she? Where did she come from? Where did she go? Whose baby was it, and where are they now?

But most of all, with the knowledge of her father's indiscretion newly coalescing in her heart, Joanna found there was one question that trumped all the others: *Is she my very own Mona Tipton?*

CHAPTER 11

"MOM," JENNY CALLED FROM THE BEDROOM DOORWAY. "YOU'D better get up. Butch says you're going to be late for work."

Joanna opened her eyes and peered at the clock. Seven-fifteen. She staggered out of bed and headed for the bathroom. The hot shower helped get her on track, but no amount of makeup could fix the ravages of her relatively sleepless night.

"And here I thought Dennis finally slept through the night," Butch said, examining her face as he handed her a mug of coffee. "Turns out I'm the only one who slept. Obviously you didn't. Sorry about that."

"It's okay," Joanna said, choosing not to mention that her sleepless night had very little to do with poor little Dennis.

"Toast?" Butch asked. "English muffin?"

Joanna shook her head. "Thanks. I'd better just go. And I'll probably have to drive up to Tucson later on this morning, after the briefing. I don't know how late I'll be."

"Call on my cell," Butch said. "Jeff will be here in about an hour with that group of high school kids he rounded up for the cleanup job. We'll be at the other house most of the day."

"How's the wash?"

"I walked down and checked on it earlier," Butch said. "It's still running some but passable—as long as you have four-wheel drive. Maybe it's time to think about unloading that Crown Victoria."

"Not right now," Joanna said. "The department's budget is already in a world of hurt. Believe me, buying new four-wheel-drive patrol cars isn't in the cards."

Outside, the sky overhead was a clear cobalt blue. After several days of rain, weeds and grass that had lain dormant in the desert floor were suddenly springing to life and spreading a carpet of unexpected green. Normally, Joanna would have rejoiced at seeing that miraculous green. Today she saw the transformation, but her heart was too heavy to respond. Hank Lathrop was dead. Now her memories of him were dying, too, and poking holes in her memories of Andy in the process.

Joanna made it into the office by ten after eight. She was pulling herself together to face the morning briefing when she heard a woman yelling out in the lobby. "They've taken him, Jaime," she screamed. "They've got him and it's all your fault. What are you going to do about it?"

Joanna hurried to her office door. Jaime Carbajal, standing in front of Kristin's desk, was trying to fend off the blows from a young dark-haired woman who was flailing away at him with both fists clenched.

"Enough," Joanna ordered. "Stop it. What's going on here?"

As the infuriated woman turned to look at Joanna, Jaime succeeded in grabbing her wrists and holding them still. "This is my sister," Jaime managed. "Marcella Andrade, Luis's mother."

"And he's gone, I tell you," Marcella raged. "Luis is gone. If he hadn't come to see you, if you hadn't let them put his name in the paper—"

"Slow down, please, Marcella," Joanna said. "Tell us what's going on. Who has Luis? When did you lose him?"

"I didn't lose him!" Marcella declared furiously. "You make it sound like I put him down someplace and forgot where I left him. When I came home this morning, he was gone. Oh, God. They've taken him, I know they have. What'll they do to him? What if I never see him again? What if I've lost my baby forever?" Suddenly the fury that had propelled her to attack her brother seemed to dissipate. Sobbing, she sagged against Jaime's chest as he struggled to hold her upright.

"Why don't you come into my office?" Joanna suggested. "Let's try to get to the bottom of this."

Jaime led Marcella into Joanna's office. While he eased her into one of the captain's chairs, Joanna handed her a box of tissues. "You think someone has taken your son?"

Marcella nodded numbly.

"Do you know who?"

Marcella didn't answer right away. "Some bad guys, I guess," she said finally. "Some of Luis's father's friends—Marco's used-to-be friends."

"What kind of friends?" Jaime asked.

Marcella bit her lip. "Dealers," she said. "Drug dealers. Marco was working with them for a while, and they thought he ripped them off."

"Did he?" Jaime asked.

Marcella shrugged. "Maybe."

"So what happened?"

"Marco told me he was afraid that the dealer would try to take Luis in order to get even for what Marco did. That's why I left Tucson. That's why Luis and I came back home to Bisbee. I didn't think he'd know to look for us here."

"Does this guy—this dealer—have a name?" Joanna asked.

Marcella nodded. "Juan," she answered. "His name's Juan Francisco Castro. Everybody calls him Paco."

Joanna made a note of the name.

"So, like I said," Marcella continued, "we came back here. We rented a house and we were getting along just fine until Luis found those damned bones. Yesterday morning Jaime let somebody put his name in that newspaper article, and now he's gone. What if they found out where we were from that? If Paco's got him, there's no telling what he'll do."

The idea that Jaime had any control over what went into a newspaper article was almost laughable. Besides, the drug dealers Joanna knew personally weren't exactly news junkies. Still, she supposed it was remotely possible that Paco Castro or one of his cronies could have seen the name in the Tucson papers and put two and two together.

"When did you find out Luis was gone?" Jaime asked.

Marcella paused for a moment before she answered. "When I got home," she said at last.

"What time was that?"

"About four," she admitted. "I was out partying with a friend."

From what Jaime had said about his sister's exploits the day before, Joanna had an idea about what kind of a friend that might be as well as what kind of party, but she didn't say a word. Neither did Jaime.

"I suspect Luis was gone much earlier than that," the detective said quietly. "Pepe and I stopped by after his Little League game to check on him."

Marcella was suddenly furious again. "You came by the house again? I thought I told you—"

"That was a little after eight," Jaime continued. "So either Luis refused to come to the door, or else—" He let the end of the sentence drift away unfinished.

"Is there a chance that Luis may have gone off with his father someplace?" Joanna asked.

Marcella shot Jaime a furtive glance before she answered. "No," she said. "No chance."

"Why not?"

"Because Marco's in prison in California right now," she answered with a defiant glare in her brother's direction.

"And is Mr. Castro under the impression you and your son may have in your possession whatever it was Marco took from him?"

"Marco took Paco's money," Marcella replied. "Drug money. Paco knows he's not getting his money back. The cops confiscated it when they arrested him. This isn't about the money. It's all about getting even."

"Back to your house, then," Joanna said. "When you came home, was anything out of place? Did you see any sign of a struggle?"

Marcella shook her head. "No," she said. "None."

"She might have missed something," Jaime said. "I should probably go by the house and check."

"I already told you," Marcella insisted. "It's my house. I don't want you there."

"You don't have a choice about this, Mrs. Andrade," Joanna told her firmly. "In order to help your son, we need to know whether or not a crime has been committed. Your brother is a detective, but because he's also been to your house, he would be in a better position to spot something out of the ordinary. Of course, if you'd rather I sent a different investigator—"

Marcella sighed. "Okay," she said. "It's all right, I guess."

"So go," Joanna told Jaime. "Go now."

"Before the briefing?"

Joanna nodded. "And take Dave Hollicker along with you, just in case."

In case it turns out to be a crime scene, Joanna thought. *In case Luis really has been kidnapped.*

"What about that trip to Tucson?" Jaime asked.

"Don't worry about it," Joanna said. "I'll see if Ernie's available or maybe even Deb Howell. The cases they've been working are pretty much under control. Wanda Mappin's case isn't."

Nodding, Jaime rose to his feet. "All right, then. Come on, Marcella," he said gently. "Let's go take a look."

Joanna followed the two of them out into the lobby, where she found Frank Montoya waiting outside her office, coffee cup in one hand and laptop in the other. "What's up?" he asked, watching as Jaime escorted Marcella down the hall and away from the conference room. "Who's that and where's Jaime going? I thought we were going to have the briefing."

"That's Jaime's sister, the mother of Luis, the kid who found Wanda Mappin's bones," Joanna explained. "Luis has gone missing and Jaime's on his way to their house to try to figure out whether or not foul play is involved. Let Dave Hollicker know I want him to go along with Jaime, and before we convene the briefing, I'd like you to take a look at this guy," she added. She handed Frank the piece of paper on which she had jotted Juan Castro's name.

"Who is it?" Frank asked.

"Somebody named Juan Francisco Castro. His street name is Paco, and he's supposedly one of Luis Andrade's father's not-so-nice drug-dealing associates. Marcella thinks he may have something to do with her son's disappearance. Just for the fun of it, let's see what's on his sheet."

By the time the briefing started ten minutes later, Frank had a copy of Juan "Paco" Castro's very extensive rap sheet. The man had been in prison for the better part of the last ten years. He'd gone down once for attempted murder and once for aggravated assault. He also had a string of lesser offenses, including grand theft auto and several drug-related charges.

"For somebody who's only twenty-seven, this guy is quite the gangster," Frank said. "In jail or out of it, I don't think I'd want to be on Paco's bad side. Jaime can't be too thrilled to have his family mixed up with these kinds of individuals."

That was an understatement. "He's not," Joanna said.

"Should we put out a BOLO on Luis Andrade?" Frank asked.

"BOLO" was cop-speak for be-on-the-lookout.

"Wait until we hear back from Jaime on that," Joanna suggested. "Let's see what he finds at his sister's house before we make life any more complicated for them than it already is."

True to its name, the briefing proved to be brief. A weekend during which far too much had happened in Cochise County had been followed by a Monday in which very little had happened.

Other than a few routine traffic stops and assorted minor fender benders, Patrol had very little to report. For a change neither the jail nor Animal Control was caught up in some kind of unexpected crisis. Once everyone had been brought up to speed on the fact that Luis Andrade had gone missing, Joanna turned to her detectives.

"What about the Beasley situation?" she asked.

"Sandra Wolfe and Samantha Edwards seem to have buried the hatchet for the moment," Deb Howell reported.

"Thank God for small blessings," Frank murmured.

"There's an announcement from them in this morning's paper," Deb continued, "an announcement about Alfred and Martha's joint funeral service—a memorial service rather than a funeral. It's scheduled for Higgins Funeral Chapel Thursday morning at eleven. They're due to be cremated prior to that. Anybody care to guess where they want their ashes scattered?"

"Montezuma Pass?" Joanna ventured.

"You've got it," Deb Powell answered. "Norm Higgins gave me a copy of the list of final instructions the Beasleys had on file at the mortuary. It's complete down to the last detail. And that means Martha may not have been at the wheel of the vehicle, but she was almost certainly the driving force behind making all these complex arrangements. I've talked to several of their friends and neighbors, and they've all told me the same thing—that Alfred had really lost focus in recent months. I don't think he would have been capable of pulling these detailed specifics together."

"What do you mean, 'lost focus'?" Joanna asked.

"Even though Doc Winfield found no obvious signs of Alzheimer's, several people mentioned they thought Alfred had been losing ground, mentally if not physically. Time and again they told me the same thing—that Alfred wasn't himself; he seemed dazed and confused. He'd seem fine—almost normal—in the mornings, but by late afternoon and evening he'd barely know his own name."

"So there was something wrong with the man, even if we don't know what it was," Joanna said.

Deb nodded. "According to Sandra, she had been actively involved in trying to find an assisted living facility where they could both be properly looked after."

"Looks like Alfred's response to that was a definite no," Frank said. "But we've still got a problem with the Beasleys' house. So far today I've had two separate calls from Sandra Wolfe's attorney asking when we're going to be releasing it to them. He says that since it can't be considered a crime scene in the ordinary sense of the word, Sandra and her sister need to be able to go in and start sorting through things."

Joanna glanced at Deb. It was her case and her call. "What do you think?" Joanna asked.

The detective shrugged. "I suppose it's okay to let the daughters do whatever they need to do," she said.

Joanna noticed Deb Howell's singular lack of enthusiasm for the subject, but Frank Montoya apparently took her words at face value. "I'll call Federer, then, and let him know it's a go," he said. "I'll also tell Bisbee PD that they can take down our crime scene tape to allow Sandy and Samantha access."

Joanna turned to Ernie Carpenter. "What's on your agenda today?" she asked.

"I have a meeting with Tom McCracken in a little while," Ernie said. "He's been telling everyone who'll listen that the Sundersons set fire to his place. I thought I'd give him a little reality check and bring him up to speed on what the DPS investigator told us. I won't mention this to him, but if he was aware the wiring was hazardous, Carol Sunderson might be able to take *him* to court."

That possibility was enough to make Joanna smile. She turned to Casey Ledford, who as usual was sitting quietly in the far corner of the room and doodling in her notebook.

"What about you, Casey?"

"I'm still working on those plastic bags," the fingerprint tech said. "And I'm still hoping to find something, maybe not on the bags themselves. The sand pretty well scrubbed all of that clean. But there are dozens of feet of duct tape there, and I'm going over every inch of them. That takes time."

Joanna looked around the conference table. "Anything else?"

Shaking their heads, people stood and headed out, but Joanna called Detective Howell back before she made it out the door.

"You clearly didn't want to turn that house over to the daughters," Joanna said. "How come?"

Deb shut the conference room door and returned to the table. "Something about this isn't right," she said. "It's nothing I can put my finger on—just a feeling I have."

"Women's intuition?" Joanna asked with a smile. Since her arrival at the Cochise County Sheriff's Department, Joanna herself had been derided for relying on that on more than one occasion, although she had been proved right more often than not.

"I guess," Deb admitted.

"Look," Joanna said. "What the guys call 'gut instinct' is fine, but calling it 'women's intuition' will get you in trouble every time. So give me your best gut instinct."

"I don't like the man," Deb said. "I don't like him at all."

"Who?" Joanna asked.

"Larry Wolfe," Casey replied with a shudder. "Sandra's husband. He gives me the creeps; makes my skin crawl. And if they're so broke, how can they afford a hot-shot defense attorney like Irwin Federer? Lawyers like that don't come cheap."

"The Wolfes are broke?" Joanna asked. "Who says?"

"Relatively broke," Deb said. "Relative to how they were before."

"Before what?"

"Before they lost it all," Deb said. "Years ago they lived in Texas. Houston, I believe. He was an executive for some big company that went broke."

"Enron, maybe?" Joanna asked.

Deb nodded. "That's the one. When that whole thing went south, the Wolfes pretty much lost everything—their savings, their retirement money, their house. When they moved back to Arizona—to Tucson—Alfred and Martha Beasley fronted them enough money—seventy-three thousand dollars—to make a down payment on a house. It was supposed to be a loan, but to this point none of it has been paid back, so that amount plus interest will have to be deducted from Sandra's share of the estate."

"How much?" Joanna asked.

"By the time the house is sold and after expenses, Sandra and Samantha should both come away with close to two hundred thou, maybe even more."

"If Larry Wolfe's retirement went bye-bye, what's he doing now?" Joanna asked.

"Wearing an orange apron and working at Home Depot in Tucson. Plumbing supplies."

"And what is it you don't like about him?"

Deb thought about that for a moment. "For one thing, I didn't like the way he looked at me. When guys look at you that way—like they're trying to undress you—while their wives are sitting right there, it makes me want to puke."

Joanna had endured a few leering looks of her own on occasion, with much the same reaction. It didn't help to think that Larry Wolfe would have to be a good twenty-five to thirty years older than Casey.

"And if he was the least bit sorry about Sandra's parents being dead," the detective continued, "he sure as hell didn't bother acting like it. I overheard him talking on the phone. He was chatting with one of his pals and setting up a golf game for late Thursday afternoon—twilight golf out at Palominas at the Rob Roy Links."

"The same day as Alfred and Martha's funeral service," Joanna observed. "So he isn't planning on spending the whole day in deep mourning or consoling his wife. The man may be an uncaring jerk, but that doesn't make him a killer."

"No," Deb agreed. "It doesn't, especially since he has an airtight alibi for the day Alfred and Martha went off that cliff. He was at work the whole time—punched in at eight in the morning and out at four, and we have that suicide note. I just flat didn't like the guy, but he's part of the Beasleys' family, and I wanted to talk to him."

"You didn't?" Joanna asked.

Deb shook her head. "He bugged out before I had a chance. Sandra said he needed to get back to Tucson because he had to be at work early this morning."

"Tell you what," Joanna said. "How about if we kill two birds with one stone. I need to drive up to Tucson to talk with the head of the Flannigan Foundation about Wanda Mappin. If you'll ride along while I do the first interview, I'll go with you to talk to Larry Wolfe."

"When will we be back?" Deb asked.

"Probably late this afternoon. Why?"

"Let me check with Katy," Deb said. "I want to be sure it's not a problem if we don't turn up right on time."

Katy Rawlins was Deb's younger sister. She was also Deb's live-in babysitter for Benjamin, Deb's six-year-old son, but the presence of a new boyfriend in Katy's life had complicated their arrangement and made her less available than she had been previously.

Jaime called while Joanna was waiting for Deb to return. "What have you got?" Joanna asked.

"Not much," Jaime answered. "According to Marcella, Luis's school backpack is missing and some of his clothing, although the place is such a mess, I don't know how she'd know what was there and what wasn't."

"He left on his own, then?"

"So it would seem. Their next-door neighbor, Mrs. Dumas, said she saw Luis leave the house just before sunset last night. He was alone at the time and wearing his backpack."

"No kidnap, then," Joanna said. "No evil drug dealers."

"Evidently not. More like a runaway. I finally got Marcella to admit that the two of them had a huge fight after I brought him home the other day. Luis may have just gotten fed up with her and decided to strike out on his own."

"At age fourteen," Joanna said. *The same age as Jenny,* she thought. "Does Marcella have any idea where he might have gone?"

"She gave me a few names and numbers," Jaime said. "I'll be checking them out."

"What about an Amber Alert?" Joanna asked. "Or a BOLO?"

"A BOLO maybe, but not an Amber Alert," Jaime said. "Frank just called me with Paco Castro's rap sheet. Plastering Luis's name and face all over radio and TV might help us find Luis, all right, but it could also lead Paco and his crew straight to Marcella's front door as well. Not a good idea."

Deb reappeared in Joanna's doorway and gave her a thumbs-up sign. "You do what you think is best, Jaime," Joanna told him. "Meantime, Deb and I are on our way to Tucson to have a chat with your Mr. Dietrich."

"Good luck with that," Jaime said, but he didn't sound particularly hopeful.

Delayed by a couple of phone calls, it was after ten before Joanna and Deb headed for the parking lot. By then Joanna's energy level was flagging. Driving in that condition didn't seem wise.

Joanna unlocked the Crown Victoria and then tossed the keys to her detective. "Do you mind?"

"Not at all," Deb said. "Ben's been sleeping through the night for years now. I can tell you're not that lucky."

Joanna gave Deb the address for Flannigan Foundation and then climbed into the passenger seat. She was asleep before they ever made it over the Divide. She stirred briefly when they slowed for Tombstone and again for Benson. When she opened her eyes again, they were already in Tucson and turning off I-10 onto Valencia. It was after noon by then. Not having had any breakfast, Joanna was both groggy and starved.

"Lunch first," she said.

They stopped at a tiny Mexican food dive near the airport. Over greasy tacos and several cups of bitterly strong coffee, Joanna brought Debra Howell up to speed on the Wanda Mappin case.

"What if Don Dietrich refuses to talk to us?" Deb asked.

By then, revived by both sleep and food, Joanna Brady was feeling a whole lot better. "No problem," she said with a cheery smile. "We'll park ourselves with him until he does."

Flannigan Foundation was housed in a handsome glass-and-stucco edifice on the road that led to the Executive Terminal. They parked in a visitor's slot and then walked into a spacious marble-floored lobby that looked more like an upscale hotel than it did your basic nonprofit. There were several people already in the lobby, including a pair of sales representatives, a man and a woman, each dressed in business attire and armed with wheeled sample cases and laptops. A young woman wearing a telephone headpiece held sway behind an ultramodern teak desk that barred the way to a pair of ornately carved double doors.

"May I help you?" she asked with a smile.

Jaime had thought Joanna would charm her way past Don Dietrich's gatekeepers. She opted instead for being hard-nosed. "We're from the Cochise County Sheriff's Department," she announced, producing her ID wallet and handing it over. "I'm Sheriff Joanna Brady and this is Homicide Detective Debra Howell. We're here to see Mr. Dietrich."

The receptionist's welcoming smile faded. "I'm afraid Mr. Dietrich is very busy today," she said. "Do you have an appointment?"

"We're investigating a murder," Joanna replied coolly but without lowering her voice. Deb Howell wasn't in uniform, but

Joanna was, and she was more than happy to create a scene. "That kind of work doesn't generally lend itself to making appointments in advance. We'll be glad to wait—however long it takes. That's him, isn't it?" she added, gesturing toward a framed black-and-white photo that hung on the wall just to the left of the door. By then the two sales representatives were all ears. The receptionist nodded grimly but said nothing.

"Good," Joanna said. "Mr. Dietrich shouldn't be too hard to miss. Keep an eye on the parking lot," she added to Deb. "It would be a shame if he tried skipping out by some other door."

The ploy worked. Within minutes two separate people came to collect the sales representatives. As soon as they were safely out of sight, the double doors glided open and Don Dietrich himself marched into the lobby. He was a tall, painfully thin man with his sparse gray hair molded into an appalling comb-over.

"What's going on here?" he demanded.

Joanna once again produced her ID wallet and showed it to him. "As I told your receptionist, we're investigating a homicide— the death of one of your clients, Wanda Mappin. Since you've been unable to return my investigator's calls, Detective Howell and I decided to stop by and see you in person. We could do this here, or, if you'd rather—"

"Come along," Dietrich said abruptly, heading back toward the double doors. "This way. We'll go to my office." He turned back to the receptionist. "Hold all my calls, Cindy," he barked over his shoulder. "This shouldn't take long."

He led them down a short hallway to an expansive and well-appointed corner office. He gestured them into visitor's chairs and seated himself behind a magnificent polished wood desk. By then he seemed to have gathered his resources.

"You're right," he said smoothly. "I'm sorry to say, I've been far too busy with critical matters here, and I haven't been able to get back to"—he glanced around his desk and settled on a yellow message form before finishing the sentence—"to Detective Carbajal, I believe it was. Thankfully, though I've managed to contact Ms. Mappin, Wanda's mother, to express my sincere condolences at her loss. Losing a child, even a special-needs child, is always terribly traumatic. I've asked her to stay in touch and keep me apprised of where and when Wanda's services will be held. We'll want to send flowers, at the very least."

"Of course," Joanna said. "I should think so."

Don Dietrich's bland facade hardened a little. "What do you mean by that?"

"When an organization like yours is charged with caring for vulnerable people, I would think you would take that responsibility very seriously, and when you lose them—"

"Sheriff Brady," he interrupted. "Let me point out that as soon as Wanda Mappin missed that first midnight bed count, our people immediately reported her missing. We also launched an extensive search of the neighborhood surrounding Holbrook House. We utilized a search and rescue group with dogs and people and canvassed every inch of a three-square-mile area. As you said, these are exceedingly vulnerable people. From time to time, a few of them do wander off. When that happens, we treat it very seriously because we understand the risks. Special-needs people are often loving and trusting, which leaves them terribly susceptible to some of the evils this wicked world has to offer."

"Yes," Joanna said. "I'd have to agree that being trussed up, taped into a plastic bag, and then having your skull beaten in is pretty evil."

Don Dietrich paled. "As I said to Ms. Mappin, we're outraged and appalled by what happened to poor little Wanda. It is a tragedy in every sense of the word."

Little? Joanna thought. *Wanda Mappin was a size twenty. You didn't even know her, you worthless jerk!*

"So in the course of their missing persons investigation, did detectives from Tucson PD speak to people at the group home—to staff members and clients?"

"I'm sure we made our staff members available for questioning, although I don't know for sure whether or not any of them were actually interviewed," Dietrich said quickly. "As for our clients, I doubt detectives would have been allowed access to them. We have an obligation to protect client privacy, something else we take very seriously."

"How many clients do you tend to lose in any given year?" Joanna asked.

Dietrich's eyes turned stony, but he answered smoothly enough. "As I said earlier, clients do wander away from time to time, but we usually find them somewhere in the near neighborhood and are able to bring them back."

"What about Wayne Hamm?" Joanna asked.

"Who?"

"Wayne Leroy Hamm," Joanna repeated. "He was another one of your clients—a friend of Wanda's, we believe—who went missing from a place called Warwick House—another Flannigan Foundation facility—on May 12, almost two months after Wanda disappeared. He, too, has never been found."

Dietrich frowned in concentration. "Now that you mention it, I do seem to remember the name. Again, another very unfortunate circumstance."

"Is it possible there's a pattern here, Mr. Dietrich?"

"I'm not sure what you mean."

"Could it be that some of the people who work for your organization are in fact victimizing the very people they're supposed to be caring for and protecting?"

"That's an outrageous accusation," Dietrich declared. "Our caregivers are all highly qualified. Our employees go through a rigorous security check before they're ever hired, and we offer the best in-house continuing-education training program in the caregiving business."

"Were Wanda Mappin and Wayne Hamm ever in the same facility?" Joanna asked.

"No!" Dietrich said categorically. "We don't have any coed kinds of facilities. Many of our clients may be developmentally disabled, but their hormones aren't necessarily limited in the same fashion. We have the occasional picnic, trips to the Desert Museum, and other supervised social events, but staying in the same facility is an absolute no-no."

"Is it possible that Wayne Hamm and Wanda Mappin might have met at one of those 'social occasions' and become friends?"

"I don't know that for sure, but if they were clients at the same time, I don't suppose it would be out of the question, no."

"Why, then, would some of your people—your well-trained caregivers—tell Lucinda Mappin that it wasn't possible for Wanda to have a friend named Wayne, that he was someone she had made up?"

"Someone told her that?"

Joanna nodded.

"I'm sure Ms. Mappin was going through a very difficult time," Dietrich said. "It's possible that she's simply mistaken. She might have been told one thing and have understood something else."

"It's also possible she was lied to," Joanna said.

Don Dietrich leaned back in his chair and crossed his arms. "If you're going to make these kinds of wild accusations, I believe this interview is over."

"Yes," Joanna agreed, rising to her feet. "I believe it is, but don't be surprised if you see a lot of my investigators and me in the next little while, Mr. Dietrich. We're going to be combing through your records, talking to your people."

"Not without a warrant."

"Oh, we'll have warrants, all right," Joanna returned. "This is a homicide investigation. Any expectation of patient confidentiality went away the moment someone bashed Wanda's skull in and stuffed her into those two garbage bags. I don't know for sure where she was murdered, but her body was found in Cochise County. That means I'm going to find out who did it and why. You may not be overly concerned about who did this to one of your most vulnerable clients, but I am. As sheriff, that's my job. Believe me, I take that responsibility the same way you take yours, Mr. Dietrich—very seriously."

CHAPTER 12

"HE WAS LESS THAN HELPFUL," DEB COMMENTED AS THEY WALKED back to Joanna's Crown Victoria.

"I noticed," Joanna said. "Where to now?"

Deb glanced at her watch. "It's a little past one. How about if we try Home Depot next? Larry Wolfe works at a store that's just off Broadway, the one at El Con Mall. Want me to drive?"

Joanna nodded and climbed into the passenger seat. With the midday sun bearing down on them, the car was like an oven. Joanna was grateful for the Civvie's downscale cloth seats. In the fierce heat, leather would have been impossible. As they drove from the airport into town, with the air-conditioning struggling to gain headway, Joanna picked up her notebook and paged through it until she found the place where she had jotted down the Tucson PD case numbers for Wayne Hamm's disappearance and for Wanda Mappin's as well. Moments later, with the help of directory assistance, she was on the phone introducing herself to a records clerk for Tucson PD.

"The investigating officer assigned to Wanda Mappin's case is Detective Ramsey," the clerk told Joanna in answer to her question. "Detective Rebecca Ramsey. Do you need her number?"

"Sure," Joanna said. "Thanks. And then I'll need to ask about a second case—another missing person."

"Which one?"

"Wayne Leroy Hamm? He disappeared in May of this year."

Joanna heard a keyboard clicking in the background. "Here it is," the clerk said. "That case was assigned to Detective Maldonado— Richard Maldonado."

"Do you have a phone number for him?"

The clerk sighed. "Sorry, Sheriff Brady," she said. "I'm afraid you won't be able to reach him. Period. Rick retired on July first of this year. Unfortunately, he died on July fourth. Self-inflicted gunshot wound. His wife left him."

Four brief sentences, Joanna thought, *holding a whole lifetime's worth of tragedy.*

"Who's handling Detective Maldonado's cases, then?" she asked.

"The active ones have all been transferred to other detectives. But Mr. Hamm's case is a couple of months old now, and it's also relatively cold. As far as I can tell, it hasn't been reassigned to anyone in particular."

It took another few minutes before Joanna was able to reach Detective Ramsey by phone.

"I heard your people had located the remains," Becky Ramsey said. "I figured I'd be hearing from someone on this before long.

I have Wanda Mappin's case file right here on my desk. I pulled it first thing this morning."

"So you remember it, then?" Joanna asked.

"Wanda's mother has called me once a week ever since it happened, but I'd remember Wanda Mappin even without the case file," Becky said. "I have a cousin named Sally who's also developmentally disabled and probably has a lot of the same issues Wanda did. Sally's one of the lucky ones. Her parents are still able to keep her at home. Everyone kept telling them that Sally needed to be institutionalized, but my Aunt Jane absolutely refused. It hasn't been easy for them, but I've always respected that decision. Dealing with Wanda's case brought me face-to-face with the reality of how those places work. Now I respect my aunt and uncle that much more."

"What do you mean?"

"If you study the Flannigan Foundation Web site, they claim to provide their clients with quality care in a 'comfortable, home-like atmosphere.' The words paint a pretty picture. Pardon me if I'm not convinced."

"Did you visit Holbrook House, the place where Wanda Mappin lived?" Joanna asked.

"You'd think so, wouldn't you," Detective Ramsey said bitterly. "Logic dictates that most missing persons investigations start from where the person lived and where he or she was last seen. When I tried to gain access to Wanda Mappin's place of residence, I was turned down cold. According to their rules and regs, having outside visitors of any kind is an absolute no-no due to client confidentiality considerations. I was told I could interview employees but only off-site, and I did so. What I wasn't allowed to do was to have any kind of interaction with Wanda's

housemates, even though they might well have had some knowledge of when and why she disappeared."

"Couldn't you have gotten a warrant?" Joanna asked.

"Tried that," Becky said, "but it didn't work. My supervisor
shot it down. Told me we didn't have jurisdiction."

"Jurisdiction or not, you'd think the people from Flannigan
Foundation would have bent over backward to help you. Why
didn't they? Are they hiding something?"

"That's pretty much what I decided," Detective Ramsey answered.

"What?"

"I suspect a lot of human warehousing goes on in places like
that."

"What do you mean?"

"Docile clients that don't cause trouble are easily ignored. As
for the troublemakers? I wouldn't be surprised if the caregivers
tend to keep those folks overmedicated and zoned out of their
gourds to the point of being comatose. It would make them easier to handle."

"Which category did Wanda Mappin fall into?"

"Definitely the second one."

Joanna was taken aback. "Really?" she asked. "Wanda a troublemaker? From talking to her mother, I would have thought
Wanda would fall into the sweetness-and-light category."

"You can't always trust mothers," Detective Ramsey observed.
"They're blinded by love, so all they see is the best in their kids no
matter what. Betty Saroyan is the one who gave me the lowdown
on Wanda."

"Who's she?"

"The housemother at Holbrook House. Betty was the only

person from Flannigan who agreed to see me, and the two of us had several long talks. She told me that there were times when Wanda was docile and cooperative, but if you happened to cross her or if something made her mad, she could turn into a hundred eighty pounds of pure trouble. She was also something of an escape artist."

"She was able to get out? From what Lucinda said, that sounded impossible."

"Mothers don't always know best," Becky observed. "Wanda evidently got out time and again. Betty said that sometimes she made it back home on her own. Other times they'd have to send out a search party. They usually found her wandering in the near neighborhood without ever having to report her missing. The only incident where they went so far as to call in an actual report was the last time it happened, when she took off and didn't come back."

"And ended up dead in a pair of duct-taped trash bags a hundred miles away," Joanna added.

Becky nodded. "I'm sure her mother is devastated, but family members usually prefer knowing the worst to not knowing anything."

"That's probably the case," Joanna agreed. "Lucinda Mappin came down to Bisbee yesterday and identified some of her daughter's effects. She also mentioned a friend of Wanda's, someone named Wayne. She wasn't able to provide any details but she said Wayne had disappeared and that his being gone had Wanda upset and out of sorts."

"Oh, yes," Becky said. "I remember the Wayne part of the story and the fact that Wanda had complained to her mother that he was gone. The whole bit reminded me of that old Jimmy

Stewart movie, the one where his character can see an enormous rabbit that no one else can see. But after Lucinda mentioned it to me, I did ask Mrs. Saroyan about it. She claimed she'd never heard of anyone by that name, either in Flannigan Foundation or out of it. She wondered if maybe Wayne was someone Wanda had met when she was out on one of her illicit jaunts. I checked on this mysterious Wayne character to the best of my ability and finally gave it up as a lost cause."

"What if I told you we've now uncovered a second missing person case involving a Flannigan Foundation client?" Joanna asked.

"Another one?" Becky asked. "Who is it and when did this happen?"

"The guy's name is Wayne Leroy Hamm. He was reported missing from a Flannigan Foundation group home called Warwick House off South Swan and East Twenty-fourth. That was on May twelfth."

"You think this may be Wanda's mysterious Wayne?"

"That's what we're trying to find out."

"But how is this possible? I was already investigating a case involving a Flannigan Foundation client. How come I never heard one word about it? Who's working the case?"

"It was assigned to someone named Detective Maldonado."

Becky let out her breath in what sounded like a whoosh of frustration. "Not good," she said. "Not good at all."

"Why not?"

"It's not nice to speak ill of the dead," Becky replied, "so let's just say Rick was a troubled guy. If he was handed this case in May, it probably didn't get much attention because by then Rick Maldonado had lots of other fish to fry."

"I know," Joanna said. "The records clerk told me what happened to him."

"Would you like me to take a look at his case book and give you a call back?"

"Please," Joanna said. "I'd really appreciate it."

"Give me your number."

By the time Joanna put down the phone, Deb was driving north on Alvernon. As they neared Home Depot, Joanna found herself beset by a swarm of second thoughts. Homicide detectives routinely find it necessary to question their victims' grieving family members, friends, and associates. Talking to people who knew the deceased is the only way to find out what was going on in the victim's life just prior to the time of death.

Larry Wolfe was Alfred and Martha Beasley's son-in-law. Interviewing him would have been routine except for one small thing. The last Joanna had heard, Larry Wolfe was at war with her department. His attorney had threatened a police brutality lawsuit against the Cochise County Sheriff's Department in general and against Sheriff Joanna Brady in particular. Had she consulted the county attorney on this score, he probably would have advised her against being anywhere near Larry Wolfe. At this point, not seeing the man wasn't an option, but Joanna knew that if he pursued the police brutality charge, she needed to defend herself.

Best cover your butt, girl, Joanna told herself.

As soon as Deb stopped the car, Joanna grabbed her briefcase out of the backseat. She rummaged through it until she located the tiny tape recorder she kept there. Naturally, when she tried switching it on, the batteries were dead. No matter. They were going into Home Depot—replacement-battery central.

"Do we need that?" Deb asked, looking questioningly at the recorder.

"Yes, we do," Joanna said. "Better to have it and not need it than the other way around."

Inside the store, Joanna went straight to the nearest checkout stand. After purchasing her batteries, she stood there and fixed the recorder. When she and Deb finally went searching for their quarry, the recorder was already humming away in the breast pocket of Joanna's uniform.

It turned out that Deb's plumbing department tip was in error. They finally tracked down a floor supervisor who was able to explain Larry Wolfe worked in electrical rather than plumbing. "I heard about the situation with his in-laws," the man said. "Very sad. If you need to talk to Larry in private, you're welcome to use my office out back. Tell him Mr. Dorn said it was fine."

They found Larry administering a treatise on dimmer switches to a man with a shopping cart full of rolls of wire, junction boxes, and electrical fittings. Joanna and Deb had been standing in the aisle listening for several minutes before he noticed them. Once he recognized Deb Howell, Larry did a classic double take. The look he threw in Deb's direction could have been a glare or a leer. Although Deb Howell was certainly leer-worthy, Joanna wasn't sure which it was.

Realizing he had two police officers for an audience seemed to take the wind out of Larry Wolfe's dimmer-switch sales pitch. Shutting down the discussion, he sent his still befuddled customer off in the direction of the checkout stands and wheeled on Deb.

"What are you doing here?" he demanded. "Can't you see I'm working?"

"This will only take a few minutes," Deb assured him quickly. "We've already cleared it with your supervisor, Mr. Dorn. He said we could use his office."

"But why—"

"It's just routine," Deb continued placatingly. "It would have been more convenient if we could have done this yesterday in Bisbee, but you got away before I could catch you."

Clearly unhappy about it, Larry gave in. "All right," he said brusquely. "If we must. Come on, then. Mr. Dorn's office is out back."

He set off at breakneck speed, with Deb Howell following on his heels. "Tell your little partner there to get a move on," he added over his shoulder. "Otherwise we'll lose her."

Joanna had been about to introduce herself. Wolfe's erroneous assumption and abrupt departure caught her off guard. *Partner?* she thought. *He thinks I'm Deb's "little partner"?*

But after a moment's consideration, she let the assumption ride and set off after them. What Larry Wolfe didn't know might just hurt him.

He led them through a door into the stifling back area of the warehouse, where air-conditioning failed to penetrate. He wandered past jumbled tangles of incoming and discontinued merchandise. He stopped in front of a keypad-managed door that allowed them into a small cramped office with a battered metal desk, two grubby chairs, and a mass of boxes stacked floor to ceiling. The place was a mess, but at least it was air-conditioned. Joanna and Deb helped themselves to the chairs. Larry stood leaning against the desk, his arms folded across his chest.

"I talked to Sandy earlier," he said. "She told me the medical examiner has released the bodies for burial. I assume that means he must be satisfied as to the cause of death. If the investigation is over, what do you want from me?"

When medical examiners finally get around to releasing victim remains, family members are usually relieved to know that they can finally move forward with making final arrangements. They focus on that. By deciding the investigation into Alfred and Martha Beasley's deaths was over and done with, Larry Wolfe was making a leap of logic worthy of the most dedicated *Court TV* aficionado. It was enough to pique Joanna's interest, but by then Deb had brought out her notebook and sat with pencil poised at the top of a blank page.

"How long did you know your wife's parents?" she asked.

"Only fifteen years or so," Larry said. "This is Sandy's second marriage. My third. Believe me, I can't say a bad thing about Al and Martha."

"You had a good relationship with them?"

"Absolutely. No one could have asked for better in-laws. They were great, and I cared about them a lot. It hurt to see them failing, of course, and they were failing. Al especially was clearly losing ground."

"Losing ground mentally?" Deb asked. "Physically?"

"I'd say both. When I first met them, Al was sharp as could be, but not lately."

"Did that upset him?"

"I'm not sure if you know that Alfred's mother had Alzheimer's, even though he didn't talk about it much. And I'm sure Alfred was bright enough to figure out it was probably coming for him, too. Because Martha was so dependent on him, we hinted around to them that they should probably consider assisted living. Alfred was adamant that wasn't for him; said he'd rather die first."

"He actually said that?" Deb asked. "That he'd rather die?"

Larry frowned. "I'm sure he did. I don't remember exactly where or when."

"Did his not wanting to go into assisted living have anything to do with money?" Deb asked.

"No," Larry declared. "Not at all. The two of them had enough dough socked away that they could have afforded the best care money could buy. Alfred simply didn't want to go. Didn't want to give up his independence. I think he wanted to go out in a blaze of glory. He did, too," Larry added admiringly. "You gotta respect him for that. Like that old Paul Anka song says—Alfred did it his way."

"Is that how your wife feels about it, too?" Joanna asked. "That her father did it his way?"

Larry had been staring at Deb while he answered her questions. Now he turned to face Joanna. "Probably not," he said with a shrug. "They were her parents, after all. As I tried to explain to her when we first got the news, that's what happens to people our age. We lose our parents. They get old and die on us. It'll happen to us, too, eventually. One of these days we'll just keel over and drop dead. The fat lady'll sing, and it'll all be over.

"I know, I know," he added. "You probably think I'm some kind of heartless bastard, but I'm not. I'm a realist, and I know how it feels. I understand exactly what Sandy's going through right now because I lost my parents, too—just last year. My mother died of congestive heart failure in a nursing home. She had been ill for years, but once she died, my father was gone within weeks. He just went home, went to bed, and gave up the fight. Not nearly as spectacular as the stunt Alfred pulled, but I think, in his own way, Dad made the same decision. He didn't want to go on without my mother. That's what they call true love, right?"

"Your parents sound like nice people," Joanna said. "Midwesterners?"

"Missouri," he said. "How did you know?"

"Lucky guess," Joanna told him.

Larry glanced as his watch. "Look," he said. "We're always shorthanded at lunchtime. If there's nothing else, I should get back to the floor."

"When's the last time you saw Alfred and Martha?" Deb asked.

He sighed. "Last Thursday evening. Thursday is my usual day off. I like to play golf, but I'm not golf-crazy enough to try to play here in Tucson in this killer heat. So I drove down to Palominas. I played a twilight round out at the Rob Roy, then I drove to Bisbee and stopped by to see them on my way home."

"Thursday," Deb mused. "That would be the night before it happened. How did they seem?"

Larry frowned. "Alfred seemed a little out of it. Spacey, even. I asked Martha about him, but she said to pay no attention, that he'd be fine in the morning. I figured she knew him better than anyone. If she said he was fine, he was probably fine."

"Did they make any mention of their plans?"

"No. None at all. If they had, I swear I would have moved heaven and earth to stop them."

"About your wife's sister," Deb began. "Can you tell us anything about her?"

Larry shook his head. "Not a thing, other than the fact that she's a complete nut job."

"You don't get along with her?"

"How could I? I don't even know her. Sandy and I have been together for fifteen years. Until yesterday I had never met her sister. Now that I have, I'll be happy to have another fifteen years pass me by before I have to deal with her again. But that's the other reason I took off like a shot yesterday afternoon and didn't hang around long enough to talk to you. Sandy and her Sammy." Using his fingers, he mimed quotation marks around the diminutive name. "The two of them may be all hunky-dory at the moment, but I'm not. Last Saturday night Samantha Edwards tried to beat the crap out of my wife, and I have no intention of forgetting it or letting bygones be bygones. Once we make it through this funeral business, that woman is out of our lives. I don't want to have anything more to do with her ever again."

Inside Joanna's breast pocket the tape recorder gave a tiny lurch and a click as it came to the end of the tape. She held her breath wondering if Larry had heard or noticed, but he hadn't.

"That's all I have," Deb said. "Can you think of anything else?" she asked.

Joanna shook her head. "I think we have everything we need. Thanks so much for sparing us the time."

"You're welcome," he said. "After all, it isn't often a guy like me gets a chance to be locked in the boss's office with a pair of attractive young ladies."

And there was no question at all about the look he gave them on his way out. That one really was a leer.

"I told you Larry Wolfe is a jerk," Deb said.

"Yes, you did," Joanna agreed. "He is that—in spades."

"And if he liked his in-laws as much as he claimed, what's he doing back at work today? Why isn't he in Bisbee with his wife?"

"Good question," Joanna said.

Her phone was ringing before they ever made it back through the store. Detective Rebecca Ramsey was on the phone, and she was outraged.

"I think Rick Maldonado buried this case," she railed. "I don't think he ever lifted a finger about it. I don't think he did any interviews or tracked down any leads. This case landed on his desk and died. Between the time I talked to you before and now, I've done more work on it than Rick ever did."

"And?"

"I'm not sure what Wayne Hamm was doing in Arizona or how he ended up at a Flannigan Foundation care facility. He's from California originally, but he's a ward of that state."

By then Joanna and Deb had made their way back to the Crown Vic. They were inside it now, with the engine idling and the air-conditioning running full blast. Instead of pulling out, Deb sat waiting for marching orders.

"No relatives?" Joanna asked.

"Not that I can find. And that's probably why Rick didn't have a problem letting Wayne's investigation die on the vine. Unlike me with Wanda, Detective Maldonado didn't have Wayne's frantic mother calling him every week or so to see what was happening."

"So how long was he here in Arizona?"

"A couple of years."

"All of it at the place out on South Swan?"

"That's the interesting part," Becky said. "Wayne got moved to Warwick House off South Swan on March eleven. Prior to that he was at a place called Blythe House—where do the Flannigan people get these names?—at 3031 East Hedrick."

"So?" Joanna said.

"You don't know Tucson geography," Becky told her. "If you did, you'd know that East Hedrick is only a few blocks from East Copper. In other words, Blythe House and Holbrook House are only a matter of blocks apart."

"You're saying he and Wanda really might have known each other."

"Yup," Becky replied, "but once he got transferred all the way across town, they wouldn't have been able to see each other."

"Which squares with what Wanda told Lucinda."

"But if Wayne existed, why did everyone at Flannigan claim Wanda had made him up?"

Joanna remembered something Donald Dietrich had said earlier about why they didn't have coed facilities. "What if Wanda and Wayne's relationship was starting to morph from friendship to something else?" she asked. "Could Flannigan Foundation have been held liable if she had turned up pregnant while under their care and supervision?"

"That's an interesting idea," Becky said. "They probably could have been."

"If that's the case, if Flannigan had uncovered the fact that Wayne and Wanda were carrying on, they might have tried to squelch any kind of sexual entanglement by simply separating them—by moving Wayne out of what they thought was harm's way," Joanna said thoughtfully. "Now Wanda's dead, and Wayne is still missing."

"A neat little coincidence," Becky said. "I don't like coincidences much. What do you think the chances are that Wayne Hamm is every bit as dead as Wanda Mappin? The only difference is, so far no one's found his body, and maybe we never will."

That was Joanna's expectation as well. Wayne Hamm was developmentally disabled. He wouldn't have had the mental capability to engineer a complete escape from his keepers. If he had fallen off the edge of the earth, it was likely someone else helped him do it.

"For starters," Joanna said, "we need to ascertain whether or not Wayne and Wanda were acquainted. The way we do that is to go after Flannigan Foundation records."

"I already told you," Becky Ramsey said. "When I came looking for information, they clammed up completely."

"For a missing persons case, maybe," Joanna said. "As I pointed out to Mr. Dietrich, the Flannigan Foundation executive director earlier today, this is now a homicide investigation. Two homicide investigations really—an actual homicide and a possible. That changes the rules of engagement. We will have warrants."

"Good," Becky said, sounding relieved. "It's about time."

Joanna thought about that. Clearly Detective Ramsey was more than interested in this case. What had happened to Wanda Mappin was personal for her. She might have been thrown off track earlier, but Joanna sensed that wouldn't happen a second time. Not only that, having local investigators putting pressure on the Flannigan Foundation might be a lot more effective than whatever she could do with her very limited resources from a hundred-plus miles away.

"What about conducting this as a joint operation between Cochise County and Tucson PD?" Joanna suggested. "At this juncture your department and you know a whole lot more about the people involved than we do. You'd be able to move forward while my people are still getting up to speed."

"A joint op?" Becky repeated. "I like it, but don't ask me. I'm just a worker bee."

"If I were going to sell this concept to your brass," Joanna said, "where would you suggest I start?"

"Assistant Chief Paul Dougherty," Becky Ramsey said at once. "He's ex-homicide. He's also a good guy. Hold on a sec. I'll get you his direct number."

While Joanna waited for Becky to come back on the line, her cell phone buzzed twice. She recognized Frank Montoya's cell phone in the caller ID box, but she didn't want to hang up on Becky. She was still waiting when Deb Howell's phone began to ring. She answered, listened briefly, and muttered only a curt "Got it."

Without another word, Deb activated both the emergency lights and the siren and sent the patrol car hurtling out of its parking place.

"What's going on?" Joanna demanded.

"That was Chief Deputy Montoya," she said. "Samantha Edwards has evidently gone off the deep end again. She's holding her sister hostage and has barricaded herself in the back bedroom of her parents' house."

"She's armed, then?" Joanna asked.

"Evidently," Deb Howell said grimly. "City of Bisbee PD is requesting our assistance."

Becky Ramsey came back on the line and delivered Paul Dougherty's phone number. As soon as that call ended, Joanna dialed Frank back.

"What's going on?" she asked. "The last time I saw Samantha Edwards, she was overwhelmed with gratitude that she and her sister were friends again. What changed?"

"You tell me," Frank said. "First we received a call from Ms. Edwards reporting items being stolen from her parents' home. Next the 911 operator received a call from Sandra Wolfe's cell phone saying that there was some kind of new altercation with her sister. When the call ended and she didn't answer the phone again, officers responded. They're the ones who reported the hostage situation. Unfortunately, the back bedroom of the house is where Alfred Beasley kept his gun collection."

"I'm a hundred miles away," Joanna said. "Less than that now. Deb is driving like hell, but why is Bisbee PD calling us? What do they expect us to do that they can't do for themselves?"

"Bisbee doesn't have a SWAT team. They also don't have an official hostage negotiator," Frank said.

"Do they want to use our SAT guys?"

Inside the Cochise County Sheriff's Department, the letters SAT had nothing to do with scholastic aptitude testing. The letters referred instead to Joanna's newly constituted Special Assault Team. It was an elite group of seven officers, her best-qualified deputies. In addition to extensive law enforcement experience, each member of SAT was required to be a crack marksman. They had all undergone a rigorous course of supplemental training that included everything from hostage negotiation to conducting tactical vehicle pursuits.

"Not at this time," Frank answered. "They're asking for you."

"Me?" Joanna echoed. "But I'm not a trained hostage negotiator, either."

"Doesn't matter," Frank said. "The responding officers managed to use the Beasleys' landline to make contact with the two women. Sandra Wolfe asked for you specifically. She seems to think you're the only person on the planet who can reason with her sister."

"Great," Joanna said. "So where's this house?"

"Tombstone Canyon," Frank said. "Just west of the first exit from Highway 80. We've got a perimeter set up around the place. You won't be able to miss it."

"All right," Joanna said. "We're coming as fast as traffic, lights, and sirens will allow. Is there anything else going on I should know about?"

"According to Jaime, there's still no sign of Luis Andrade," Frank said. "None at all."

Great, Joanna thought. A day that had started out badly was now on its way to being a whole lot worse.

Joanna ended the call and turned to Deb. "You're wearing your vest?"

"Yes, ma'am," Detective Howell replied.

"Good," Joanna said. "You're probably going to need it."

That was small comfort, however. In hostage situations there was only so much a Kevlar vest could protect.

After a moment, Joanna picked up the phone. When Butch didn't answer his cell phone, she dialed the home number, where Jenny, there looking after Dennis, answered the call.

"Butch still isn't back from the other house," she said. "He probably didn't hear his phone ring. Do you want me to give him a message?"

"Yes," Joanna said. "Tell him something's come up. I'll probably be late for dinner." She ended that call and then turned to Detective Howell. "Want me to call Katy and give her the same message?"

"Please," Deb Howell returned.

She did so, utilizing the same kind of bland language she had used with Jenny. "Something's come up," Joanna told Katy Rawlins. "We may be late."

Joanna didn't say, "Deb and I will be home as soon as we finish laying our lives on the line." That would have scared Deb's sister to death.

It would have scared Joanna Brady, too, and since they were driving at something close to ninety miles an hour into the teeth of a hostage situation, scaring herself silly wasn't a good idea.

CHAPTER 13

DREADING THE UPCOMING CONFRONTATION, DEB HOWELL AND
Joanna drove most of the way to Bisbee in an uneasy silence
punctuated only by the sound of the siren. "Do you think we
should call Larry Wolfe at work and let him know what's happening?" Deb asked.

Having distraught relatives show up in the middle of hostage
situations was generally a surefire recipe for disaster. "Let's leave
it be for the time being," Joanna said.

Deb nodded and said nothing.

Just north of the Mule Mountain Tunnel they drove past a
police roadblock that had shut down the old Divide Road to all
traffic. The same was true for the first exit into Old Bisbee. That
one was closed in both directions.

Deb stopped the Crown Vic at the far edge of the cluster of

police and emergency vehicles from a variety of jurisdictions—
City of Bisbee, Arizona Department of Public Safety, and Cochise County Sheriff's Department—parked haphazardly along
the street. Joanna stayed in the vehicle for a moment, assessing
the situation.

The officers in attendance—all of them wearing vests and
maintaining positions that kept them out of the line of fire—
appeared to be focused on a small one-story frame house on the
north side of Tombstone Canyon. Like its near neighbors, it was
old-fashioned, complete with a tin roof and a screened front
porch. Someone had installed a homemade wheelchair ramp that
looked much too steep to meet code but probably served its purpose anyway. The tiny graveled yard was surrounded by a
chain-link fence. A narrow walkway led from the front of the
house around to the back, where only the walk and the fence
separated the house from a bank of rocky hillside that rose
abruptly behind it. Unless someone was prepared to do genuine
mountain climbing, there was really only one way in or out of
the yard—through the front gate.

A hulking fire truck was parked in the street. Behind it, shel-
tered from the house, Joanna spotted Frank conferring with Bisbee's police chief, Alvin Bernard.

Joanna opened the car door and got out. Bisbee was a good
ten degrees cooler than Tucson, but it was still hot—close to a
hundred.

"Stay with the car," Joanna ordered Deb Howell. "I'll check
with Frank and see where we're needed."

Careful to keep a screen of vehicles between herself and the
Beasleys' house, Joanna approached Frank and Alvin. The city's
police chief had been less than welcoming when Joanna was first

elected sheriff. He, like many others, had been skeptical about whether or not she'd ever turn into a "real" police officer. Five years into her administration, however, those early jitters were pretty much gone. Most of the time the two of them had a reasonably good rapport, and if Alvin had a problem with Joanna's being in charge of a department that was several times larger than his, he didn't let on.

"What's the situation?" she asked.

"We're going on two hours now from when Ms. Edwards first called our office," Frank explained. "She asked for you specifically. Kristin told her you were out, and asked if she could take a message. Samantha reported that someone had broken into her parents' home and was stealing their stuff. Kristin advised Samantha to dial 911 and report it, which she did. When officers from the City of Bisbee showed up, however, they were greeted by a hail of gunfire. They backed off and tried reaching the residence by phone—on the Beasleys' landline. That's when Sandra told the officers once again that Sheriff Brady is the only one her sister, the hostage taker, was willing to talk to. You're the only one she trusts."

"What's happening now?" Joanna asked.

"Not much," Alvin said. "Playing a waiting game and listening to that god-awful singing."

"Singing?" Joanna repeated, not sure she'd heard him properly. Joanna had spent an hour and a half and a hundred miles mentally preparing herself for a life-and-death confrontation. In a hostage situation that included an armed assailant, singing had never been part of the equation. "What do you mean, 'singing'?"

"Listen," Frank said, holding up his hand. Sure enough, in the background and over the subdued crackle of police radios, Joanna heard someone warbling a barely recognizable version of "Down in the Valley."

"There's an open window in that bathroom," Frank said. "The sound is coming from there."

"Is she drunk?" Joanna asked.

"Could be," Frank said. "When I first got here, she was singing 'I'm a Little Teapot.' She went from that to 'Where Have You Been, Billy Boy.' Now this. If she's drunk, though, she's an armed and dangerous drunk."

"Any chance of her passing out?" Joanna asked.

"One can hope," Frank said. "But I doubt we'll be that lucky."

"What about Sandra Wolfe's cell phone?" Joanna asked. "Has anyone tried calling that?"

"We did," Frank said. "Sandy picked up. Samantha ordered her to put it down. As soon as she did, there was a gunshot and the call ended."

"She shot her sister?"

"That's what we thought at first, but then we heard Sandy scream, 'You shot my phone! You shot my phone!' We're guessing Samantha plugged the cell phone."

Joanna breathed a sigh of relief. "What about the gun she's using? Where did that come from?"

"Alfred Beasley had several guns that I know about," Alvin Bernard told them. "He was quite the hunter back in his younger days. When he quit that, I'm guessing he never bothered getting rid of the guns."

"He was losing his mental faculties but he still had guns?" Joanna muttered under her breath.

"That's the way the Second Amendment guys want it," Alvin

growled. "And old age isn't strictly speaking, a medical disorder."

It was hardly a time to launch into a heated discussion of gun control, and Frank stepped in to short-circuit it.

"That's not the point," he said. "Our problem right now is that however many guns Alfred Beasley may have had, they've fallen into the hands of his certifiably nutty daughter. We need a plan."

"I'm not a trained hostage negotiator," Joanna said. "But since she asked for me, should I try talking to her?"

Alvin handed her a cell phone. "Be my guest," he said. "The Beasleys' landline is the last number I called. All you have to do is punch the green button twice. That'll activate the redial."

"You talked to her, then?" Joanna asked.

"I said I called the number," Alvin corrected. "Samantha Edwards wouldn't talk to me except to say she wanted you here. After that she hung up. She did the same thing to Frank."

Joanna put the cell phone on speaker and then punched the button. Moments later, when the phone rang inside the house, the singing ended abruptly.

"Samantha?" Joanna said when the call connected. "It's Sheriff Brady. They said you wanted to talk to me. What's going on in there?"

"Are you here now?" Samantha asked.

"Yes. I'm just outside," Joanna said. "If you can see the fire truck out in the street, I'm on the far side of that."

Something must have set her off, Joanna thought. *What could it be?*

"You were fine when I saw you earlier," Joanna said. "What happened? And how's your sister? Is Sandy all right?"

"There's a strange woman in here who claims to be my sister, but she's not," Samantha declared. "Whoever she is, I think she may have done something to Mother. Mom is missing and so is Dad, and there are all kinds of people—really bad people—standing around outside the house. If you don't do something to stop them, I'm afraid they'll try to steal Dad's stuff."

Joanna was stunned. Somehow Samantha Edwards had forgotten that her parents were both dead and she had no idea that the woman she was holding at gunpoint was her long-estranged sister. Not only that, in Samantha's state of mental befuddlement she had somehow convinced herself that the cops surrounding her parents' house—officers summoned by her own 911 call—were actually a band of thieves.

Joanna covered the cell phone's speaker. "It sounds like she's suffered a complete psychotic meltdown."

Frank and Alvin nodded in agreement. They thought so, too.

"If Samantha's this screwed up, how does she even know who I am?" Joanna asked.

Alvin shrugged. "Beats me," Frank said.

While Joanna was off the line, Samantha wandered into a relatively tuneless but still recognizable version of the Joan Baez classic, "500 Miles." It was as though all those different songs were connected by some invisible string in Samantha's subconscious, with one leading seamlessly to the next with no obvious connection.

Joanna took her hand off the speaker. "Why did you want to talk to me?" she asked.

"Who are you again?"

"Joanna Brady," Joanna said patiently. "Sheriff Joanna Brady. They told me you asked to talk to me. Why? What do you want?"

"A bean burrito enchilada-style," Samantha answered at once. "I'm hungry. Did I miss lunch?"

Considering the circumstances, that improbable answer was almost as jarring as her singing, but in the world of hostage negotiations, granting a simple request was a possible starting point, and Joanna latched onto it.

"A bean burrito enchilada-style," Joanna repeated. "I'm writing it down. I'll have to send someone to go get it. Once the food gets here, I'll trade you the burrito for your weapon, okay?"

"Only if you get all those other people out of here," Samantha said.

With Sandra Wolfe's life hanging in the balance, banishing the police presence wasn't an option.

"We'll talk about it when the food gets here," Joanna countered. "Okay?"

Noisily Samantha hung up the receiver. A moment later she resumed her plaintive song.

Joanna turned to Frank. "Have Dispatch call Deb. Ask her to go to Daisy's, pick up that burrito, and bring it back here."

"Right," Frank said, picking up his phone. "Enchilada-style. I'm on it."

Moments later, Deb Howell sped away from the clutch of parked cars while Joanna once again punched redial on Chief Bernard's phone.

"What about the other woman who's there with you?" Joanna asked when Samantha answered again. "Is she all right?"

"She was crying earlier," Samantha said. "She stopped now."

"Can you put her on the phone?" Joanna asked. "Can I talk to her?"

"I guess," Samantha said. "Just a minute. I'll ask her."

The song resumed, starting up in the same place where it had stopped. Then, to Joanna's amazement, Sandra's voice came through the phone.

"Sheriff Brady?" she whispered shakily. "Can't you do something about this? Can't you make her let me go?"

It was Joanna's first real chance to get information—vital information—about the situation inside the house and she didn't want to blow it.

"We're trying," she said. "How many guns does she have?"

"Four that I can see," Sandy answered. "Daddy's old .22 pistol, two shotguns, and a rifle."

"Are they all loaded?"

"I don't know for sure. Probably."

"How did this happen?" Joanna asked.

"Beats me," Sandra said. "We were going through Mom's Christmas-card list, contacting people and letting them know what's happened. Everything seemed fine. No problems. We stopped for lunch—"

"But she said she was hungry," Joanna objected.

"I don't know why," Sandra replied. "Sammy ate like a horse. Then, a little while later, she started acting funny. Weird. She got up and left the room. I thought she was going to use the bathroom. Instead she came back with an armload of guns and with the pistol stuck in the pocket of her jeans. The next thing I knew, she pulled the .22 out of her pocket and pointed it at me. She asked me who I was and what the hell was I doing in our parents' house. It was like one minute she was fine and the next minute she was stark raving crazy. She's better when she's singing. When she stops it's like she gets agitated and starts to lose it even more."

"Food's here," Frank said softly from behind Joanna.

She looked up from concentrating on her phone call and was surprised to see Deb Howell pulling back into the group of parked cars in far less time than it should have taken her to drive to Daisy's and back. That was when Joanna realized Frank had managed to pull off a bean-burrito relay of some kind.

"Put Samantha back on the phone," Joanna said. "I need to talk to her again."

By now, the woman was warbling the second verse of "On Top of Old Smokey." For the first time, Joanna realized that her entire uniform was drenched in sweat. Perspiration was running into her eyes and burning them. It was dripping off her chin.

Focus, she ordered herself. *Stay calm. Maintain a normal voice. Don't act excited.*

"Hello?" Samantha said. "Who is this?"

"It's Sheriff Brady," Joanna said. "Your food's here."

"What food?"

"The bean burrito you wanted, remember?" Joanna said. "You told me you'd trade it for your guns."

"I did?" Samantha sounded utterly mystified. "When did I say that?"

She doesn't know which end is up, Joanna thought. *That's the one thing you have going for you. Go with it. Use it.*

"Anyway," Joanna continued. "I was just talking to your dad. He and your mom thought you'd like to come join them for lunch."

"Daddy's out there?" Samantha asked.

"They both are," Joanna said. She turned to Frank and gave him the high sign. He spoke into his radio. As though they were one man, the officers maintaining the perimeter drew their weapons.

One of Alvin's uniformed officers, a younger man Joanna didn't recognize, vaulted over the fence on the far side of the house and then belly-crawled until he was lying prone next to the bottom of the porch.

Joanna was torn. If Samantha came out with guns blazing, the young cop was a dead man. On the other hand, if Joanna ordered Samantha to emerge with her hands in the air, that kind of demand was likely to raise too many red flags.

"Just leave the guns inside, okay?" Joanna said calmly. "As for that other woman, the one who's in there with you? Leave her inside as well."

"But what if she gets away?" Samantha demanded. "I think she was here robbing the place."

"Don't worry," Joanna assured her. "I have officers stationed out back. We'll make sure she doesn't get away."

For the next space of time, the universe seemed to come to a standstill. Nothing happened. Nothing at all. Holding her breath, Joanna was afraid that Samantha's singing would resume once more, but it didn't.

Someone nearby whispered, "Watch it. She's coming out."

With the screened front porch obscuring Joanna's view, she couldn't tell if Samantha was armed or not.

"Dad?" she called. "Mom? Where are you?"

"Out here," Joanna answered. "On the far side of the street."

Slowly the door on the screened porch swung open, and the officer in the yard sprang to his feet. The moment Samantha's figure appeared in the doorway he tackled her, sending both of them sprawling back onto the porch.

"Don't shoot her," Sandra screeched from inside the house as officers descended on the porch and yard from every direction. "I've got her guns. All of them. I'm coming out the back way."

The fierce battle raging inside the screened porch went on for what seemed an eternity. Samantha Edwards may have left the guns inside the house but not her determination. A pair of lawn chairs crashed to the floor. Several flowerpots tumbled and shattered. In all it took five officers to wrestle Samantha to the floor and cuff her. By the time they finally had her in custody, Joanna was dimly aware of the sound of a helicopter circling overhead— a news helicopter, no doubt, dispatched from one of the stations in Tucson.

Sandra Wolfe was hysterical when a pair of Joanna's deputies, followed by Deb Howell, met the woman at her parents' back door. When they relieved her of her armload of weapons, Sandra fell weeping into Deb Howell's arms. Meanwhile other officers half led and half carried Samantha out to the sidewalk. "Mom? Dad?" she shouted, looking desperately in every direction. "Where are you? What have they done to you?"

Frank came up behind Joanna and clapped her on the shoulder. "Way to go, boss!" he exclaimed. "Pretty impressive!"

"Where should they take her?" Chief Bernard asked as officers led Samantha past the fire truck and toward one of the city's waiting patrol cars. She was no longer fighting or resisting. Instead she had started singing again, Roger Miller's "King of the Road."

"To the county hospital," Joanna said. "She'll need a police guard and a complete psychological workup."

"Your nickel or mine?" Alvin asked.

That was what it always came down to—a question of whose

budget was about to be dinged. But Samantha Edwards had started out as Joanna Brady's problem. No matter where she was at the time she was actually taken into custody, she still was.

"We'll take care of it," Joanna said. "My department will be responsible."

Frank gave Joanna one of his "What-are-you-thinking?" looks, but he nonetheless hustled around arranging transport. In the meantime Joanna set Deb Howell the task of collecting the names and jurisdictions of all officers on the scene. The way the world worked these days, it was likely the sheriff's department would need that information and statements from everyone present in order to prove that Samantha Edwards had been taken into custody in the course of an entirely lawful procedure.

Jaime Carbajal showed up while Deb was still collecting names. "Any luck finding Luis?" Joanna asked.

"Not so far," Jaime said. "I spent the whole day looking, too. Marcella is a basket case. She's been dogging my heels all day, raising hell, holding me responsible. I wanted a break. I heard about the hostage situation over the radio and told Marcella you needed me to come help out, but it sounds like everything's under control." He stopped and looked at the house. "Wait a minute. Isn't this where the Beasleys lived?"

Joanna nodded. "Yes, it is. And you're right. The hostage situation has been resolved, but I do need you. This whole area is a crime scene. If you wouldn't mind taping it off—"

"Sure thing, boss," Jaime said. "I'll get right to it."

While he was doing that, Joanna led a still shaken Sandra Wolfe over to the parked Crown Victoria, let her into the backseat, and offered her a bottle of water. "I need to call my husband

and let him know I'm all right," Sandy said. "But my phone is wrecked."

"Here," Joanna said, offering hers. "Use this."

Joanna opened her own bottle of water. Then, sinking into the driver's seat, she leaned back and closed her eyes. *I did it,* she told herself. *I talked her out of her weapons. Nobody died. No one got hurt. We all get to go home tonight.*

Then dimly, in the background, she became aware of what Sandra was saying. "I couldn't believe it, Larry; Sammy just went completely nuts. This morning she was fine, but then right after lunch she started going bananas. It was like someone had flipped a switch. She was a totally different person. She decided I was a stranger who had broken into the folks' house to rob them blind. There was no reasoning with her. When she grabbed Dad's gun and turned it on me, I thought I was a goner. She shot my cell phone to smithereens. That's why I'm using Sheriff Brady's. If it hadn't been for her—"

Like someone had flipped a switch. The comment triggered something in Joanna's head. Hadn't Deb said something just like that about Alfred Beasley? That the neighbors had claimed he was fine in the mornings but by late afternoon and evening he barely knew his own name? Larry Wolfe had said something to that effect—that Martha had said not to worry about it. She had told him on Thursday night that Alfred would be fine by morning.

In a chilling instant, Joanna knew she was onto something— that she had found part of the answer. She sat very still with her heart hammering in her chest, waiting for Sandra Wolfe to finish her phone call.

"Thank you," Sandy said, handing the phone back to Joanna.

"Larry's on his way down from Tucson. He said he'll be here as soon as he can."

"What did you have for lunch?" Joanna asked.

"For lunch?" Sandra returned. "There was food in the folks' fridge. Since it was just going to go to waste, Sammy and I helped ourselves."

"What food?"

"Some tuna salad that was already made, a couple pieces of bread, and some canned peaches. I had those for dessert. Sammy had ice cream—ice cream with chocolate syrup and Spanish peanuts. That was always Dad's favorite, and Sammy's, too. Dad never had a problem with his weight, and it's what he always had for dessert at lunchtime—a chocolate sundae. Mom didn't like ice cream that much, but she definitely didn't like chocolate. Her top choice was caramel. In all the years Mom and Dad were married, that's one thing they always disagreed about—the right kind of syrup for ice cream. As for me? I'm a little like my mother. I don't despise chocolate the same way she did. I can take it or leave it. But when it comes to caramel, I'm there."

"And your father always had his sundaes at lunchtime?" Joanna asked. "Not at dinner?"

"Always at lunch," Sandra said. "There's caffeine in chocolate, you know. He claimed that if he had chocolate any later in the day, he couldn't sleep at night." She paused. "Wait a minute," she said. "Why all the questions about ice cream?"

But Joanna knew it wasn't about the ice cream at all. It was about the syrup. She remembered hearing that's how meds were sometimes administered to recalcitrant seniors and to little kids, too—ground up and served in chocolate. What were the chances that someone had been delivering mind-altering drugs to Alfred

Beasley in hopes of convincing him that he was losing his mind? And now his daughter had certainly lost hers.

"Just curious," Joanna said casually.

Leaving the Crown Victoria, she hustled over to where Deb Howell had finished talking to the last of the officers and was closing her notebook.

"How soon can you get Judge Cameron to issue a search warrant for this house?"

Deb glanced at her watch. "It's almost five," she said. "It'll depend on whether or not he's still at the courthouse. But why? What kind of a search warrant? What are we looking for?"

"Attempted murder," Joanna said. "We need to collect all the food in the Beasleys' refrigerator, but most especially, any and all chocolate syrup. I think someone may have been tampering with Alfred Beasley's food for some time, and I've just figured out how it was done. This afternoon Samantha got a dose of the same thing."

"I'm on it," Deb said.

"Ask Frank to give you a ride wherever you need to go. I'm going to need my car to take Sandra back to the office."

While Deb jogged off after Frank Montoya, Joanna went looking for Jaime Carbajal. "Deb's on her way to get a search warrant for this place," she said. "Find a couple of deputies and have them stay here to keep an eye on things. Tell them that no one is to go in or out until after that warrant has been executed. Then you and Ernie probably better come down to the Justice Center to take Sandra Wolfe's statement."

When she got back to the car, Sandy was still sitting in it with the car door open. For the second time that day, Joanna handed Sandy her cell phone.

"You should probably call your husband back. We'll be going

back to my office to take your statement while my officers search this place. Mr. Wolfe can pick you up there."

"Back to your office?" Sandra repeated. "Why? You're not going to put me under arrest again, are you?"

"No," Joanna said. "You're a victim here. Our job it to lock up assailants, not victims."

"Where have you taken Sammy?"

"To the county hospital down in Douglas. They've got a unit with a padded cell down there, and that's what your sister needs. In her current condition, when she's a danger to herself and others, a padded cell is a better alternative than an ER someplace or one of the holding cells at my jail."

"Oh," Sandra said, and she began punching numbers into the phone.

As they drove down through Bisbee and out toward the Justice Center, Joanna listened as Sandy explained to her husband where he should come to find her.

"No," she said finally. "You can't stop by the house. It's off-limits, and we can't stay there, either. We'll have to see if there are any rooms available at the hotel. I checked out today, but they may have a vacancy." She paused and listened to her husband. "Why is the house off-limits?" she resumed. "Because it's been declared a crime scene again. That's where Sammy attacked me and held me at gunpoint, so I guess that means there has to be an investigation." There was another long pause. "Okay, then. If you don't want to stay at the hotel, fine. We can always drive back home."

Sandy gave the cell phone back to Joanna. "Men!" she muttered. "The Copper Queen isn't nearly as expensive as some of the places where we used to stay, but I'll be glad when things settle down. Larry won't have to stress so about every miserly penny he spends. Maybe he'll finally be able to retire and play more golf."

"You said when things settle down," Joanna said. "Are you talking about when you receive your inheritance?"

"Not just my inheritance," Sandy said. "Larry's due to receive one, too—from his parents. They both died last year. Within months of each other. His brother, Mark, his older brother—the asshole—is the executor. Larry and Mark get along about the same way Sammy and I have, which is to say not at all. And Mark has done everything in his power to keep Larry from getting what's due him. We keep hearing the first of the money is going to show up any day now, and it'll be a relief when it finally does. The last couple of years have been tough. I give Larry a lot of credit. Taking that job at Home Depot was a big comedown for someone like him. He used to be a high-powered executive and all, back when we lived in Houston. So when he starts stressing about money, I usually give him a pass. Wouldn't you?"

"I suppose I would," Joanna agreed, but at the same time she was wondering how stressed Larry was about money, and how much were they talking about? He and Sandy were about to reap close to a quarter-million-dollar bonanza from her dead parents, but the way she was talking about Larry's situation, it sounded as though his folks had amassed a far larger fortune than the cool half million put together by his blue-collar in-laws.

"So Larry's parents were fairly well-to-do?" Joanna asked.

"Oh, yes," Sandy said. "They lived in Kansas City, Missouri, but Larry's father owned auto-parts stores all over the Midwest. He sold the whole works to one of the big auto-parts chains in the early nineties and made himself a fortune in the process. Jonathan said he'd had enough of cold weather by then, so he and

Fern retired to Florida. They loved it there, right up until Fern got so sick."

Sandy lapsed into silence. Glancing in the rearview mirror, Joanna could see the woman was crying. Finally she blew her nose.

"It's just so sad," Sandy said. "They don't make people like that anymore—like Larry's folks and mine—people who got married and stayed together through thick and thin for fifty-plus years. I'm sorry that generation is gone."

"So am I," Joanna said as they pulled into the Justice Center parking lot. "Very sorry."

She escorted Sandy into the building through her private entrance and seated her in the conference room. "Coffee?" she asked.

"Please," Sandy said. "That would be very nice."

Joanna went down to the break room. There was nothing but dregs left in the pot. She made a new one. While she stood there waiting for the coffee to brew, she looked up at a photo that hung on the wall over the pot. It was a foam-core-mounted panoramic photo of the Justice Center with Joanna's predecessor, Sheriff Walter McFadden, and most of his staff posed in front of it. When Joanna had taken over the department, she had removed the photo from her own office. Someone had rescued it from the scrap heap and it had found its way to the wall in the break room. Joanna went there so seldom that she had actually forgotten about the photo. Now, studying it closely, Joanna found what she was looking for—an image of the blonde she remembered so vividly from Andy's funeral.

In the photos, the sworn officers, including deputies and jail personnel, were all in uniform. The blonde wasn't. She stood at the end of the front row, tucked in among the support personnel—clerks, dispatchers, and secretaries—who had also been part of Sheriff McFadden's administration.

Who are you? Joanna wondered. *Where did you go?*

Just then her cell phone rang.

"I tracked down Judge Cameron," Detective Howell said. "I got the warrant, and we're in. Now what?"

"I want you to take every bit of food out of the fridge," Joanna said. "I want it bagged, labeled, and stored. Same goes for whatever you find in their pantry and cupboards. If it's edible, take it."

"Where are we going to put it all?" Deb said. "We don't have enough cold storage."

"We'll find enough cold storage," Joanna said determinedly, "if I have to go out and buy another refrigerator and stick it in the evidence room. You're there right now?"

"Yes. In the kitchen, standing in front of an open fridge that's way cleaner than mine is."

"Do you see any chocolate sauce in there?"

"Yes," Deb said. "Right here in the door. Tante Marie's Chocolate Sauce, a product of Canada. And here's another bottle. This one's Tante Marie's Caramel Sauce. I've never seen this brand before. I don't think you can buy it at Safeway."

"Let's hope not," Joanna said. "That would be far too easy."

"Okay," Deb said. "We're on it."

Joanna closed her phone just as the last of the coffee sputtered into the pot, but she was still staring at the photo. There was a part of her, the reasonable, commonsense part, that was counseling Joanna to leave it alone and let sleeping dogs lie. If Andy had been carrying on with this woman, what did it matter? He was dead and gone. But there was another part of her, too, the part of Joanna that was undeniably her mother's daughter, that wouldn't let it go.

One way or the other, I'm going to find you, Joanna told herself and the image smiling back at her from the photo. *No matter how much it hurts, I need to know the truth.*

CHAPTER 14

WANTING ALL HANDS ON DECK FOR SANDY'S INTERVIEW, JOANNA had summoned Ernie Carpenter to be there along with Jaime. Joanna sat in as well. During the interview Sandy repeated most of what she had told Joanna earlier. She and Samantha had gone to their parents' house as soon as Deb Howell had told them they could. They had sorted out clothing to take to the mortuary for the cremation. While in the process of contacting friends and relatives about the service, they had paused for lunch. Shortly after that Samantha, who had seemed fine all morning, started acting strangely.

"Is your sister prone to these kinds of episodes?" Jaime asked. "There was the situation the other night—"

"That was different," Sandy said. "Then we'd both had too

much to drink and things came to a head. But we were over that—at least I thought we were."

"Maybe, without your knowledge, Samantha had something to drink today, too," Jaime suggested.

"No," Sandy declared. "Absolutely not. If Sammy had been drinking, I would have smelled it on her breath. One minute she was fine and the next minute she had no idea who I was—like I was a complete stranger who had turned up in the folks' house for no reason. And then she started saying totally bizarre things—wondering when our parents would be back home. I tried to explain to her that our parents were dead—that we were there planning their memorial service! It was weird. At first I thought she was just joking around, but then when she brought Dad's guns out of the back bedroom . . ." Sandy shook her head as though she still couldn't quite grasp the reality of what had happened.

"Is it possible your sister has a problem with some other drug besides alcohol?" Jaime asked. "People on crack and meth often carry on like they've got a few screws loose."

"I suppose a drug problem of some kind is a possibility," Sandy conceded. "My sister and I have been estranged for a long time, Detective Carbajal. There's a lot I don't know about her and a lot she doesn't know about me. Still, I didn't see any evidence of her popping pills or smoking anything."

The whole time Joanna had been sitting in on the interview, she'd been thinking about Alfred Beasley's chocolate topping. With her laptop open in front of her, she'd been quietly surfing the Net. She found the official Web site for Tante Marie's Toppings, based in Montreal, Quebec. The company motto, plastered over the top of their home page in bright red letters, proclaimed: "If Your Sweetheart Has a Sweet Tooth, Doesn't She Deserve the Very Best?" The text claimed that Tante Marie's Toppings were made from only the highest-quality ingredients. Not available in stores, Tante Marie's products were shipped to discerning customers all over the globe, with a discount for case-lot orders. Visa, MasterCard, and Amex accepted.

In other words, there should be some way to trace the jars of caramel and chocolate syrups that had found their way into Alfred and Martha Beasley's fridge. Joanna wanted to find a way to bring the food issue into the official interview without necessarily letting Sandy know where the questions were leading.

"Is it possible Samantha had an allergic reaction to something she ate?" Joanna asked.

"Maybe," Sandy said. "But I've never heard any mention of that."

"Still, it might be worthwhile for you to tell Detectives Carbajal and Carpenter exactly what you and Samantha had for lunch, just in case."

While Sandy launched into that discussion, Joanna continued surfing. This time she located obituaries for Jonathan and Fern Wolfe—two obituaries each, one in Tampa, Florida, where they were living at the time of their deaths, and another in Kansas City, Missouri, where they had lived prior to retirement. The one in Tampa was clearly a paid obituary. The second one seemed more like an ordinary news article.

Longtime Kansas City businessman and philanthropist Jonathan Wolfe, whose empire of auto-parts stores once blanketed the Midwest, was found dead in his Tampa area retirement home yesterday afternoon, mere weeks after his wife, Fern, succumbed to congestive heart failure.

According to his son Mark, his mother had been ill for a number of years, and her ever-deteriorating condition had taken its toll on his father's health. "My parents were married for sixty-seven years. I guess it's not so surprising that he didn't want to go on without her."

Wolfe Brothers Auto Parts was started by Jonathan Wolfe and his younger brother, Benjamin, in 1956. They began with a single Kansas City location, and operated the business as a partnership until Benjamin's death in 1972. By the time Mr. Wolfe sold the enterprise in 1991, Wolfe Brothers had grown to eighty-seven stores located in sixty-three cities.

"My father was a smart businessman who saw a need and decided to fill it," Mark Wolfe said. "He liked the idea of shade-tree mechanics and was one himself, but as vehicles became more and more computerized, he began losing interest. I think the changing technology bothered him. He said he wanted to get out before he turned into a dinosaur."

The sale of the Wolfe Brothers franchise to onetime competitor Complete Auto made Complete a major auto-parts player in the region and gave the company a leg up in creating a nationwide retail presence.

"When he retired, Dad put away his wrenches in favor of a driver and a putter," his son said. "Until Mother got sick, he played golf every day—winters in Florida and back here in Missouri during the summers. He and his golf-playing cronies outshot me every time."

In 1993, Fern and Jonathan Wolfe created and funded a

scholarship program that bears their name. It is designed to help deserving Kansas City high school students who choose to attend in-state schools of higher education by paying their tuition expenses. Five four-year Wolfe scholarships are awarded each year.

"My father never had a chance to go to college," Mark Wolfe said, "but he thought education was important. He created the scholarship fund to help young people who might otherwise not be able to go on to college."

Reading that passage, Joanna understood what Sandy had meant earlier when she had burst into tears. Alfred and Martha Beasley and Fern and Jonathan Wolfe were part of the last of a very special breed.

Funeral services are pending in Florida. A joint memorial service for Fern and Jonathan Wolfe will be scheduled here in Kansas City at a later date. Mr. Wolfe is survived by his two sons, Mark of Saint Louis, Missouri, and Lawrence of Tucson, Arizona, and by two grandsons, Tom and Richard Wolfe of Oklahoma City, Oklahoma.

There was no way to tell from the article or the names which of Jonathan's two sons—Mark or Larry—was the father of the two grandsons.

There was a tap on the conference room door. Closing her laptop, Joanna went to the door. Wendy Cochran, one of the public office clerks, was standing outside.

"Sorry to disturb you, Sheriff Brady," she said. "But there's a man out in the lobby who's causing a disturbance and demanding to see his wife."

"Mr. Wolfe?" Joanna asked.

Wendy nodded. "That's the one."

"Mr. Wolfe's wife is here in the conference room," Joanna said. "You can bring him on down." She waited by the door. When Wendy returned with the man, Joanna escorted him into the conference room. "This is Larry Wolfe," she told Ernie and Jaime. "Mrs. Wolfe's husband."

As soon as Larry came through the door, Sandy leaped to her feet and rushed to embrace him. "Oh, Larry!" she exclaimed. "I'm so glad to see you. I was so afraid—" The rest of her words were muffled by her husband's shirt as he wrapped his arms around her.

"It's okay now, Sandy. I'm here." He sent a hard look in Joanna's direction. "What about her crazy sister? Where's she?"

"In the county hospital," Joanna said. "Under observation."

"And hopefully under lock and key," he said. "From what Sandy told me, it sounds as though Samantha is totally nuts."

Sandy pulled away from him. "This is my husband, Larry," she told the detectives. "And these two nice men are Detectives Carpenter and Carbajal. They've been going over everything that happened today. They think Samantha may have been on drugs."

"Could be," Larry said. "Knowing she was on drugs won't fix anything, but it might at least explain what happened."

"Actually, Mr. Wolfe," Jaime said, "we were just finishing up."

"I can go, then?" Sandy asked.

Jaime nodded.

"Good," Larry said, holding her close. "I'm sure she could do with some rest. I did what you said, baby," he added. "I've gotten us a room for the night at the Copper Queen."

"Thank you," Sandy said. "That was so thoughtful of you."

He was doing an excellent impersonation of a loving husband, but Joanna wasn't entirely convinced.

"If they brought you here, where's your car? Do we need to go pick it up?"

"It's out front," Joanna said. "I had one of my deputies drive it here."

Just then Deb Howell showed up in the hallway behind Joanna. "Okay," she said. "We've finished. Deputy Hogan is unloading the—"

Before Deb had a chance to blurt out anything more, Joanna took her by the arm. Drawing her away from the conference room door, Joanna steered Deb into her office and closed the door behind them.

"You've collected all the Beasleys' food?" Joanna asked.

"Every bit of it," Deb returned. "The evidence room guys aren't thrilled, but I managed to squeeze the stuff from the fridge into the evidence room cold-storage locker after all. I left Deputy Sloan up at the house to keep an eye on the place in case we need to take another look around in the daylight."

"Good thinking," Joanna said.

"Now what?" Deb wanted to know.

"Were there serial numbers on those two Tante Marie syrup bottles?" Joanna asked.

"I noticed what looked to be batch codes," Deb said. "We may be able to tell from that when the product was sold and where it was shipped."

"Good," Joanna said. "I'm guessing we'll need that information. Now let's go talk to Ernie and Jaime."

The Double Cs, as Detectives Carpenter and Carbajal were known around the department, were not amused when Joanna told them what Deb and Deputy Hogan had been doing and why.

"If you think eating a chocolate sundae was what sent Samantha Edwards over the edge, wouldn't it have been nice if you had mentioned it during the interview?" Ernie demanded. "Why the hell did you leave us stumbling around in the dark?"

"I didn't want to tip my hand to Larry Wolfe," Joanna said.

"So you're thinking he's the bad guy here?" Ernie asked.

"A bad guy who seems to be perpetually short on cash. This may well be a case of murder for profit. If it hadn't been for Samantha, he might have gotten away with it. The longer Wolfe goes without knowing we're looking at him, the better off we'll be."

Somewhat mollified, Ernie nodded. "So what now?"

"It's getting late. Let's call it a day. Tomorrow morning first thing, I want you and Deb to track down everything there is to know about Larry Wolfe. Sandy's the one who mentioned their financial woes to me. I want to know what the situation really is. I also learned that Larry's parents both died in Tampa last year within a few weeks of each other. It sounds as though the father was a self-made millionaire several times over. The brother, Mark Wolfe, lives in Saint Louis, Missouri. He's the executor of the parents' estate. Again, from what Sandy said, the two brothers have been estranged for a long time. Larry has been expecting disbursements from his parents' estates to bail him out of the soup, but those have evidently been a long time coming."

"Are you thinking Larry may have had something to do with his parents' deaths as well?" Deb asked.

"It's worth looking into," Joanna said.

"What about me?" Jaime asked. "While Deb and Ernie are tracking on Larry Wolfe, what do you want me to do?"

"Keep working on Luis," she told him. "We'll hope he's surfaced by then. If not . . ."

Jaime nodded. "You're right," he said. "Luis it is."

Joanna was home by seven—two hours later than she was supposed to be, but several hours earlier than she had expected to be. Dinner turned out to be pizza—cold pizza—the remains of several different kinds.

"Where did these come from?" she asked, munching away on a piece of garlic/artichoke.

"It turns out the kids Jeff brought down wanted to earn some money," Butch said with a laugh. "But they work harder for food, especially if whatever is being served happens to be part of the pizza food group."

"You got a lot done, then?"

"An amazing amount," Butch said. "Especially since I didn't have to go get the pizza."

"You had it delivered? Since when did Pizza Palace start delivering?"

"They don't," Butch replied. "Your mother picked it up and dropped it off."

"My mother?"

"She called right after you left this morning. She was in a great mood and has evidently forgiven me for ratting her out to you. She said she knew you were busy and wanted to know if there was anything I needed. When I told her I could use a couple of pizzas, she brought same. She even let down her hair enough to have a slice or two with us. I don't think I've ever seen pizza pass Eleanor's lips before."

Joanna didn't remember ever seeing that happen, either.

"Anyway," Butch continued, "she and Jeff were talking about

the benefit the churchwomen around town are getting ready to do for the Sundersons next week. Your mom came up with a brilliant idea. Carol Sunderson and her grandkids don't have a place to live right now, and we happen to have an extra house that's currently vacant. Eleanor suggested maybe Carol would be interested making a trade. What if we offered her and those kids of hers a place to live. They could stay in our old house rent-free or at a minimal rent in exchange for her helping out around here as needed. It would sort of be the reverse of when Clayton Rhodes was alive and helping you with the chores at the old place."

Clayton had been Joanna's longtime neighbor who had owned the adjoining ranch. After Andy's death and despite the fact that Clayton had been well into his eighties by then, the man had been unstinting in helping Joanna and Jenny with the many chores associated with old High Lonesome Ranch. Later, when he died, Joanna had been astonished to find that the old man had left his ranch to her. The ranches were still deeded separately, but Butch and Joanna had built their new home on the site of Clayton's old one at the mouth of Mexican Canyon on what they sometimes referred to as the "new" High Lonesome Ranch.

"If we had some extra help around here, so I didn't have to worry about you having to handle everything on your own, maybe I could do that book tour. Jenny thinks it's a great idea, by the way," Butch added. "She's all for it."

Joanna was instantly irate. "I thought my mother was going to help out while you were doing that," she said. "And you've already discussed this with Jenny?"

"Not me," Butch said. "Your mother discussed it with Jenny. And don't blame me. Eleanor's the one who evidently changed her mind about helping out during the tour. As I remember, you weren't exactly thrilled at the prospect of her hanging around. Still, Joey, just because your mother came up with the idea doesn't make it bad."

"It doesn't make it good, either," Joanna said. "I'm going to go change my clothes."

And try to bury my temper tantrum while I'm at it, Joanna thought. *What gives my mother the right to come waltzing in here, buying pizza, and interfering with our lives?*

It was one of those nights when Dennis had no intention of being put into his crib without a fight—one that lasted for the better part of two hours. While Butch fought that battle, Joanna cleaned up the kitchen, emptied and loaded the dishwasher, took a load of clothes out of the dryer, and generally made herself useful. The fact that the three dogs stuck with her like glue the whole time told her that Jenny had to be off spending the night someplace. Dennis was still crying at the top of his lungs when the phone rang. Calls that came in at this hour of the night seldom brought good news. This one did.

"You'll never guess where I found him," Jaime Carbajal announced.

"Luis?" Joanna asked. "You mean he's all right?"

"Yes, he is, but the little twerp is lucky I didn't knock his block off. I sure as hell wanted to."

"Where was he?"

"Hiding out in the toolshed in my own backyard," Jaime said, relief ringing in every word. "Can you believe it? After dinner I came into the kitchen and caught Pepe smuggling food out of the fridge. When I asked him what he was doing with it, he said he was taking it to Luis. He's been right here under my nose the whole time I've been looking for him. He caught a ride with someone from Naco to here and was waiting out back when Pepe and I came home from the ball game. After Delcia and I were asleep, he knocked on Pepe's window and asked him for help. The two of them rigged up a cot out in the toolshed with an air mattress and an old bedroll. They even found an old fan and plugged it in. As hot as it was last night, it's probably a good thing he had a fan."

Joanna was still playing catch-up. "I don't understand," she said. "What was he doing there? Why did he run away?"

"I asked Luis the same questions, but he wouldn't answer. He claims he can't tell me anything until he talks to his mom. After being in the same clothes for a couple of days, he was pretty ripe. Right this minute he's in the shower while Delcia runs his clothes through the washer and dryer. Once he's cleaned up and present-able, we'll go see Marcella. I already tried calling her, but there was no answer."

"Good job, Jaime," Joanna said. "I'm thrilled to know he's okay."

"That goes double for me."

Dennis finally settled down. Butch came back into the living room just as Joanna was hanging up the phone. "Do you have to go in?" he asked.

"No," she said. "Jaime's nephew has been among the missing, and now he's been found."

"Good," Butch said.

"And speaking of being among the missing, where's Jenny?"

"Spending the night with Jim Bob and Eva Lou. They asked and I let her go. It's not a problem, is it?"

"No," Joanna said. "Of course not. How could it be?" But it

was a problem. *She could have mentioned it when I talked to her on the phone,* Joanna thought.

"So how much did you and your crew get done?" she asked.

"Hauled out most of the garbage. The plumbing is pretty well trashed. We'll have to replace both toilets, and they weren't that old. We should put in a new kitchen sink and dishwasher, too, while we're at it. Tomorrow, I'll have the kids finish mucking out the floors. Then I'll tear out that old linoleum. I want to lay tile in the kitchen, laundry room, and bathrooms. They all should have been tiled to begin with. After all that, once we put on a coat of paint, it'll be like new."

Even after a long day of hard physical labor, Butch's enthusiasm for the job was infectious. Joanna knew he loved tackling remodeling jobs almost as much as he enjoyed writing. The two tasks might be at seemingly opposite ends of the creativity spectrum, but Butch was good at both. Their renter had managed to demolish the house before reneging on his rent and taking off. Instead of focusing on the disaster, Butch was determined to fix the house and make it better.

"So what went on in your world today?" Butch asked. "Jenny told me that you'd called and said you'd most likely be late. What was that all about?"

Joanna sat down on the couch. Lady climbed up next to her and put her head in Joanna's lap. Stroking the dog's smooth head may have been comforting for the dog, but Joanna knew it was good for her, too.

"We had a hostage situation, but it worked out all right," she said offhandedly, without adding that she'd been right in the thick of things, doing the negotiations with an armed assailant. If there was media coverage of the standoff, Butch would probably learn what had really gone on, but right that minute, Joanna didn't want to discuss it.

"One of the two sisters from the other night—the ones whose parents drove off the cliff the other day—had some kind of mental meltdown," she continued. "Once we had her in custody, we shipped her down to the county hospital for observation." Joanna didn't mention that there was a possibility of poisoning being involved. "We made some progress on the case involving those bones that showed up out of the wash down by Naco the other night. Now that Jaime's nephew has been found safe, I'd have to say it was a pretty good day."

And I'm on the trail of a woman who may have been having an affair with Andy, Joanna thought to herself, *a woman who may have been pregnant with Andy's child.*

Joanna couldn't help noticing how much she was leaving out of the conversation. That was how cops got through their lives on a daily basis—how they coped—by editing what they told their families about what had gone on at work. They downplayed the stuff that was dangerous or hurt too much; they told stories about good guys and bad guys, making sure that what they were saying was relatively light. They probably thought they were editing their stories for their family's benefit, but Joanna suspected it was also a matter of self-defense. That was how cops managed to keep the tough stuff they saw from themselves, too. By holding things at arm's length, they managed to stave off their own mental difficulties.

Butch sat down on the couch as well, leaving a space for Lady in the middle. "I didn't mean to upset you with that thing about Carol Sunderson," he said. "It just seemed like an idea that might be good for all concerned."

"I shouldn't have been so upset," Joanna returned, taking his hand. "I guess I was just starting to come to terms with the idea of Mom helping out. I'm surprised to hear she's changed her mind. Did she say why?"

"No."

"As for Carol? We can talk to her, but we need to charge her a going-rate rent and pay her going-rate wages for whatever work she does for us. If we do anything else, we run the risk that the next time I'm up for reelection my opponent will be able to claim we worked out a barter arrangement in order to avoid having to pay taxes."

"So you'd be willing to talk to her about it?" Butch asked. "You'd be willing to discuss it?"

"Butch, we already did discuss it," Joanna said. "Your publisher wants you to go on tour for *Serve and Protect*, and you need to be able to do that with a clear conscience. You won't be able to do a good job if you're worried about things falling apart here at home. And if Carol Sunderson can't or won't do it, we'll find someone else."

"Should we talk to Marianne and see if she can help us set up a meeting?" Butch said.

Joanna nodded. "And Carol should have someone with her during the discussions so it doesn't seem like we're pressuring her. That's easy to do when it's two to one."

The phone rang again. It was Jaime. "Marcella's not here. Her car's gone. Her clothes are gone. Mrs. Dumas, their next-door neighbor, seems to keep an eagle eye on the place. She says she saw Marcella loading stuff into her car before she drove off late this afternoon. Luis's clothes are still there at the house."

"Wait a minute," Joanna said. "You're saying Marcella just

took off—maybe even moved out—without waiting around for Luis to be found?"

"That's right."

"How could she?" Joanna asked. "And why?"

"Remember how she told us that Luis's father ripped off one of his pals?"

"Yes," Joanna said. "His name was Castro, Paco Castro."

"That's right. And she also told us that Paco's money was confiscated when Marco Andrade was arrested. That part was evidently a lie. She still has it—some of it, anyway. I don't know how much."

"Is that why she was so scared Paco would come looking for them? Is that why Luis ran away, because he was scared?"

"Luis ran away because he was mad," Jaime said. "Because he finally figured out that his mother has been lying to him. She kept telling him they were broke when she was anything but. He didn't find out about it until she lit into him over the newspaper article. She berated him for being so stupid, for letting Paco find out so he could come take their money away, yada, yada, yada. After playing the 'poor me' game all this time, she finally let the cat out of the bag. Luis was pissed. He's pretty broken up about it and couldn't believe Marcella had played him that way. I told him welcome to my world."

"What are you going to do now?" Joanna asked.

"He's inside their house gathering up his stuff and loading it into some trash bags I found in the kitchen. Why Marcella had trash bags, I can't imagine. She obviously never used them. Anyway, I've called Delcia to let her know I'm bringing him back up to the house. He'll be sleeping on the couch in the living room tonight, not in the toolshed."

"Where do you think she went?"

"Who knows?" Jaime said. "And right now, who cares? Tomorrow will be time enough to figure that out. For tonight, Luis is hurting, and he's my main concern."

"He's lucky to have you," Joanna said.

"Thanks, boss," Jaime replied. "I hope so."

While Joanna had been on the phone, Butch had let the dogs out one last time, locked up the house, and was in the process of turning off the lights. "Bedtime," he said. "No doubt little mister will wake us at the crack of dawn."

But it wasn't Dennis who woke them. It was the phone. "It's Deputy Sloan," Tica Romero from Dispatch announced in Joanna's ear. "He's dead."

Butch groaned and pulled a pillow over his head while Joanna felt the bile rise in her throat. Deputy Dan Sloan, twenty-five years old, was a newbie who had graduated from the academy only six months earlier. Married. What was his wife's name again? Joanna couldn't quite remember, but she knew the couple was expecting a baby—sometime soon.

Joanna stepped around Lady and grabbed clothes out of the closet and underwear from the dresser as she made her way into the bathroom. "What happened?"

"Deputy Sloan didn't report in when he was supposed to, and we weren't able to raise him on the radio," Tica said. "We knew he was supposed to be keeping an eye on the Beasley house up Tombstone Canyon, so I dispatched someone to check on him. He was found inside the house, shot dead on the kitchen floor."

"Did you call out the troops?" Joanna asked.

"Yes," Tica said. "Standard operating procedure. Then I called you."

"Good," Joanna told her. "Let everyone know I'm on my way."

I did this, Joanna thought as she pulled on her clothing and ran a brush through her hair. *If Larry Wolfe had known we'd already executed the search warrant, he wouldn't have gone back to the house looking for his damned chocolate syrup. Danny Sloan wouldn't be dead.*

Joanna tiptoed out of the bathroom. Before she reached the bedroom door, Butch sat up in bed and switched on the light. "What's going on?" he asked.

"One of my deputies just got shot."

"Is he going to be all right?"

Joanna came over to the bed and kissed Butch good-bye. "He's not all right," she said. "He's dead. I have to go."

"Be careful," Butch told her. "I love you."

CHAPTER 15

DRIVING DOWN THE WASHBOARDED DIRT TRACK FROM THE ranch house to High Lonesome Road, Joanna's sense of self-recrimination came to a full boil. Deputy Dan Sloan was dead and it was her fault; her responsibility. She hadn't fired the fatal shot that had killed him—hadn't pulled the actual trigger—but she knew his death could, would, and should be laid at her door-step. The baby that Dan's wife was expecting would grow up without a father as a direct result of the way Joanna and her de-partment had been conducting their investigation into the deaths of Alfred and Martha Beasley.

This wasn't jumping to conclusions; this was fact. Joanna her-self had called for the execution of the search warrant. Then, during the interview of Sandra Wolfe, she had deliberately with-held the search warrant information. That decision alone had allowed Larry Wolfe to think that he might still be able to re-move any incriminating evidence left behind in his in-laws' house.

Detective Howell was the officer who had asked Deputy Sloan to remain on the scene in the aftermath of the search. She had done so because she had been concerned someone might come there hoping to destroy or remove evidence. Subsequent events proved Detective Howell's assessment to be one hundred per-cent correct, but her decision—the one that had put Dan Sloan in harm's way—was in tune with what Joanna herself would have done had she been on the scene. That put Joanna at the top of the chain of command that had left a relatively new officer to be slaughtered by a suspected killer.

Just how new was Deputy Sloan? He'd been on the force for less than a year, but he had graduated from his state-accredited police academy training with high marks. He had also been work-ing his way through a program of individualized continuing education Joanna had purchased for members of her depart-ment. The program included a comprehensive set of computer-ized tutorials, including several that dealt with failure to call for backup. But just because Dan Sloan had read something and suc-cessfully completed a quiz on it didn't mean he had internalized the material enough so that it would become second nature in a life-and-death decision-making process.

Joanna knew full well that in the days and weeks ahead there would be plenty of Monday-morning quarterbacks ques-tioning whether or not Deputy Sloan had been properly trained and supervised, but now wasn't the time for those discussions. Tonight was all about finding and apprehending his killer. Joanna had a pretty fair idea of who that was and where to look for him—unless Larry Wolfe had already taken off for parts unknown.

As Joanna swung off Double Adobe Road onto Highway 80, she switched on her flashers and reached for her radio. "Who's securing the scene?" she asked.

"That would be Detective Carbajal and Deputy Raymond," Tica responded. "Raymond is the officer I dispatched to the scene initially. He's the one who found the body. Detective Carbajal lives nearby. That's how he got there so fast. Detectives Howell and Carpenter are both on the way. Uniformed officers from the City of Bisbee are also on the scene."

Deputy Sloan was a Cochise County deputy. Unfortunately he had died inside Bisbee's city limits. That would make for one more layer of jurisdictional complication.

"What about Frank?"

"Chief Deputy Montoya is coming from Sierra Vista," Tica said. "He's probably half an hour out."

Sierra Vista again, Joanna thought.

"Contact Ernie and Deb. Tell them to meet me at the Copper Queen Hotel," she ordered. "And press the SAT button. I want those guys there, too."

"That'll take a while," Tica said. "They're scattered all over the county."

"However long it takes is how long it takes," Joanna returned. "Tell them to meet me at the bottom of Brewery Gulch. They should approach with caution and with flashing lights only. No sirens. Once you do all that, patch me through to Jaime."

The better part of a minute passed before Tica came back on the line. "Okay," she said. "Here's Detective Carbajal."

"How does it look?" Joanna asked.

Jaime paused before he answered. Joanna knew him well enough to realize that he was fighting for control.

"Pretty rough," he answered at last. "Dan's patrol vehicle is parked in front of the house and apparently undisturbed. I'd say something—a noise, maybe breaking glass—must have alerted Dan that someone was here at the back of the house. He came around to check it out and confronted the intruder. There was a struggle, and boom—that was it."

"Gunned down with his own weapon?" Joanna asked.

"His Glock might be here somewhere," Jaime said. "So far I don't see it. So being killed with his own weapon is a very real possibility. Are you coming?"

"Not right away. I've asked Ernie and Deb to meet me at the Copper Queen. SAT, too. I'm hoping Larry Wolfe is still there."

"You're calling out SAT?" Jaime rasped. "Good luck, then," he added. "I hope you nail this SOB."

He means it, too, Joanna thought. And she knew why. Jaime Carbajal was the one who had urged Dan Sloan to apply to work at the department.

"Sheriff Brady," Tica said. "Patching through Detective Howell."

"Where are you?" Joanna asked.

"At the hotel," Deb returned. "I was almost at the scene when I got called back here. Ernie's right behind me. What are we doing?"

"I'm on my way there, too," Joanna said. "Do we know what kinds of cars the Wolfes drive?" Joanna asked.

"Yes," Deb said. "I already checked. He drives a three-year-old Dodge Ram pickup truck. She drives a 1999 Lexus. I just spotted his pickup. It's right here in the hotel lot. So far there's no sign of the Lexus. Ernie's on his way inside to talk to the desk clerk."

"Okay," Joanna said. "I'll be there in a matter of minutes." As she put the radio down, her cell phone rang. Answering, she could see that Frank Montoya was on the line, and she wondered why he was calling on her cell rather than using the radio.

"I heard you're bringing in SAT," he said. "Are you sure calling in an assault team is a good idea?"

Frank's question took Joanna by surprise. "Why?" she returned. "Do you think it's a good idea to pound on Larry Wolfe's hotel room door without a hallway full of firepower backing us up?"

"The man's a suspected cop killer," Frank pointed out. "What if one of Deputy Sloan's buddies gets trigger-happy and decides to take him out?"

Joanna knew then why Frank had called on her cell. He was questioning one of her orders, but he didn't want to countermand her in public. Furthermore, she had to admit Frank had a point. What were the chances that one of her SAT guys, pumped up by what had happened to Deputy Sloan and fueled by a need for vengeance, would open fire on Larry Wolfe if he emerged from his room holding, say, a television remote rather than a weapon? If that was to happen, Joanna's department would be embroiled in charges of using excessive force. The resulting lawsuits would most likely long outlast her second term in office.

But Joanna had made a very public decision to deploy SAT, and she wasn't ready to unmake it. "That's a risk I'm willing to take," she returned.

"All right, then," Frank said. "Where do you want me?"

Joanna heard the undertone of disapproval in her chief deputy's voice and didn't want to deal with it—not right then. "How about if you go to the scene and check in with Jaime?" Joanna suggested. "Then maybe you can see about rousting Judge Cameron out of bed and getting us another search warrant—this one for the hotel room and for their vehicles as well. Deb has the details on those. We're going to need a warrant in hand, and the sooner we have it, the better."

"All right," Frank said. "Will do."

As Joanna pulled into a parking spot at the mouth of Brewery Gulch, Ernie came trotting down Howell Avenue. She hopped out of her car and waved him down.

"What's up?"

"I just talked to Darla MacPherson, the Copper Queen's desk clerk. She remembered seeing Larry Wolfe go out around nine and come back later. Sometime after eleven. The hotel has several security cameras, and I got her to rewind the tape. One of them shows Wolfe riding the elevator down to the lobby at nine-oh-two and exiting via the front doors. He returned at eleven-twenty. When he left, he was wearing a Hawaiian shirt. When he came back, the Hawaiian shirt had been replaced by a torn T-shirt."

"I want those security tapes taken into evidence," Joanna said.

"Already done," Ernie said.

"In other words, Larry Wolfe probably got blood on his shirt. That's why he ditched it," Joanna said. "But if he'd already shot Dan, why did he come back here in the first place? Why not just take off?" Joanna glanced at her watch. "That was a good hour and a half ago now. Is he still here?"

"I doubt it," Ernie said. "I'd be willing to bet that he's managed to sneak out some other way without the desk clerk seeing him."

"What about Sandy?" Joanna asked. "Where's she?"

"No sign of her," Ernie said. "Not in the tapes I saw, anyway. Darla hasn't seen her either."

"And what about Deb?"

"On the far side of the hotel," Ernie told her. "She's searching the upper parking lot to see if the missing Lexus is parked in one of those. Since it wasn't listed on their registration form, it isn't parked in the regular lot. I'm thinking we should probably put out an APB on it. If we wait until we know more—"

He let the rest of that sentence go unfinished, but Joanna heard the unspoken part loud and clear. If Larry Wolfe had already made a run for it, every minute they delayed in launching an APB and starting a systematic search would allow the man more time to make good his escape. If he had gone north, he could be back in Tucson by now—in Tucson or beyond it. If he'd traveled east, he could be a long way into New Mexico. Or he might have gone south and crossed the international border at Naco. Joanna hated to think how many more miles he'd be able to cover by the time Frank arrived with a newly minted search warrant and her SAT guys got their gear together and converged on the scene as well.

"Do it," Joanna said. "For now he's a person of interest, but he's to be considered armed and dangerous. He's already killed one cop. I don't want him to take down another."

Nodding, Ernie headed for his car and his radio. Back in her patrol car, Joanna monitored the radio transmissions that were shooting back and forth. Casey Ledford and Dave Hollicker had now arrived at the crime scene in upper Tombstone Canyon. George Winfield was there as well. Just then the first member of the SAT team arrived at the base of Brewery Gulch.

Deputy Jimmy Williams, the SAT team leader, hopped out of his Explorer and hurried over to Joanna's Crown Vic. "My guys are all en route," he told her when she rolled down her window. "They've been apprised of the situation. Is the perp still inside the hotel, and where do you want me?"

"Talk to Ernie," Joanna said. "He's been in and out of the hotel lobby. You two decide."

Williams hustled off while Joanna picked up her phone. "Where are you now?" she asked Frank.

"Just coming up the far side of the Divide."

"All right. Let Jaime know Larry Wolfe left the hotel at nine and returned a little after eleven. Somewhere along the way, he ditched his shirt—a Hawaiian shirt. We need to find it."

"What about notifying Dan's wife?" Frank asked. "Do you want me to handle that? Or should Jaime do it?"

"Definitely not Jaime," Joanna declared. "He's too close to them. I'll handle it myself, but not yet. When I tell Sunny Sloan about this, I'd like nothing better than to be able to say we already have the guy in custody." The name of Dan's wife had come back to her unbidden.

"Don't wait too long," Frank cautioned. "This is a small town. Things have a way of getting out."

As if to prove him right, there was a sudden sharp rap on the window beside Joanna's head. When she turned to look, Joanna was dismayed to find Marliss Shackleford standing next to the Crown Victoria, notebook and pen in hand.

"Gotta go," Joanna said to Frank. "I'll have to get back to

you." She rolled down the window. "What are you doing here?" she demanded.

"Good morning to you too, Sheriff Brady," Marliss said pleasantly. "And what I'm doing is my job. One of the few advantages to being menopausal is the insomnia that goes along with it. Whenever I can't sleep, I entertain myself by monitoring the police channels. Tonight I hit the jackpot."

"This is a police matter, Marliss," Joanna said. "We need you to leave the area at once."

"I've learned that one of your deputies died tonight," Marliss continued, pointedly ignoring Joanna's terse order to leave. "I understand his name hasn't yet been officially released, but anonymous sources tell me it was Sloan, Deputy Daniel Sloan. Would you care to comment on that?"

Let me get my hands on one of those "anonymous sources," Joanna thought savagely. "No," she muttered. "No comment."

Joanna reached for the window control, but Marliss beat her to the punch by jamming her leather-bound notebook into the opening to keep the window from closing. Not wanting to burn up the control, Joanna gave up and left it open.

"I noticed that the alleged shooting took place at the home of Alfred and Martha Beasley," Marliss continued. "Does what happened tonight have anything to do with the deaths of Alfred and Martha last Friday?"

"I said 'No comment,'" Joanna repeated. "I mean no comment."

But Marliss was nothing if not determined. "According to the Beasleys' next-door neighbor, Maggie Morris, one of Martha and Alfred Beasley's daughters—I believe it was Samantha—was involved in some kind of difficulty yesterday afternoon. I understand police were called to the residence, shots were fired, and someone was taken away by ambulance, possibly to the county hospital down in Douglas. Your public information officer, Chief Deputy Montoya, issued a blanket statement on the topic early yesterday evening, but I've been unable to contact him for an additional comment or details. Could you confirm whether or not Samantha Edwards was the person taken away by ambulance?"

Thank you so much, Maggie Morris, Joanna thought. *There's nothing like a little small-town gossip to fan the flames of rumor.*

"I'm confirming nothing; I'm denying nothing," Joanna returned.

"Getting back to Deputy Sloan—"

"Look, Marliss," Joanna said. "I can't say it any more plainly than I already have. No comment means no comment."

A car pulled up directly behind her. She expected and hoped that the new arrival would be another member of her SAT unit. That hope was soon dashed.

"Hello, Chief Bernard," Marliss said, greeting Bisbee's chief of police by name. "We seem to be having quite a night around here."

"What are you doing here, Marliss?" the chief growled.

"My job," she said.

"Well, clear out."

Two uniformed officers trotted up behind Chief Bernard. "Get her out of here," he ordered, nodding in their direction.

"Where do you expect me to go?" Marliss asked.

"I'd prefer to have you on the far side of the moon," Bernard replied uncharitably. "But for right now, I'll take what I can get. We're setting up a perimeter on the far side of Main Street. I'd suggest you wait over there in the parking lot. That should be far enough to keep you out of harm's way."

Marliss looked as though she was prepared to argue, but finally, removing her notebook from Joanna's window opening and still protesting the injustice of it all, she allowed herself to be led away. As soon as she was out of earshot, Chief Bernard rounded on Joanna.

"Who the hell do you think you are, Sheriff Brady?" he demanded. "I'm sorry as hell that you've lost one of your officers, but still, you can't set up an armed confrontation in the middle of my jurisdiction without saying one word to me about it beforehand."

Joanna knew he wasn't wrong to be pissed. "Sorry," she said. "I was just—"

"Never mind. What's the deal here?"

"We believe the armed killer who gunned down Deputy Dan Sloan may be holed up in a room in the Copper Queen. My people are coming here to take him down before he has a chance to get away."

"You're bringing in your SWAT team?"

"SAT," Joanna corrected.

"Whatever!" he returned. "And you're planning on staging a shoot-out right here in the middle of town?"

"It's not going to be—"

"Think about it," Chief Bernard advised. "You're upset. Your people are upset, and why wouldn't they be? But somebody else needs to handle this. Your guys are too damned close to it. Don't get me wrong, so am I. Danny Sloan played Little League for me for three years when he was a little shaver, and I'm mad as hell that he's dead. But I've only got one detective. Phil Lester's a hell of a nice guy, but it's been years since he's worked a homicide."

Bernard seemed to be washing back and forth between being pissed at Joanna and being reasonable; between telling her to shove off and asking for her help, wanted or not.

"What are you suggesting?" Joanna asked.

"We should bring in DPS," Chief Bernard said. "Let the Arizona Department of Public Safety handle this."

Joanna knew Alvin Bernard had a point—almost the same one Frank Montoya had expressed earlier. But what would DPS do if she ran up the flag to them? They certainly had far greater numbers of highly qualified personnel to bring to bear on the situation than either she or Chief Bernard did. The question was: Would they? Would an agency with statewide law enforcement responsibilities give Deputy Sloan's murder the kind of attention Joanna thought it deserved, or would they do lip service only?

"Maybe later," Joanna said. "But not tonight. They wouldn't get here soon enough to do any good. How about if we leave DPS out of it and handle it ourselves?"

Alvin Bernard blinked. "As in a joint operation?"

"You have one homicide detective. I have three. That would give us four altogether. With all of our people pulling in the same direction, maybe we can get this creep off the street."

Joanna could see Chief Bernard was mulling over her proposition when Ernie lumbered over to the car. He was practically giddy with excitement. "They found the shirt!" he announced gleefully. "A blood-spattered Hawaiian shirt."

"Where?" Joanna demanded.

"In a trash bin three houses down the street from the Beasleys' place. And Frank says to tell you that—"

A bloodcurdling scream cut through the still dark night. At the sound of it, a shocked hush fell over the collection of mismatched police officers gathered at the bottom of Brewery Gulch.

Joanna remembered her mother telling her that, back in the old days when the hospital was still located in Old Bisbee and air-conditioning wasn't an option, women in the delivery room would often bring the whole of uptown to a standstill with their soul-shattering screams. The same thing happened now. The whole crowd stood transfixed while one horrendous scream after another echoed off buildings and steep canyon walls.

Moments later, a young woman shot out through the front door of the hotel. She bounded down the front steps and raced down the street to where the officers were assembled. Ernie Carpenter was the one she seemed to know, and she focused in on him.

"Come on," she yelled, gesturing frantically. "It sounds like he's killing her."

"Which room?" Ernie demanded.

"The one you were asking about earlier. Number 218. The Wolfes' room."

Joanna had seen Darla MacPherson on occasion and knew that she worked part-time as the Copper Queen's night desk clerk. Having delivered that chilling piece of information, Darla turned and raced back up the hill. Hot on her heels were Detective Carpenter, Lieutenant Williams, and Deputy Ed Singleton, Joanna's latest SAT arrival.

As the horrific screams continued to pulse through the night, Joanna knew that waiting for the rest of her team was no longer an option. Delaying until the arrival of a search warrant was also out of the question. With someone in physical danger—someone suffering bodily harm—all of the usual checks and balances evaporated.

She turned to Alvin Bernard. "Do we have a deal?"

The chief nodded. "Yes, Sheriff," he replied. "I believe we do."

"All right, then," she said. "We're going in. Get your people and the rest of mine to shut down the streets and keep them clear. I've got somebody up at the top of Howell Avenue, so that end of the street is covered, but Deb could probably use some reinforcements. Send someone around to the back of the hotel in case he tries to get out that way. And if he tries to make a break for it, stop him. Make sure everyone knows the score—armed and dangerous."

"Will do," Chief Bernard replied. "Good luck."

As he began barking orders to the remaining officers, Joanna dashed up the hill while the appalling screams went on and on. Joanna crashed through the double glass doors into the hotel lobby to find that Ernie and the others had disappeared. Trembling and out of breath, Darla was the only person visible. She was planted in front of the elevator door, pointing up the carpeted stairs.

"They went that way," she gasped. "Second floor. To the left. End of the hall."

"Can you shut down the elevator?" Joanna wanted to know.

Darla nodded wordlessly.

"Do it, then," Joanna ordered. "Do it now."

As Darla reached for the set of keys that hung on her side, Joanna scrambled up the stairs. As she raced down the hall, doors opened along the corridor as startled hotel guests, awakened by the racket, peered out of their rooms to see what was going on.

"Shut your doors," Joanna told them. "Stay inside. Don't come out until we tell you it's safe."

She caught up with the others, standing with their weapons drawn, at a door marked 218. Using the door frame for cover, Lieutenant Williams rapped sharply on the wood-paneled door. Nothing happened. No one came to the door, and the screaming never changed, either. After waiting the better part of a minute, Williams knocked again. Still nothing. Finally he tried turning the knob. It moved in his hand, but the door didn't open. That meant the dead bolt was fastened from the inside. The door would have to be opened with a key—or a kick.

"Wait," Lieutenant Williams said. "I'll do it."

Joanna and Ernie stayed to one side while Williams took a running start at it. He slammed into the door, shoulder first. The wood shuddered under his weight but held firm. He hit it again, this time with a waist-high kick. Wood splintered under the blow as the door began to give way. A second powerful kick sent the door flying. Forward momentum carried Jimmy into the room and almost across it. Ed Singleton rushed in directly behind him, but the keening screams didn't stop or even change.

"Clear," Jimmy shouted, followed a moment later by Ed shouting the same thing from inside the bathroom.

Pausing in the open doorway, Joanna was surprised to see Sandra Wolfe, stark naked and completely alone, standing in front of the closed closet door, screaming her lungs out. Her hands were empty. She apparently had no weapon, and she didn't appear to be injured. There was no visible sign of blood. She seemed completely unaware that anyone else had entered the room.

"Sandra?" Joanna asked tentatively, holstering her own weapon. Deputy Singleton and Lieutenant Williams kept theirs at the ready, just in case.

"Are you all right?" Joanna asked. "Has something happened? Are you hurt?"

Still staring at the closet door, Sandra Wolfe appeared to be entirely oblivious to the fact that someone was speaking to her. All the screaming made hearing impossible.

Careful to make no sudden moves, Joanna crossed the room toward the distraught woman. Passing the bed, she plucked a floral-patterned bedspread from the mound of covers. Holding the spread at arm's length, Joanna moved closer. When she reached Sandy, Joanna placed the bedspread over the woman's bare shoulders and wrapped it around her. For her part, Sandy never stopped screaming.

"Is someone in there?" Joanna demanded. "Is he hiding in the closet?"

When Sandy didn't respond, Joanna grabbed her by the shoulders and spun her around. "Talk to me," she urged. "Tell me what's going on. Did he hurt you?"

For a scant second a look of comprehension crossed Sandy's face, then she tuned up again. As a two-year-old, Jenny had pitched some screaming fits. In Joanna's bag of motherly tricks there had been only one countermeasure that actually worked.

"Quick," she ordered over her shoulder to Ernie and the others. "Bring me some cold water. Throw it in her face."

Frank looked at Joanna as though she were nuts, but Jimmy Williams was an experienced father of five. He knew how it worked. Instead of heading for the bathroom as Joanna expected, he backed out into the corridor, where a guest from a neighboring room—someone who, despite Joanna's warnings, had ventured into the hallway and listened to the whole exchange—handed him a champagne bucket full of icy water. Jimmy brought the bucket into the room and flung the ice-laced contents full into Sandy Wolfe's face. She gasped, sputtered, and fell quiet. Out in the hallway, Sandy's neighbors applauded the welcome silence before her screams changed to hopeless sobs.

"What is it, Sandy?" Joanna asked. "What's wrong?"

"My face," she managed between racking sobs. "It's my face."

Joanna was looking Sandy full in the face. She saw no blood and no bruising, and no sign of damage other than the scabbed-over scratches and purple bruises Samantha had inflicted during their bar fight on Saturday night.

"What about your face?" Joanna asked. "What's the matter with it?"

"Don't you see?" Sandy demanded shrilly. She turned back to the closet door and pointed. "Look," she said, pointing. "See there? It's gone."

The problem was she was pointing at a door—a plain wood-paneled door covered with layers of white enamel. There was no mirror on the door—and no way for Sandra Wolfe to see her reflection or her "missing face."

She started sobbing again, sobbing and shivering. "Please," she begged, moaning. "Please give it back to me. I need it."

Joanna turned to Ernie. "I think she's been dosed with the same thing Samantha took earlier. Call an ambulance. Jimmy, help me get her on the bed, and then shut the door."

While Ernie reached for his phone to summon help, Jimmy picked Sandy up and deposited her on the bed. She lay there weeping. "I need my face," she whimpered over and over. "People can't live without faces. I need it."

But at least she's not screaming, Joanna thought.

An open suitcase sat on a stand next to the bed. Joanna rummaged through the contents until she found a lightweight track suit. While Ed Singleton and Jimmy Williams faded discreetly into the background, Joanna set about getting the woman dressed. It took lots of coaxing and prompting, but eventually she succeeded. Joanna didn't want Sandy to suffer the indignity of having the EMTs haul her through the corridors and out the hotel's front doors dressed in nothing but a bedspread.

Ernie closed his phone. "The EMTs are on their way," he announced. "They'll be here in a few minutes."

"Good," Joanna said.

Lieutenant Williams had taken advantage of the relative quiet to return to the bathroom. "You'll never guess what's in there in the garbage," he said when he reemerged. "A used syringe and an empty vial labeled ketamine. That stuff is wicked. No wonder the poor woman is out of it. If he gave her the whole dose, it's a miracle she's not dead."

But Larry Wolfe is long gone, Joanna thought. And maybe that was a good thing. If he was out of the county, Frank Montoya's "excessive force" worries would prove groundless. Still, she was sick at heart that she could no longer delay going to see Dan Sloan's widow. Not only would Joanna have to tell Sunny Sloan that her husband was dead, she would also have to admit to the grieving woman that so far the bastard who had killed Danny had gotten away clean.

Joanna turned to Ernie. "You need to call Dispatch and amend that APB," she said. "Then call Jaime and let him know that as soon as the EMTs get here, I'll be on my way to notify the next of kin. And one more thing."

"What's that?"

"I still haven't made it to the crime scene up Tombstone Canyon. Let Doc Winfield know that he's not to move that body until I get there. Once the next-of-kin notification is out of the way, the crime scene's my next stop."

"Got it, boss," Ernie Carpenter said. "I'll tell him."

CHAPTER 16

IT WAS WELL AFTER THREE O'CLOCK IN THE MORNING BEFORE Sandy Wolfe's ambulance pulled away from the front of the Copper Queen. With a heavy heart Joanna got into her vehicle for the drive to Bisbee's Warren neighborhood and to the house at the top of Congdon where she'd been told Dan and Sunny Sloan lived in a basement apartment.

In five years, Sheriff Joanna Brady had done her share of next-of-kin notifications, but she dreaded this one far more than any of the others. This was a first for her. Dan Sloan was one of her own, an officer who had died in the line of duty.

On the trip down the canyon she worried about what she was going to say, and she remembered, with some regret, her earlier confrontation with Marliss. Since Joanna had refused to give the frustrated columnist any help, what if she had decided to move forward on her own? What if Marliss, in order to get back at Joanna, had done her own ham-fisted version of a next-of-kin notification?

As Joanna drove around the long flat curve of Lavender Pit, she noticed that a vehicle—another wide-bodied sedan—had dropped in behind hers and seemed to be mimicking her every move. It stayed with her around the traffic circle and all the way through Warren.

What do you want to bet this is some jerk of a reporter determined to get a scoop? she asked herself.

At the corner of Congdon and Arizona Street, Joanna pulled over to the curb and stopped. As soon as the trailing car, a Mercury Marquis, went past her, Joanna turned on her flashers and signaled for the driver to pull over. When she ran the plates, the vehicle came back as belonging to Saint Dominick's Parish.

She approached from behind, with one hand perched warily on her holstered Glock. "Driver's license and registration, please," she demanded.

"You're Sheriff Brady, aren't you?" a male voice asked. "What seems to be the problem?"

Peering inside the car, she saw a middle-aged man wearing a clerical collar. "I am Sheriff Brady," she told him. "Were you following me?"

"Yes," he admitted at once. "I'm Father Rowan, Father Matthew Rowan, the new priest at Saint Dominick's. Jaime Carbajal is one of my parishioners. So are Danny and Sunny Sloan. Jaime called and asked if I'd mind tagging along when you went to tell Sunny. I got to the hotel just as you were leaving. Since I'm new to town and don't know my way around yet, I decided to play follow-the-leader."

A priest, not a reporter! Joanna's anger turned to relief. "I'm glad to meet you, Father Rowan," she said, waving aside his proffered ID. "I'm sorry I stopped you, but with everything that's happened tonight—"

"Think nothing of it," he said. "Perfectly understandable."

"And thanks for coming," she added. "I'm sure Sunny will be glad to have you there." *I know I am!* "Their house is just a few blocks up the hill here," she said, pointing. "I'll lead the way."

A few minutes later, with the comforting presence of Father Rowan at her side, Joanna Brady approached Dan and Sunny Sloan's apartment. The lights were off inside. Most likely Sunny was still asleep and had no idea that her husband was dead.

There was no doorbell. Behind a flimsy screen door was a substantial mahogany one, an old-fashioned model with three stair-step panes of glass near the top. The bottom of the lowest piece of glass was still inches above the top of Joanna's head.

Squaring her shoulders, Joanna pulled open the screen door and knocked. Nothing happened. No light came on; no one answered the door. After waiting the better part of a minute, she knocked again, louder. Finally a lamp was switched on somewhere inside the house. Seconds later the door cracked open the length of a brass security chain.

"Who is it?" a woman's voice asked. She sounded anxious and wary and more than a little tired.

"It's Sheriff Brady," Joanna said. "I'm sorry to awaken you, Sunny. We need to talk."

"Sheriff Brady?" Sunny repeated. "What are you doing here? What's wrong?" As she spoke she fumbled with the lock, pulled the door open, and stood there in backlit disarray with her pregnant body swathed in a lightweight summer nightgown.

"May Father Rowan and I come in?" Joanna asked.

"Father Rowan?" Sunny gasped in surprise. "What are you doing here?" she asked. Then her eyes widened in comprehension. "Oh, no. It's Danny. Something's happened. Is he all right?"

Joanna shook her head. "I'm afraid he's not all right," she replied softly. "I'm so sorry to have to tell you this—" she began, but Sunny Sloan didn't bother to hear her out.

With her face blanching, she backed away from the door, holding up her hands as if to fend off Joanna and the news she was about to deliver.

"No!" Sunny wailed, her voice rising in anguish. "No, please. It can't be. It isn't possible. Don't tell me he's dead. Danny can't be dead. We're expecting a baby!"

Without a word, Father Rowan moved past Joanna into the small living room. He took Sunny by the elbow, guided her to an armchair, and helped ease her ungainly body into it. Closing the door behind her, Joanna followed them inside and took a seat on a faded flowered couch. While she waited for Sunny to quiet down, Joanna struggled to find the right words. What could she possibly tell this grieving woman that would offer any kind of consolation?

"I'm so sorry," she said again. "Your husband was on duty and attempting to apprehend a suspect in a homicide case. Shots were fired. Dan was struck at close range, possibly with his own weapon. He died before our officers found him."

Sitting as though frozen in place and with her face stark white, Sunny listened numbly to the news. Only the last sentence provoked a response.

"He died?" she repeated. "You're saying Danny's dead? That can't be. You must be mistaken. Doctors do all kinds of things to save gunshot victims these days. Surely there's something they can do."

Denial, Joanna thought. *The first stage of grief.*

"No one knew there'd been a problem with Dan until he didn't call in on schedule," Joanna explained. "An officer was dispatched to the scene, but by the time he arrived, it was too late. Your husband was already gone."

Gone, Joanna thought. *Why do people say 'gone' instead of 'dead'? They mean the same thing.*

For the longest time after that, Sunny Sloan simply sat there with one hand resting on her bulging belly. She appeared to be staring straight at Joanna but it seemed likely that she wasn't seeing anything at all.

"Did he suffer?" she asked at last.

There it was again—the same question Lucinda had asked about the death of her daughter—the same question survivors always asked. Joanna had been so caught up with trying to apprehend Larry Wolfe that she had yet to visit the crime scene. Still, although she knew from talking to Jaime that Dan's death had been ugly, she didn't have to say that to his widow.

"No," Joanna answered at once. "I'm sure he didn't."

Sunny covered her eyes with both hands. "Thank God for that," she said despairingly, and burst into tears once more. When that paroxysm finally abated, Joanna handed Sunny one of her cards.

"We won't release Dan's name to the media until you give us the go-ahead," she said, "but once you've notified close friends and family, please let me know."

Sunny nodded. "I will," she said.

"Is there someone we should call right now?" Joanna asked. "Someone who can come stay with you tonight?"

"My dad," Sunny said. "My dad and my stepmom. They live out in Bisbee Junction."

Using his own phone, Father Rowan placed the call that rousted Fred and Anne Coyle out of bed. Joanna stayed on until they arrived. Then, as she prepared to leave, Father Cowan followed her out to the car.

"I think I'll hang around a while longer," he said. "Try to make myself useful."

"I really appreciate your coming," Joanna told him. "Having you here was a huge help."

He nodded. "No problem," he said. "Glad to be of service."

Joanna opened her car door and then paused. "I hope you'll look in on Jaime a little later," she said. "He and Dan were close. He's taking it pretty hard."

Father Rowan nodded. "I'll make it a point to stop by and see him," he said. "But you take care, too."

Joanna nodded her thanks and then ducked into her vehicle without saying anything more. After turning her key in the ignition, she reached for the radio.

"I'm on my way back uptown," she told Tica in Dispatch. "What's happening?"

"Doc Winfield is ready to transport, but he's holding off until you get there. Chief Deputy Montoya delivered the search warrant to Ernie and Deb Howell. They're still at the hotel. Frank is back at the crime scene in Tombstone Canyon. He asked me to call in some of our off-duty officers to serve as an honor guard when it's time to bring out the body."

I should have thought of that, Joanna thought. *It's a good thing Frank did.* He may have disagreed with her handling of things as far as SAT was concerned, but her chief deputy continued to be as indispensable as ever.

"Chief Bernard said to tell you that his detective—"

"That would be Detective Lester," Joanna supplied. "Phil Lester."

"Detective Lester went by that little 7-Eleven up the canyon. He wanted to check with them because he was pretty sure they had installed state-of-the-art surveillance cameras. He's got a tape showing what looks like the suspect's vehicle driving up Tombstone Canyon at nine forty-five. The tape shows a red Dodge Ram going up the canyon, but there's no sign of it coming back down. Still, he says the resolution of the tape image is very good. We may be able to enhance it enough to ID the driver."

"That's good news," Joanna said.

We'll need all that stuff, she thought. *Finding Larry Wolfe is only the first step. We also have to have enough evidence to convict him.*

A mile away from the crime scene Joanna could already see the wild pattern of flashing emergency lights pulsing off the steep canyon walls. Closer to the Beasley place, the street was parked full of haphazardly positioned vehicles, blocking driveways and jammed onto sidewalks. They filled both sides of Tombstone Canyon, with more on side streets as well. Joanna herself was forced to pull into a spot three blocks downhill from the crime scene and walk from there.

Making her way up the sidewalk, she encountered countless clutches of hush-voiced neighbors and concerned bystanders, some of them still in their nightclothes. They gathered in anxious little knots to speculate about what had happened. Some of them recognized Joanna on sight. She nodded as she walked past, but she said nothing. They'd find out the ugly details soon enough.

She found Jaime in his Econoline van talking on the radio.

"What's happening?" she asked when he put down the microphone.

"Between here and the parking lot across from the hotel, we've already got a sizable media presence, with more news teams expected all the time," he told her. "Chief Bernard is going to handle the public-information end of things. He's scheduled a press conference at his headquarters down on the traffic circle in about half an hour. He's doing it there to get the reporters out of our hair here. He also said that since I was the first detective on the scene, he'd like me to act as lead investigator."

It all made perfect sense. "Good thinking," Joanna said.

"Chief Bernard wanted to know if we're ready to release the officer's name."

"Not yet," Joanna told him. "Not until Sunny Sloan gives me the word."

"Please tell me she isn't coming here," Jaime said.

"No, she isn't," Joanna told him. "Her dad and stepmother are with her down in Warren. So's Father Rowan. Sending him along was a good call."

Jaime nodded.

"What's going on inside?" Joanna asked, gesturing toward the house.

"Casey and Dave are still working the crime scene. I told them to take as much time as they need. We want this done right. We don't need it done fast."

Exactly, Joanna thought.

"You heard about the surveillance tape from the 7-Eleven?"

Joanna nodded.

"Finding that was a real stroke of luck."

It wasn't luck, Joanna thought. *It was good police work. It happened because Phil Lester knows what's happening in his jurisdiction. It happened because I took Frank's advice and Alvin Bernard's advice and didn't try going it alone.*

"We've had officers out canvassing the neighborhood," Jaime continued. "They've pretty well narrowed down the time of death. Ron Davis, who lives across the street, said he heard what he thought was someone setting off firecrackers just after ten-thirty, about the time Jay Leno was doing his monologue. Maggie Morris, who lives next door, says she heard a vehicle of some kind—a loud vehicle—speed off a little before eleven. That gives us a pretty clear idea on the timing."

"Speaking of timing," Joanna said. "It's time for me to go in."

Jaime shot her a dubious look. "You don't have to."

"Yes, I do, Jaime," she said. "Deputy Sloan was one of my deputies. I owe him."

Joanna leaned against the back wall of the Beasleys' house long enough to don a pair of paper crime scene booties. The outside screen door had been dusted for fingerprints. It had been propped open to allow for ease of access and also to reduce the amount of handling.

Careful, she reminded herself. *Don't get that stuff on your clothes.*

Taking a deep breath, Joanna paused for a moment in the open doorway and gathered herself. Finally she moved forward. Just inside the back door, a sprinkle of shattered glass littered the floor—jagged shards of glass with a trail of bloody shoe prints leading through them. The door itself was a Dutch door with a dinner-plate-sized hole broken out of the window section. A chunk of river rock the size of a man's fist lay on the floor nearby.

No doubt that was how the killer had gained entry to the house—by breaking the window. Joanna found herself agreeing with Jaime's theory that the sound of breaking glass might be what had summoned Dan Sloan to his doom.

Doing her best to avoid both the glass and the bloodstained footprints, Joanna stepped into Martha Beasley's old-fashioned kitchen. She stood there, next to an expanse of fern-patterned wallpaper and allowed the awful scene to sear itself into her soul.

A few feet into the room, Dan Sloan's body lay sprawled in a horrifying pool of blood. He had been tall—well over six feet. His long lanky frame stretched from one end of the tiny kitchen almost to the other. His right sleeve was soaked in blood, and the back of his head lay tipped up at an odd angle against the broiler drawer of a vintage electric range, while the toes of his polished boots pointed toward the open door of the completely empty refrigerator.

That was what hit Joanna the hardest—the open refrigerator door. She was convinced that the fridge was where whatever drugs Larry Wolfe had used on Alfred Beasley had been concealed. The killer had come there tonight in hopes of destroying any remaining incriminating evidence. That was why Dan Sloan was dead. Larry Wolfe had been doing damage control.

Standing stock-still, Joanna forced herself to examine Dan's body and catalog each gruesome detail. There were at least two wounds, one that had nearly severed the right arm. The other had torn through his abdomen just under Dan's Kevlar vest. Blood spatter marred the shiny surface of Martha's knotty-pine cabinets and dotted the garish wallpaper. A shockingly vivid pool of the copper-smelling stuff crept out from under Dan's uniform and spilled across the faded linoleum of Martha Beasley's kitchen floor. Joanna knew how much blood there should be in a living human body. Seeing the size of the puddle confirmed for Joanna that she hadn't told Sunny Sloan the truth—and rightfully so. Dan hadn't died instantly, and he had suffered, too, lying there alone and helpless as his life's blood oozed from his body.

The realization was almost enough to buckle Joanna's knees. She reached out to catch her balance, but when she spotted blood spatter there, too, she somehow managed to pull herself back together.

This is how military commanders must feel, she thought. *When they issue orders that send troops into an armed engagement, they know this can happen, will happen. People will die.*

George Winfield appeared in the doorway at the far end of the kitchen. "Are you okay?" he asked.

"I will be when we catch the son of a bitch who did this," Joanna declared. "How long did all this take?"

"For him to die once he was shot?"

Joanna nodded.

"Ten, fifteen minutes or so. There's no sign of any movement in his legs. He stayed exactly where he fell. That means we'll probably find that the shot that killed him also severed his spinal column. With his right arm useless, he couldn't turn himself over, much less crawl."

"Why didn't he call for help?"

Jaime Carbajal, appearing in the kitchen doorway, answered that one. "Maybe he tried to, but whoever did this turned on both the swamp cooler and the television. On the TV they turned the volume as loud as it would go. The two of them made enough racket that even if Dan had called for help, the neighbors wouldn't have heard him. And from the amount of blood loss, he was probably unconscious within a matter of minutes."

"What a cold-blooded bastard!" Joanna exclaimed.

Jaime nodded. "I'll say," he agreed.

It surprised Joanna to realize that she felt no grief right then, only a cold and determined fury.

"Did you find a weapon?"

"His reserve Glock is still in his ankle holster," Jaime said. "He never had a chance to draw it. His service pistol is still missing."

There was a muffled gasp from the kitchen doorway. Joanna looked up to see Deb Howell standing there with one hand clasped to her mouth attempting to muffle a sob.

"It's my fault," Deb managed. "I should never have left Dan here on his own. I should have—" Unable to continue, she broke off. Jaime moved as if to comfort her, but Joanna beat him to it. Reaching up, she lay a consoling hand on her grieving detective's shoulder. "It's not your fault," she countered.

Even though Joanna meant the words—for Deb if not for herself—they still rang hollow.

"But it is," Deb responded. "I should have remembered how new he was and how little experience—"

"Dan Sloan was a trained police officer," Joanna interrupted. "He knew he was on the lookout for a homicide suspect, didn't he?"

Deb nodded. "Yes," she said. "I told him."

"In other words, he knew that if the guy showed up, he could be dangerous. It isn't your fault that Deputy Sloan went in without calling for backup, Deb. He did that on his own."

"But—"

"But nothing," Joanna said firmly. "He knew better but he did it anyway. That's why they call failure to call for backup 'tombstone courage'—because officers who do it can die."

She turned to Jaime. "And it's not your fault, either," she told him. "Understand? Dan wanted this job. He signed on to do it. And if we stand around blaming ourselves, who's going to be left to go after Dan's killer?"

Leadership 101, Joanna thought. *Buck up the troops.*

"So come on," she added. "Let's leave Doc Winfield and Casey to finish up here while the rest of us go do our jobs."

They went back outside and time passed. Joanna wasn't sure how much. It could have been minutes—or hours. Dave Hollicker had set up a pair of enormous highway construction lights next to the spot where Detective Sloan's patrol car was still parked. On his hands and knees, he was doing a painstaking nighttime search of the surrounding area in hopes of locating any bit of trace evidence that didn't quite fit.

Sometime during the wait, Joanna's phone rang. "Dennis woke me up. Are you all right?"

"Yes."

"Can you talk?"

When it came time to discuss the night's appalling events with Butch, Joanna wanted to be far away from anyone else's prying eyes and ears. But right now, in order to be an effective leader, she had to hold it together, exhibiting strength instead of weakness.

"Not right now," she said.

"I love you."

"Thank you."

A few minutes later, Marianne Maculyea called as well. "I wasn't on the list for tonight, but someone called me anyway. Do you want me to come there?" she asked.

Of course I want you to come here, Joanna thought. *But at the first sign of sympathy I'm going to fall apart. Then I'll be useless.*

"No," she said. "We're working. The scene's still pretty chaotic. You'd just be in the way."

As the sky gradually lightened in the east, Joanna was still huddled with Jaime in his van, where he was trying to keep tabs on the APB. Without warning, George Winfield hustled out through the Beasleys' screened front porch, down the center walkway, and out through the gate. The ME got in his Dodge Caravan and immediately started the engine. He seemed to be leaving.

Joanna hopped out of Jaime's vehicle and hurried over to George's. She tapped frantically on the Caravan's window just as George put it in gear.

"Wait a minute," Joanna said when he rolled down the window. "Where are you going? What are you doing?"

"If you'll get out of my way," George said, "I'm going to move my van."

"But why?" she asked. "I thought we were gearing up for you to do the transport."

"I am gearing up to do the transport," George said. "Have you looked out at the street lately?"

Joanna hadn't, but now she did—she turned and looked. To her amazement, on both sides of the street behind her stood two unbroken lines of officers, some in uniform, some not. The lines stretched from the house next door to the Beasleys' and from the one across the street down the hill and all the way around the next curve, where they finally disappeared from sight. The officers close enough for Joanna to see were standing at ease. They had assembled throughout the night in solemn silence. Speaking in hushed tones, they had organized themselves at a distance that was far enough away from the crime scene so as not to interfere. Now, in the welcome cool before dawn, they simply stood and waited.

"Who are they?" Joanna wanted to know. "Where did these people come from?"

"I have no idea," George answered, "but those guys didn't come here to watch my van drive down the street. They came to pay their respects to a fellow fallen officer, and we're going to let them do it."

George pulled out of the parking place, made a sharp U-turn and then drove down the street until the van vanished from sight. While Joanna waited for George to return, she caught the occasional flash of a camera. People gathered on the sidewalks were taking pictures. Whether the photographers were professionals or not, no doubt the resulting pictures would make their way into the media. The world wasn't going to allow the Cochise County Sheriff's Department to grieve for Deputy Sloan in private. Everything they did or said would be on full public display. It was important to get it right.

George Winfield understood that completely. "Showtime," he said when he reappeared after hiking back up the street. "Who's going to do the honors?"

"You lead the way," Joanna said. "The three of us—Jaime, Frank, and I—will handle the gurney."

"It's a steep grade," George cautioned. "We'll put Jaime in front and use him for braking. Joanna, you steer. Frank, you walk alongside, and be prepared to grab for it if it starts to get away."

They followed George around the side of the house to the back, where a wheeled gurney, already loaded with the zipped body bag, waited just outside the door. With Jaime pulling and Joanna pushing, they moved the gurney around the house. They pushed it through the front gate, with Dave Hollicker and Casey Ledford standing at attention on either side. Someone shouted a command. Down the line the assembled cops came to attention, standing ramrod-straight with their hands covering their hearts or else raised to their foreheads in a somber salute. And on their badges—the badges Joanna could see—each of them wore a thin black band.

Seeing those made Joanna swallow hard. She looked away quickly, pretending that she had to pay attention to the gurney as they guided it along the sidewalk, down the driveway curb cut, and then out into the street—the middle of the street—devoid now of all traffic.

Only a few days earlier, this very same stretch of Tombstone Canyon had been lined with throngs of cheering spectators assembled to watch Bisbee's annual Fourth of July coaster races. This morning, with the sky just starting to turn to lavender, there were probably several hundred people in attendance, but the street was deathly quiet. There wasn't a sound. Not one.

As they started downhill, Joanna glanced from side to side, trying to tell who all was here. She was able to pick out officers she knew from police and fire personnel agencies all over southern

Arizona—from Sierra Vista and Benson, Bisbee and Douglas, Willcox and Fort Huachuca—along with countless officers she didn't know. All of them had answered Tica's call. They had come out in the middle of the night and waited patiently until dawn to fulfill their sacred duty.

All night long, Joanna had refused to shed a single tear. Afraid of showing any sign of weakness, she had kept herself focused on what had to be done. Now, though, seeing those assembled men and women, her long-delayed tears could no longer be held in check. Unbidden, they spilled out of her eyes and coursed down her cheeks.

Joanna Brady had plenty of reason to cry. Some of the tears were tears of grief over the terrible tragedy of losing a promising young officer. But there were also tears of gratitude because so many wonderful people had shown up during the night to help Joanna and her department bear their awful burden.

George Winfield proved to be completely right about the steepness of the grade. Once they moved off the sidewalk and onto the pavement, gravity exerted its full force on the body-laden gurney. It took all of Jaime's and Joanna's strength—both of them gripping the handles with both hands—to keep Dan Sloan's body from getting away from them and careening downhill like one last ghostly coaster racer.

But keeping both hands on the gurney meant there was no hand left for Joanna to use for anything else, including grabbing a tissue to wipe away her tears. She caught Frank Montoya looking at her questioningly, as if asking if she wanted his help, but she shook her head and told him no. This was her job. She was determined to see it through.

As cameras flashed, Joanna also knew full well what would

be on television and on the front pages of any number of newspapers at the very first opportunity—photos of the sheriff of Cochise County crying her eyes out.

Too bad! Joanna thought fiercely. *What did they expect? That's what they get for electing a woman.*

CHAPTER 17

WHEN THE GURNEY WAS FINALLY LOADED INTO THE M.E.'S VAN, Jaime walked off and stood by himself for a few minutes, his shoulders heaving. Joanna turned to find Frank with his face damp with tears as well. Once again he offered her the use of his handkerchief. This time she gratefully accepted. She was using it to mop her face when the phone in her pocket sprang to life.

"It's Fred," her caller announced. "Fred Coyle, Sunny's dad. She wanted me to let you know that we've called the people we need to call."

"So we can release Dan's name to the media?"

"Yes, but Sunny wants to know if you've caught the guy yet."

"No," Joanna said. "Not yet. Tell her we're working on it." She ended the call and returned Frank's soppy hanky. "We can release Dan's name," she said.

"Good," Frank said. "We should let Chief Bernard know he's good to go for the ID press conference. It's a good thing, too. I've already had one call about an article the *Bisbee Bee* is set to publish first thing this morning. Since they're going with Dan's name, we need to bring everyone else up to speed. If one outlet gets way ahead of everyone else . . ."

Tired as she was, Joanna felt her adrenaline kick back in. "Let me guess," she said. "The one going off half-cocked would be Marliss Shackleford?"

"None other," Frank replied.

Without another word, Joanna picked up her phone and dialed Chief Bernard. He answered on the second ring. "Any news?"

"We haven't caught Larry Wolfe, if that's what you mean," Joanna said. "But we've got a brewing media situation."

"Marliss?" Chief Bernard asked.

Joanna had always thought of Marliss Shackleford as her own personal cross to bear. Obviously the woman was a continuing problem for Alvin Bernard, too.

"Exactly," Joanna said. "We just received permission to release Dan's name. We need to get it out there to everyone else as soon as possible."

"That won't be a problem," Chief Bernard replied with a mirthless chuckle. "You should see my parking lot. It's swarming with reporters. The press conference is here, but you're the one who should make the official announcement."

Joanna knew he was right. "I'll be there in ten minutes, so we can get started."

She closed her phone.

"If there are going to be cameras, you might want to take a

look in the mirror," Frank suggested diplomatically. "And you're going to need one of these." He handed her a black band for her badge. He was already wearing his. She put hers on and patted it into place.

"Thanks," she said. "I don't know what I'd do without you."

Once inside her vehicle, Joanna pulled down the visor, opened the mirror, and did what she could to fix her face. Frank was right. She looked awful. She hadn't put on any makeup when she left the house. That turned out to have been a good thing because it would have been washed away. She had a compact and some lipstick and a hairbrush in her purse, but that was about it. She ran the brush through her hair, dabbed at her nose with the powder, and then slapped on the lipstick.

It's a press conference, not a beauty pageant, she told herself.

"Sheriff Brady?" Tica's voice came over the radio before Joanna made it out of Old Bisbee.

"Yes."

"I have Sheriff Barnes on the line. He needs to talk to you."

Joanna was well acquainted with her fellow sheriffs in Arizona. The name Barnes didn't ring a bell. "Who's he?" she asked.

"Sheriff Ralph Barnes," Tica replied. "Of Hudspeth County, Texas. I think you're going to want to talk to him."

"Patch him through."

"Morning, Sheriff Brady," Ralph Barnes said in what Joanna recognized as a west Texas drawl. "So sorry for your loss. Hurts like hell to lose one of your guys, but I think I've got some good news on that APB you put out."

Joanna's heart leaped to her throat. "You caught him?"

"Not exactly," Barnes returned. "Let's just say, whoever was driving that '99 Lexus won't be bothering anybody ever again. He came through the Border Patrol checkpoint at Sierra Blanca about forty-five minutes ago. When they tried to wave him over, he took off like a shot. Border Patrol called us, and one of my deputies gave chase at speeds up to a hundred miles an hour. In the rain. Fifteen miles east of Sierra Blanca he hydroplaned. He went airborne, slammed into a bridge abutment, and then went end over end. The driver was alone in the vehicle, and he was ejected. Must not have been wearing a seat belt. My deputies were right behind him, but it still took 'em ten minutes to locate the body. Turns out the car landed right on top of the sucker—smashed him flat."

"So Larry Wolfe is dead, then?" Joanna asked.

"Somebody's dead," Barnes returned. "As a damned doornail. That's the name on his license, by the way—Lawrence Alan Wolfe—but it's gonna take more than eyeballing what's left of the guy to figure out for sure who he is. You happen to have any fingerprints or dental records on this yahoo? If you do, have 'em sent to Dr. Ken Dohan, the Hudspeth County M.E. There's nothing I'd like better than to know we've got your man."

"Me, too," Joanna said, "but I'm driving right now and can't write down anything. Tica," she added. "Are you still on the line?"

"Yes, I'm here."

"Please patch Sheriff Barnes through to Chief Deputy Montoya so Frank can get all the specifics. Then I'll need to talk to Detective Carbajal. Sheriff Barnes, before you go. Did you happen to find a weapon—a Glock? We think Deputy Sloan was killed with his own weapon."

"No, ma'am. We haven't found anything like that yet, but I'll let you know if we do," he said. "The sun's up now. We'll be searching every damned inch of the debris field, but it's pretty extensive. Once we do ID him, what about next of kin?" Barnes added. "According to the amended APB, he's suspected in the deaths of his in-laws and he may have tried to take out his wife as well. Should we notify her about what's happened?"

"Sandra Wolfe was taken away by ambulance earlier this evening," Joanna said. "She's in no condition to be notified about anything. Once she is, though, we'll handle that."

"Anyone else, then?" Sheriff Barnes asked.

"Larry Wolfe's parents are both dead. His brother lives in Saint Louis." Joanna had to think for a few seconds before she was able to dredge up the brother's name. "I'm pretty sure the brother's name is Mark. I don't have a middle initial or an address."

"We'll be able to sort that out," Barnes said.

"From what I understand, the brothers have been estranged for some time."

"No matter," Barnes said. "Next of kin is next of kin. We'll be responsible for finding Mr. Wolfe and notifying him. It sounds like you and your people have your hands full."

"Thank you," Joanna said. "And, Sheriff Barnes . . ." she began.

"Yes, ma'am?"

Joanna had to swallow hard before continuing. "Thank you so much for all your help," she said. "You have no idea what this means to me."

"Oh, yes, I do," Sheriff Barnes replied. "All too well. Lost my K-9 officer and his dog to an escaped convict two years ago. Shot 'em down in cold blood before Deputy Franklin ever got his gun out of his holster. I cried like a baby when they caught that worthless son of a bitch. He's on death row in Huntsville right now. I'm planning on being there in person on the day they put him down."

"I'm on my way to a press conference, so I'm going to have to put you through to my chief deputy. Frank Montoya will take down all the pertinent information."

"I heard," Barnes said. "But in the meantime, you take care of yourself, you hear?"

"Yes," Joanna said. "Yes, I will." Seconds later, she was on the horn to Jaime Carbajal. "Did you hear any of that?"

"Yes. It's great news!" Although, from Jaime's voice, it didn't sound as though he thought it was all that great.

"I want you to be the one to tell Sunny we think we've caught him. In fact, I'd like you to do it as soon as you get off the phone with me."

"All right," Jaime said. "I'll give her a call."

Joanna knew that the longer he waited to face that particular demon, the worse it would be. "No," Joanna said. "Not over the phone. You need to go there yourself, Jaime. Give her the news in person. Be there for her."

Jaime said nothing, so Joanna changed the subject.

"What's happening with Sandy Wolfe?"

"She's completely out of it—worse even than when we saw her. One of the EMTs told me her blood pressure was off the charts. When the ER docs at the Copper Queen Hospital found out it was most likely a ketamine overdose, they made arrangements to airlift her to Tucson Medical Center. They're afraid she'll go into full respiratory failure."

"In other words, not much chance of talking to her anytime soon."

"Talking to her about . . . ?"

"According to Sheriff Barnes, we're going to need dental records for a positive ID on the guy driving the Lexus, but as long as Sandy's non compos mentis, we're not going to be able to ask her."

Joanna drove for a few moments before speaking again. "Tell you what," she added. "Once we know Sheriff Barnes has notified Larry's brother in Saint Louis, we should check with him. He may not know Larry's most recent dentist, but he may know of one from years ago. Old records would be better than no records. And if Casey found any fingerprints tonight, ask her to rush whatever she has into AFIS. I doubt Larry's prints will be on file, but if he's our guy, we should be able to match prints from our scene with prints from the dead guy in Texas."

As Joanna signed off, she was pulling into the Bisbee Police Department parking lot. Chief Bernard had mentioned that the place was crawling with reporters, and that was absolutely true. They came running toward her car, surrounding it in a milling throng as soon as she turned in from the street. Once she was out of the car, the reporters followed her toward the building, shouting questions. She was grateful when an officer wearing a Bisbee PD uniform opened a side door and ushered her inside and down the hall to where Chief Bernard waited in his office. He rose to greet her.

"Sorry to say we don't have a room big enough to do this inside, so we've set up to do it out front."

"Wherever," Joanna said. "Let's just do it. I want this over and done with."

Frank Montoya usually handled media interaction for Joanna's department for the very good reason that Joanna had virtually zero tolerance for the task. The most difficult part for her was announcing Deputy Sloan's name. She had steeled herself to stifle her emotions when she did so, but that was easier in the planning than it was in the delivery. After that, she gave a brief overview: Both Samantha Edwards and Sandra Wolfe had been hospitalized for undisclosed medical reasons. A man who was a person of interest in that case who had fled the area was presumed to be the victim of a car crash that had occurred on I-10 in west Texas. No, his name could not yet be released.

Once she had finished reciting the information that could be discussed, Joanna had to ward off dozens of questions, rephrased several different ways, asking for details that could not be released. That was the part Frank Montoya excelled at—deflecting those questions with easy good grace. Joanna had to battle to keep her temper under control and to keep from saying what she really meant, as in, "What part of N-O don't you understand?"

She was within moments of losing it completely when she was saved by the ringing of her telephone. Pulling the blaring phone from her pocket, she glanced at the screen and saw a number she didn't recognize. *Probably another reporter,* she thought, exasperated. Even so, she was glad for even the slimmest of excuses to abandon the bank of microphones and leave the reporters along with their ongoing barrage of questions to Chief Alvin Bernard.

Joanna melted through the door and went back into the building, answering the call as she went.

"Is this Sheriff Brady?" a male voice asked.

"Yes," she replied. "Who's this, and how did you get this number?"

"From Sheriff Barnes in Texas. I'm Mark Wolfe, Larry's brother."

"I'm so sorry for your loss—" Joanna began.

"Never mind all that," Mark interrupted. "I just need to know if what Sheriff Barnes told me is true."

"That your brother's dead? We're trying to confirm that, but—"

"Not that," he said impatiently. "I want to know about the rest of it—about Larry shooting a cop and possibly poisoning his father-in-law and attempting to poison his wife and her sister as well."

The man sounded upset. If he was convinced of his brother's innocence, Joanna didn't want to antagonize him further.

"We don't know any of that for sure," Joanna said. Wary of his fury, she tried to soft-pedal the bad news. "So far it's all conjecture. My investigators are still working the crime scene. It's still far too early to be able to say anything definitive. The fact that your brother fled the state immediately after the shooting leads us to believe—"

But Mark Wolfe wasn't easily deflected. "What about the poisonings?" he asked determinedly.

"The alleged poisonings," Joanna corrected, trying to deescalate the situation. "We don't know any of that for sure, either. An empty vial that we believe had once contained ketamine was found in his wife's hotel room. We'll be doing forensics analysis of any residue in that, as well as of any number of substances taken from Mr. and Mrs. Beasley's—the in-laws'—home here in Bisbee. We'll also be conducting toxicology screenings on all possible victims. Once we do that, we'll have a better idea of what really happened."

"I already know what happened," Mark Wolfe said bitterly. "Larry did it."

That wasn't what Joanna expected to hear. "Wait a minute," she said. "You think he's guilty?"

"Absolutely," Mark returned. "Guilty as sin. Why wouldn't he be? He got away with murder at least once before. Why wouldn't he try it again?"

"What do you mean, he got away with it?" Joanna asked. "What are you talking about?"

"My parents," Mark Wolfe replied. "The hospital listed my mother's death as heart failure. That may or may not be true, but I'm almost sure Larry helped my father along. He was there with Dad at the time he died. The M.E. in Tampa listed cause of death as an accidental overdose due to a combination of alcohol and an over-the-counter sleeping aid. I know my father, though. Dad never would have done such a thing—not intentionally, and not by accident, either."

"You weren't there at the time it happened?"

"No. There had been some bad blood between Larry and my parents—a dispute that had gone on for years. Although my father never disinherited Larry, they didn't speak for a long time. Then, when my mother ended up in the hospital that last time, Larry came riding home, and both my parents welcomed him with open arms. The whole prodigal-son bit just pissed the hell out of me. After Mom's funeral in Kansas City, I came back to Saint Louis. Larry took Dad back to Florida. The next thing I knew, he was dead. Larry didn't bother contacting me until after he'd had Dad cremated. When I finally heard about it, I went to Tampa and raised hell. I tried to convince the local authorities to open an investigation, but they wouldn't. They told me lots of old people come to Florida to die. I even tried talking to the local prosecutor. He declined to press charges."

Mark stopped for a moment. "Now, though," he said when he resumed speaking, "if what Sheriff Barnes told me is true, several more people are dead or in the hospital. What happened to them is all my fault."

Joanna Brady, who was currently dealing with her own self-recrimination issues, couldn't quite connect the dots. "You can't possibly hold yourself responsible for what a prosecutor did or didn't do."

"It's what I did," Mark Wolfe said. "I hired a private eye and did some checking around. I found out my brother was in a financial bind. He needed his inheritance sooner rather than later, but since I'm the executor, I've been stalling—because I could. Because I wanted to stick it to him; because I wanted to rub his nose in it. I knew how desperate Larry was—how badly he needed the money. I, more than anyone else, understood exactly what he was capable of. Now, because of me—"

Mark's voice broke and he couldn't go on. Joanna waited patiently on the phone, giving the man a chance to pull himself back together.

"So tell me about his wife," he said. "Sandy. She's his second wife. Although they've been married for years, I've never met the woman. Is she going to be all right?"

"I don't know," Joanna answered honestly. "She received a massive overdose of ketamine. She's been airlifted to a hospital in Tucson."

"And her sister?"

"We think Samantha Edwards received a somewhat smaller dose. She's hospitalized right now, too, but she's probably going to be all right."

"Thank God," Mark said. "Do you have my number?"

"No," Joanna said. "And I can't take it down right now. If you'd call my office—"

"Of course," Mark said. "Please ask Sandy and her sister to be in touch with me when they can. I'll do whatever I can to help. And Sheriff Brady, I'm so very sorry about your deputy."

"I know," Joanna said. "I am, too. And I'm sure that my investigators are going to need to talk to you as well."

"As I said, I'll do whatever I can."

"Did your brother have a dentist?" Joanna asked quickly.

"A dentist?" Mark Wolfe repeated. "I wouldn't know about that. We've been out of touch for years."

"Not a current dentist," Joanna said. "An old one. One he might have gone to when he was a kid."

"Dr. Randall," Mark Wolfe answered at once. "Kansas City, Missouri. We went to Doc Randall until we both graduated from college."

"Is he still in business?" Joanna asked.

"Old Doc Randall has been dead for years," Mark replied. "I believe his granddaughter is running the practice now. Do you want the number? I don't have it right now, but I'm sure I can get it."

"Good," Joanna said. "Someone from my department will be in touch."

Joanna closed her phone and then slipped out the side entrance, intent on getting back to her office, where she knew a huge tangle of officer-involved-in-shooting paperwork would be waiting. Joanna was dismayed to find Marliss Shackleford leaning against the front bumper of her Crown Vic.

"Any comment on Deputy Sloan's death now?" Marliss asked, notebook at the ready.

Joanna stared at the woman, wanting nothing more than to rip into the reporter and give her a piece of her mind. But then Joanna thought about Dan Sloan and about Sunny. This wasn't the time to allow herself to be suckered into some kind of petty grudge match.

"Deputy Dan Sloan's death is a terrible tragedy," Joanna said with as much dignity as she could muster. "He will be missed."

With that, she got in the car, closed the door, and drove away. When Joanna reached the Justice Center she discovered that not all the media crews had stayed focused on the scheduled press conference at Bisbee PD. There were plenty of reporters milling around in her parking lot as well. She was glad to be able to park out back and duck into her office unnoticed.

It was only a little past seven when she got there, but she was surprised to find Kristin, black band on her wrist, already at her desk and fielding phone calls.

As soon as she put her purse down, Joanna called home. Jenny answered. "I heard, Mom," Jenny said. "Are you all right?"

"I'm okay," she said. "I'm back at the office now. I don't know how long I'll be here."

"Here's Butch," Jenny said.

"Hi, Joey," he said. "Sounds like you had a pretty bad night."

It hadn't been the worst night of Joanna's life. That would have been the night Andy was shot, but it was certainly the worst night of her career.

"Yes," she murmured. "Yes, it was."

"You're at the office?"

"Yes."

"Come home when you can. You can't go without sleep forever."

"Thank you," she said. "I know."

As the call to Butch ended, Kristin came into Joanna's office and dropped a stack of message slips onto the desk. "Terry was coming in early this morning, and I did, too. I thought you'd need me, and I was right. The phone's been ringing off the hook, everyone's calling because . . ." Kristin stopped speaking. Her eyes filled with tears.

Joanna remembered seeing Terry Gregovich and his eighty-five-pound German shepherd, Spike, standing at attention with a group of fellow Cochise County officers as she had followed Dan Sloan's gurney down Tombstone Canyon.

"Thank you for coming in, Kristin," Joanna said. "It was a bad night and it's going to be a worse day." She picked up the stack of messages and shuffled through them. There were calls she would have to return, but right that moment, she wasn't ready. She looked up Mark Wolfe's number on her incoming-call list, jotted it down, and passed it over to Kristin. "This is Larry Wolfe's brother's number. His name is Mark. Give him a call a little later. He'll give you the number of a dentist's office where we may be able to get Larry Wolfe's dental records. Once you have the number, hand it off to Ernie or Deb. They'll know what to do."

Nodding, Kristin took the note. "Would you like something to eat?" she asked. "According to the front office, people have been coming by all night long, bringing food. The break room is full of casseroles."

The way Joanna felt right then, she didn't want any food, but she knew she needed it. "That's probably a good idea," she said.

Pushing her tired and achingly stiff body away from her desk, Joanna rose and followed Kristin down the hall to the break room. "Have a seat," Kristin said, then brought Joanna a cup of freshly brewed coffee. "And let me get you a plate. We have biscuits, tamales, three different kinds of quiche, tamale pie, and green chili casserole. Butch brought that. He dropped it off just after I got here."

Following Kristin's orders, Joanna sank gratefully onto one of the hard plastic chairs. Her secretary bustled around the room, filling a plate, putting it in the microwave, gathering plastic silverware. While she was doing that, Joanna stared up at the photo on the wall over her head. The blonde was still there, staring back.

Please, Joanna found herself praying silently, *please don't let there be any surprises like this for Sunny Sloan.*

Kristin set the steaming plate in front of Joanna. There were two tamales, one red and one green, some of Butch's casserole, and a chunk of quiche that looked like it was probably from Costco.

"Are you sure you shouldn't go home for a while?" Kristin asked. "I mean, you look—"

"Awful?" Joanna finished for her.

Embarrassed, Kristin ducked her head and nodded.

"No," Joanna said, using a plastic fork to cut into the red tamale. "I have to be here. As soon as I finish eating, I need to talk to Jaime, but I'm curious about something. That blonde there in the picture, the one at the end of the front row. I can't quite place her. Who is she?"

Kristin went over to the picture and squinted up at it. "Oh, her," she said. "What was her name again? Sue . . . Suzy . . . No, Suzanne. That's it. I remember now. Suzanne Quayle. She was working here as a dispatcher, but she quit right after all that bad stuff happened with Sheriff McFadden. I think she moved to Tucson not long after that and hired on as a 911 operator up there. I'm pretty sure I heard she has a little boy. He must be five or six by now. Why?"

A little boy? Joanna thought as her stomach clenched into a hard ball. It was all she could do to keep that first bite of tamale where it belonged. *Andy had a little boy? Was that possible?*

Suddenly Joanna was in an emotional free fall. Andy had been dead for years, but the hurt of this potential betrayal was astonishingly present. Her heart pounded in her chest. She thought she was going to hyperventilate.

Was it possible that everyone in town had known Suzanne Quayle was pregnant when she left town? Did that mean everyone also knew who the father was? Everyone, that is, except Andrew Roy Brady's wife!

"Are you all right?" Kristin asked, concern in her voice and on her face.

Joanna shrugged and tried to act as though she wasn't overly interested. "It's just that I know most of the rest of the people in that photo," she said as offhandedly as she could manage. "She's somebody I didn't recognize."

"That's because she quit the department long before you got here," Kristin said.

Yes, Joanna thought. *For good reason, and I'm pretty sure I can figure out what that reason was.*

As two of the front-office clerks came into the break room, Joanna pushed her plate aside. "Thanks, Kristin," she said, "but I'm afraid I can't eat anything right now."

CHAPTER 18

JOANNA STAGGERED BACK TO HER OFFICE, WHERE SHE NO LONGER had time to agonize over personal considerations. There was too much to do. Just after eight, her people turned up for a hurriedly assembled morning briefing. Everyone had been out working most of the night. The men were unshaven. Deb's makeup was a shambles; her long hair was a tangled mess. Without checking a mirror, Joanna knew she was in a similarly bedraggled condition. They gathered around the table in their rumpled clothing, swilling coffee and looking shell-shocked and weary.

Of all of them, Jaime Carbajal was in by far the worst shape. The death of Deputy Sloan, Jaime's protégé, had left the detective devastated and angry. Drumming his fingers impatiently on the table and looking ready to explode, he listened along with everyone else while Joanna brought them up-to-date on what she had learned from Mark Wolfe.

"I'm sure Larry's brother is right," Ernie observed when she finished. "If the guy got away with it once, he figured he'd be able to do so again. It's a good thing he's dead, though. For sure he was never going to be brought to trial over what happened to his father, and I doubt we would have been able to make charges stick with Alfred and Martha Beasley, either. So our only shot at him would have been—"

With a glance at Jaime's thunderous face, Ernie wisely chose to shut up.

Yes, Joanna thought. *Our only shot at convicting him would have been for killing Dan Sloan, and we probably wouldn't have been able to prove premeditation.*

"Where are we on crime scene investigation?" Joanna asked.

"We've had Larry Wolfe's pickup towed to our impound yard," Dave Hollicker told her. "We've found what looks like blood smear on the steering wheel and tiny shards of glass in the driver's foot well. It's going to take time to sort it all out."

Joanna nodded and turned to Deb. "What about the food from the Beasleys' refrigerator?" she asked. "What's happening with that?"

"I've called the DPS Crime Lab in Tucson and let them know I'll be bringing it to them today," Deb Howell replied. "They'll test everything, but I'm betting the most likely culprit will turn out to be Alfred's chocolate syrup. I've already called that company in Montreal, Tante Marie's Toppings. I've ordered another jar of the same stuff to be FedExed directly to the crime lab. They'll need that for comparison.

"And I've been reading up on ketamine. Long-term use can

lead to short-term memory loss and mental confusion. The same kind of symptoms we've been told Alfred Beasley was exhibiting."

"The same kind of symptoms as the poor man's worst nightmare," Joanna said. "No wonder he thought he was coming down with Alzheimer's. What happens with a massive dose?"

"Everything from psychotic episodes to complete respiratory failure."

"Do we have any idea where the drug came from?" Joanna asked.

Dave Hollicker was the one who answered. "I'm checking with the manufacturer on the vial we found in the hotel bathroom," he said. "They're looking into tracking the serial number. It's possible Larry just hopped the prescription bus, rode down to Nogales, and bought it over the counter."

Just then Casey Ledford let herself into the room and closed the door. She looked as tired as the rest of the people in the room, but she was smiling when no one else was.

"Do you have something for us?" Joanna asked.

Casey nodded. "I managed to get only one decent print from the bloody ones we found on the scene last night. I've sent that off to the M.E. in Texas."

"Good work," Joanna said as her team members nodded in somber agreement.

"But that's not all," Casey added. "There's something more."

"What?"

"Late last night I finally found one usable partial on the duct tape from Wanda Mappin's plastic bags," she said. "I was in the process of enhancing it when all hell broke loose last night. I finished it just now. As soon as I put the print into AFIS, it came back with a hit."

"Whose is it?" Joanna asked.

"His name's Carmichael," Casey said. "Billy Carmichael. He's currently being held in the Pima County Jail, where he's doing six months for breaking and entering."

Any other time having an AFIS hit in an unsolved homicide would have been cause for celebration and high fives all around.

Not today, Joanna thought.

"Excellent," she said. "But what's Carmichael's connection to Wanda?"

"No way to tell from this," Casey said. She stood up and distributed a set of papers that contained Billy Carmichael's rap sheet. "You can see he's been in and out of trouble for a long time—drug possession charges, petty theft, and possession of stolen goods. Most of the time he's gotten away with slaps on the wrist. This is his first stint of doing any real jail time."

"Want me to go have a talk with him?" Jaime offered.

Wanda Mappin's case had been Jaime's originally. Ordinarily doing follow-up interviews would have fallen to him automatically, but Joanna thought the intensity with which Jaime asked the question made it sound like he'd just as soon beat the crap out of anyone who got in his way. Joanna was surprised Jaime had shown up for the briefing and doubted if he should be on duty. In his current condition, turning him loose to interrogate a suspect was completely out of the question.

"No," Joanna told him. "Deb's on her way to Tucson to take the food to the crime lab. She can stop off at the Pima County Jail and handle the preliminary interview with Carmichael. You've got plenty to do around here."

"What?" Jaime demanded. "We already know Larry Wolfe is

dead. Surely you don't expect me to sit around doing stupid paperwork that nobody's going to worry about—"

"I said Deb will handle it," Joanna said firmly.

Jaime was pissed but he stifled his anger. "Whatever you say," he muttered.

"Anything else?" Joanna asked.

Frank raised his hand. "I've had a call from Samantha Edwards. She expects to be released from the county hospital later on this morning after her doctor does rounds. She says she's okay. Once she gets out, she'll need transportation back to her vehicle so she can drive up to Tucson. I gave her an overview of what happened last night and let her know that Sandra is in TMC."

"She knows Larry is dead?" Joanna asked.

Frank nodded. "I told her. She said she'd tell Sandra about it. Samantha is also calling the mortuary to put the Beasleys' memorial service on hold until Sandra gets back on her feet."

"Where's Samantha's car?" Joanna asked.

"Where she left it yesterday morning," Frank said. "Still parked outside her parents' house up Tombstone Canyon."

"Can you take care of having someone pick her up?" Joanna asked.

Frank nodded. "Will do."

A few minutes later, with the rest of the agenda items cleared, everyone stood to go, but Joanna beat Jaime to the door and kept him from leaving.

"What?" he asked sarcastically. "Shouldn't I be getting started on all that life-and-death paperwork?"

"How are you doing, Jaime?" Joanna asked. "How are you doing really?"

Grimacing, he didn't meet her gaze. "Not so hot, I guess," he admitted ruefully.

"You saw Sunny?"

"Yes," he answered. "I saw her, and it hurt like hell. She was glad to know the guy who most likely did it was dead, but I don't see why I had to be the one . . ."

"It's going to hurt like hell for a very long time," Joanna interrupted. "It's going to hurt you and it's going to hurt Sunny, but I want you to handle that end of it for us, Jaime. I want you to be the official liaison between our department and Deputy Sloan's family."

"But—"

"This isn't optional," Joanna said. "It's an order. I'm guessing you were closer to Danny than anyone else in the department. That means you're also closer to Sunny. I need you to help us coordinate whatever funeral arrangements she needs to make, so we can help out by doing whatever she wants us to do. Afterward, I want you to stay in touch with her. If she needs help filling out claim forms or filing for Social Security or whatever, I want you in on it. Danny was one of our own. That means Sunny is, too. Understood?"

"Yes," Jaime said. "I see what you mean." He reached for the door handle, but Joanna stopped him.

"How's Luis?" she asked.

"Okay, I guess," Jaime said with a shrug. "He's at the house with Delcia and Pepe."

"Has he heard from his mom?"

"Not a word."

"Keep me posted on that, too," Joanna said.

Jaime nodded. "Anything else?"

"Yes," Joanna said. "Before the day is out, you're to go see Father Rowan; not for Sunny—for you."

He nodded again. "All right, boss," he said softly. "I will."

This time when he reached for the door handle, Joanna let him go. She returned to her office and tried to get a start returning phone calls—not only the ones that had come in earlier but also the additional stack that had come in while she was off in the break room and conducting the briefing. The most interesting call was from Detective Rebecca Ramsey of Tucson PD. Joanna returned that one first.

"So sorry to hear about your deputy," Becky said, once Joanna had identified herself. Dan Sloan's death was right at the top of that day's news cycle, and Joanna knew some variation of that theme would be the beginning of every telephone conversation for days to come.

"Thank you," Joanna said. "It's pretty tough times around here at the moment. Do you have anything for me?"

"I went to pay a call on your friend Donald Dietrich at Flannigan Foundation," Becky said with a laugh. "You must have made quite an impression on the man. He wasn't thrilled to see me to begin with, and when I mentioned your name, my chilly reception turned downright frigid."

"Not surprised," Joanna said, because she wasn't.

"So I told him I'd been assigned to follow up on a missing person who had disappeared from one of his facilities. When I told him I needed Wayne Leroy Hamm's dental records to put into our missing persons database, he went into a whole song and dance about how he couldn't possibly give them to me due to client confidentiality concerns. When I threatened to go public with his deliberately stalling the search for one of his missing clients, he folded. He says he'll make the dental records available as soon as he can locate them."

Folded, Joanna thought, wondering if it was possible Detective Ramsey played poker, as did Joanna. An all-girl, all law-enforcement poker game might be fun sometime, but she let that idea pass.

"As soon as he can locate them?" Joanna asked. "I suppose that means sometime in the far distant future."

"No," Becky said. "I gave him twenty-four hours to produce them or I go to the media. Flannigan has a reputation to protect in this town. I don't think Dietrich'll risk having his money-raising capability damaged."

Definitely a poker player, Joanna thought.

"I'll let you know if anything comes of it," Becky continued.

Joanna stayed on in the office until almost one, but by then she could no longer hold her head up. "I'm going home for a nap," she told Kristin on her way out. "If you need me, call."

Once at the house, she stripped off her clothes and fell into bed. Then she surprised herself by falling into a deep sleep. Hours later, a loud clap of thunder brought her wide awake. If the noise hadn't awakened her, Lady would have. Joanna's spooky little Australian shepherd was terrified of thunderstorms. She vaulted onto the bed and then burrowed, shivering, under the covers to cuddle up next to Joanna. For the next few minutes, while the worst of the storm blew over, Joanna lay there comforting the frightened dog as rain pelted down outside. Finally, with the thunder receding, Joanna booted Lady out of the bed and got up herself.

Wrapping her robe around her, she went out to the kitchen, drawn there by the sound of voices and the smell of burned bread. There she found Butch at the table plugging a ravenous Dennis full of rice cereal while Jenny, spatula in hand, presided over the stove. On the counter next to the stove top was a platter containing several grilled cheese sandwiches, some of them more than slightly charred.

"Butch is teaching me to cook," Jenny said happily when her mother appeared in the doorway. "I let the pans get a little too hot."

"They'll be fine," Butch assured her. "Cooking takes practice." He turned to Joanna. "How are things?" When Joanna had come home earlier, she had been too tired to talk. While she had been asleep, Deputy Sloan's death was out of her head. Now she could think of nothing else.

She walked over to the fridge and went looking for something to drink, settling on the pitcher of iced tea she found there.

"It was a rough day and it's going to be a rough week," she said. "After we eat, I should probably get dressed and go back in for a while."

"No," Butch said, using the spoon to scrape some escaping food from Dennis's chin as the baby greeted his mother with a toothless grin. "It's been raining for the better part of an hour and the washes are already running. You'll have to wait until the water goes down again."

Running several simultaneous murder investigations in the middle of the monsoon season was complicated.

"Here, Mom," Jenny said. "Try this." She dropped one of the sandwiches, pretty-side-up, on a plate and set it in front of her mother. "I hope it's okay," she added nervously.

It was more than okay. For one thing, the grilled cheeses were made to Butch's specifications. That meant there was enough chopped jalapeño to more than offset the taste of charred toast. And since Joanna had eaten nothing since that taste of tamale much earlier in the break room, she quickly scarfed down one whole sandwich and willingly accepted another half.

Jenny put a sandwich-laden plate in front of Butch, then sat down with one of her own. "Are you going to tell her?" Jenny asked.

"Tell me what?" Joanna wanted to know.

"About Mrs. Sunderson," Jenny said.

Butch shot his stepdaughter a warning look.

"What about her?" Joanna asked.

"I talked to my editor this morning," Butch replied. "She called as soon as they opened up on the East Coast. She told me that in order to set up any kind of tour appearances, she had to have an answer today. So I talked to Marianne. She brought Mrs. Sunderson down here for an interview just before noon. I hired her on the spot."

Joanna was dumbstruck and more than slightly offended. "You hired her?" she demanded. "Just like that?"

"Yes, just like that," Butch replied. "She worked in preschools for years before her husband got so sick that she had to stay home with him. She's not exactly inexperienced as far as taking care of kids is concerned. I like her. Jenny likes her. She's thrilled that she'll be able to rent our old house—"

"You did all this without consulting me?" Joanna asked.

"Maybe not this morning, Joey, but I did consult you. Remember?" Butch said. "The last I heard, you said you wanted me to go on tour. I had to give New York a yes-or-no answer today.

With everything you were dealing with at work, I didn't think you were in any condition to have a long heart-to-heart discussion about it or to schedule an interview."

Joanna had to admit that much was inarguable. She had been up to her neck in work-related issues. There wouldn't have been time for her to deal with a domestic crisis as well.

"I really do like Mrs. Sunderson," Jenny put in. "And just think, this way there'll be some kids living right next door."

Now that the news had been broken, Butch hurried on with outlining arrangements. "Mrs. S. and the boys will stay at the motel until the middle of next week. Even with a full crew, that's the soonest I'll be able to complete the fix-up on the other house. Marianne said that will give her time to gather up some donated furniture for them to use. Once they get moved in, she'll start working for us right away while the boys are still out of school for the summer. That way, by the time the tour rolls around, she'll be familiar with our routines, know where things go, and so forth."

"But—" Joanna began.

"Look," Butch said, "you hire the best people you can find to do your job, and I'm doing the same thing. Having her here will help her because it'll be a job she can do without having to worry about day care for her boys. It'll help me because I'll have some time for writing when I'm here and I won't need to worry about how things are being handled when I'm gone."

Jenny stood up abruptly. "There's no sense in sitting around here if all you two are going to do is fight," she declared. "Want me to burp him?" she asked Butch, reaching for Dennis.

"That would be nice," Butch said. "But this isn't fighting. It's discussing."

"It sounds like fighting to me," Jenny said. She grabbed Dennis up. With all three dogs at her heels, Jenny flounced out of the room.

Butch picked up his now cold sandwich and munched on it in silence. Sitting there with him, Joanna knew there was a good deal of truth in everything he had said. Butch ran the household without complaint, but the very fact that he'd willingly accepted help from her mother was an indication that he sometimes had difficulty keeping all the balls in the air. And they did want his career to move forward. Both of them wanted that, and for that to happen he needed to go on tour.

"Can we afford the extra expense of hiring Carol Sunderson to help out around here?" Joanna asked at last.

"I don't think we can afford not to have her," Butch said. "It'll be tight," he admitted, "but I'm convinced it's going to be a good thing for everyone concerned—Jenny and Dennis included."

"All right, then," Joanna said.

Butch gave her a grateful smile. "So now that you know about my day, how about if you tell me about yours."

It turned out to be a very long story, from the time she had left the house overnight until she'd finally dragged herself home in the early afternoon. At that juncture, Joanna and Butch's conversation was interrupted by the realities of life—of doing the dishes, straightening up the kitchen, getting Dennis put to bed. When things quieted down once more and Joanna resumed her recitation, she was tempted to skip mentioning the part about Suzanne Quayle and Andy. In the end, she didn't. Butch's response wasn't what she had expected.

"Just because your dad was having an affair doesn't mean Andy was," Butch observed when she finished.

"Wait a minute," Joanna said. "Now you're defending Andy? What's this all about? I suppose it figures that men would stick together."

"I'm not defending him," Butch returned. "But, if you ask me, you're a long way from having probable cause. You've learned that someone Andy worked with was pregnant when he died. Since she didn't kiss up to you at the funeral and left town shortly thereafter, you've developed this whole scenario of what may or may not have happened between them. I think you're jumping to unwarranted conclusions. This isn't what I'd call a slam dunk."

Joanna bit her lip and said nothing.

"What are you going to do?" Butch asked.

Joanna shrugged. "Look into it, I suppose," she said.

"What if you find out it's true? What if Jenny has a little half brother or sister? What will you do then, tell her or not tell her?"

"I don't know," Joanna admitted. "I hadn't thought that far ahead."

"You'd better think about it," Butch warned her. "As you've already figured out this week, those kinds of family secrets have a way of bubbling to the surface at all the wrong times."

Their conversation was interrupted by a ringing telephone. For a change, the call was for Butch instead of Joanna.

"That's right," he told Jeff Daniels. "I'll pick up the tile tomorrow morning in Sierra Vista. If you could get the painting crew started while I'm doing that, it would be a huge help."

Butch paused, listening. "Tell Marianne thanks but that we've got that covered," he said. "Eleanor said she'd be here as early as I need her."

Jenny's right, Joanna thought. *We are fighting.* On the evening of Joanna's worst day as sheriff, the last thing she needed was to be wrangling with her husband.

"My mother's coming over again?" she asked pointedly once Butch got off the phone.

"Eleanor knows how much work it's going to be to have the house ready by next week. She said she'd be glad to do whatever she can to help."

"Oh," Joanna said. "With any kind of luck, I'll be at work by the time she gets here."

Except she wasn't. Eleanor, smiling brightly, was in the kitchen drinking coffee with Butch by the time Joanna got out of the shower the next morning. "Come outside and see my baby," she told Joanna. "I worried about driving her through the wash for fear we'd get hung up on a rock or something, but we made it okay."

Joanna, accompanied by Jenny, followed her mother outside to a spot just beyond the garage, where Eleanor had parked her bright red Mazda Miata.

"What do you think?" Eleanor wanted to know.

Joanna didn't know what to think. "It's really something," she said.

"Will you take me for a ride later, Grandma?" Jenny asked. "Can we put the top down?"

"Once Butch gets back," Eleanor replied. "It's a good thing you're as tall as you are," she added. "It'll be a long time before Dennis can ride with me because of the passenger air bag."

Butch chose that moment to abandon ship. "Gotta run," he said, dashing up and giving Joanna a peck on the cheek.

"Well," Eleanor asked, once they were all back in the kitchen. "What do you think?"

Joanna had lain awake for hours that night doing just that—thinking—and not just due to her long nap that afternoon. If her mother was so damned eager to help Butch out right now, why was she equally adamant about *not* helping when Butch was going off on tour? It made no sense, and Joanna was still grumpy enough about it that it was difficult for her to feign any enthusiasm about her mother's automotive purchase.

"It's cute," she allowed, "but it doesn't look like it'll hold much luggage."

"We won't need room for luggage," Eleanor said with a dismissive shrug. "When we travel, all of that will be in the Newell. We'll tow the Miata."

Eleanor seemed to be speaking a foreign language. "Excuse me?" Joanna asked.

"The Newell," Eleanor repeated firmly. "The motor home. It's older than Margaret and Donald's, but it's bigger, too."

It took a moment for Joanna to realize her mother was referring to Butch's folks, Margaret and Donald Dixon. Months earlier, just before Dennis was born, the Dixons had shown up in their RV. As far as Joanna was concerned, Maggie Dixon had ridden in on her broom. But Joanna was finally getting the message. Her mother and George had decided to get on board the RV bandwagon.

"You and George have bought a motor home?" she asked. "An RV?"

"Exactly," Eleanor beamed. "It comes with a towing package. That means we'll be able to drag the Miata with us wherever we go."

"You're going somewhere?" Joanna asked. "You're taking a trip?"

Eleanor's bright smile faltered. "You mean George didn't tell you? I thought he was going to."

"Tell me what?"

"I gave him a choice," Eleanor said. "It was work or me. He chose me. He's resigning immediately. George has a cabin on a place called Big Rock Lake in Minnesota. Or maybe it's Big Stone. I'm not sure which. The cabin was supposed to be rented for the whole summer, but the people who had booked it for August called just last week and canceled. Some kind of family crisis. So George and I are going to head up there next week. The end of next week, actually. We'll stay for the rest of the summer."

Joanna was stunned. "You're going to Minnesota?" she asked, surprised at the accusatory tone in her voice, as in, "You did this without consulting me." "When will you be back?" she asked.

"Probably right around Thanksgiving," Eleanor answered. "Too late to help out with the tour, of course, which is why I told Butch I'd do everything I could for him right now."

"Does Butch know about this?" Joanna asked. "Is he aware you're leaving town?"

"Oh, no," Eleanor said. "I couldn't possibly tell him about it until after I'd told you."

"And why didn't you tell me before?" Joanna wanted to know.

"Oh, Joanna," Eleanor said. "We've become so close since little Dennis was born. I was afraid you'd be disappointed in me. If I did something to hurt you, it would just break my heart."

CHAPTER 19

IT TOOK A WHILE FOR JOANNA TO EXTRICATE HERSELF FROM home. As soon as she drove away from the ranch, she dialed George's office number. "You're leaving?" she demanded when he answered. "Just like that?"

"Ellie told you, then?" George returned mildly.

"She pretty much had to," Joanna replied. "Since you're taking off the end of next week in that new RV, she couldn't very well put it off any longer."

"It's not a new RV," George said. "It's used and very affordable."

"Whatever," Joanna said. "But you're quitting?"

"Resigning," George said. "Effective immediately."

"But why? I don't understand."

"No," George agreed. "I don't suppose you do. You're probably too young. I made plenty of mistakes in my first marriage, Joanna. The most critical one was working more than was good for me or for the relationship. From what Ellie tells me, I believe your parents' marriage suffered from the same malady. Until your mother took off this week, I had no idea how unhappy she was with the way things were going. Now that Ellie's managed to get my attention, she and I are determined to do something about it. Neither one of us wants to make the same mistake twice. We've decided to spend however much time we have left just that way—together."

Joanna had to admit that she didn't remember her mother ever looking as radiant as she had that morning. Joanna had thought her high spirits were all related to her brand-new little red sports car, but clearly there was a lot more going on than buying a car.

"I hope you'll be very happy," Joanna said.

The words sounded halfhearted and grudging, but she meant them when she said them. Still, there was a part of her that felt lost and bereft. She liked George. They worked well together. She would miss him terribly, not only at work but also for the special role he played in her family life. And no matter how much Eleanor had driven Joanna crazy over the years—no matter how often the two of them had locked horns over every little thing—it had been reassuring to know her mother was right there where she had always been—in the little house on Campbell Street. Now Eleanor Lathrop Winfield would be gone from there, probably for months at a time.

You've got to watch out what you wish for, Joanna thought. Then, because she had to, she switched gears.

"What about Dan's autopsy?" she asked.

"I'll do it this afternoon—about one. Chief Bernard is sending Detective Lester. Do you want someone there, too?"

"Ernie Carpenter," Joanna said at once. "I'll let him know."

"If I can release the body to the mortuary later today, the funeral could be scheduled for either Friday or Saturday. According to Jaime Carbajal, the widow is hoping for Friday. She wants it to be sooner rather than later."

Joanna understood that. The days between Andy's death and his funeral seemed to have gone on for weeks. She was also glad to hear that Jaime was doing what she had asked him to do—running interference for Sunny Sloan. It wasn't easy to be a twenty-something widow. There was too much you didn't know at that age—too much you shouldn't have to know. The same thing was true for the people in Joanna's department as well. They were all in unfamiliar territory. As they spent time and resources arranging the many details of a fallen-officer funeral, they'd be learning lessons none of them wanted to learn.

"All right," Joanna told George. "Keep me posted if there's anything you think I should know."

Pulling into the Justice Center, she swallowed hard when she saw the flags hanging at half-mast. Stacked near the door was a mass of floral bouquets that had been dropped off in memory of Deputy Sloan. Joanna had no doubt there was another mountain of remembrance flourishing outside the Beasleys' house in Tombstone Canyon. The other thing she noticed in the parking lot was the inevitable collection of media vans. They were empty, which meant the newsies were all assembled in the public lobby waiting for her.

Once again accessing her office through the private entrance, she sat at her desk for a moment gathering herself for the onslaught. Outside her window, the hillside leading up to the towering limestone cliffs had turned a brilliant green. And the usually stick-thin, spiny ocotillos were covered with dark green leaves that left them looking fat as bottle brushes.

That's how the desert responds to life-giving rain, Joanna told herself as she collected her paperwork to go to the morning briefing. *And we'll get through this, too.*

Inside the conference room, the mood was nothing short of somber. Like Joanna, everyone had managed to get some sleep overnight. They had all come back to work, but their hearts weren't in it.

"What have we put together on Larry Wolfe?" she wanted to know, addressing Dave Hollicker.

"We've got blood transfers in his truck, on the steering wheel and on the armrest," he answered. "I also found bloodstained glass shards in the foot well of the vehicle that would be consistent with debris being dropped off the soles of his shoes."

"You'll be testing all those?" Joanna asked. "Finding out whether or not DNA from the stains match Dan's?"

"Absolutely," Dave said. "But what's the point? Why spend a lot of time and effort on this—"

"The point is that regardless of who pulled the trigger, the media will be holding our department responsible for Dan's death," Joanna answered. "They'll be questioning our policies and procedures. They'll be wondering whether or not Deputy Sloan was properly trained. We're going to conduct this investigation as vigorously as if it were going to trial because it will be—just not in a court of law. Got it?"

"Got it," Dave replied. Everyone else nodded in agreement.

"That's why Ernie will be joining Bisbee's Detective Lester at Dan's autopsy this afternoon. It's also why we'll be shouldering the expense of testing all the foodstuffs taken from the Beasleys' kitchen."

"But I'm not sure we can afford—" Frank began.

Joanna already knew why he was objecting, and she cut him off in midsentence. "Yes, I know," she said. "Doing that testing and contracting for DNA examination of all blood evidence will be expensive. Can we afford to do it? My position is we can't afford *not* to do it. Have we heard any more from Sheriff Barnes over in Texas?"

Ernie nodded. "Hudspeth County CSIs found Dan's Glock at the scene of the rollover accident. Until Doc Winfield retrieves the bullet, we won't know for sure that was the weapon that fired the fatal shot."

Joanna turned her attention to Jaime, who winced visibly at that bit of news. "How are you doing?" she asked.

"All right," he said, but he didn't look all right.

"Any word on funeral arrangements?" she asked.

"Father Rowan has reserved Saint Dominick's for a service at ten A.M. on Saturday," Jaime replied. "That's all tentative, of course, based on whether or not Doc Winfield releases the body to the mortuary today."

"And once those arrangements are finalized, you'll be responsible for getting the word out?" she asked. "I'm expecting that there will be officers from all over the region who'll want to attend."

Jaime nodded. "I'll let everyone know," he said.

Joanna turned to Deb. "What about the guy in the Pima County Jail—the one whose fingerprints Casey found on the Wanda Mappin trash bags? Did you talk to him?"

"I did," Deb replied. "He was more than a little surprised

when I showed up. Initially he claimed he didn't know anything about anything. Couldn't imagine how his fingerprint could have ended up on that trash bag. He's lying, of course. He knows way more than he's saying."

"Do you think we might be able to flip him?" Joanna asked.

"Possibly," Deb said.

"All right, then," Joanna said. "Let's keep that in mind as we gather more information."

Most of the investigators departed the room, leaving Frank and Joanna to dispose of their routine business. They were almost done when Joanna mentioned the news about George Winfield's pending resignation.

"Funny you should mention that," Frank said with a surprisingly guilty expression on his face.

"So you already knew about it?" Joanna asked.

"Not George's pending resignation," Frank returned. "Mine."

Joanna could barely believe her ears. "Yours?"

"Sierra Vista's chief of police is taking early retirement," Frank said. "I've applied for the position. I heard yesterday that I'm one of the three finalists."

Two of her rocks, George Winfield and Frank Montoya, were abandoning ship. How could that be? It seemed as though Joanna's carefully constructed professional world was falling apart.

"You're leaving, too?" she demanded.

"It's not a sure thing," Frank told her. "They're supposed to make a final decision by August fifteenth. If they offer the job, I'll take it—no hard feelings. I've been happy being your chief deputy, honored, even. But five years is a long time to play second banana to anyone. I'd like the chance to run my own shop. Besides, with LuAnn and her kids out there, it would be a lot easier if I wasn't spending half my life running back and forth between Sierra Vista and here."

"LuAnn as in LuAnn Marcowitz?" Joanna said. "As in Dr. Marcowitz?"

Frank nodded.

"The lady you told me you'd been having fun with."

"Quite a bit more than just fun, I suppose," Frank admitted.

"You're serious about her, then?"

"Pretty serious."

It took a moment for Joanna to summon a smile. "I suppose my loss is LuAnn Marcowitz's gain," she said. "And of course, you'll get the job. They'd be stupid not to offer it to you."

"Thank you," Frank said. "I hope you're right."

He left the room then. Once he was gone, Joanna sat there for a while longer, feeling bereft and wondering how she'd manage without him. She cringed at all the times she'd been less than diplomatic with the man. How many instances had there been like the one earlier in this very meeting, when she'd ignored Frank's opinion or run roughshod over what he'd been trying to say? Yes, on occasion she had treated him like a second banana. No wonder he was actively searching for other opportunities.

Lost in thought, worrying about where she'd find a new chief deputy and whether or not she'd be able to work successfully with the new medical examiner, Joanna was startled when Kristin tapped lightly on the conference room door.

"Sorry to interrupt," Kristin said. She stuck her head inside and glanced around the otherwise empty room. "Oh, I thought the meeting was still in progress."

"What is it?" Joanna asked.

"Phone call for you. A Detective Ramsey. From Tucson PD."

"Thanks," Joanna said. "I'll take it in here." She grabbed up the phone as soon as it rang. "Did you find Wayne Hamm?" she asked.

"Yes, I did," Becky Ramsey said. "All we had to do was enter his dental records and we had a hit."

"Where is he?"

"Buried in the pauper's grave corner of Evergreen Cemetery."

"In Bisbee?" Joanna asked.

Becky laughed. "In Tucson's Evergreen Cemetery."

"He's dead, then?"

"Very. He broke into the apartment of a U of A grad student named Lauren Dayson and she shot him dead. She had broken up with her violent boyfriend some time earlier. The boyfriend had threatened her with bodily harm. She had a restraining order against him. When her dog started barking like crazy in the middle of the night, she thought he was making good on that threat. She pulled a loaded weapon out from under her pillow and shot him to pieces. Except it turned out the dead guy wasn't her ex. She claimed to have no idea who the victim was. There was no ID at all. We got a hit on AFIS. The victim's prints had shown up at the scene of several unsolved residential burglaries here in Tucson. The prints were found and linked but never identified. John Doe was shot dead on March 10. When no one came forward to declare him missing or to claim the body, the county finally went ahead and buried him on April fifteenth."

"Wait a minute," Joanna said. "You're saying someone shot Wayne Hamm dead on March tenth? How's that possible? From what I was told, he wasn't reported missing from the group home until some time in May."

"That's right," Becky answered. "May the twelfth, to be exact."

"You're telling me Wayne was dead for more than two months *before* he disappeared?"

"What makes it even more intriguing is that I have copies of records stating that the State of California Department of Health and Human Services was paying full fare for Wayne's care right up until he was declared missing. Since he was dead a good two months before they admitted he was gone—"

"Someone at Flannigan Foundation was pulling a fast one," Joanna concluded.

"At the very least," Becky replied. "More likely they were committing outright fraud."

"Anything else?" Joanna asked.

"I've reviewed the case file. When Wayne was found, he had no ID. The only personal property found with him is a single earring, presumably a woman's earring, in the pocket of his jeans."

Joanna's heartbeat quickened. "An earring?" she asked. "What kind of earring?"

"Pink is what it says here in the written report—a pink pierced earring with the gold back still on it. It's probably locked away in an evidence room somewhere. Why? Do you know something about an earring that I don't?"

"We found one rose zircon earring in the plastic bag with Wanda Mappin's bones," Joanna said. "One earring, not two. The other one was missing."

"And if they're a matched pair, we've just connected the dots between these two cases."

"Exactly," Joanna said. "And I've got some even better news. Yesterday my latent fingerprint tech came up with a print from the plastic bags and got a match off AFIS to a guy who's currently being held in the Pima County Jail, a guy by the name of"—Joanna had to pause for a moment long enough to find the suspect's name in her notes—"Billy Carmichael. He's locked up on charges of petty theft. He claims that all he did was help dispose of Wanda's body—that she was already dead when he saw her. Deb is of the opinion that, given enough encouragement, Carmichael might be persuaded to spill the beans. He seemed wobbly when she was talking to him about one murder. Now that a second homicide has been added into the mix, maybe it's time to turn up the heat."

"Should I go see him?" Becky asked.

"We should both go see him," Joanna said.

"Want me to set up the interview with Pima County?"

"No," Joanna said. "I'll do that once I know exactly when I'll get there, and I'll bring Deb Howell along. We'll all go see him together. You locate your earring. I'll locate mine. Then we'll put the screws to him."

"Wait a minute," Becky said. "You're not thinking of trying to offer some kind of plea deal, are you? We're not authorized—"

"Absolutely not," Joanna said. "No plea agreement of any kind. I'm going to give this poor mope an opportunity to tell us the truth about what happened. We'll let him know that he's already been linked to Wanda's murder. If he doesn't come clean about that one, he's likely to be held responsible for Wayne Hamm's death as well."

"Do you think you'll be able to bluff him into confessing with a pair of earrings?" Becky Ramsey asked. "That's not much of a hand."

"Let's add in a couple of face cards," Joanna said. "Bring along any photos you happen to have of Wayne Hamm."

"As in crime scene photos?"

"Absolutely," Joanna said.

She stopped by the evidence room long enough to go through the Wanda Mappin evidence box and emerged carrying a copy of the photo Dave Hollicker had taken of the earring that had been found with Wanda Mappin's remains, as well as a photo of the diamond-studded locket. Along with those she collected a set of crime scene photos and a picture of a much younger Wanda, one her mother had submitted as part of the original missing persons report. With the file folder of photos in hand, Joanna dialed Deb Howell's extension.

"What are you doing?"

"Paperwork," Detective Howell admitted. "Mounds of it. Stacks of it. There wasn't time yesterday."

"And there probably won't be time for it today, either," Joanna said. "Let's take a ride."

"Where to?" Deb asked, sounding relieved.

"Tucson," Joanna told her. "To the Pima County Jail. I want to pay a visit to your good friend Billy Carmichael. You drive. I need to make some calls."

The first one was to Pima County Sheriff William Forsythe. Joanna's interactions with Bill Forsythe had never been particularly cordial, especially after she had cleaned his clock in the formerly boys-only annual poker game at the Arizona Sheriffs Association meeting in Page several years earlier. Now, though, on her way to interview an inmate in Forsythe's jail, she owed the man the courtesy of a phone call.

"I hear you're dealing with some mighty tough stuff, Sheriff Brady," Forsythe said, once she had him on the line. "Losing a deputy that way is hell. If there's anything at all my department can do to help out, just say so. In fact, as soon as you know when the funeral is, give me a call. I can probably have some of my off-duty officers head down there to handle routine patrol duties while your guys attend the services. Mutual aid and all that. In fact, I may even be able to send along some admin folks so your office people can attend the funeral as well. And I have a line on the bagpipers we've used in the past."

This may have been Joanna's first line-of-duty fallen-officer funeral, but clearly Bill Forsythe had already been there and done that. His gruff and entirely unanticipated offers of help caught Joanna off guard. Maybe the thin blue line wasn't as thin as she sometimes thought it to be.

"Thank you," she murmured at last. "That's very kind."

"Have your chief deputy contact my administrative assistant," Forsythe said easily. "We'll get those shifts covered. Now what can I do for you today?"

"Detective Ramsey from Tucson PD and I are working to link two separate cases together. We need to interview one of your jail inmates, a guy named Billy Carmichael. We're on our way to see him right now."

"What's your ETA?" Forsythe wanted to know. "I'll call my jail commander and let him know you're coming. I'll also have him book an interview and make arrangements to bring Carmichael out of lockup. That way he'll be there ready to go by the time you get there."

As Joanna finished the call, she couldn't help marveling at how things had changed in the space of a few short years. The acceptance she had earned from people like Chief Alvin Bernard and Bill Forsythe hadn't come easily. Now that she had it, she realized that it was possible she had opened doors for other women who might want to follow in her footsteps.

Joanna closed her phone and turned to Deb. "Okay," she said. "Give me a preview of Mr. Carmichael."

"Not all that bright," Deb said at once. "Whatever was going on, he was a grunt. He certainly wasn't the brains of the outfit."

"What's his connection to Flannigan Foundation?"

"I asked him that yesterday," Deb said. "He claimed he'd never heard of them."

"We already know that's a lie," Joanna said. "That'll be as good a place as any to start."

As they crossed the Divide heading for Tucson, Joanna saw a group of vehicles pulled off on either side of the road. Joanna slowed, expecting to find the remains of a recent car wreck. Instead of wreckage, however, they found people standing with cameras pointed up the mountainside. Days of record-breaking storms had done their magic. Today a tumultuous waterfall roared off the mountainside at a spot where the red-rock cliffs were usually dry as bone.

It was beautiful. It was inspiring. *It's something Dan Sloan never lived to see,* Joanna thought sadly.

They met up with Detective Ramsey in the Pima County Jail's utilitarian public lobby, where a quick visual comparison of the two earring photos seemed to indicate they were a pair. Minutes later they were joined by a uniformed guard. After helping the visitors deposit their weapons in individual lockers, he led them to a small room adjoining the interview room, which gave them a view of a gaunt young man in a jail jumpsuit sitting at a metal table and drumming his fingers nervously on the table's surface.

"Which one of you is going in with him?" the guard asked.

"We all are," Joanna answered at once.

"But it's a very small space," the guard objected. "Are you sure—"

"The more crowded it is, the less wiggle room Mr. Carmichael will have."

"All right," the guard agreed reluctantly. "If you'll give me a minute, I can bring in a couple more chairs."

"That's not necessary," Joanna said. "One of us will sit. The others will stand. It'll be fine."

She led the others into the room and then took the empty chair opposite Carmichael while Deb and Becky Ramsey assumed positions next to the one-way mirror. Without a word, Joanna dropped her collection of photos on the table and said absolutely nothing. As the silence lengthened, Carmichael stared curiously at what he could see of the photos. Finally, he nodded toward Detective Howell.

"I know who she is," he said. "She was here yesterday talking about some kind of fingerprint crap and a dead body that I don't know nothin' about. But who are you?" he demanded of Joanna. "And who's she?" He pointed at Detective Ramsey.

"I'm Sheriff Brady," Joanna said. "Detective Ramsey is with Tucson PD. This interview is being recorded, by the way." She nodded toward the video equipment attached to the wall just under the ceiling. "We're investigating the disappearance of this man."

She extracted the crime scene photo of Wayne's gore-spattered body from the stack and slid it toward him across the table. There was no way to disguise the shock of recognition that flashed in Billy Carmichael's eyes.

"So you knew Wayne Hamm?" she asked casually.

"I didn't say that," Carmichael replied.

"You didn't have to," Joanna returned with a smile. "I could see that you did. And because of these," she added, plucking out the two earring photos, "we can now link you to two separate homicides."

"Two," he echoed faintly.

"Two," Joanna repeated. She extracted Wanda Mappin's photo from the stack. "You see her?"

Carmichael glanced at the photo and then looked away. "What about her?"

"This is one homicide victim. Her name is Wanda Mappin. We found her bones in the plastic bag with your fingerprint on it. And this earring—one of a pair of earrings—was found in the bag along with her remains. And this identical earring"— she produced the other earring photo and pushed it over to Carmichael—"this one we found among the personal effects of our other victim, Wayne Leroy Hamm, who, as it turns out, was shot by a startled homeowner when he broke into her home."

"Like I already said," Carmichael grumbled. "I had nothing to do with it."

"But the two deaths are related," Joanna insisted. "We know that because of the pair of earrings, and we're guessing that if you were involved in the one murder—and we have physical evidence linking you to that one—that you probably also know about the other one as well."

"But I didn't *do* it," Carmichael insisted suddenly. "All I did was help Tommy dump the body. She was already dead. If she would have just shut the hell up about it—if she would've let it go—nothing would have happened to her. She wouldn't be dead. I mean, who cares if there's one less retard in the world?"

"You mean she wouldn't shut up about Wayne," Joanna said. "About him being gone."

Billy gave Joanna an appraising look, then he nodded. "Tommy said that's all she would talk about. For weeks. People were starting to get suspicious. He had to do something."

"Tommy," Joanna said. "Who's Tommy?"

"If I tell you, will you make sure I don't get charged with this?" Billy asked. "With the murder, I mean. I swear I didn't have nothin' to do with that. All I did was help Tommy get rid of the body. We took it down to Bisbee and buried it. The tape came loose. There was stuff leaking out. I helped tape it back shut. But I didn't kill her."

"Who's Tommy?" Joanna asked again.

"Tom Bidahl," Billy answered. "My ex-roommate. He had a sweet deal going. He used those guys—guys like Wayne—for recon."

"Excuse me?" Joanna asked.

"You know. To scope out places," Billy answered. "To figure out which places were locked up tight and which ones weren't and would be good to rob. Tom would turn Wayne loose in a neighborhood to check things out. Once Tom's crew knew which houses were easy marks, in they went; no muss, no fuss. If Wayne or one of the other dopes got caught in the process, so what? They're not competent. They can't be tried and convicted of anything. Those poor bastards have the ultimate get-out-of-jail-free card. All Tom had to say was that they got out and went wandering on their own. That worked fine, right up until Wayne got the bright idea to go solo and got himself killed in the process. Even that wouldn't have been so bad if Wanda had just kept her mouth shut. She kept harping on it and harping on it until people started asking questions. That's when Tom decided to do something. He put her out of her misery. I mean, he had to, didn't he."

"And how did you get roped into helping?" Joanna asked.

Billy Carmichael shrugged. "I sell stuff. I used to sell stuff. On eBay. For a percentage. Most people don't care where something comes from as long as they're getting a bargain."

"In other words, you were Tom Bidahl's fence."

Billy nodded. "I guess so," he agreed. "But like I said, I had nothing to do with killing this woman. She was already dead. You understand that, right?"

"Absolutely," Joanna agreed. "I understand that completely. But where's Tom Bidahl now? Whatever happened to him? You're not still roommates, are you?"

"Oh, no," Billy said. "I still live in the same place, an old house just off Euclid. That's where I'll go when they let me out of here, but Tom went on to bigger and better things. We were roommates before he ever went to work for Flannigan Foundation. First he was just an hourly attendant for them. Once he got a job as a resident manager, he didn't need an apartment anymore."

"Where is he now?"

"I heard he went to work for corporate—for the guy who runs Flannigan."

"At the Flannigan headquarters?"

Billy nodded.

"Were there other people like Wayne?" Joanna asked. "Other Flannigan clients who got used for recon purposes and then went away once they outlived their usefulness?"

"I wouldn't know about that."

Joanna stood abruptly and began to gather her papers.

"You're going to help me, aren't you?" Billy asked. It was a whine more than a question.

"Help you what?"

"Prove that I didn't do it. That I wasn't responsible for killing that woman. Tommy's the one who did it. All I did was—"

"Mr. Carmichael, you talked to us this afternoon of your own free will. We'll be turning a videotaped copy of everything you said here over to the prosecutors in question. What they eventually decide to do with it is entirely up to them."

"But I thought we had a deal."

"That wouldn't be the first mistake you ever made," Joanna told Billy. "And I doubt it'll be your last."

"But I didn't do anything to her. I didn't. I can prove it."

"And my people are going to be working day and night to prove that you did," Joanna returned smoothly. "So if somebody happens to be generous enough to give you the opportunity to turn state's evidence, I'd suggest you do it in a heartbeat."

"You didn't read me my rights."

"Deb Howell read you your rights on this yesterday, didn't she?"

"Well, yes, she did," he admitted, "but—"

"But nothing. You agreed to talk to her again today, didn't you?"

"Yes."

"There you are," Joanna said. "Once Mirandized, always Mirandized. Have a nice day."

CHAPTER 20

BY THE TIME THEY GOT THEIR WEAPONS AND WERE OUTSIDE AGAIN, Becky Ramsey was in a fit of temper that had nothing to do with the 104-degree temperature scorching the parking lot pavement.

"What do we do next?" Deb Howell asked.

"We don't stand around here talking," Joanna told her. "Not in this heat."

In the end they settled on stopping at one of Becky Ramsey's favorite hangouts, the Crossroads on South Fourth. There, in the air-conditioned cool of a Mexican-food dive, they settled in over tacos and iced tea to strategize.

"So if Wanda was murdered in Tucson and dumped in Bisbee," Becky said, "we should probably bring my homicide guys in on it. By the time they finish grilling Billy Carmichael, we'll be able to take down Tommy Bidahl."

Joanna was relieved to be able to hand off the Wanda Mappin murder investigation to someone else. "Sounds good," Joanna said. "Have whoever's put in charge of the investigation contact Detective Howell here. She can give them whatever we have."

"But bringing in Bidahl isn't going to be the end of it," Becky declared hotly. "Flannigan Foundation is supposed to be in the business of caring for at-risk people. Instead they're letting their clients wander around unsupervised and leaving them in situations where they're even more vulnerable."

"With two dead that we know about already," Joanna put in.

Becky nodded. "The organization may have been started with the very best of intentions," she said, "but those have long since gone by the board. Now Flannigan is being run by a bunch of profiteering creeps who have apparently hired caregivers who are literally getting away with murder."

"Too many patients and not enough oversight," Deb Howell said.

"Exactly," Becky agreed. "But that stops here. I'm going to see to it that someone takes a long hard look at all those halfway houses of theirs and finds out what's really going on inside them."

Joanna thought about her encounter with the less than helpful Donald Dietrich. *Yes,* she thought. *There's a man who deserves a long hard look.*

Her phone rang then. Frank was on the line telling her that the autopsy had been completed and that Dan Sloan's funeral had now been confirmed for Saturday morning. She passed along everything Sheriff Forsythe had said about helping out with staffing issues as well as having access to a bagpipe brigade. When she finished the call, Deb was reading a copy of a newspaper article which she passed over to Joanna.

"What's this?" she asked.

"Read it," Deb told her.

On a cold night in March, Lauren Dayson's dog, Mojo, alerted her to the presence of an intruder in her bedroom. Terrified by a former boyfriend's threats of violence, Ms. Dayson was prepared. She pulled a fully loaded weapon out from under her pillow and fired away, shooting the intruder and killing him on the spot.

There was only one problem with this whole scenario—the dead man wasn't Ms. Dyson's ex-boyfriend, the man who had actually threatened her with bodily harm. To this day, the intruder she shot dead in her bedroom doorway remains unidentified.

Tucson PD homicide investigators have spent countless hours trying to identify the shooting victim, who was finally buried in an unmarked plot at Evergreen Cemetery in mid-April—a grave Ms. Dayson visits once a week, bringing flowers.

"That's the part that eats away at me," she said in a telephone interview. "That I don't know who he was. I thought I was in danger at the time. Maybe I was and maybe I wasn't. Did I shoot some poor guy because he was in the wrong place at the wrong time? I wish I could tell his family how sorry I am. I wish I could explain to them that when you've been a victim of domestic violence, you don't ever get over it. And when someone wanders uninvited into your bedroom in the middle of the night, you may do something you'll live to regret."

As for the former boyfriend? It turns out he's no longer a danger to anyone, Lauren Dayson included. Shortly after the shooting incident, he was injured in a diving accident at a Phoenix area hotel. His neck was broken. Now a quadriplegic, he is being cared for by the very woman he once threatened.

"It's a way of evening the score," she says. "I took a life and now I'm giving one back. I pray for forgiveness every day. I hope God is listening."

"I have Lauren Dayson's address," Detective Ramsey said quietly. "Do you want to go visit her and let her know we've identified her victim?"

Joanna's first instinct was to say no, that she and Deb needed to get back to Bisbee and handle whatever needed handling there. She didn't, though, and she was glad. Lauren Dayson and Rick Mosier lived in a one-level town house at the far end of Grant, where the ringing doorbell was greeted by the frantic barking of what sounded like a tiny dog.

Mojo, Joanna thought.

The woman who opened the door was a careworn woman holding a squirming dog. "Ms. Dayson?" Becky asked.

The woman nodded. She was a lithe blonde whose figure said she was probably somewhere in her twenties, but her haggard face made her look far older. "I'm Lauren Dayson," she said. "Who are you?"

"Police officers," Becky said, holding out her ID. "I'm Detective Ramsey. This is Sheriff Joanna Brady from Cochise County, and this is one of her detectives, Debra Howell. May we come in?"

"Who is it?" a man's voice bellowed from somewhere out of sight. "What do they want? And can't you get that damned dog to be quiet for even a minute?"

Lauren glanced toward a room that must have been a bedroom, but she didn't reply. "I guess," she said, opening the door and gesturing the three women into the unit. "What's this about?"

"It's about the man you shot," Joanna said. "Now that we've identified him, we thought you'd want to know."

Clutching the dog close to her body, Lauren Dayson staggered away from the door and dropped onto a couch. "Who was he?" she asked.

They stayed there talking with her for the next forty-five minutes, telling her everything they could about Wayne Leroy Hamm. The whole time they talked, the conversation was interrupted time and again by Rick Mosier summoning Lauren from the living room to the bedroom for one bogus reason or another.

"What an incredible jerk!" Deb exclaimed as they made their way back out to Joanna's Crown Victoria. "He treats her like crap. Why does she even bother?"

"Guilt," Joanna replied.

"But why? She didn't make Rick Mosier dive into the shallow end of a pool. That was his own stupidity."

"And you didn't make Danny Sloan walk into that ambush, either," Joanna reminded her. "You didn't, Jaime didn't, and neither did I."

"Oh," Deb Howell said quietly, fingering the black band around her badge. "I see what you mean."

—+—

The next few days were hell. Preparing for Dan Sloan's funeral and then getting through it occupied Joanna's every waking moment. The day started with an inspiring standing-room-only service at Saint Dominick's that came complete with all the necessary pomp and circumstance and what seemed to be hundreds of officers visiting from other jurisdictions. Jaime Carbajal ended the funeral itself by delivering a moving eulogy. After that came those other essential pieces—the wailing bagpipes; the presentation of the folded flag; the last call; and a luncheon at the high school cafeteria put on by firefighters from all over the county.

Much later that afternoon, more than a week after their deaths, Martha and Alfred Beasley were quietly laid to rest as well. The only good thing about their joint memorial service was that their two daughters, both out of the hospital, sat through it all side by side. They were there together and no longer feuding. They said they would be scattering the ashes at the top of Montezuma Pass at sunrise the next morning. Would Samantha and Sandy's truce last long enough to get though Larry Wolfe's upcoming funeral? That was anyone's guess.

At the end of the day Joanna had to conclude that, by any standard, it was way too many funerals in far too short a time.

The following Monday morning, Joanna came out to the kitchen feeling emotionally spent and not nearly ready to start a new week. She was surprised to find several newcomers gathered there—Carol Sunderson and her two grandsons. While the boys mowed through multiple bowls of cereal, Butch was explaining Dennis's sleeping, eating, and bathing schedule to an attentively listening Carol Sunderson. Within a matter of days, Carol and her boys fit into Butch's and Joanna's lives like an essential piece of a picture puzzle that they hadn't known was missing. By the end of that first week, neither Butch nor Joanna could imagine how they had ever managed without Carol.

On Thursday Dick Voland dropped by Joanna's office.

"The feds are calling off the dogs," he said. "You and Butch are in the clear."

"Really?" Joanna asked.

"Really," he replied. "So that makes us even. Right?"

"Right," she said.

Friday of that week was when Joanna was finally able to go before the Board of Supervisors and get permission to retool Animal Control with Jeannine Phillips in charge. That Friday was also George Winfield's last day on the job. Until a permanent replacement was hired, the county would be contracting with other medical examiners in the area.

George and Eleanor came to High Lonesome Ranch that night for a farewell dinner.

"You're all packed up, then?" Butch asked as they sat around the dining room table eating some of Carol Sunderson's freshly made peach cobbler.

"Yup," George said. "Packed and ready to rumble. When we get home tonight, I'll put my car on the trickle charger in the garage and we'll bring Ellie's along on the tow bar. We'll be up and out bright and early in the morning. It's going to be fun."

Joanna glanced at her mother's shadowless face. Eleanor was actually glowing. In fact, Joanna had never seen her happier.

The realization that George and her grandmother were really going away had finally penetrated Jenny's world, and she wasn't at all happy about it. "I'm going to miss you," she said almost tearfully. "Are you sure you'll be back in time for Thanksgiving?"

"Definitely," Eleanor declared. "We wouldn't think of being

anywhere else. Jim Bob and Eva Lou have already invited us to have Thanksgiving dinner with all of you at their place." With that she turned to her son-in-law. "Did you make this cobbler?" she asked.

"No," he admitted. "Carol made it."

"I thought so," Eleanor said. "It's not nearly as good as yours."

Later, when it was time to say good-bye, Eleanor hugged Joanna close. "You've got a good one there," she said. "Be sure to treat him that way."

"You've certainly brought my mother around," Joanna said to Butch as they lay in bed that night.

"Eleanor's not so hard to figure out," Butch said. "As long as I make you happy, she's happy."

"George seems to have her number, too."

"Yes, he does," Butch agreed. "They're both having a ball."

Moments later, Butch was snoring. Joanna lay awake thinking about all that. From the outside, it seemed as though George had quit working because Eleanor had pressured him into doing so, but since they both seemed so ridiculously happy with what they were doing now, did it really matter what had caused it? Wasn't it likely that George had been ready to quit all along and had just been waiting for some kind of catalyst? And if it was that easy for George to make Eleanor Lathrop happy, why hadn't Hank Lathrop been able to do the same thing?

That was the real question—the one that stayed with Joanna for the rest of the night. By the time she finally fell asleep, she knew she would have to ask it. The next morning she got up and dressed in plainclothes rather than a uniform, but it was clear she had no intention of hanging around the house.

"It's Saturday," Jenny objected. "Do you *have* to go in?"

Joanna nodded, but that wasn't quite true. She drove straight past the Justice Center and up to Old Bisbee. About ten past ten she pulled up in front of the small wood frame house at 305 Quality Hill. Mona Tipton's house. Kristin hadn't looked up the information for her. Joanna had found it herself.

Now, though, peering at the house, Joanna paused, filled with uncertainty and a sense of disloyalty, too. This was none of her business. Her father's love life was his love life. And if Hank Lathrop had betrayed her mother once long ago, what did it matter? And yet Joanna understood that she had based much of her adult antagonism toward her mother on her father's presumed perfection. In her mind, Hank had always been the wronged party. Maybe it was time to set the record straight by finding out the truth of the matter. That was the only way Joanna was going to get over it once and for all.

Finally, she climbed out of the car and made her way up the short flight of stairs. She rang the bell and then waited as someone called, "I'm coming. I'm coming. Who is—?"

When Mona Tipton opened the door, she stopped in midsentence. "Oh," she added after a pause. "It's you. Come on in. I wondered if you'd ever get around to asking me about your dad. Have a seat. Would you like some coffee? I just made a new pot."

That was surreal. Here Joanna was in the home of the woman who had been her father's lover, and Mona was offering her coffee as if this were a perfectly normal event. As though their meeting like this was nothing out of the ordinary.

"No, thanks," Joanna said. "I'm fine." Although she wasn't fine. She was *anything* but fine.

"If you don't mind, I'll go get mine, then," Mona said. "There's no sense in letting it get cold."

Mona returned with a cup that announced she had donated money to NPR. She was still an attractive woman. Her dark hair, now broken by several strips of white, was pulled back in a French twist that was held in place by a pair of old-fashioned tortoise-shell combs. She was slender and graceful enough that Joanna found herself wondering if maybe she had been a dancer once. And even on this Saturday morning at home, she was wearing a skirt and blouse, stockings, and a pair of low heels.

"I can see how you had to wait until your mother left town before you could come see me," Mona said. "What is it you want to know?"

That meant that long after D. H. Lathrop's death, Mona Tipton still kept track of her rival's comings and goings.

"I read my father's journals," Joanna answered quietly. "I know you and he were involved."

"Yes," Mona said, thoughtfully sipping her coffee. "Yes, we were. Your father was a wonderful man. He was loyal and strong, but what I loved most about him was his sense of humor. No matter how bad my day was, he always found a way to make me laugh. I don't think your mother ever appreciated that in him. I don't think she ever appreciated him at all."

Joanna didn't doubt the appreciation bit was true. Eleanor had always been as hard on her husband as she had been on her daughter, but Joanna was beginning to realize that was how Eleanor Lathrop showed her love—by being toughest on the people she cared for most.

"I hear she gave that new husband of hers the same kind of

deal—my way or the highway," Mona continued. "And I heard she won that round, too, won it hands-down. Your mother's a very fortunate woman to be able to wield that kind of influence on the men in her life."

"Wait a minute," Joanna said after a pause. "What do you mean, 'won that one, too'?"

"Because your father chose her instead of me," Mona said quietly. "He called me that Saturday morning—the morning he died—before he went to pick you and your friends up from that camping trip. He told me he had made up his mind—that you and your mother came first. He said I'd have to leave the sheriff's department—that he'd give me good references but that it wouldn't work for me to stay on. Hearing it broke my heart, of course. Then he died, and that broke it even more. I don't know how your mother found out about it. I thought we'd been very discreet, but that's the way small towns are. She knew. She called me up and told me that if I dared set foot anywhere near the funeral, she'd tear me apart. I believed her, and I didn't go."

Mona's eyes filled with tears. The woman's hurt was still there. And somehow Joanna understood that D. H. Lathrop had loved her, too—just as deeply as she had loved him. Making the difficult choice must have hurt him, too.

"He talked about you in his journals," Joanna said softly. "He may have chosen my mother and me, but I know he loved you, too."

"Thank you for saying that," Mona said. "Thank you very much."

When Joanna left Mona Tipton's house an hour later, she felt older but not much wiser. She had come away with a sense that her parents were real people in their own right. That they had existed in ways that she'd known nothing about. On the surface they were still the same people they had always been. Now they were more than that. And less.

Joanna could have stopped then. She could have come down to the bottom of Quality Hill and turned her car around and driven right back to the Justice Center or back to the ranch. But one piece of unfinished business still haunted her. She had one more ghost, one that she either had to lay to rest or learn to live with. With that in mind, she headed for Tucson.

Suzanne Quayle's house wasn't hard to find. Her name and address, well, her initial, anyway, and address were right there in the phone book. "S. Quayle." She lived in one of the newer housing developments off Kino out near the airport. The homes were on the smallish size—affordable places in a neighborhood where newly planted landscaping was just barely taking hold.

Suzanne Quayle's house didn't have trees in the fenced front yard, but there was a swing set with two little boys, one with blond hair and one with brown, playing on it, swinging as high as their little legs could pump. It was getting on toward noon and very hot by Bisbee standards, but these two little desert dwellers—laughing and flying through the air—seemed totally unaffected by the heat.

Joanna studied them closely, searching both tanned small faces for some resemblance to Andy. If it was there, it wasn't readily apparent. She walked up to the gate.

"Is your mommy home?" she asked.

One of the two, the one with a mop of brown hair, skidded to a stop. "She's inside," he said. "I'll go get her."

He dashed away before Joanna could stop him and returned a moment later with a woman—the same small blond woman

Joanna remembered from the sheriff's department's group photo—following behind. "Jimmy, I don't know who—" She saw Joanna and stopped short.

"Oh," she said. "What are you doing here? How did you find me?" She glanced nervously in her son's direction.

"It wasn't hard," Joanna said. "You're in the book."

"What do you want?"

"To talk to you."

"Let's go inside, then," Suzanne said. "Jimmy, you and Gus stay out here for a little while longer, then we'll have lunch."

For the second time that day, Joanna was led into a home—an "other woman's" home. As soon as they were inside, however, Suzanne Quayle ditched any pretense of being polite.

"You've got no business coming here," she said. "No right bringing up the past. I've done my best to put it behind me. I'm listed in the book because I've got nothing to hide. I'm proud of my little boy, but if you're here to cause any kind of trouble—"

Joanna's heart was breaking. This was every bit as bad as she had expected. "I'm not here to make trouble," she managed. "But he is Andy's, then? Was your son's father my husband?"

"Excuse me?" Suzanne demanded.

"Your little boy," Joanna said again. "Was Andy his father?"

"Absolutely not!" Suzanne declared. "How could you even think such a thing?"

"But I—"

"Of course Andy wasn't the father. It turns out Jimmy's father wasn't a father, either. He wanted me to have an abortion instead of a baby. He wanted me to 'get rid' of him. If Andy hadn't helped me, I don't know what I would have done. He was the only one who said it didn't matter what the father said. That if I wanted to have the baby, I should have the baby. And I did. That's why Jimmy's named the way he is—James Andrew—after your husband."

"Oh," Joanna said sheepishly. "Do you mind if I sit down for a minute? I think I'm feeling a little woozy."

When Joanna left Suzanne Quayle's house some time later, it was with a profound sense of gratitude. Her mother was a fortunate woman, and so was she. They had both chosen wisely. Twice.

Even then, she might have gone home, but she didn't. She was learning the painful truth that even though change hurts, it isn't all bad. There was one more thing she needed to do, something she wanted to buy that wasn't available in Bisbee.

It took a while to find the right dealer. Then, once she had made her purchase, it was hell finding someone who would gift-wrap it. Eventually, though, she succeeded. When she got back to Bisbee, she didn't even slow down for the Justice Center. She drove home.

Butch was at the kitchen table, writing. "The kids are at the other house," he said, not looking up from his computer. "Carol said if she took them all to her place, maybe I'd have a better chance of getting some work done."

"Fine," Joanna said, "but right now you have to stop and open this." She set the gift-wrapped package in front of him.

"What is it?" he asked. "Am I in trouble? Did I forget a birthday or an anniversary?"

"It's a surprise," she said.

"Why?"

"Because you're a good man," she said. "And I've decided to give you your heart's desire."

"What is it?"

"Open it up and find out."

When he unwrapped the box and saw what was inside, he looked back at Joanna with some consternation. "But I don't need this," he said. "I already have a motorcycle helmet."

"It's not for you," she said. "It's for me."

"But I thought you said it would be a cold day in hell before you'd ever get on that damned Goldwing with me."

"Something like that," Joanna said with a smile. "So get out your leather jacket. I have a feeling we're in for a very cold day."